'This is my stop,' I told Ji-yeong. 'Coming?'

'Do I have a choice?'

'Sure,' I said. 'You can try to fight your way back to the bridge and gate out while they're busy. You know the castle; you might manage it. Or you could join up with Anne. She's recruiting at the moment.'

'What happens if I do that?'

'You get possessed by a jinn for two or three days.'

'Just two or three days?'

'Yes.'

Ji-yeong started to answer, then paused. 'What happens *after* two or three days?'

'An army of mages invade this shadow realm and kill you.'

'Okay, that last bit?' Ji-yeong said. 'I think you should have told me that part first.'

By Benedict Jacka

Alex Verus novels

Fated
Cursed
Taken
Chosen
Hidden
Veiled
Burned
Bound
Marked
Fallen
Forged
Risen

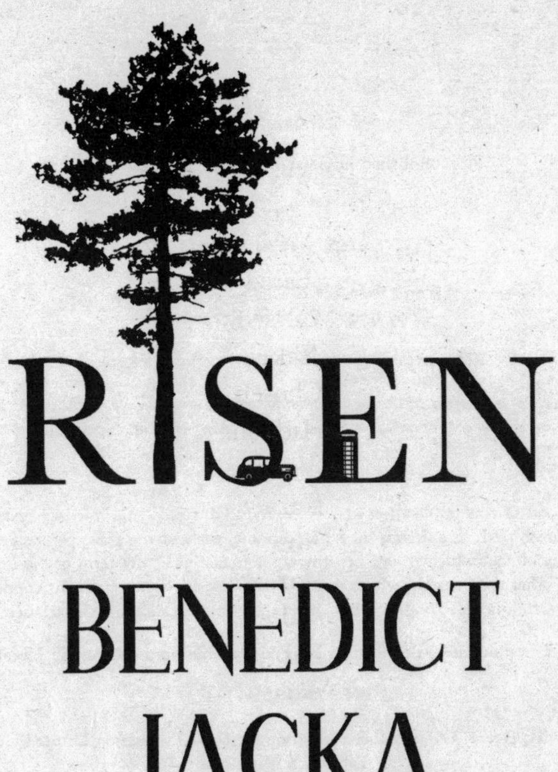

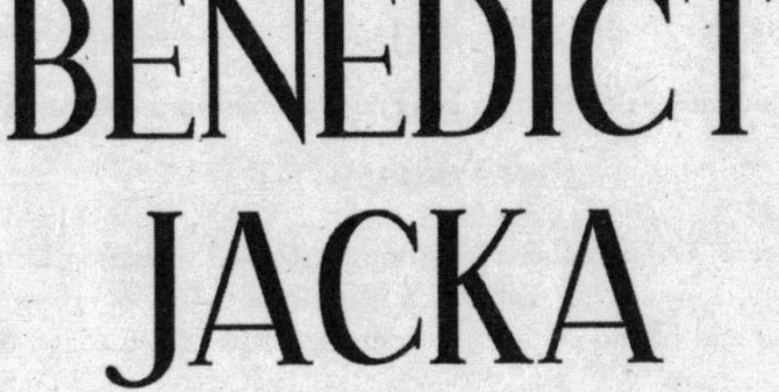

orbitbooks.net

ORBIT

First published in Great Britain in 2021 by Orbit

1 3 5 7 9 10 8 6 4 2

A CIP catalogue record for this book is available from the British Library.

ISBN 978-0-356-51117-7

Typeset in Garamond 3 by Palimpsest Book Production Limited,
Falkirk, Stirlingshire
Printed and bound in Great Britain by Clays Ltd, Elcograf S.p.A.

Papers used by Orbit are from well-managed
forests and other responsible sources.

Orbit
An imprint of
Little, Brown Book Group
Carmelite House
50 Victoria Embankment
London EC4Y 0DZ

An Hachette UK Company
www.hachette.co.uk

www.orbitbooks.net

For my parents

1

The castle was falling.

Walls and battlements of yellow stone stretched into the distance, fading into the haze of the noonday sun. I was on top of the tallest tower on the eastern wing, and from my vantage point I could see the battle raging. Two black armies fought in the haze, clashing on high walkways and in the courtyards below. They blended in a sea of violence, tiny figures striking each other down, the bodies tumbling into space to wisp away into nothingness.

The attacking army was made up out of jann, slender humanoids that seemed to have been sculpted from living darkness. They moved with a darting grace, murderous and quick. The defenders were shadow constructs, smoky bodies with glowing white eyes. They were slower and clumsier than the jann, but they didn't die – when their bodies were destroyed they would simply re-form at their place of creation. A steady stream of them were flying from the tombs, flapping through the sky with heavy wingbeats to rejoin the combat.

But the jann and the shadows were only pawns: it was the mages who would decide the battle. Few in number, they were hidden behind rooftops and ramparts, but their power made them simple to track. Here a swarm of jann vanished into a building, but never came out. Farther south, a flock of shadows descended into a courtyard;

light flickered briefly off the walls, and a few minutes later a new cloud of black specks emerged from the distant tombs.

The castle belonged to a Dark mage called Sagash. Or *had* belonged; I'd been watching for twenty minutes and it was clear Sagash's forces were losing. The cathedral overlooking the southern quadrant had held out for a long time, lightning striking down any jann that came close, but ten minutes ago there'd been a flurry of battle magic and the lightning had stopped. The last time I'd been in this castle I'd fought one of Sagash's apprentices, a lightning mage called Sam. I had the feeling it was him I'd sensed in that cathedral. I also had the feeling I knew who'd silenced him.

As I watched, I noticed an offshoot of the battle moving in my direction, shadows fighting a running skirmish against a pursuing force of jann. Both sides were taking losses, but the jann were receiving reinforcements and the shadows weren't. From the shadows' movements they seemed to be protecting something, but I couldn't see what.

I scanned through the futures, searching for information. In one possibility ninety seconds away, I caught a glimpse of a figure on a rooftop, fighting alone against a swarm of jann. I couldn't get a look at their face, but I could make a good guess at who it was.

I considered a moment, then stepped off the tower, letting myself fall.

By the time I arrived, the shadows had all been destroyed, the last two dissolving into smoke as I stepped out onto the yellow stone. The battle had gained height and we were on a flat rooftop, iron spike railings and low parapets guarding against a sheer drop on three out of the four sides. Huge buildings to the north and south were separated by yawning gaps, the walls dropping away down and down to courtyards far below. Wind rushed across the roof in a low, steady roar, whipping at my hair and clothes.

There were three jann standing over the remains of the shadows, and as I arrived on the rooftop they turned and loped toward me, claws outstretched. I left all three burning on the stone. At the end of the rooftop, a flight of stairs descended out of sight; the bulk of the jann were clustered around it, their attention focused on something below. A small square-topped tower rose twenty feet above roof level, and I jumped up onto it.

From my new vantage point I could see that the flight of stairs descended to what might once have been a bridge but which now ended in a ten-foot stone platform. Beyond was a jagged break and a sheer drop. Standing on the square was a young Korean woman, dressed in blue and grey. She carried a short-sword and a small shield, and was crouched in a fighting stance, facing the stairs. It was probably the same sword she'd tried to stab me with on my last visit.

The stairs were packed with jann, crowded tightly all the way up to the top. They were focused on the woman, but weren't attacking. Instead they clustered just out of range of her sword, their stance low and predatory, wolves facing a cornered deer.

The jann and the woman were focused on each other. They were over a hundred feet away; between the distance and the roaring wind, neither had yet noticed me. I reached out through my dreamstone, finding the woman's mind and touching it delicately. *Yun Ji-yeong, wasn't it?* I said through the link.

I saw Ji-yeong start. Her mouth moved.

Talk through your thoughts, I told her. *I'm on the towertop at your two o'clock.*

Ji-yeong turned her head and saw me, then something made her jerk back toward the jann. *Who are you?* she demanded. Her thoughts were rough and scratchy, but clear.

My name's Alex Verus. We met four years ago.

Verus? Ji-yeong sounded startled. *You were with—* The mood of her thoughts changed. *Ah, shibal.*

Yes.

Ji-yeong said something angry in Korean, then switched back to English. *You know, fine! You want me? Call off your dogs and come get me yourself!*

You mean the jann? I asked. *They're not mine.*

You came with her, didn't you?

I'm not on her side, and I'm not on yours.

Ji-yeong paused, and when her thoughts came again they felt more cautious. *What do you want?*

Information, I told her. *Here's the deal. Answer my questions and do as I say, and in exchange I'll get you out of your current mess and keep you safe.*

Sagash isn't going to let you— Ji-yeong began, then cut off abruptly and lashed out with her sword. The nearest jann jumped back; a ripple went through the crowd, and other jann edged closer.

I don't think Sagash is your biggest problem at the moment, I told Ji-yeong once the jann had settled down.

What the hell are you going to do? Ji-yeong demanded.

Her thoughts were keyed-up, tense. *If you aren't with her, those things aren't going to obey you.*

No.

You're a diviner, right? You going to kill them from up there?

No.

So what are you going to do? Stab them all to death?

Yes.

Ji-yeong laughed. *I'd like to see you try.*

Do we have a deal?

Sure. Why not? It's not like I've got anything to lose.

Good.

I hopped down to ground level and started walking across the rooftop. As I did, I spun my weapon into a ready position. It was a polearm called a *sovnya*, a slightly curved scimitar-like blade mounted on the end of a long shaft. I held it one-handed, arm extended, the blade low above the flagstones.

I was clearly visible on the empty rooftop and it didn't take long for the jann at the back of the crowd to notice me. Two of them turned, faceless and eyeless; any sound they might have made was carried away by the wind. I kept walking and the two of them loped forward, splitting up to come at me from both sides.

Futures unfolded before me. The one on the left would feint, trying to draw my attention from the one on the right. If I turned right, the one on the left would strike instead. A simple attack, a simple counter.

The jann moved into their attack pattern and I showed them what they were expecting. The right one hovered just out of reach as the left lunged. Without turning to look, I reversed the *sovnya* and thrust, feeling the shudder as the weapon bit. The jann in front hesitated; I waited exactly one second, then brought the *sovnya* around to meet its lunge. The blade bisected it at the shoulder, the jann's shadowy flesh igniting with red light. Its body fell to the stone in two halves, flaming and burning. The *sovnya* pulsed greedily, hungry for more.

In the time it had taken me to kill the first two jann, five more had noticed me. They turned and attacked, fanning out to come from all directions.

Four died in eight seconds. The fifth backed away as the rest of the crowd finally started to take me seriously.

In the old days, I would never have taken this fight. My divination shows an enemy's weaknesses, tells me what to expect and where to move, but against this many enemies, that's not enough. Sooner or later you'll get tired, or they'll come from too many angles, and you'll get overwhelmed.

But in the old days I hadn't had a set of reactive armour that could shed a strike from a jann's claws, stiffening at the point of impact to deflect the blow. And I hadn't had the *sovnya*, a weapon forged to kill magical creatures. The polearm burned with a fierce light, its blade cutting through the jann's bodies like a flaming sword through cobwebs. I'm better with a knife than with a spear, but the *sovnya* knew how it wanted to be used; it was less like wielding a weapon and more like fighting with a very close partner.

And most of all, I had the fateweaver. As I danced through the futures, I didn't just see them, I changed them. Small touches to possibilities, closing off some paths, widening others. I nudged the movements of the jann so that they were never quite co-ordinated, never attacking in exactly the right way. Every time one was in a position to threaten me, I'd shift things so that I'd have an extra half-second to react before they could strike.

Superior intelligence; superior weaponry; better defence; fate manipulation. You can overcome one of those advantages, if you have an edge of your own. Maybe two. Not all four.

The jann died, their bodies falling to the stone to burn from the inside out as the *sovnya* consumed them. The only sounds were the stutter and scrape of footsteps, and the roar of the wind, interrupted by the high-pitched whine of the jann's death screams. By the time the remaining jann realised that they should run, it was far too late. They were backed down onto the stairs, trapped between Ji-yeong and me with an endless drop on both sides.

Six jann left. Four flung themselves at me, trying to escape. Three, then two, then one. The last managed to pass me and almost made it to the top of the steps before the *sovnya* took off its leg.

The two at the back went after Ji-yeong. I could have moved in to finish them, but instead I stopped to watch. Ji-yeong engaged the first, blocking with the shield, stabbing with the sword. Her movements were unnaturally quick; in my magesight, I could see the green lace of life magic twined around her limbs.

The first jann opened up a gash on Ji-yeong's arm; blood welled up but she ignored it and closed the distance, ramming her sword into the thing's body over and over again until it shuddered and fell to the stone. The second jann ripped Ji-yeong's back with its claws;

she whirled and slammed it with her shield. The jann stumbled back over the edge, falling silently down and down to disappear into the haze below.

Ji-yeong turned to me, breathing hard.

'You've gotten better,' I told her.

The green light of Ji-yeong's life magic wove around her wounds. The gash on her arm stopped bleeding and pulled together, the edges of the cut binding to leave smooth pale skin. A glow from behind showed that the same was happening to the tear on her back. In only a few seconds, she was healthy again. She straightened and looked at me, her eyes flicking to my weapon and armour.

I turned and climbed the stairs. Once back on the rooftop, I walked twenty feet, then turned and waited.

Ji-yeong followed me up. She moved out onto the rooftop cautiously, glancing from left to right. 'Decision time,' I said, raising my voice to be heard above the wind.

'What?'

I gestured to the open rooftop. 'You want to try and take me, now's your chance.'

Ji-yeong hesitated for a long second, futures flickering. Battle, flight, submission. One future eclipsed the others as she made her choice. Her stance relaxed slightly and she wiped off her sword, then slid it back into its sheath.

I nodded. 'Follow me.'

I took a winding route back across the battlements, Ji-yeong trailing me at a distance. Once I reached the tower I'd been using as a vantage point, I stopped in front of the doorway. That door led into a spiral staircase that would take me to the top of the tower. I crouched, then leapt.

Air magic surged from the metal headband around my brow and a rush of wind hurled me upward, bearing me thirty times farther than I could have jumped on my own. I soared up and over the tower's parapet and landed lightly on its roof. Then I turned toward the open stairwell leading down into the tower, and waited.

If you're going to have a problem with someone, it's best to settle it early. I'd already given Ji-yeong the chance to fight. Now I was giving her the chance to run. She was fifty feet away and out of sight; if she wanted to flee, she'd never have a better opportunity. Again I saw the futures waver, but this time she made her decision quickly.

Two minutes later footsteps sounded and Ji-yeong's head appeared in the open stairwell. She looked around the towertop, saw me, and walked across. The sword was still sheathed at her hip. 'You could have given me a lift,' she told me, raising her voice above the wind.

I wasn't actually sure if I could. The copper headband I'd been using to make these jumps was an imbued item that employed air magic; I'd taken it from Levistus's shadow realm only two days ago, and while it was willing to carry me, passengers were another story. 'Something wrong with your legs?' I asked Ji-yeong.

Ji-yeong looked unimpressed.

I turned to the parapet. 'Let's get to work.'

The battle had moved on while we'd been busy. The areas closer to us had emptied; all the fighting was far away now, around the central keep. Jann and shadows clashed in waves, looking like black dots, a steady stream of reinforcements flying in from the tombs. I pointed toward the tombs. 'Who's fighting who?'

'You mean who started?' Ji-yeong asked. 'Or who's left?'

'Start at the beginning.'

Ji-yeong made a face. 'This is humiliating.'

'Let me guess. First you got beaten by Anne, now you had to get rescued?'

'And now you want me to tell you the story.'

'You're alive,' I said. 'Which means you're doing a lot better than most people who've gone up against Anne lately. Now start at the beginning.'

'Fine. A couple of hours ago the breach alarm went off. When we got to the gatehouse, there were three people waiting on the other end of the bridge. The one in the middle was that Anne Walker girl.'

'Other two?'

'Western woman, Western guy. Oldish, forty or something? The woman was a fat earth mage, the man was a force mage in a nice suit. We went out to meet them.'

Caldera and Barrayar. 'Who's "we"?'

'Me, Aether and Jethro.'

'Who?'

'Aether's Sam. He took that name after Sagash made him Chosen. Jethro's the new kid.'

'What happened to Darren?' I asked. He'd been the third of Sagash's apprentices.

'Killed in a raid two years back. Anyway, the Walker girl did all the talking. The other two just stood there like statues. She threatened me and Sam a bit, but she was really here for Sagash. She called him out.'

'Did he come?' I asked with interest.

'Kind of,' Ji-yeong said. 'Talked via projection. We backed off so I didn't hear what they were saying, but when it was done Sagash didn't sound happy.' Ji-yeong paused. 'Well, he never does these days. He shifted his projection to in front of us, told us to defend the castle and vanished.'

'He didn't come to join you?'

Ji-yeong shook her head. 'Been months since he left the keep. And he's been getting more unpredictable. I was actually starting to think about . . . well. Guess it doesn't matter now.'

I waited. After a moment Ji-yeong carried on. 'So we decided it was worth a shot. I mean, three on three's not so bad, right? And we'd have the shadows backing us up.' Ji-yeong was silent for a moment. 'Yeah. That did not go to plan. First she calls up an army of summoned monsters in ten seconds flat. I mean, that's not even supposed to be *possible*. Sagash spent ten years building up those shadows and there's a whole ritual arrangement in the tombs. You need set-up. She just did it –' Ji-yeong snapped her fingers. '– like that. And then there was her. I mean, the Walker girl's a life mage, sure, but Sam and I dealt with her last time, we knew what she could do. Or we thought we did.' Ji-yeong shook her head. 'It was nothing like last time. She's got some new kind of magic. Sam and I went at her from both sides and she held us both off and I don't think she was even trying. It was like fighting Sagash.'

'What happened?'

'Jethro's dead,' Ji-yeong said. 'He tried to run and the guy in the suit got him in the back. I saw him go off one of the walkways. Aether – Sam – last I saw, he was facing Anne Walker. I stopped sensing his magic a minute later. For all I know he's dead as well.'

'Does that bother you?' I asked.

'Why?'

'Just curious.'

'You don't expect other apprentices to be your friends.'

'But?'

'But what?' Ji-yeong shot me a challenging look. 'You want to see if I'm going soft?'

'Anybody else in the castle?'

'Just the shadows.'

I nodded and stepped away. 'All right. We're done here.'

Ji-yeong frowned. 'I thought you wanted information.'

'I've got all I need.'

Ji-yeong pointed at the keep in the distance. Black flashes of battle magic lit up its walls; even from this distance I could sense the power in the spells. 'You don't want to see who wins?'

'I already know.'

'I've never seen Sagash lose a fight.'

'Doesn't matter,' I said. 'This is the problem with setting yourself up as ruler of your little pocket kingdom. You get isolated. If Sagash had stayed in touch, he might have got wind of what was coming. He wouldn't have won, but he could have set up a bolt-hole.' I pointed in the direction of the battle. 'Those two other mages, Caldera and Barrayar, they're possessed by ifrit jinn. Anne is possessed by a marid. There's only one way this is going to end.'

I started walking toward the stairs. Ji-yeong fell into step just behind me. 'So what's going to happen?'

'Anne is going to smash through Sagash's defences and take him down,' I said. 'Once that's over, she's going to do a sweep of her new shadow realm.'

The inside of the tower was cool and dusty, beams of light passing through arched windows to splash across the spiral staircase. 'What happened with you two anyway?' Ji-yeong asked. 'Last time you were . . .'

'We were what?'

I hadn't raised my voice, but there must have been something in my tone because Ji-yeong didn't finish her sentence. We descended a flight of stairs in silence.

'How much do you know about Anne's history with Sagash?' I asked.

'He doesn't talk about it.'

'Sagash kidnapped Anne and brought her here nine years ago. She was eighteen at the time. He wanted an apprentice-assassin and when Anne didn't turn out murderous enough for his liking he decided to change her by force. It had some lasting effects. When Richard Drakh showed up looking for a host for that marid, he decided she was the perfect candidate.'

'Drakh?'

'Recognise the name?'

'Well, yeah,' Ji-yeong said. 'He made kind of an impression. He met with Sagash after you escaped.'

'What did he want?'

'I don't know, but whatever it was, Sagash turned him down.'

I nodded. That decision had probably sealed Sagash's fate.

We came out of the tower at ground level. Grass grew in between weather-worn structures of pale stone. 'Wait,' Ji-yeong said. 'So *all* of this has been about this Anne girl? First Sagash wanted her, then Crystal wanted her. And now you're saying Drakh's been chasing her too?'

'Pretty much.'

'I don't get it,' Ji-yeong said. 'All these master mages, fighting over one life apprentice who doesn't even want to join them?'

I glanced back at Ji-yeong. 'You think they should have found a volunteer? Like you?'

Ji-yeong looked defensive. 'Well, why not?'

'The traits that Sagash and Richard Drakh valued in Anne were exactly the ones that guaranteed she would never willingly join them.'

'It's still stupid.'

'Well, in the long run, it was,' I said. 'Sagash and Drakh both tried to mould Anne into the kind of person that would suit them. And they weren't the only ones. A rakshasa called Jagadev, a Councillor called Levistus . . . they put Anne on a path, forced her to keep walking down it. Trouble was, once she got to the end of that path . . . it turned out what they'd actually been creating was a monster.'

'She didn't look like a monster last time,' Ji-yeong said. 'More like a victim.'

'A lot of monsters start out that way.'

We stopped in a corner of a grassy courtyard. Sagash's shadow realm had wards that made it impossible to gate in or out except from the platform at the end of the bridge. But it's hard to make a gate ward strong everywhere, especially over a place as big as this castle. There was a small vulnerability in this particular spot, between two of the nodes; every now and again, the ward coverage would weaken just enough to allow a gate. The next window wasn't due for another thirty-six hours, but I'd already used the fateweaver to adjust that. Maybe this was how Richard had broken in all those years ago. 'This is my stop,' I told Ji-yeong. 'Coming?'

'Do I have a choice?'

'Sure,' I said. 'You can try to fight your way back to the bridge and gate out while they're busy. You know the castle; you might manage it. Or you could join up with Anne. She's recruiting at the moment.'

'What happens if I do that?'

'You get possessed by a jinn for two or three days.'

'Just two or three days?'

'Yes.'

Ji-yeong started to answer, then paused. 'What happens *after* two or three days?'

'An army of mages invade this shadow realm and kill you.'

'Okay, that last bit?' Ji-yeong said. 'I think you should have told me that part first.'

I leant on the *sovnya*. 'So what'll it be?'

Ji-yeong watched me suspiciously. 'You're giving me a lot of chances to walk away here.'

'As one of my old teachers used to say, I prefer willing servants.'

Ji-yeong tapped her sword hilt. The futures hovered, then settled more solidly this time. Ji-yeong gave a little sigh. 'You can't start dancing until someone plays the drum.' She inclined her head. 'Lead on, Master.'

I nodded and turned back to the grassy corner. A few touches with the fateweaver, then I channelled through my dreamstone, linking our world to Elsewhere.

'I've still got my gate focus,' Ji-yeong said. 'But it won't do any good unless we can—'

The air shimmered and became an oval portal. Beyond the portal was another castle, this one made of black stone instead of yellow.

Ji-yeong stopped. 'How did you do that?'

Somewhere in the distance, the battle was still raging. I wondered how long Sagash would last. Anne wouldn't want to kill him quickly. She'd been looking forward to this for a very long time.

I stepped through into Elsewhere. After only a moment's hesitation, Ji-yeong followed and I let the gate close behind us.

2

I walked through a castle of black stone, brooding storm-clouds gathering overhead, a hint of rain in the air. I bent the world around me, and the stones beneath my feet became dusty and pale, the black castle transforming piece by piece into an ancient abandoned city.

Behind me I felt Ji-yeong's steps falter. 'Keep up,' I told her.

'What's going on?' Ji-yeong sounded disorientated. 'I can't feel . . .'

'Just stay close.'

The wall ahead reshaped itself into an old wooden door. I reached out and turned the handle; daylight rushed in. I stepped through, making sure to hold the door open until Ji-yeong had followed me before letting it swing shut.

We'd come out into a small park in London. Birds sang in the trees, the sun shone down from above, and the breeze blew with the first hints of autumn. Everything was normal and sane again.

Ji-yeong looked back but the door was gone. 'What was *that*?'

'Elsewhere.'

'Else— wait. Elsewhere? *That* Elsewhere?'

'Mm-hm.'

'I thought that was just a story?'

'It's that too. I wouldn't recommend visiting on your

own.' I reached out through the dreamstone, searching for a familiar set of thoughts. 'I have to make some calls.'

Ji-yeong stayed quiet and I turned away, walking absently across the grass as I reached out to find the mind I was searching for. There's a moment of vertigo when I make contact with the dreamstone, like stepping over a gap that's a foot wide and a thousand miles deep. *Luna.*

Luna replied instantly. Emotion overlaid her words, worry and tension and determination. *Did you find him?*

Her, yes. Him, no.

Frustration joined the other feelings. *Where's she hiding him?*

I don't know, but wherever it is, I don't think he'll be staying. Anne wasn't alone: she had two mages fighting on her side. Caldera and Barrayar.

Possessed?

Safe bet. That's two out of four. Vari's probably going to be number three. I think next time we run into him, he'll be on her side.

Luna was silent. *It's time for the meeting*, I told her.

I want to come.

No.

Alex!

Once this is over, I want you to have a life to go back to, I said. *And as far as that goes, walking in by my side is going to leave a* terrible *impression. I promise I'm not going to shut you out of this, but right now this is a negotiation and there's nothing you can do to help.*

The silence lasted longer this time. *Fine*, Luna said at last.

I've got to go. Call you later?

Okay.

I broke the connection. Luna wasn't taking this well. I couldn't really blame her, but right now I couldn't spare the time to watch her. I hoped she wouldn't do anything stupid.

I took out a communicator focus and channelled a thread of magic through it. 'Hello,' I said. 'Testing.'

A voice sounded from the focus instantly. 'Verus? Where are you?'

'Getting ready to gate.'

Talisid's voice was sharp. 'You're thirty-five minutes late.'

'I think once you hear what I've got to tell you, you'll appreciate why.'

'That remains to be seen. Hurry up, please.'

'On my way.'

Talisid is a political operative high up in the Council, and we've had a long relationship. Mostly it's been good, recently it's been bad, and a couple of days ago it hit rock bottom when he led a group into a deep shadow realm in an attempt to kill me. I felt as though our relations should improve from here on out, given that there really wasn't any way they could possibly get worse.

I cut off the focus and slid it into my pocket as I walked back to Ji-yeong. 'We've got a meeting.'

'A meeting with who?'

'The Senior Council. Or two or three of them, anyway.'

Ji-yeong laughed.

I just looked at her.

Ji-yeong stopped smiling. 'You're serious?'

I fished out a new gate stone. It looked like a pebble of smooth glass carved with an insignia. 'But the Senior

Council doesn't meet with outsiders,' Ji-yeong said. 'Especially Dark mages.'

'They've been pushed a little out of their comfort zone lately,' I said. 'Once we're inside, just follow my lead. I'll let you know what to do.'

Ji-yeong and I stepped through into the bubble realm of Concordia. The gate closed behind us and there was silence.

Concordia is one of the oldest of all created worlds, and it's been used by the Councils of the various magical nations for over a thousand years. The Concord was negotiated here, and it wasn't the first major treaty to take this place's name. Among mages, the name 'Concordia' carries the sound of power and history and decisions that shape the world. I'd never expected to see it in person.

We'd arrived in a circular antechamber. Huge slate-grey columns rose to a ceiling ringed with small windows that glowed with orange-yellow light. The floor was decorated with circular mosaics. Everything was absolutely silent. The air smelled sterile and clean.

A slender construct, mechanical-looking and copper-coloured, inclined its head toward us. Its face was a blank, curved plate with a cross-shaped glow of yellow light. 'Welcome,' it said in a melodious voice. 'May I please have your names?'

'Alex Verus,' I told it.

The construct didn't answer, but its head tilted towards Ji-yeong.

'And guest,' I added.

The construct bowed again. 'Please follow me.'

The construct led us into a hallway, huge and spacious, light filtering down from windows far above. Arches to our left and right gave views onto a vast pillared hall, but everything was deserted. Ji-yeong and I followed the construct at a distance, the sounds of our footsteps echoing in the emptiness.

'What are we doing here?' Ji-yeong said. Her voice was barely above a whisper: something about this place made you want to keep quiet.

'Richard Drakh told me yesterday that Anne Walker and that jinn were about to cause a national disaster,' I said quietly. 'He took it to the Council proposing a truce.'

'Drakh's meeting with the Council?'

'As of yesterday, I've got a seat at the table. You're here to give evidence as to what just happened in Sagash's shadow realm. Just tell the truth and keep to the point. I'll handle the rest.'

Ji-yeong muttered something under her breath. 'I woke up this morning thinking it was going to be a boring day.'

The hallway ended in a set of double doors. The construct stopped and gestured forward with a bow. I pushed the doors open and walked through.

Beyond was Concordia's main audience chamber. The room was huge and circular, divided into five equal-sized segments like a pie chart. The borders of the segments were marked by low walls, silver-grey and twelve inches high, and the tops of each wall glowed yellow, projecting an invisible vertical barrier. Those barriers protected against magical and physical attack, and were supposed to be completely impenetrable. The effect was to divide the room into five sections; people in different sections could talk to each other but were completely unable to harm them. The fact that this is their premier negotiation site probably says something about how mages tend to get on with one another.

At the narrow wedge of each segment were chairs and a low table, arranged in an arc so that the chairs of all five segments formed a ring. Four out of the five segments, including ours, were empty. The fifth was not.

The segment across and to our right was filled with people. Standing on the flanks, and guarding the doors at the back, were a dozen armed men. They were more heavily armed than normal Council security: their body armour was magically enhanced, and the assault rifles slung across their chests looked to have been upgraded. Half of them tracked us as we crossed the floor; the others were watching the exits. Looming over the men were four mantis golems, bulky silver-and-gold constructs that watched us from faceted eyes.

The golems and the security men were dangerous enough; four mantis golems and a dozen elite security were more combat power than most mages would ever see in one place in their whole lives. But compared to the six men and one woman around the chairs, they weren't important at all.

There were three people standing, and four sitting. The ones standing were a square-faced mage in his fifties giving me a distasteful look, a long-faced, mournful-looking man with straw-coloured hair, and a much smaller and younger man who was avoiding my gaze completely. They were Nimbus, the Director of Operations of the Order of the Star; Maradok, Secretary to the Council from Council Intelligence; and Sonder, a Keeper auxiliary and time mage.

Sitting in the first and fourth chairs at the table were Talisid and Lyle. Both were mages I'd known for a long time; both had been my friends once, and both were my enemies now. Talisid gave me a glance before shifting his eyes to Ji-yeong; Lyle looked nervously away.

But it was the two people seated at the middle who really mattered. One was a man, bearded and barrel-chested and running to fat, the other a woman with a lined face and very straight grey-brown hair. Their bodies were opposites, but their eyes were the same, watchful and sharp. Their names were Druss and Alma, and together, they formed forty per cent of what was left of the Light Council, the governing body of the most powerful magical organisation in Britain. I kept walking until I reached the chairs twenty feet away from them, then I stopped. Ji-yeong shadowed me, staying a pace behind. I looked down across the forcefields at Druss and Alma. The last echoes of our footsteps faded into silence.

Alma spoke. 'You're late.'

I didn't answer.

'Do you have a reason?' Alma asked.

'Yes.'

Alma raised her eyebrows as if waiting for an explanation. I looked back at her calmly. The silence stretched out.

Druss broke it, rapping his thick fingers sharply on the table. 'Well,' he said, 'since you've finally shown up, maybe you can tell us when Drakh's going to grace us with his presence.'

I pulled out one of the chairs. It slid smoothly on the polished floor, and I sank into the soft leather. To my right, Ji-yeong followed my lead. 'Oh, he's here already,' I said. 'He's just deciding when to make his entrance.'

'Then,' Alma said sharply, 'perhaps you should tell your master to make it.'

'He hasn't been my master for a very long time,' I told Alma, 'and he's not my master now. If you want to pass him a message, I'm sure you can find a way.'

No one else on the Council side seemed inclined to speak. Lyle, Talisid, Nimbus and Maradok are all important in their own ways, but Druss and Alma are in a totally different league. Ji-yeong was also staying quiet. Dark mages pretend sometimes that they're above the Council, but any of the mages sitting opposite us could crush Ji-yeong with a word, and she clearly knew it.

Alma made a disgusted noise. 'This is a waste of time.' She glanced at Druss. 'We should leave.'

'You aren't going to leave,' I told her.

'You're giving us orders now, Verus?'

'You came out here with two Senior Council, five other mages of varying seniority, four mantis golems, and a bunch of security,' I said. 'You wouldn't have done that if you were planning to walk out.'

'That what you think?' Druss said.

'What I think,' I said, 'is that as soon as Drakh got in touch with you last night, you called up Alaundo and Helikaon and every other diviner you keep on retainer. You told them to drop whatever they were doing and find out whether Drakh was telling the truth, right now. And after they got done being pissed off about being hauled out of bed, they did exactly that. Now, what they said when they got back to you, I don't know, but just from the fact that you're sitting here at this table, I can make a good guess.'

Druss and Alma looked at me. Their eyes gave away nothing, but the silence was an answer.

I leant back in the chair. 'So why you two instead of Bahamus? With Sarque gone, I would have thought he was the obvious choice.'

'We aren't here to make small talk,' Alma said.

'Because he doesn't want to get close to you,' Druss said.

Alma shot a lightning-quick glare at Druss. 'Oh, no one gives a shit, Alma,' Druss told her. The big mage stifled a yawn before looking back at me. 'Bahamus was your ally. After what you did, he's keeping his distance.'

'Apparently not that committed an ally.'

Druss shrugged. 'You get caught breaking the law, that's what happens. Who's the girl?'

Alma's eyes moved to Ji-yeong, her flash of temper already gone. The mages behind her followed her lead. I saw Sonder frowning slightly, as if trying to remember who she was. 'This is Yun Ji-yeong,' I said. 'Up until forty-five minutes ago, she was a senior apprentice under the Dark mage Sagash.'

'So?'

'You want to know what happened forty-five minutes ago?'

'I don't give a shit about some Dark apprentice,' Druss said. 'What's she doing here?'

'She's here,' I said, 'because Anne Walker just went into Sagash's shadow realm with an army of jann and either killed or took control over every human being inside it.' I nodded at Ji-yeong. 'Except for her. Given what Richard told you about Anne's plans, I think you can see the relevance.'

'And why should we believe the word of a Dark mage?' Alma asked.

'Yun Ji-yeong has agreed to give evidence as to today's events in exchange for safe conduct,' I said. I waited just long enough for Alma to open her mouth before going on. 'She's under my protection, so if you'd like to question her, I would request that you do so politely.'

Alma gave me a hard, flat look before switching her gaze to Ji-yeong. 'Very well,' she said. 'Apprentice Yun Ji-yeong. At your convenience, perhaps you could see fit to inform us as to Anne Walker's activities.'

'I wasn't aware that Anne Walker was targeting our shadow realm,' Ji-yeong said. Her voice was calm; she'd obviously taken the time to steady herself. 'The first I knew of what was happening was when the perimeter alarms sounded. I travelled to the bridge and . . .'

Ji-yeong told the story simply and clearly. I sat quietly, studying the futures as Alma and Druss kept interrupting. They wanted to know tactical details: how many jann had Anne summoned, how many other mages had been supporting her, how much combat power she'd displayed. Ji-yeong answered honestly, but her answers didn't seem to make them happy.

Once Ji-yeong began to repeat herself, Druss cut her off with a gesture. 'All right,' he said. 'Well, Verus, you're the diviner, so here's a question. What happens if we gate to that shadow realm and go after Walker right now?'

'That . . . would depend on a lot of things.'

'Are you one of those things?'

'What do you mean?'

'What Druss is asking,' Alma said, 'is this. If we were to follow your old master's plan and attack Anne Walker, whose side would you be on?'

I hesitated. Suddenly I was very aware that everyone in the room was watching me. 'Anne is in the process of being possessed by the marid jinn from Suleiman's ring,' I said carefully. 'I consider that jinn to be an enemy.'

'You do understand what "possession" means, right?' Druss said. 'If the jinn's an enemy, so's she.'

'I would prefer to find some way to separate them.'

'And what if you do *not* find one?' Alma said. She clasped her hands in front of her, leaning toward me. 'What if there is no way to separate them? What if the choice is between eliminating Anne Walker, and allowing the jinn to achieve its goals?'

I met Alma's gaze. There was a clear path behind me, yet suddenly I felt trapped. Seconds ticked by.

Then the *boom* of an opening door echoed through the chamber. Richard had arrived.

Most of the Council group turned towards the sound. The Council security adjusted their formation, shifting to face the new threat. I saw Nimbus take a battle stance, and Druss's hand twitched as though he'd like to do the same.

Richard entered with two people flanking him. On his left was Vihaela, a tall, predatory woman with dark skin. Her gaze swept the room like a raptor scanning for prey, and she noted and dismissed me before focusing on the Council group. On Richard's right was what looked like a swirling mass of grey-black darkness, vaguely humanoid with a faceless blur for a head. I knew that it was a man, even if it didn't look like one: his name was Tenebrous, a radiation mage. He wore that shroud everywhere, and as far as I knew, no one on the Council had ever seen his face. He'd been one of Richard's cabal for a while. Apparently with Rachel and Morden gone, he'd been raised to the inner circle.

But it was Richard who drew my attention. Shorter than both Vihaela and Tenebrous, he was (after Sonder) probably the least physically imposing person in the room. But it was he who'd summoned the Council, not the other way around. The Council forces outnumbered Richard's group eight to one, but given a choice between the Council group and Richard's three, I knew which I'd rather have as an enemy.

'Alma,' Richard said as he walked closer. His voice rang through the chamber, commanding as always. 'Druss. And Verus.' He gave me a nod. 'I'm glad you were able to make the journey.'

'And we're glad you deigned to show up,' Alma said sharply. 'I was starting to wonder if you were intending to win this war by waiting for us to die of old age.'

'I can't imagine you dying of old age, Alma,' Richard said with a smile. He pulled out a chair and sat. Vihaela dropped into the chair at his side and put her feet up on the table. Tenebrous stayed upright, silent and brooding.

'Let me first say,' Richard began, 'that I appreciate you all coming on such short notice.'

'Piss off,' said Druss.

Richard raised his eyebrows. 'Excuse me?'

'We know what you are, Drakh,' Druss said. 'We don't like you, we don't trust you, and you're only here 'cause you want something. Get to the point.'

'I'm afraid I have to agree,' Alma said. 'We have waited more than long enough.'

'I see,' Richard said. He turned to me. 'Verus? Do you feel the same?'

I'd been watching the back and forth. 'You know why I'm here,' I said simply.

'Yes,' Richard said, and turned back to the Council. 'Well, then. I have brought you here today because we have a problem.'

'We have a lot of problems,' Druss said. 'But I'm guessing you mean Anne Walker.'

'Correct.'

'I am more interested,' Alma said, 'in your use of the word "we".'

'How so?'

'Because,' Alma said, 'I would consider it more accurate to say that *you* have a problem. You arranged, at significant time and expense, to free that jinn from the Vault and to have it possess Anne Walker. You then proceeded to use it as a weapon until the jinn, quite predictably, broke free and attacked you instead. At which point you came to us. So no, Drakh. I don't think we have a problem. I think that you are attempting to make *your* problem into *our* problem.'

'As I recall, Anne Walker killed one of your companions on the Senior Council just last month,' Richard said.

Druss's eyes narrowed dangerously. 'She killed Sarque during *your* attack!'

'And this month, she was involved in the death of a second Senior Councillor,' Richard said. He raised his eyebrows. 'Two months, two empty seats. It seems to me that she's become your problem already. Although on the positive side, if she keeps whittling down the Senior Council at her current rate, it might not be long before your and Alma's votes are enough for a majority.'

Druss slammed his fist on the table with a bang. 'You think this is funny?' He leant forward, glaring at Richard. '*You* started this, Drakh! You and your insane war!'

'Who was it who had Anne captured and tortured, Druss?' Richard asked calmly. 'Who sentenced her to death and attempted to have her assassinated? Not me. If you believe she has any reason to think kindly of the Council, I assure you, you are very much mistaken.'

'Why don't we let them handle it?' Vihaela said lazily. 'They'll figure it out soon enough.'

Alma spoke over her, her voice rising. 'You have the nerve to come here and attempt to lay this at *our* feet—'

'Enough!' I shouted.

I hadn't really expected it to work. But for some reason, Richard, Vihaela, Alma and Druss all stopped and looked at me. It caught me off guard but I plunged forward. 'Everyone here shares some blame for this,' I said, my voice hard. 'In fact, by my count, the only ones in this room who *haven't* contributed one way or another to Anne's current situation are Tenebrous and those four mantis golems.'

'I didn't—' Sonder began.

'You provided the evidence that got her arrested. Now, we can sit around this table arguing over whose fault this is, or we can decide what to do.'

There was a moment of silence. I forced myself to stay still. 'All right, Verus,' Druss said. He leant back in his chair. 'What's your call?'

All of a sudden everyone was looking at me. *Why are*

they acting like I'm in charge? 'We are here because of Mage Drakh,' I said. 'He has claimed that the marid, acting through Anne, is in the process of taking actions that will have catastrophic consequences. He has also claimed that a truce between him and the Council is the best way to prevent those consequences.' I looked at Richard. 'I would like to hear him justify these claims.'

First Druss, then Alma turned with me to look at Richard. One by one, the rest of the Council group followed their lead. Vihaela just looked bored.

'A reasonable request,' Richard said. He raised his eyebrows toward Alma and Druss. 'If you have no further objection?'

Druss snorted but didn't reply. 'Then let us hear it,' Alma said.

'The jinn possessing Anne Walker is the marid sultan from the Jinn Wars,' Richard said. 'Now that it has been freed, it intends to continue that war. To fight a war, it needs an army. It intends to acquire one.'

'How?' Druss asked.

'I assume you are familiar with the consequences of Suleiman's binding ritual?'

Alma gave a curt nod. 'Which consequences?' I said.

'The ritual bound a jinn to an item, and in doing so permanently destroyed its ability to manifest,' Richard said. 'If the item was subsequently destroyed, the jinn was banished. A banished jinn could be resummoned by a free jinn of higher rank, and as such the mages binding jinn were careful to safeguard the items. But that was close to a thousand years ago, and while the binding items are resilient, they are not invulnerable. Enough have been destroyed that, by now, banished jinn greatly outnumber bound ones.'

'So a banished jinn can be resummoned by another of higher rank?' I asked. 'Isn't the one possessing Anne the *highest*-ranked?'

'The resummoning process is slow and is subject to limitations,' Richard said. 'At present, the marid sultan has only been able to resummon a small number of ifrit. If left to its own devices, this will shortly change.'

'Get to the point, Drakh,' Alma said.

'The point,' Richard said, 'is that the marid intends to use its new base in Sagash's shadow realm to conduct a ritual. This ritual will grant the marid's host – that is to say, Anne Walker – the ability to summon greater jinn quickly and efficiently. This process requires only another human, and a banished jinn of lesser rank than the sultan. And, as Verus has noted, that is a *great many* jinn.'

'How many?' I asked.

'At the very minimum, more than all Light and Dark mages in Britain put together.'

There was silence.

'Oh,' Richard added. 'And as I understand, the marid has already demonstrated an ability to use this summoning ability upon hostile mages. It seems unlikely that any of you would be more successful at resisting the possession than Mages Caldera and Barrayar.'

The reason that Anne – that the marid – had been able to do that to Caldera was because of me. I pushed that thought aside. 'How fast can it summon a jinn to possess a target?'

'At the moment? Hours or days. If it completes its ritual? Minutes or seconds.'

More silence. In the quiet, an image played in my mind of Anne's group of jinn-possessed humans spreading like a virus, their numbers increasing with each mage they defeated. Sagash's shadow realm had been heavily fortified and defended, and Anne had conquered it in a matter of hours. That had been with three jinn. What could she do with a hundred?

Alma spoke up. 'A pretty story, Drakh. But why should we believe it?'

Richard sighed. 'Alma, please stop wasting time. You and Druss have already contacted your diviners to ask that exact question. If they had not confirmed what I just told you, you would not be here.'

I looked at Alma and Druss. 'Is it true?'

'We have . . .' Alma said, choosing her words carefully, 'not received any information that directly contradicts Drakh's story.'

'Ugh,' Vihaela said loudly, and thumped her head back against the cushions of the chair. 'I *told* you this was a waste of time.'

I ignored her. 'I didn't ask if you could disprove it,' I said to Alma. 'I asked if it were true.'

Druss gave Alma a look.

'Medium-term divinations . . .' Alma said reluctantly, 'have produced . . . irregularities. Within a certain time band, a majority of projected futures contain widespread attacks on magic-using power centres across the country. These attacks ramp up in a manner which is consistent with, though not proof of, an escalating threat.'

'How large a majority?'

'In the absence of intervention, greater than ninety per cent.'

'And this time band would be . . . ?'

Druss answered. 'Seventy-two to ninety-six hours from this morning.'

I sat back in my chair.

There was a long silence.

'Well,' I said at last. 'It sounds as though we *do* have a problem.'

'A problem, yes,' Alma said. 'The cause of that problem is another question.'

Richard raised his eyebrows at her.

'We did our homework, Drakh,' Druss said. 'Swarm of greater jinn. You're telling the truth about that part.'

'And what part do you have doubts about?'

'How it happens,' Alma said. 'We have not sat idle during this war, Drakh. We know precisely what kind of man you are. And summoning a vast number of greater jinn to possess your enemies is *exactly* in line with your methods.'

'If that is the case,' Richard said calmly, 'why would I be approaching you now?'

'You fucked up?' Druss said.

'To lure us into a trap?' Alma said.

'Bit of both?' Druss said. 'Point is, we don't trust you.'

'Your level of trust in me is interesting but irrelevant,' Richard said. 'Your current enemy is the jinn.'

'And how do we know you're not controlling the jinn?' Alma said. 'Or working together with the Walker girl? As Druss says, we simply cannot trust you.'

'Then it seems we are at an impasse,' Richard said. He looked at me.

He wants me to step in. I kept my mouth shut.

'Verus?' Richard said.

Damn it. 'All right,' I said with a grimace. 'Alma, Druss: if you're asking why you should trust Drakh – you shouldn't. But as to his relationship with Anne and the jinn . . . he is not controlling her, and he is not working with her.'

'And you know this because . . . ?'

'Because up until four weeks ago, he *was* controlling both her and the jinn. Via a dreamstone that he got from a deep shadow realm.' I glanced at Talisid. 'The same one I trapped you in, if you're interested. During the battle in Sal Sarque's fortress, I destroyed that dreamstone. That freed Anne, and she and that jinn have been Drakh's enemies ever since.'

Talisid did not look amused. 'And how do we know that *you* aren't working with Drakh?' Alma said.

'Alma, I'm going to be frank,' I said. 'I don't like you. You supported Levistus while he was alive, and you voted to sentence me to death, not once but over and over again. If you were to drop dead of a heart attack, I wouldn't lose a moment's sleep. But Richard is a far worse enemy to me than you will ever be. If I were in a room with you, Richard and a gun with two bullets, I'd shoot Richard twice. Does that answer your question?'

Alma looked back at me, stone-faced. Richard had been watching our exchange with an expression of mild interest. Druss looked amused. Vihaela just seemed to be enjoying the show.

'We will pause this meeting to confer,' Alma said, her voice flat. 'We will resume in twenty minutes.'

'We will be waiting,' Richard said.

*

The Council delegation had withdrawn into the anteroom from which they'd entered. Four Council security had been left in the hall; they stood with weapons ready, watching us closely.

Ji-yeong and I stood near the middle of our section, alone in the giant empty space. 'You did well back there,' I told her.

'Why did you introduce me as an apprentice?' Ji-yeong asked.

'Because if I hadn't, they've have treated you as an adult mage.'

'I *am*—'

I spoke over her. 'An adult mage is a legitimate target. An apprentice is not. I told you I'd keep you safe, and this is the simplest and most effective way to do it.'

Ji-yeong made a face and looked away. 'I thought I was done with this,' she said after a moment.

'Needing protection?' I said. 'Sagash was a big fish in a small pond. You're going to have to get used to bigger ponds.'

Over Ji-yeong's shoulder, some distance away, I saw Richard rise from his chair and walk towards us. 'Stay here,' I told Ji-yeong, and moved to intercept him.

Our paths met on opposite sides of the barrier, close to the wall. 'Richard,' I said.

'Alex,' Richard said. He glanced toward Ji-yeong. 'A new protégé?'

'She's temporary,' I said. 'So are the Council going to say yes?'

'Isn't that a question you should be asking them?'

'I don't think you'd be going to all this trouble if you didn't already know their answer.'

Richard smiled slightly. There was a pause.

'What's your angle?' I asked.

'I'm sorry?'

'What do you want?'

'If you're asking why I've approached the Council . . .' Richard made a small open-handed gesture. 'I would have thought you of all people would be very familiar with the realities of a common enemy.'

Off to one side, I could see Vihaela talking with Tenebrous. The Dark life mage was leaning back on her chair with her feet up, while Tenebrous stood stone-still.

'A common enemy, yes,' I said. I tilted my head at him. 'A common goal? Not so much. If that jinn really is about to cause this much devastation, why not just leave the Council to deal with it? Hole up for a while, let your two enemies fight.'

'Leaving two enemies to fight,' Richard said, 'is only of benefit if both have a chance of victory.'

I looked at Richard. 'You don't think the Council can win.'

'Without my assistance? No chance at all.'

'You haven't answered my question,' I said. 'Why do you care?'

'Alex, I'm not some sort of genocidal maniac,' Richard said. 'Winning this war will bring me no benefit if there isn't a country left at the end of it. And I assure you, if Anne's jinn succeeds, there will be *very* little left.'

I tapped my elbow but didn't reply.

Richard sighed. 'Come on, Alex. No one in this room wants to see the Jinn Wars come again. Is it really so hard to believe that our interests might align? You were happy enough to work with me once. I don't see why we shouldn't be able to do so again.'

I stared at Richard closely. His face was relaxed and calm. Neither his expression nor the futures gave anything away.

A creak and a boom sounded from the far end of the room. Turning, I saw the Light delegation crossing the floor, heading back toward their tables. The Council had made its decision.

3

'So?' Luna demanded. 'What did they say?'

We were in the Hollow, side by side on a fallen tree. I was sitting facing the grass, while Luna was straddling the trunk, leaning in towards me. Through my mage-sight, I could see the silver-grey mist of her curse twisting around her body, just barely out of range. The blurry, half-real sun of the shadow realm was above the treetops, its rays barely catching us as the afternoon faded into evening.

'Oh, they had plenty to say,' I said. 'They argued for hours.'

'Okay, let me rephrase. I don't actually care what they said. What about Vari?'

'Barely mentioned,' I said. 'But I did pick up on a couple of things. You remember Ares?'

Luna shook her head.

'Council Keeper of the Order of the Shield. Fire mage. Tried to kill me on that trip to Syria.'

'And?'

'He was found dead at his home this morning,' I said. 'Someone tore through all his wards, destroyed his body-guard constructs, and engaged him in a fight. There wasn't much left. Apparently once he figured out he was losing, he blew himself up and most of the house as well.'

'So one more out of all the people who've tried to kill you is dead. Why does this matter?'

'It matters,' I said, 'because the previous time he took a shot at me, he got Anne instead. It was nasty.'

'And what, you think this was payback?'

'Not payback,' I said. 'Recruitment.' I leant back on the tree. 'I've been thinking back over the past ten years, counting up all the people Anne would have a good reason to hold a grudge against. Ares – burned her. Zilean and Lightbringer – had her tortured. Sal Sarque and Levistus – gave the orders to have her tortured. Solace and Barrayar – they were the aides to Sal Sarque and Levistus. Caldera – beat her down and captured her. Crystal – mind-controlled me into hurting her. There are plenty more. Sagash. Sagash's apprentices. Jagadev and Jagadev's men. They're nearly all dead. And the ones that aren't dead, Anne's captured.'

'So?'

'The marid can summon greater jinn to possess human hosts,' I said. 'We were already pretty sure that was what Anne was doing. But she doesn't want random people off the street. She wants people who matter to her, that she's got a connection to. She's tracking down her best friends and worst enemies, and turning them into jinn-possessed slaves.' I was silent for a moment. 'I think, in a way . . . she's trying to replace us. The way she sees it, we betrayed her by not taking her side. So she's creating herself some new companions, ones who'll never betray her because they're mind-controlled so that they *can't*.'

Luna made a face. 'When you put it like that, it sounds even creepier. Do you . . . You think she's done that to Vari?'

'Anne captured Caldera and Barrayar two days ago,

and they were fighting on her side today,' I said. 'Vari was captured yesterday, so . . . I'd say it's a good bet. Richard said it takes a while to do the summoning and binding, but it's going to be easier now she's got a base.' I looked at Luna. 'She didn't pick that spot at random, either. Dark Anne was born in that shadow realm. Not a coincidence that when she needed a fortress, that was where she went. Pretty safe bet that we'll find Vari there, too.'

Luna looked down at the grass.

'What's wrong?' I asked.

'When you say "we", you mean the Council as well,' Luna said. 'Don't you?'

'It's going to be a full-on invasion, yeah.'

'And the Council aren't going there to rescue Vari.'

'They say they'd prefer to banish any jinn they find rather than killing their hosts.'

Luna just looked at me. There was no need to say what we both were thinking. The Council would place some value on Variam's life – he was a Keeper, after all – but if he got between the Council forces and Anne, they'd kill him without a second thought. And 'between the Council forces and Anne' was exactly where Anne would put him.

'I shouldn't have let it get this far,' Luna said.

'What happened yesterday wasn't your fault.'

Luna shook her head. 'Before that. When she came to the shop. The way she talked . . . She looked like Anne, but it was like watching someone walking around in her skin. Like there was hardly anything of her left. I knew something was going to happen.' Luna exhaled. 'I just didn't want to admit she was gone.'

I looked down. Luna wasn't the only one who'd made that mistake.

We stayed silent for a minute, then Luna looked up. 'All right. You said they'd prefer to banish the jinn. That must mean they know some way to do it.'

'Kind of, but there's a catch,' I said. 'Remember that anti-jinn weapon we heard about last week? The one the Council was working on as a secret project?'

'Oh yeah, the one—' Luna stopped. 'Wait. Didn't Richard steal that?'

'Yep.'

Luna threw up her hands. 'Oh, *come on*!'

'Which he was using as a bargaining chip in the negotiations, by the way.'

'You've *got* to be kidding!' Luna said. 'Wait, wait, wait, let me see if I'm getting this right. First Richard steals Suleiman's ring, the one with the marid, out of the Vault. Then he manipulates Anne into picking it up. Then he uses Anne and that marid to start a war against the Council. *Then* when they make an anti-jinn weapon to try and stop her, he steals *that*. And *now*, after he's finally lost control of Anne and that jinn, he's asking for an alliance. Did I miss anything?'

'You missed the fact that when he came to see us yesterday he blamed the whole thing on me,' I said. 'For smashing his dreamstone and letting Anne loose.'

'Jesus. Is there even a *word* for that?'

'"Chutzpah".'

'Okay, he's a chutzpah.' Luna shook her head. 'I can't stand the Council and he's making *me* want to take their side.'

'You can see why they weren't keen on a truce,' I said.

'The Council had already decided to go after Anne, before they even walked into that meeting. And that meant putting their war with Richard on hold whether they liked it or not. *Working* with him, though . . . that's something else. Richard told them that they'd have to, or he wouldn't share the details on the marid's ritual. Druss told him they didn't need the details: they could just go in and kill everyone. Richard said they wouldn't be able to get into Sagash's shadow realm without him. Alma said they'd find a way. Richard said that if they didn't involve him then they could kiss goodbye to their special weapon. I'm giving you the short version; the whole thing took hours.'

'Yeah, that's why I'm never getting into politics. So?'

'They hammered out a compromise,' I said. 'Richard and the Council are going to attack the shadow realm separately. Multiple simultaneous gates, multiple points of entry. They were cagey about committing to anything, but my read is there are going to be four groups. First two are going to be Council-led, third is going to be Richard's cabal. Fourth group is me.'

'And me,' Luna said without hesitation.

'And you.'

'When?'

'The Council has the ritual pegged to go off between seventy-two and ninety-six hours starting from 8 a.m. today,' I said. 'So somewhere between Sunday morning, and the early hours of Monday. They're planning to go in tomorrow, Friday evening. That gives them the Friday night and all of Saturday to work with in case something goes wrong.'

Luna gave me a sharp look. 'You think it will?'

I was silent for a long while. 'I'm not sure,' I said at last. I rose to my feet. 'There's one more thing I'm going to try. I'll keep in touch.'

I stepped out of the gate and into the warmth and quiet of an English summer evening. Trees rose up around me, with the tops of buildings just visible over their branches. From outside the park, the sounds of London filtered through, quiet and muffled. The sun had disappeared behind the trees, but its rays still reflected from the buildings above.

'Sorry about the wait,' I told Ji-yeong. 'You ready to go?'

The Dark life mage was sitting in the shadows, leaning against a tree with her head tilted back. 'I suppose.'

I nodded. 'Head to the park's south gate, that way. There's a cab waiting that'll take you to a hotel. There's a reservation under your name. Take a shower, get some rest. There'll be someone coming with some new clothes, so pick something out. Oh, and ask at reception and they'll give you a phone. The contact number in its memory will put you in touch with someone who should be able to handle anything you need.'

Ji-yeong gave me an odd look. 'What?'

'We're pretty much done here,' I said. 'You came out of Sagash's shadow realm without a phone or bank cards, and I know you don't have a base here in London, so I figured you could use a place to stay. The Council will probably want to interrogate you tomorrow about the wards on the shadow realm, so don't be surprised if they track you down, but they shouldn't be too pushy about it. If there are any problems, give me a call.'

'How did . . . ? Wait.' Ji-yeong got to her feet. 'When did you have the time to do all this?'

'Can't expect me to tell you all my secrets.'

'Okay . . .' Ji-yeong said. 'Then why?'

'Tell you secrets?'

'Why are you helping me?'

'Why not?'

'That's not an answer.'

'Yes, it is. It's just not the one you expected.'

'No one does favours for nothing.'

'We had a deal, and you held up your end,' I said. 'I don't have any further obligations towards you, but I've got the ability to make the rest of your day much less unpleasant, and all it'll cost me is some money, which, in my current position, isn't something I much care about. So, again –' I shrugged. '– why not?'

'And that's it?' Ji-yeong asked. 'I just walk away?'

'That's right.'

Ji-yeong stared at me for a long moment. 'I don't understand you,' she said at last.

'You don't need to,' I said. 'Goodbye. I doubt we'll meet again.'

I travelled a little way east, to Canonbury. There, on an ordinary-looking street, I found a place under an ordinary-looking tree, opposite from an ordinary-looking house. I leant against the tree and waited.

When I'd talked to Luna about everyone Anne might carry a grudge against, I'd listed people from the magical world. But Anne had had a life before becoming a mage. The house opposite me right now was the home of the foster family with whom she'd spent most of her childhood, and deep down, she probably hated them as much as everyone else on that list put together.

I stood under the tree as the light faded and the sun sank below the horizon. Above me, the sky faded from cyan to royal blue to deep purple. Around me, the sounds of traffic rose and fell, carried on the breeze. I let the sounds of the city wrap around me, trying to take what calm from it I could. And somewhere beyond, through another sense, I watched the shifting futures.

The phone in my pocket buzzed, breaking me out of my trance. I glanced at who it was, then reached out through the dreamstone. *November?*

Oh good, you're there. November's thoughts feel different from those of a human: smoother, more precise, like blocks of machined glass. *I hope I'm not distracting you.*

It's fine. How did everything go?

Your new acquaintance checked in at reception one hour and thirteen minutes ago, November said. *Since then, she's activated her new phone, made two calls to mobile numbers in South Korea, picked out three sets of clothes from those made available to her, had a shower, and called for room service. Twice.*

Sounds like she's doing fine. Any news?

The Council net is highly active, November said. *All the data I can intercept is consistent with preparations for a major military strike.*

At least they're taking it seriously.

It certainly appears so, November said. *And I gather from your location that you are . . . waiting.*

Yes.

It seems highly improbable that Anne Walker would choose to visit her family home under these circumstances, November said. *If detected by the Council, she would face a significant risk of being traced and overwhelmed. All tactical considerations would push her toward remaining in her new shadow realm.*

You see the future through probability distributions, I told November. *I see that too, but I also see choice. And Anne's been thinking about coming here all evening.*

What's the probability that she will?

It's not that simple, I said across the link. *I've been watching the futures for hours, and they keep shifting. If it was just her making up her mind, it wouldn't look like this. Something's affecting her ability to make the decision.*

But her arrival is still a possibility?

Yes.

Then you really should not be standing there, November said bluntly. *If Anne Walker gates to your vicinity, you will be in extreme danger. Even were I to immediately raise the alarm, it would take a minimum of three to five minutes before any reinforcements could reach your position. The probability of your capture or death would be high.*

Sounds accurate.

Then forgive me for asking, but why are you exposing yourself like this?

I sighed, resting my head against the tree. *Because it feels like this might be my last chance to talk to her.*

That isn't a very good answer.

I suppose it isn't.

Given Anne Walker's recent history, any attempt at negotiation would be highly dangerous without access to close and overwhelming force in the event of an attack. I strongly advise that you bring in support.

If I bring in other mages, Anne will spot them a mile off and won't come anywhere near.

It seems to me that her not coming anywhere near would be altogether the best outcome.

I was silent. I didn't have a comeback, and I wasn't willing to leave.

Well, November said at last. *If you insist on staying, I'll monitor as well as I can. But I must once again urge you to reconsider.*

Thanks.

I stayed there as the sky above faded from purple to black. The futures shifted and jumped, but the ones in which Anne arrived kept shrinking, the possibilities dwindling and petering out until the futures in which she appeared on the street were only a blank void.

I stared across the street. The lights in the house were on, on both the ground and first floors. Anne and I had gone there for dinner a couple of months ago. It had been my first time meeting her family, and once had been enough. If Anne hadn't been struggling with the after-effects of a childhood like that . . .

A wave of anger rose up inside me. I thought about crossing that street, kicking the door down, and picking up those foster parents and slamming them into a wall so that I could shout into their faces *do you know what you've done?* It was more tempting than it should have been. Who was going to stop me?

Anne's foster family hadn't been dark tyrants like Richard, or sadistic monsters like Vihaela, or cold manipulators like Levistus. They'd just been selfish and petty. But having to grow up in a family like that, being treated for years and years as though she didn't matter, had damaged Anne just as surely as any of the enemies we'd fought, and it had been a kind of damage her magic couldn't heal. It had left cracks in her mind, cracks into which Sagash and Jagadev and Richard had driven wedges, splitting her personality into light and dark. And it had been that split that the marid had taken advantage of to possess her.

The people in that house really *did* deserve to pay for that.

I let out a long breath, taking my anger and resentment and setting it aside. Going after Anne's foster family wouldn't do anyone any good, not now. Still, a thought lingered. Anne had considered coming here – probably would have, if something hadn't stopped her. She'd wanted to go back to her beginnings. Maybe I needed to do the same.

The futures were silent and still. I turned and left.

'. . . throughout the realm's boundaries,' Karyos said. 'The creatures of the Hollow will warn me the moment Anne sets foot in this shadow realm. But that may be too late.'

'You can't figure out any way to deactivate Anne's key specifically?' I asked.

Karyos shook her head. 'My magic is of growth and life. I have little understanding of the wards you and your friends created. I could pull them down, but . . .'

'But then Anne could just walk in anyway,' I finished. 'Along with anyone else.'

Night had fallen in the Hollow, and Karyos and I were standing in the doorway to my cottage. Karyos was barely visible, a slight, starlit figure blending in with the trees and grass. In the shadows, the hamadryad's golden skin and bark-like hair were hidden to the point that you could have mistaken her for a young girl.

'I am sorry I cannot do more,' Karyos said.

'Not your fault,' I said. 'We spent weeks setting up these wards. Can't expect to find a way to shut her out this fast.'

'Will she come again?'

'Not in any of the futures I can see,' I said. 'Her number one reason for coming here was Luna, and we've moved Luna out. Also, right now, she's probably got as many prisoners as she can handle.' I paused, looking at Karyos. 'But if she does come back, I'll be ready. I won't let her walk in here like that again.'

'Thank you.'

'Can you do me a favour?' I asked. 'That meditation technique you use, calling back old memories? Could you try to remember everything you can about jinn? Especially anything that might tally with what Richard said in the negotiations.'

Karyos nodded. 'Very well.'

I stepped into my cottage and shut the door.

I walked to my desk, then carefully slipped the copper headband up over my hair and laid it down on the wooden surface, well away from everything else. I could feel the item's spirit, restless and swirling; it didn't want to be put down. I stood there for a few minutes, maintaining the connection, harmonising it until the item had quieted, before I finally took my hands away. Next I removed my armour, the plate-and-mesh coming off my limbs and body one piece at a time. It's heavier these days than it used to be. The armour's been damaged many times over the years, and each time the broken plates and material have grown back thicker. My armour's more willing than the headband to be taken off, but I still had to take some time reassuring it that I wouldn't be in danger overnight. Once I was done, I glanced at the *sovnya* leaning in the corner. The polearm was the easiest of the three to put down, but the hardest to wield – it wanted to kill, and every second that it was in my hands, I could feel its bloodlust. Karyos had told me to take it out of her shadow realm, but I didn't have anywhere else to put it and I didn't trust it to be out of my sight. For now at least, it seemed stable.

Imbued items are dangerous. Wielding one is less like using a tool, and more like riding a very powerful, half-trained animal – you can influence the item, but it can influence you right back. Most mages will only use imbued items when they absolutely have to. Wielding two at once is much harder than using one – the items fight with both their wielder and each other, pulling in different directions. I'd been using three.

It was only the dreamstone and Arachne's training that let me do it. With my experience of Elsewhere, I could stabilise the links between myself and the items, riding the waves of their desires. The armour pushed me to be guarded and safe; the headband wanted to be high up and watchful and always on the move; the *sovnya* wanted to attack and kill. Instead of fighting the urges, I'd cycled between them, allowing each of the items free rein when the time was right, and playing them off against each other when it wasn't. But keeping it up was a strain, and right now I felt like I'd been carrying heavy weights all day.

There were other weights, though, that I couldn't put down.

The Hollow was still and quiet. Karyos had retreated

back to her tree, and to her strange dryad form of sleep. Luna was far away, hiding in a place where Anne couldn't find her. The night was mine alone. I stepped out of my cottage and closed the door.

Out in the night, under the stars, I could breathe more easily. I've always liked the darkness, ever since I was a child. In the shadows, when all is empty and quiet, life seems to slow down to a calmer pace. There's time to think.

I walked the paths of the Hollow, slipping between the trees. The birds in the branches above were sleeping, heads tucked beneath their wings. The only movement was the rustle of the leaves in the breeze, and the occasional skitter of a night-time creature. As I drew closer to the Hollow's north side, I came to a small rise, rocks and grassy earth forming a hillock ten feet tall. A pair of amber eyes gleamed from above.

'Hey, Hermes,' I said. I climbed the hillock, my steps quick and sure. The blink fox had been sprawled on a flat patch of rock at the top of the rise, lying on his side with his chin hanging over the edge. As I climbed up next to him, he rolled onto his belly and looked up at me.

'How are you doing?' I said.

Blink.

With a sigh I sat down next to the fox. 'So how was your day?'

Hermes yawned, shutting his mouth with a snap of teeth.

'Wish I could trade.' I looked past Hermes into the darkness. 'We're going to be launching an invasion tomorrow. Sagash's shadow realm. Well, I guess we should call it Anne's shadow realm now. Same place I met you, come to think of it.'

Hermes tilted his head.

'I'm not sure how many people are going to be coming back. Anne and the jinn are one thing. But then there's the Council to worry about as well, and Richard's cabal. All three of those groups hate each other. It's pretty much a guarantee that things are going to go wrong.'

Hermes seemed to consider that, then gave what could have been a shrug.

'I know, not your problem. But it is mine. I have to somehow figure out all of the ways in which this can go to hell, and stop them from happening, and also hold everything together long enough to make this work. And if I don't, then it's all going to fall apart, because there isn't anyone else. All the people I've got on my side, they're good at what they do, but there's no one else who can do what I can.'

Hermes blinked.

'It was never like this before,' I said. 'There always used to be someone above me. First it was Richard, then it was Helikaon. Then for the longest time it was Arachne. I mean, I had people depending on me. But if it was ever too much, I had someone I could go to. I can't do that any more. There's no one above me, not even the Council. I make a mistake, it's just me.' I was silent for a moment. 'You know, when I was dealing with Ji-yeong today, I was acting a role. But it's starting to feel like I have to do the same with everyone. If Luna and Karyos have problems, they expect me to have answers and sound like I know what I'm doing. Because if I don't, they'll think "Oh crap, if *he's* worried things must be really bad." I wonder if that was how it was for Arachne? She was so powerful, but always alone. And when I'd come to see her, it'd usually be because I needed her help.' I smiled as I remembered those visits, sitting amid the sofas and the rolls of silk. 'God, I must have been *so* annoying. Every couple of months, I'd be bringing her some new problem. Usually something that was my own fault, too. And I'd expect her to be wise and patient and tell me how to fix it. And she would.' I stared into the darkness, my smile fading. 'She never talked about her own problems. Even right at the end, when she knew what was coming. I used to wonder why. I think I understand a little better now. She didn't talk about herself because she really didn't have anyone she *could* talk to. And now it's the same for me.'

Hermes yawned again.

I laughed and looked down. 'Except you. I can lay all this stuff on you and it won't bother you at all, because you really don't care. Because you're a fox.'

Hermes blinked.

'Today was her birthday,' I said. 'September seventh. She just turned twenty-seven. Remember the party we did for her last year? Me and you and Luna and Vari? The war was heating up so we couldn't do much. Still made her happy. Didn't realise it was going to be the last time.' I was silent for a moment. 'I thought about leaving her a birthday card. Even planned out how I'd do it. Put it in an envelope, leave it with a beacon marker somewhere in the castle courtyard so she'd find it once we were gone. Was a stupid idea. Would have had to fight through those jann to get there, then fight my way out again. Risking my life for nothing. But a bit of me still wishes I'd done it.'

Hermes looked up at me, then reached across and touched his nose to my left hand. I glanced at him and smiled, then scratched his head. We sat there for a while under the stars.

I slept badly that night. Strange currents tugged at my dreams, making me twist and turn. I felt as though a voice was calling to me, but every time I'd start half-awake and listen, I'd hear only silence.

It felt as though someone was seeking me in Elsewhere. I slipped into a dreamshard and extended my awareness, searching for the brush of another consciousness against mine. I waited like that for a long time, but nothing came. I was alone.

At last I gave up and slipped back into normal sleep. The voices didn't come again.

4

I woke next morning to the sun streaming through my window. I lay on my futon for a little while, listening to the birdsong, then sat up and looked down at my right arm.

From the tips of my fingers all the way up to my shoulder, my arm was smooth, too white and pale to be living flesh. It flexed and moved like a normal arm, but without wrinkles or tendons or veins. It looked like an animated statue. Only at the curve of the shoulder did the material meld into normal skin, but white tendrils were already reaching into my shoulder blade and collarbone.

Klara, the life mage who'd studied me after I'd replaced my hand, had told me that the fateweaver was going to continue transmuting my body until one of three things happened: it reached a stable equilibrium, it reached my brain, or it reached my heart. She'd been fairly confident that the last one would happen first, probably within a few months. Right now, that estimate was looking very optimistic.

I've made a lot of enemies in my life. Light mages, Dark mages, magical creatures. Over the years, as that list had got longer and longer, I'd had a growing feeling at the back of my mind that it was more than I could handle. Sooner or later one of the people I'd pissed off was going to catch me at the wrong time, and I'd be too slow or too outmatched or just unlucky. One of them would get me – the only question was which.

But over the last couple of weeks, I'd changed my mind. My enemies weren't going to kill me; this would. I didn't have any evidence and I hadn't seen it in any of my divinations, but the feeling didn't go away.

I did a short workout. I've had to change my exercises over the past month, as the fateweaver spread to transmute more and more of my arm. Push-ups don't work any more: my right arm is too strong. Barbell lifts had the same problem. Instead I did dumbbell exercises on my left side, then some leg and abdominal work. Once I was done, I washed and shaved and walked out.

The air of the Hollow was fresh and clean. A glance through the futures told me that Karyos wouldn't be up until the afternoon, so instead I reached out through the dreamstone to Luna.

Luna responded instantly to my mental touch, with no trace of drowsiness. *You're up early*, I told her.

Couldn't sleep. Anything?

On Vari? No. I need your help with something.

Okay.

The invasion's going to launch this evening, I said. *Between then and now, find out what you can about what Richard's adepts are up to. Preparations, mobilisations.*

Richard? Luna said. *Not the Council?*

The Council are going to be coming to me.

And what about when they get Vari in their sights and decide he's acceptable losses?

Then they'll start being a problem again, yes. Until then, my bigger worry's Richard.

Luna was silent for a moment. *All right*, she sent. *I'll handle it.*

Thanks. I'll be in touch.

I broke the connection and started reaching out through the futures. It was time to look up an old friend.

A cold breeze hit me as I stepped out of Elsewhere and let the gate close behind me. I was standing on a mountaintop, granite and close-cropped grass dropping off around me down and down into the valleys below. The sea glittered in the distance, and the sky above was bright and blue.

A few hundred feet north of me was an old hut, hidden by the rocks. If I followed the ridge around the boulders, the hut would appear, and it would be empty and deserted. Door hanging open, cold burnt sticks in the fireplace. Someone had been there, perhaps recently, but they were gone.

I terminated the path-walk and explored a different future where I left the ridgeline and approached the hut from the other side. This time I'd see the fireplace first. Once again, there'd be nothing there. My future self entered the hut, searching nooks and crannies. Empty.

New future. I circled all the way around and crept up from the back. Once the future Alex had reached the hut's back wall, he moved swiftly around to the door.

Empty.

I paused, then started walking. I kept a very close eye on the futures of the empty hut. For a moment, I thought I saw them quiver.

I came around the boulders, still watching the futures.

My divination told me I'd see a cold fireplace, an empty hut with an open door . . .

The hut's door was closed, the rock in front of it neatly swept. A small campfire was burning, the flames licking at the bottom of a pot. And sitting on a flat stone was an old man with bleached-white hair, dressed lightly despite the cold, glaring right at me.

'Goddammit,' Helikaon said in a tone of pure disgust.

I used to believe that my divination always told the truth. When it failed, I'd assume that it was my fault, that I'd made some kind of mistake. But gradually, over the years, I'd noticed that those mistakes seemed to happen a lot more often around certain people. Specifically, other diviners.

I'd finally figured it out last month. Master diviners could project illusionary futures, make other seers think that something was going to happen when it wouldn't. That was how Richard had been able to trick me in the past, and how Helikaon had tried to trick me today.

'I'd say it was good to see you,' I said, 'but apparently the feeling's not mutual.'

'What gave you that idea?' Helikaon jabbed his thumb back at the hut. 'Long as you're here, make yourself useful and get some cups.'

I walked forward. 'Not this time.'

Helikaon looked up at me as I stopped on the other side of the fire. His eyes were sharp, calculating. The short-sword at his side shifted as he adjusted his position.

I looked down at my old teacher and he looked back up at me. Then with a sigh I sat down on a rock, and the moment was gone. 'I was hoping you could give me some help.'

Helikaon grunted, the tension leaving him. 'Been trying to do *that* for fifteen years.'

I nodded. 'Your way was never going to work for me.'

'Of course it bloody works,' Helikaon said. 'Can't hurt someone if they're not there.'

'You can still hurt everyone else.'

Helikaon shrugged.

'I know, you don't care,' I said. 'Don't worry, I'm not here to change your mind.'

'Like to see you try.' Helikaon pulled himself upright and disappeared back into the hut, reappearing a few seconds later with a single mug.

'So you're not here for advice,' Helikaon said, leaning over to check the water in the pot. 'Then what?'

'That false vision you put up to pretend you weren't here,' I said. 'How many times have you done that?'

Helikaon poked at the fire with a stick, held a leathery hand near the water to test the heat.

'I'll be more specific,' I said. 'The times I've been in trouble and I've come looking for you for help. How many times did you see me coming and avoid me?'

'Couple.'

'A couple?'

'What d'you want, an apology? I'm not your mother.'

'What I want is for you to teach me the trick.'

Helikaon didn't answer. He checked the water temperature again, then put some more sticks on the fire. Then he checked the water a third time. Only then did he sit back.

'Both how to do it and how to counter it,' I added.

Helikaon nodded, then looked me right in the eyes. 'You want to kill Drakh.'

I was silent.

'You can stop pretending, boy,' Helikaon said. 'That spell's damn near useless. Only thing it's good for – the *only* thing – is against another diviner. Well, you're not after me, or you wouldn't be sitting there. Who's that leave?'

'Killing Richard is not my primary objective,' I told him.

Helikaon snorted.

'Believe me or don't,' I said. 'Are you going to help?'

'And if I say no?'

'I would prefer that you didn't.'

'Prefer,' Helikaon said cynically. 'What happened to that nice mild-mannered apprentice I used to have?'

'Turns out he was never all that nice.'

Helikaon grunted. 'Took you long enough to figure that out.'

'Look,' I said. 'I know you don't like getting involved in these things. But right now, if you want me to go away and leave you in peace, the easiest way to do it is to teach me what I need to know.'

Helikaon waved a hand. 'All right, all right. Shut up and I'll tell you what you want to hear. But I'm warning you, you won't like it.'

I nodded and settled back onto the stone.

'All right,' Helikaon said again. 'You'll need a channelling focus. Doesn't matter much what kind, long as it's material-effective. Anything that's not divination or sensory.'

I thought of the fateweaver replacing my hand. 'I've got something that'll work.'

'Next step. Look at the futures you're going to be

replacing. Pick a set. Once you're ready, channel through that focus, but do it *in* your future sight.'

I tried doing as Helikaon said. It was difficult. I've spent my life seeing the futures ahead of me as a passive thing, something to watch, not something to change. But my use of the fateweaver had already shifted my ways of thinking. I tried again . . .

Huh. Blurry light, connected to my thoughts, spread over the glowing lines of the futures. I studied it with interest.

'Not *over* the futures,' Helikaon said. 'If you're sculpting an *optasia*, do it over a null area, then transpose it.'

I switched my view to null futures. That was better. Now anything I did stood out clearly against the void.

I'd already decided what I'd try. For a first attempt, I'd project a future of a man arriving here on the mountaintop. I channelled through the fateweaver and light spread through the void, like sparkling paint squeezed from tubes. I tried to sculpt it.

It was harder than I'd expected. Actually, much harder. The threads of magic responded to my thoughts, and I could make them take the form of a ghost-future, shadowy and ethereal, with no more effort than it took to think. But what I was trying to create wasn't a two-dimensional image, or even a three-dimensional one. It was *four*-dimensional, sight and sound shifting through time, and as I tried to adjust some parts others would fuzz and fade. Over and over again I'd try to perfect the image, and each time my own clumsy efforts would disrupt it. At last I gave up on my original plan and cut out most of the movement and branching futures, leaving only the image of a man standing there. Even then, actually transposing it caused its own problems – when I tried to layer it over the existing futures they didn't mesh, and I had to make more corrections. At last I decided it was as good as it was going to get. I looked up at Helikaon. 'Like that?'

Helikaon had sat patiently the whole time. 'You've got the idea,' he said.

'Is it good enough to pass muster?' I said. 'Not much point me putting up a false vision if you can tell it's fake.'

Helikaon nodded agreeably.

'So what does it look like?'

'Well, let's see,' Helikaon said. 'Hard to really describe these things, you know?'

'Just tell me.'

'I know,' Helikaon said as if the idea had just struck him. 'How about a visual aid?' He poked around on the ground before picking out a flat-sided rock. '*Optasia* is like art, you know? A really good one, that's like the work of an Old Master. Every detail perfect.' He took a sharp-edged pebble and began to scratch at the rock in his hand. 'One-of-a-kind. Won't even be seen most times, but that doesn't matter. All about the craft.'

'Richard Drakh's one of your Old Masters, then.'

Helikaon nodded. 'Been a while since I saw his work. That image you were going for, man coming up behind me? Drakh was doing it, you could pick out the hairs on his head. Man'd look so familiar, it'd be like you'd seen him before.'

'So what does mine look like?'

In answer, Helikaon turned the rock around. Scratched onto the flat surface was a crude stick figure with a circle for the head. He raised his eyebrows at me.

'So I'm guessing it's not going to fool anyone.'

'Oh, I dunno, let's ask him.' Helikaon waggled the rock in his hand, talking at me out of the side of his mouth in a high-pitched squeaky voice. '"Sure thing, Master Helikaon, sir! I'm a real boy! Just look at me!"'

'Going to take that as a "no".'

Helikaon waved the rock. '"Why howdy, Mister Verus! You sure are a big shot to make something like me! Why, I bet no one's gonna notice a thing!"'

'Okay, how do I improve it?'

'"Improve? Why gosh darnit, there's nothing to improve! Just look at how—"'

'Please stop.'

Helikaon tossed the rock to the ground with a clatter.

'All right,' I said. 'It sucks. How do I make it *not* suck?'

'Six months' practice,' Helikaon said, thankfully going back to his normal voice. 'Year if you want to get good.'

'That's a little more time than I have.'

'How long do you have?'

'About half a day.'

'Then you're going to suck,' Helikaon said with finality.

I grimaced.

'Told you you weren't going to like it.'

The realistic part of me wasn't surprised. Learning new spells is a slow business. 'All right,' I said. 'How do I spot fake futures?'

'Same way you spot a forgery,' Helikaon said. 'Know what to look for and practise a lot.'

'And is that also going to take months?'

Helikaon grinned at me with a certain sadism. 'Few weeks.'

I sighed, then rubbed the bridge of my nose.

'And that's why doing this shit is dumb,' Helikaon said. 'How many years you think Drakh's been doing this? Hm? How many other mages he's gone up against? 'Course he's going to be better than you. Yeah, you can dance around, look for an angle. Wait for him to make a mistake. And maybe he will. Or maybe it'll be you.' Helikaon spread his hands. 'Why risk it?'

I started to answer, then paused. 'Why did you take me on?'

'What are you talking about?'

'When I came to you after running away from Richard,' I said. 'I was a failed apprentice on the outs with my master and the Council. Not exactly a safe investment.'

Helikaon shrugged.

'You always said not to take sides. The only winning move is not to play, right? So why'd you get involved?'

'I don't bloody know,' Helikaon said. 'Because I'm old and stupid. Or maybe you reminded me of myself a bit. Young and clueless and thinking divination would fix your problems. Who the hell knows?'

'Never knew you had a soft-hearted side.'

Helikaon scowled. 'None of your lip.'

'All right,' I said. 'I'm never going to learn to project false futures – what you call *optasia* – well enough to fool someone like Drakh. What if I didn't try?'

'What do you mean?'

'Project wide-spectrum futures across his cone,' I said. 'I've got enough power to do it. Just random images and noise.'

Helikaon frowned. 'He'd push past it.'

'I could keep adding layers. Anyway, when it comes

to something like this, it's a lot easier to make a mess than clean it up, right?'

'Suppose it is,' Helikaon admitted. 'Pretty obvious catch, though.'

I nodded. 'It'd mess up my own divination as well.'

'Only way for you to do it with your level of finesse, have to be right on top of him. Which means your cone'll overlap his.'

'If what you're saying is true, I can't beat Richard in a divination duel anyway,' I said. 'I can't fool him, but he can fool me. I have to second-guess every future I see, while he gets perfect information.' I looked at Helikaon. 'So I blind us both. Even the scales.'

Helikaon grunted. 'You know the thing about even scales? They're not tilted your way.' He threw up his hands. 'All right, all right. It's not a *completely* stupid idea. We'll give it a shot.'

Despite his complaints, Helikaon worked with me for the rest of the morning. I threw myself into the practice, pushing as hard as I could. I had far to go, and little time to do it in.

By the time we were done, I could project a fuzz of images and random noise that should screw up both short- and long-term divinations over all possible futures. Helikaon could still see through it, but only with time and effort, and he admitted he probably wouldn't be able to manage that under pressure. The big problem was range. According to Helikaon, an *optasia* master could project false futures anywhere, as long as they had a clear enough image of what they wanted the target to see. My own crude technique could only affect the area around me, and it was about as subtle as a fire alarm. The instant I used it, Richard would know exactly what I was doing, and why.

This would probably only work once. I'd have to make it count.

By eleven o'clock, I decided I'd practised enough. I said my goodbyes to Helikaon and left.

Talisid had left me a message while I'd been gone. Actually, several messages. I got in touch and after a minimum of pleasantries Talisid suggested a public place where we couldn't easily be overheard.

I reached Stratford Olympic Park a little before noon. The sun was shining through breaks in the cloud, and the grass and concrete were wet from the morning's rain. The Greenway across the Olympic Park gives an amazing view: from the embankment you can see all the way to south London and to the skyscrapers of the City. The last time I'd met Talisid here I'd turned down off the Greenway to the canal path, where we could walk without being seen. This time I stopped on the bridge over the canal, leant against the railings and waited.

A few minutes passed. People trickled by. Dog walkers, cyclists, locals. Not many children. The new school term had just started; most kids would be sitting in a classroom right now. Maybe they were staring out of the windows, watching the clouds move on the wind that was ruffling my hair right now, and wishing they were outside. I used to do that once.

A cyclist whirred past, and I turned to look at him, seeing him clearly in the second and a half that he sped by. Late thirties, English looks, thinning hair escaping in wisps from under a white cycle helmet. Light blue button-down shirt, cream-coloured trousers, dark shoes. From behind round glasses, a pair of blue eyes stared out at the path ahead with the absent-minded concentration of the practised cyclist. He looked like a civil servant, maybe a bank manager. Reasonably fit but with a sag to his cheeks that wouldn't have been there five years ago. I knew the type. He'd have grown up here in London, six years in primary school, seven in secondary. Then the round of UCAS admissions, carefully researched. A gap year to show a little independence. Thailand, maybe Australia. Then three or four years at university and out onto the career track, nine to five and a starting salary and a commute that'd become so regular he'd know the journey by heart. A flat, a shared house, eventually a house of his own. Other people, more shadowy; a wife, children? And maybe one Saturday or bank holiday he'd happen to be wandering through Camden and he'd see a shop with a funny sign and he'd go in just out of curiosity. Ten minutes staring at the things on the shelves and he'd be off again, ready with some stories for the next Friday evening drinks: *so did I tell you guys about the time I went to a real magic shop? No, not stage magic, supposed to be real. No, I didn't buy a magic wand, ha ha, missed a trick there . . .*

The bike sped away, pedals going up and down, its rider shrinking into the distance. I stared after him, trying to imagine what a life like that would be like. I couldn't do it. He hadn't looked much older than I was; if I'd been born into his place, maybe that could have been me. But I couldn't see myself there. I used to have points of connection to the normal world: my shop, my flat, buying food at the supermarket, walking in the park. I didn't have them any more. I was as far removed from that man on his bike as the Council was.

The thought left me tired. Maybe it really was time to end things.

Talisid appeared a couple of minutes after the cyclist, climbing up from the canal walk below. 'Verus,' he said, crossing the path to meet me.

I nodded.

Talisid glanced at the long sightlines around us, the Greenway stretching in both directions with the Olympic Stadium to one side and the view over London to the other. 'A little exposed.'

'Hiding isn't really an option for me these days,' I said. 'How can I help you?'

Our relationship had changed, and I could feel it in the way Talisid addressed me. For all the years I'd been meeting like this with Talisid, he'd always been the more powerful. He'd never used it to threaten me; he was too courteous for that, in his well-bred way. But always, in our dealings, Talisid had been the one to set the terms. Not any more.

'The Council has a proposal,' Talisid said. 'Actually two proposals.'

'And you got tapped to do it,' I said. 'They weren't worried that our little encounter in Hyperborea might have soured our relationship?'

Talisid looked back at me steadily. 'Has it?'

'Not really,' I said with a shrug. 'I've never had any illusions about you, Talisid. Your loyalty's to the Council. I think you do sort of like me, as much as you like anyone. But if the Council orders me betrayed and killed, you'll do it without a second thought. Or try to.'

'I . . . regret the events of our previous meeting.' Talisid was choosing his words carefully, and watching me more carefully still. 'I would have preferred to have handled things differently.'

'Really.' I raised an eyebrow. 'I didn't get much of a sense of regret. You'd been getting frustrated with me for a while because I kept refusing to play the game. I think when they finally made the decision to have me removed, you were probably relieved. A way to close the book on a messy relationship and move on to something new.'

'I wouldn't put it that way.'

'I'm sure you wouldn't.' My voice hardened slightly. 'But that wasn't what I asked. Are you going to tell me I'm wrong?'

Talisid held my gaze but didn't speak.

I let the moment stretch out, then looked away, breaking the tension. 'Relax.' My voice was easy again. 'I'm not going to take it out on you. If you vanished, the Council would just send someone else.'

Another couple of cyclists buzzed past, their wheels whirring on their axles. 'I always wondered what you'd be like if you came to understand politics,' Talisid said.

'Yes,' I said. 'So what does the Council want from me?'

'Firstly, the Council wishes to appoint you as its liaison to Mage Drakh for the duration of this operation,' Talisid said. 'With your approval, of course.'

'Why not pick someone they trust?'

'While you and the Council have had differences, we do recognise that you have a history of upholding your commitments,' Talisid said. 'Also, it was suggested that someone with a more personal relationship with Drakh might be a wiser choice.'

'What's the second proposal?'

In answer, Talisid dug into his pocket and pulled out a small grey and black focus. Looking down, I saw that a small blue light was glowing at its centre.

'A comms focus?' I asked.

'This concerns the second proposal,' Talisid said.

I tilted my head. 'You were good enough to deliver the first message. Why not the second?'

'I believe, once you hear it, you will understand why.'

There were really only a handful of people Talisid could be talking about. I'd already been checking the futures, and after an extra look just to be safe, I took the focus from Talisid's hand and channelled a thread of magic into the centre. The light switched from blue to green. 'Alma,' I said.

'Verus,' Councillor Alma said. She sounded exactly as she had when I'd met her yesterday in Concordia.

'Are you representing the Council, or is this a personal call?'

'The Council,' Alma said. 'I understand you plan to lead a team of your own into Sagash's shadow realm. Is this correct?'

'Yes.'

'Good,' Alma said. 'We want you to kill Drakh.'

I leant back against the bridge railings. 'So you've finally decided to stop dancing around.'

'We have not been "dancing", as you put it, for some time.'

'So why come to me instead of your other mages?' I said. 'Hoping to keep your hands clean?'

'Every mage going on tonight's operation has exactly the same orders as you.'

'You *are* taking this seriously.'

'Our primary objective remains as discussed,' Alma said. 'Prevent the jinn from completing its ritual, and bind or banish it to ensure that it cannot try again. Our secondary objective is Drakh's death.'

'When and how?'

'We don't care.'

'You're not concerned about people finding out?'

'Verus, you can shoot him in broad daylight in the middle of Trafalgar Square as far as I'm concerned. You can even hold up your Keeper signet and shout that you did it on Council orders, just as long as he's dead.'

'Well, that certainly simplifies things,' I said. 'So I take it you aren't buying Drakh's story?'

'I trust Drakh's story completely,' Alma said. 'All the parts of it that we can verify. Everything else is empty talk. And quite frankly, it doesn't make a difference. Richard Drakh has declared war on the Light Council of Great Britain. He is the greatest challenge to our authority that we are likely to face this century. The war must be ended, and for that to happen, Drakh must die.'

I glanced around. Talisid had withdrawn to the other side of the bridge and was studying his fingernails. A pair of middle-aged women were walking by, a chocolate Labrador panting happily between them.

'Well?' Alma said.

'Two caveats,' I said. 'First, Drakh is going to be expecting this.'

'Of course.'

'He'll have protection, and there's a good chance he'll

move first,' I said. 'This will not be a surgical strike. It will be messy and there will be casualties.'

Alma's voice was cold. 'Casualties are acceptable.'

'Second, if I do this, you're paying for results,' I said. 'As in, Drakh's death. You don't get to complain about who pulls the trigger.'

'You expect to be paid for other people's work?'

'I'm a diviner, Alma,' I said. 'If I want someone dead, most of the time it's just going to look like a very unfortunate accident.'

'We found Levistus's body stabbed through the heart with your bloody fingerprints on his robes.'

'Yes, well, I already tried the subtle approach with you guys and you didn't listen, so I decided to make the message a bit clearer the second time round. Given that we're having this conversation, it apparently worked.'

'Apparently,' Alma said. 'Are you in or out?'

'In,' I said. 'Let's talk price.'

Alma snorted. 'Of course.'

'Don't worry, I think you'll find my terms quite reasonable,' I said. 'First, I need some equipment. Standard Keeper issue. A bullet ward, a set of armour, that sort of thing.'

'Arrange it with Talisid.'

'I'm not finished. Second, I want a full pardon for Anne.'

'The entire point of this operation is—'

'To stop the jinn possessing her. If I can get it banished, I want Anne to go free of all charges.'

'This is ridiculous.' Alma sounded exasperated. 'We're trying to preserve the country, not the life of one criminal. Besides, banishing a possessing entity usually kills the host anyway.'

'In which case, any charges against her won't matter, will they?'

I heard Alma sigh. I had the feeling she was pinching the bridge of her nose.

'Look, Alma,' I said. 'You really aren't giving up very much here. If I banish the jinn and Anne dies, then any charges against her are a moot point. If I banish the jinn and she lives, then she's not a threat any more. Besides, given that she was under the jinn's influence while she did the things she was charged with, I'd argue that she shouldn't be held responsible.'

'Of course you would,' Alma said sarcastically. 'Very well. But I want you to understand very clearly that our primary objective is to stop the jinn, not conduct a rescue. The Keeper teams will not compromise their mission in order to save your . . . companion.'

'I'm not expecting them to. Oh, one more thing. The Council really needs to get back up to full strength, so I think my Junior Council place should be transferred to some other Dark mage. I'd like to retain the right to sit in on meetings, though. You can come up with a title to give me, whatever you think's appropriate. "Minister without Portfolio" or something.'

I felt Talisid start slightly. The communicator was silent. 'What are you playing at, Verus?' Alma said at last.

'I'm planning ahead,' I said. 'It's a habit I've been getting into lately. You see, once all this is over and the jinn's gone and Richard's dealt with, I think most of your Light mages are going to want to draw a line under this whole thing and go back to normal. Most of them. But there'll be a few – not naming any names

– who are going to see this as an opportunity to tie up loose ends.'

'We have already made a truce with you.'

'Which I'm perfectly happy with,' I said. 'But at some point I'm sure it's going to occur to someone on the Senior Council that they could just pass a new resolution and overrule that truce. I mean, let's be frank, you guys *do* have a bit of a track record of sentencing me to death while I'm not there. Consider this an extra safeguard.'

I could feel Alma weighing her decision. 'You ask for a great deal.'

'Yeah, well, that's the problem with downsizing, isn't it? It gets awkward when you have to hire the same people back.' I paused. 'With hindsight, it would have saved everyone an awful lot of trouble if you'd just convinced Levistus to leave me alone.'

'Levistus did not make a habit of taking advice,' Alma said. I felt the futures settle. 'All right, Verus. You'll get what you ask for. But only if Drakh doesn't leave that shadow realm alive.'

'Fair enough. I imagine you won't be taking part in the attack?'

'Of course not.'

'In that case, I doubt we'll be seeing much more of each other.'

'No. We won't.'

I deactivated the focus and walked over to Talisid. 'Did you get all that?' I asked. 'The armour's for Luna; the bullet ward's for me. We'll need them for tonight.'

'That shouldn't be a problem.'

'Good.'

Talisid turned to go.

'Oh, and Talisid?'

Talisid looked back.

'When I set that trap for your team in Hyperborea, I picked a deep shadow realm that would leave you all unavailable for a few hours,' I said. 'I could just as easily have picked one that would have erased you from existence. I chose not to. Call it professional courtesy.' I paused. 'Try anything like that again, and I won't extend the same courtesy. It's nothing personal. It's just, well, I can't keep letting people off with a warning. You understand?'

'Yes,' Talisid said. 'I do.' He gave me a nod. 'Verus.'

Talisid left. I watched him go.

5

I returned to the Hollow to find Karyos awake, sitting cross-legged in her clearing. 'You slept late,' I said as I walked over.

'Recovering the memories was difficult.'

Karyos was reborn less than a month ago, and she still doesn't remember most of her past lives. If she needs to recall something, she uses a meditation ritual. I guess when you live as many lifetimes as a hamadryad, keeping track of all those memories is difficult.

I sat down in front of Karyos. 'To understand the ritual,' Karyos began without preamble, 'you must understand how jinn die.'

I nodded.

'Jinn are immortal,' Karyos said. 'They can take a body, but only as a vessel. As clothing. When their bodies were killed – back when they had them – the jinn's essence, their soul and animating spirit, would drift, discorporated. In time, other jinn would give them form again by performing a ritual of rebirth. The elements of the world around them were sculpted into a body. The jinn would wake, and begin its new life.'

When I'd asked Sonder about jinn, he'd told me about history and war. When Richard had brought it up, he'd talked about armies and power. Now I was getting a third perspective.

'Jinn were connected to the elements of our world.

They did not fear death – the word has no meaning for them. What they feared was something else. The void. If they were to lose their connection to our world, they would be cast into the space between. Somehow, mages learned of this. They came to believe that they had found the jinn's weakness.' Karyos was silent for a moment. 'Suleiman's ritual was designed to sever a jinn's connection with our world. With that link gone, discorporation was no longer a drifting sleep. It was an eternal nightmare.'

'And that was what happened to all of them,' I said.

'The lesser jinn were reduced,' Karyos said. 'Their thoughts and consciousness degraded until they were little but husks. Those creatures that attacked us two days ago . . . they were living beings once. Perhaps they might even have been among the ones I spoke to, when I was young. If they were, they did not recognise me. Nor I them.' Karyos stared into the distance for a moment, lost in her memories. 'The greater jinn retained their consciousness. After a fashion. The void contains . . . entities. They do not live or exist in time as we understand it. But they can affect those they touch.'

'Well, that's incredibly creepy,' I said. 'You think that marid was affected?'

Karyos shrugged. 'It wanted for the humans of this world to be made extinct even before being banished to the void. From your point of view, I'm not sure it makes much difference.'

'Fair point.'

'In the waning days of the war, the jinn attempted to revive those of their kin that had been banished,' Karyos said. 'Working together, they were able to modify the rebirth ritual. Instead of creating a new body, they learned how to summon a banished jinn into a human host. Unlike a normal contract, the host's consent was not required.'

'And that wasn't enough to win them the war?'

'The ritual was too slow, and by the time they had fully developed it, too many jinn had been bound. The problem lay in the amount of energy required to bring a conscious mind through the veil. Mindless and near-mindless creatures, such as jann, could be summoned easily, but greater jinn were far more difficult. The sultan and its generals came to believe that if the veil was weakened in a specific area, this problem could be solved.'

'That's the ritual that Richard's talking about,' I said. 'So what, the sultan tried it back then and it didn't work?'

'The Council forces discovered the plan, and attacked and crushed the remaining jinn before the ritual's completion.'

'And now the same thing's happening again,' I said. I thought for a minute. 'You said the ritual weakened the veil in an area. What sort of area? Like a shadow realm?'

'Perhaps,' Karyos said. 'It may be that the ritual would not work in our world. Perhaps a smaller, separated reality is necessary.'

'Would explain why she went after Sagash's shadow realm. Well, that and for personal reasons.' I frowned. 'Wait. The ritual affects an area?'

Karyos nodded.

'Richard said the ritual was supposed to affect Anne,' I said. 'It'd give her the ability to summon greater jinn fast.'

'Effectively.'

'It doesn't modify Anne to act as some sort of conduit, or something like that?'

Karyos shook her head. 'I do not fully understand how the ritual works, but I'm quite sure that would be impossible. No living body would be able to withstand it. And even if it could, the effect would fall apart as soon as she moved. It would have to be anchored to an area.'

I kept frowning.

'Alex?' Karyos asked.

'Yeah,' I said absently. When Richard had described the ritual at the meeting, he'd implied that the way it worked was by affecting *Anne*.

It wasn't a big difference in practical terms. Instead of making new jinn-bearers on the spot, Anne would have to knock them out and drag them back to her shadow realm first. It would make things harder, but not that much harder. But if it was such a minor detail, why had Richard lied about it? Had he been trying to make the ritual sound more dangerous than it really was to pressure the Council to take action?

Or maybe Richard didn't know everything. Maybe he'd just made a mistake.

I considered both explanations. Neither felt quite right.

Karyos was waiting patiently. 'Can you think of any reason Richard would want us to think the ritual was designed to affect a person?' I asked.

Karyos shook her head. 'I don't understand how your master thinks.'

'Yeah, not many do,' I said. 'All right. Thanks for the help. One last thing. Are you hoping the marid's going to pull this off? I mean, mages haven't given you many reasons to like them.'

'Some have,' Karyos said. 'Besides, I do not believe the sultan's plan will end happily. The jinn I knew and walked in the woods with, when I was younger . . . I saw nothing left of them in those summoned forms. All that I loved in them is gone.'

I got in touch with Luna. *What's the news?* Luna asked immediately.

Richard's lying about how the ritual works, the Council want me to assassinate him and I've learned a few things about divination and jinn. Oh, and I need you to report to the War Rooms to get issued a set of combat armour.

I was hoping to hear something about Vari, but I guess I'll take what I can get. You want to hear what I've found out?

Yes, please.

Okay, Luna said. *So I've been listening in on the whisper network. Last few times Richard's launched a big offensive, we've heard rumours a day or two in advance. Right?*

Ever since the start of the war, Richard's biggest source of manpower had been his adepts. He had a network in place for passing out messages: orders would go down the pyramid from him, to his inner circle, to Arcadia-trained adepts, to other adepts. Eventually the messages would filter through to adepts who weren't so loyal, or to ones who'd been having second thoughts about signing up for Richard's 'association', and some of those people would be willing to talk, especially to a friendly shopkeeper who might have helped them in the past. *Right*, I said.

So that's not happening now, Luna said. *The long-serving adepts, the ones who were trained in Arcadia and who've been with him from the beginning, they're being mobilised for something, they don't say what. Everyone else is being told to stand down. Word is there'll be new orders issued after the weekend.*

The ritual deadline, I said, and frowned. *If you were Richard and you were doing an operation like this, wouldn't you want all the manpower you could get?*

Luna gave a telepathic shrug. *He wants a smaller team? Something more agile?*

Maybe. I thought for a moment, then shook my head. *I'm going to call November.*

November responded to my telepathic call instantly. *Oh, Alex, I was hoping you'd call. There's been no movement from Mage Walker or her jinn. My projections now place her within the shadow realm up until the time of the attack with over ninety per cent confidence.*

Can you give me the order of battle for the Council strike forces?

November replied instantly, information flowing through the dreamstone far quicker than speech. *The Council forces for tonight's operation are composed of two strike teams and a reserve. The first strike team consists of five hundred and thirty-two mages, auxiliaries and Council security personnel. It is commanded by Director Nimbus, with Captain Rain as his second. The second strike team consists of one hundred and seventy-nine mages and Council security personnel, all cleared for front-line combat. It is commanded by Captain Landis, with Lieutenant Tobias as his second. The first and second strike teams are composed of Keepers from the Order of the Star and the Order of the Shield, respectively. The reserve is still being assigned but is currently somewhere between five and six hundred strong, and contains further members of the Order of the Star, some members of the Order of the Cloak, and other mages classified as secondary combatants. Director Nimbus has field command, with Captain Landis and Captain Rain as second- and third-in-command respectively, but both are subject to Senior Council members Druss, Bahamus and Alma, who will be directly overseeing the operation.*

Bloody hell, that's a lot, I said. I'd never seen the Council deploy even half that many. *On a related note, I'm not sure what it says about Council operational security that you could find all that out.*

November sounded smug. *I am rather good at this.*

You know, back when I was planning these kinds of ops, I used to think they were secret. I shook my head. *Tell me what you know about the ward defences on the shadow realm.*

The Council gained reasonably thorough information on the shadow realm's wards during the abortive siege four years ago, and in the aftermath a team was tasked with drawing up an attack plan should it be necessary to assault the shadow realm more forcefully. This has been combined with information provided today by the Dark apprentice Yun Ji-yeong, and also with intelligence gathering over the past twenty-four hours in order to produce a reasonably complete picture. The gate wards across the shadow realm are of a standard design and—

Forget the standard wards, I said. *Ji-yeong said something about an isolation effect. What's that?*

It seems that after his previous experiences, Sagash became increasingly security conscious, and he was particularly concerned about the threat of a large-scale invasion. Rather like the one that's going to be launched today, in fact. Though probably not in the way he was expecting. Well, in any case, Sagash devoted considerable time and resources to installing an isolation ward, a large-scale defensive ward placed over the shadow realm as a whole. When activated, the isolation effect alters certain universal constants within the affected shadow realm, causing a dissimilarity between it and our world that makes it difficult if not impossible to link the two with gate magic.

You can do that?

Apparently. It's a rather experimental branch of magic.

If it's such a good defence, why doesn't everyone use it?

Well, for one thing, the similarity between a shadow realm and its corresponding location on Earth is what anchors the shadow realm to our reality. Weakening this metaphysical link could compromise the shadow realm's stability.

Okay.

Second, November said, *the Council have so far been unable to determine precisely which universal constants the isolation ward would affect.*

When you say universal constants, you mean . . . ?

The gravitational constant, the Planck constant, the parameters of the Higgs field potential . . . that sort of thing.

Um, I said. *In practical terms, what would happen if it changed the wrong ones?*

Well, scientifically, it would be very interesting, November said. *But you probably wouldn't want to be in the area while occupying any kind of physical body.*

Okay, thanks for giving me some new things to worry about.

In any case, the Council are aware of the defence system and have been studying it in detail, November said. *The isolation ward is designed to trigger only in the case of a large-scale assault. The Council's ward specialists believe that they can bypass this trigger. The isolation ward appears to be fully automatic, so once the strike teams have entered the shadow realm, it should no longer be relevant.*

Unless Anne decides to go exploring, finds a big red button somewhere, and pushes it. No, that wouldn't happen. Survival was Dark Anne's number one priority. *Anything else the Council are doing that I should know about?*

Just preparations. If it helps, I haven't seen any indications that they're planning to try to assassinate you again.

Not for the next two days, at least. Thanks, November. Let me know if anything changes.

Of course.

I broke the connection and sat back. Around me, the Hollow was peaceful and quiet. I thought back over what I'd learned this morning. My mind jumped from detail to detail, searching for connections.

I kept coming back to two things. Richard's lie about the ritual, and the isolation ward. I held the two ideas up in my thoughts. I had the feeling they fit together somehow.

I still had a few hours left, and I'd spoken to most of the people I needed. The obvious missing piece was Richard, but my instincts told me that right now, going to talk to him would be a mistake. I didn't know the right questions to ask, and I was starting to learn that letting Richard set the agenda was a very bad idea. He'd give away less than I would.

But it was Richard who was the key. It wouldn't be enough this time to just react. I needed to understand him.

I sat there in the Hollow for a few minutes, listening to the birds sing in the trees. Gradually an idea began to take form. It wasn't a particularly pleasant one, and at first I pushed it away, but each time I did, it would circle around and come back. At last, reluctantly, I rose to my feet and began making a gate.

*

The apartment block was red, with sand-coloured edgings and pale blue drainpipes running from the roof to the ground. Wrought iron balconies jutted from the flats; the balconies on each level had a different design, from half-moons to rectangles to boxes topped with spikes, as though the building had grown layer by layer over the decades with a different architect each time. The street felt too wide and the air too cold, and I watched the cars pass by for a couple of minutes before entering.

The inside of the apartment building was gloomy, with the odour of cleaning fluid trying to drown out an underlying scent of mould and beer. The lift had a notice posted on it in Cyrillic, and didn't work. I took the stairs.

The third-floor corridor ran the length of the building, with light streaming in from the window at the far end. Muffled sounds of traffic drifted in from the outside. Sitting in a chair beside the window was a woman with a lined craggy face who looked older than the building. At the sight of me, she glared and fired off a challenge in rapid-fire Russian.

I gave her a nod and walked down the corridor. When I reached the right door, I knocked.

The woman hauled herself to her feet and said something angry-sounding. She had white hair peeking from under a red shawl, and carried a thick walking stick. She stomped down the hallway, brandishing the stick.

'Relax,' I told her. 'I'm just visiting.'

Suspicious eyes glared up at me from under deep-set brows. She shook the stick under my nose.

There was a soft footstep from behind the door, and

I turned away from the woman to face the spyhole. There was a moment's silence, then the sound of a key turning in a lock and a chain rattling. The door opened to reveal another woman, taller and straighter-backed than the old lady. She stared at me.

I looked back at her.

'Well,' she said after a pause. 'You might as well come in.' She said something in Russian to the old lady, then disappeared into the flat. The old lady gave me a look of deep suspicion before stomping off down the corridor.

I walked into the flat, the door closing behind me with a soft snick. The rooms inside were quiet with a sense of age, beams of light filtering through the windows to catch motes of dust floating in the air. It smelt of old wood and cigarettes. I walked through the entry hall into the living room.

My mother was sitting in a chair near the window, her legs crossed. The chair was positioned so that the rays from the window caught her legs but left her body in shadow, and she was holding a cigarette between two fingers from which a trail of smoke drifted lazily toward the ceiling. It was a while since we'd seen each other, and I looked at her face, studying her. Not much change. Deep hooded eyes, aquiline nose, wide mouth, strong jaw. A few more lines at the eyes and cheeks. The hair was still jet-black, though it was starting to look out of place. How old would she be now? Twenty-three plus thirty-four . . . fifty-seven.

I nodded back toward the corridor. 'I see you've got a dragon guarding your door.'

'Olya,' my mother said with a faint smile. Her accent

was more pronounced than I remembered. 'She was floor manager in our building when I was a girl. Now she keeps away the Uzbekistanis. They steal things.' She nodded at a chair. 'Sit down.'

The chair was by the table, directly in the path of the window. I moved it into the shade and sat. The light from the window streamed into the room between us.

'You look starved,' my mother said. 'Isn't anyone feeding you?'

'I've had a busy few weeks.'

'And you haven't had time to eat?' She raised her eyebrows. 'Why are you here?'

'Family visit.'

'You don't visit. You didn't even come to the wedding.'

'You mean your second wedding?' I asked. 'Or have you had a third one I don't know about?'

My mother frowned at me. 'Don't be uncultured.'

'Sorry,' I said. 'But you can't expect your son to be especially excited about you divorcing his father and marrying someone else.'

My mother had been tapping her cigarette into a glass ashtray; now she shot a look at me. 'What happened to you?'

'What do you mean?'

'You said sorry,' my mother said. 'And you didn't start a fight.'

I gave her an annoyed look. 'So?'

'Oh.' My mother's eyes opened wide. 'Who's the girl?'

'What do you mean, who's the girl?'

'You've fallen in love,' my mother said. 'Who's the girl?'

'This hasn't got anything to do with a girl.'

My mother laughed. 'I know men, and I know you.'

I tried to shake off the annoyance. It didn't work. *How do parents always manage to get under your skin?* 'Given how your relationship with Dad turned out, I'm not sure you know men all that well.'

'Your father's an idiot.'

'He's a university professor.'

'He made professor? Hm.' My mother shrugged. 'Very smart idiot is still an idiot. He could have been part of the English camarilla. He knew the right people. I told him, all you have to do is not rock the boat. I would have helped. I could have been at his side, done what he couldn't. But he wouldn't listen.' My mother shook her head. 'When he came home that day and told me he was resigning from the party . . . good God, I was angry! You probably don't remember, you were too small. I was furious. A few more years and they would have been in power; all he had to do was keep his mouth shut. He said it was a point of principle. Tchah!' It was a disgusted noise. 'So he shuffled off to teach in a dusty classroom.'

'I don't much agree with my dad's principles either,' I said. 'But he is sincere about them. And looking back on it, he did try to make the marriage work.'

'Principles,' my mother said, loading the word with contempt. 'Things for rich men in rich countries. A man should put his family first.'

I didn't have an answer to that. I looked away, out the window. Unbidden, a cold, uncomfortable thought came to my mind. The things I cared about, the person I was . . . how much of that was just the imprint of my parents? How many of my problems had been me trying to reconcile two incompatible ways of looking at the world?

'I think,' I said after a pause, 'that if you and Dad had focused a bit less on why your ways of doing things were right, and focused a bit more on compromising with each other, then my life would have turned out a hell of a lot better.'

My mother sighed and seemed to deflate. Suddenly she looked much older and much more tired. 'I was young and full of fire. And stupid. I thought I could handle everything.' She studied the smouldering tip of her cigarette. 'You think I haven't had that same thought, many times? There is much time for regret, at my age.' She looked up, met my eyes. 'Do you still hate me for it?'

I took a moment to answer. 'No,' I said at last. 'I carried a lot of resentment for a long time, but . . . no. My life's my own, and so are my choices. Anyway, I've seen what happens when people hold onto grudges. It doesn't end well.'

My mother didn't answer, but I thought I felt her relax just a little.

'Richard came to visit you after I left home,' I said. 'It would have been seventeen years ago.'

My mother looked curiously at me. 'So?'

'What did you think of him?'

'What did I think?' My mother laughed. '*Now* you listen to your mother? I'm going to die of shock.'

'Better late than never. So do you remember?'

'Of course I remember,' my mother said. 'He was a *tolkach*.'

I gave her a puzzled look. *Tolkach* doesn't have a good

translation in English – 'pusher', maybe, or 'fixer'. They'd been the manipulators of the old Soviet system, wheedling and lying and bartering to make the numbers add up to what the government said they should. My mother had told me stories about them, when I was young and she'd been in a good mood. 'I don't think he lived in Russia.'

My mother waved a hand impatiently. 'Every country has *tolkachi*. Some admit it; some pretend. He was one of the ones who would pretend. Oh, he was charming and cultured and when we spoke he was very attentive. He wanted to be seen as noble, like an old Romanov. But I grew up around *tolkachi* and I know them when I see them. The look in their eyes, always thinking what they can sell.'

I almost smiled at the image. The idea of Richard as a two-bit criminal was funny. It would be nice if he was only that.

Maybe he is?

I frowned.

'I told myself it would be good for you,' my mother said. She was looking past me, lost in her memories. 'You were so rigid. I hoped it would teach you something.' She was silent for a moment. 'Some part of me knew I was being foolish, that he was a dangerous man. But what could I do? You would not listen.'

'I suppose not,' I said absently, then glanced out the window. The sun was dipping low over the St Petersburg skyline, and I rose to my feet. 'I'd better go.'

My mother tapped out her cigarette and rose with me. 'I hope you don't leave so long between visits next time.'

'No promises.'

My mother had closed the distance between us. Now her hand shot out to grab my arm, her grip surprisingly strong. I gave her a quizzical look.

'I'm not a fool, Alex.' Her voice was quiet. 'You didn't come here just to talk about your old teacher.'

'No,' I admitted. 'But you did help. Thank you.'

'I won't ask what you're going to do.' My mother's eyes were dark and intense. 'But whatever it is, you come back. Understand?'

I looked back at her for a moment before nodding. 'I'll do my best.'

'Good.' My mother released my arm. 'And stop calling yourself by that ridiculous name. My mother and father kept our family name alive through the famines and the purges and the siege, and you just throw it away?'

I sighed.

By the time I stepped out into the streets of St Petersburg, the sun was hanging low over the buildings. Long shadows stretched out across the road, and a cold wind was blowing out of the east.

I turned down the pavement and began walking, absently tracking the cars and pedestrians, lost in my thoughts. I'd come to see Richard as a mastermind, someone who was always two steps ahead. And I wasn't the only one – the Council had developed an almost superstitious fear of him. Mages like Alma liked to pretend the Council was invincible, but he'd outmanoeuvred them too many times for them to believe it.

But my mother didn't know about the war, and had only a vague knowledge of the magical world. She'd judged him as a man. Maybe she'd seen something I hadn't.

Tolkachi were manipulators and liars. Richard's reputation had built him up to be some kind of dark lord. But what if he wasn't? What if he was just an ordinary man who'd used tricks and leverage to parley up his magical talents to the point where he could punch far above his weight? Like me?

If that were true, then I shouldn't be thinking about how to beat Richard, as though he was the final boss at the end of a dungeon. I should be looking for the trick. Yes, he'd tended not to lie – at least, not directly – but he'd always used misdirection, hadn't he? In all his big operations, he'd made the Council look the wrong way before catching them off guard.

Put it all together. He'd said he needed the Council's help to defeat the jinn – probably true. He'd implied the jinn's ritual would act on Anne – definitely false. He hadn't mentioned the isolation ward, but he'd certainly know about it. And he wasn't bringing as many forces as he could.

A crazy idea surfaced in my mind. That *couldn't* be his plan, could it? But no – as I thought it through, it wasn't crazy. Audacious, yes, and you'd have to be *very* careful about calculating the risks. But wasn't that exactly Richard's style?

The more I thought about it, the more plausible it seemed.

But if I was right, then how to counter it? Richard was a diviner. If I set up anything in advance, he'd see it coming, and I couldn't project false futures well enough to fool him. There was the jamming technique I'd learned from Helikaon, but that didn't have enough range.

Well, that just left the more traditional ways of fooling

divination. Cloud the futures with randomness and individual choice, and don't give the diviner enough time to react.

I turned around on the pavement and started walking towards my gating spot. Three hours to go.

6

The War Rooms were full of noise and motion. Even out here in the entry hall, you could feel the change in the atmosphere: clerks and messengers hurried in and out through the security gates, too preoccupied to talk. They were so busy, they hadn't even noticed me come down from the surface.

I walked up to the security gates, paused to let a Council bureaucrat run by and stopped in front of the officer on duty. He was busy writing on a clipboard. 'Hi, Fred,' I told him.

'Just use the gates, we're not signing anyone in today—' Something in my voice made the security officer look up mid-sentence. His eyes went wide.

'Been a while,' I said. 'How are the wife and kids?'

Fred hesitated, his eyes darting around at the rushing crowd. 'Um—'

'Relax,' I told him. 'I'm not here to pick a fight, and if I was, it wouldn't be with you. Anyway, I guess they haven't told you about the truce. I'm not kill-on-sight any more.'

'Ah . . .' Fred said. 'Mage Verus, I'm really supposed to call this in . . .'

'Go ahead,' I said. 'But your supervisor's not going to answer and the front desk is busy. Ask them to put you through to Mage Talisid. He'll vouch for me.'

Fred looked as if he'd rather be anywhere else, but he took a few steps away and started muttering into his communicator, shooting me occasional glances. After a few minutes he turned back to me. 'He's on his way.'

Talisid arrived fast enough that he must have run or jogged. He weaved his way through the crowd towards us. 'Thank you, Officer –' He glanced at the badge. '– Davies. I'll take it from here.'

Fred Davies swiped me through the security gates and watched us go with a definite look of relief. 'Here's the bullet ward you asked for,' Talisid said, passing it to me. The focus was made of dull grey metal, designed to clip onto a wrist. 'I had to sign it out, so I'd prefer if you could return it, but given the circumstances I'll understand if you don't.'

The corridors of the War Rooms were filled with noise and bustle. Almost none of the people rushing past us would be going on the operation today, but you could feel the tension in the air: everyone knew that something big was happening. 'Are you sure it'll be enough?' Talisid asked.

'This'll do fine,' I said. Bullet wards aren't very powerful, but by the same token they don't need much energy. 'Where do you have me placed in the command structure?'

'What do you mean?'

'Technically, I'm still on the Council,' I said. I didn't mention that that was only because the Senior Council had been too busy over the past month to get around to kicking me out. 'That would make me senior to Nimbus.'

'Yes . . .' Talisid said, drawing out the word. 'I'm afraid I don't think it's politically feasible to place any troops under your direct command at present.'

I hadn't really expected that one to work, but it had been worth a try. 'I'm still going to need command access.'

'What kind?'

We came out into the Belfry and turned left, our footsteps echoing on the wide floor. Normally at this time there would be a steady flow of people leaving from the judicial and legislative wings, but not today. Instead, the movement of people was towards the west halls and the Cathedral.

'You're hoping I'll deal with your Richard problem,' I said. I didn't bother to keep my voice down: there was far too much chaos for anyone to overhear. 'I guarantee you that Richard is going to make his move before you do. When that happens, I'm going to need the Council forces to act on my direction, fast.'

'There are certain issues of trust.'

'Yes, because up until a few days ago, you and the rest of the Council were trying to kill me, so I killed a bunch of you first. Get over it. If you want this operation to have the slightest chance of working, you're going to have to put that aside.'

Talisid stopped. A woman with a sheaf of papers went hurrying between us and we leant aside to let her past. 'What are you looking for?' Talisid said.

'Comm focus access for the command staff and official status as liaison,' I said. 'Plus I need you to talk to Nimbus. He won't listen to me, but he might listen to you.'

The look on Talisid's face wasn't encouraging. 'I'll see what I can do.'

The Cathedral is the single biggest open space in the War Rooms. It's a vast, vaulted hall, stretching for hundreds of feet. In between the ribs of the vault are tall stained-glass windows, permanent lights casting a glow down over the polished stone floor. There are duelling pistes and lecterns, but usually it's empty except for a handful of people who like to wander around admiring the architecture during their breaks.

No one was admiring the architecture today. The huge open space was filled with hundreds of people, scattered in groups all the way to the far wall. To the right, a field armoury had been set up, assault rifles and sub-machine-guns and ammo boxes laid out on tables, and Council soldiers lined up in front of them doing weapons checks. The area around the duelling pistes had been cleared and mages were doing combat drills under the direction of Keepers. Sergeants and officers stood in the middle of small groups, delivering briefings. The noise was a constant roar, scores of people trying to raise their voices enough to be heard over everyone else.

A brown-haired figure detached from the nearest group and walked quickly towards us. Talisid gave me a preoccupied nod and left. 'Alex!' Luna shouted over the roar.

I beckoned and Luna moved closer. I looked her up and down; she was wearing a set of standardised black and grey combat armour of the type the Council makes available to Keepers and elite security. Rigid plates for the torso, a helmet for the head, light mesh for the arms and legs. Not as good as military body armour for stopping bullets, but it would do better against magical attacks and was a lot lighter. Good to see Talisid hadn't cheaped out. 'Looks good,' I said.

'Better than it feels,' Luna said. 'This stuff is *heavy*.'

'I need to talk to Landis and Sonder,' I said. 'And Nimbus, but not until after Talisid's found him first.'

Luna pointed. 'Landis is over there, Sonder disappeared somewhere, and I've no idea about Nimbus.'

'Find Sonder and bring him here. I'll be with Landis.'

'On it.'

Landis was near the duelling pistes, addressing a group of Council security, and he was in full cry. 'Now, you see, this simply isn't any good at all,' he was saying. 'Not at all! Take this sorry excuse for an armoured shell. Weber, just stand still for a moment, please, there's a good fellow. No, no, don't draw away. Now . . .'

The security man whose name was presumably Weber stood still with a slightly alarmed look. The men around him had unobtrusively edged away. Landis flicked out a hand and a brilliant, extremely precise blast of flame flashed out and struck Weber in the chest. Weber flinched, but it was there and gone in the time it took to blink.

'The picture of health!' Landis said, and held up an admonishing finger. 'But! That was a mere one thousand degrees. Now if we try a mild increase to two thousand—'

'Wait—' Weber began.

The fireblast was noticeably brighter this time. Weber yelped as it hit his chest.

'See?' Landis said, pointing at the chestplate. 'Look at that! Feel it. Oh, come on, come on.' He grabbed the hand of one of the other security men, who unsuccessfully tried to pull away as Landis slapped the hand directly on to Weber's chestplate. 'You feel how warm it is?'

'Yes, sir,' the man said in a long-suffering tone.

'That was a tenth of a second burst. If I'd held that spell for a mere two-tenths of a second longer, our dear friend Weber here would be on fire! Now, this is what happens when you don't properly attend to your gear. The diffusion effects absolutely *require* regular maintenance or they're no better than a fire extinguisher! Now go check out a new suit and we'll test it when you get back.'

Weber disappeared with a look of relief. 'Landis,' I shouted over the noise. 'Can I have a word?'

Landis whirled to face me. 'Verus! Capital! Carry on for a moment, boys.'

I led Landis to a slightly quieter space near the wall. A stained-glass window loomed above us, gently glowing, a mage in rainbow colours depicted in combat with a dragon. 'Now then,' Landis said cheerfully. 'How can I help our most recently instated, de-instated and re-instated Council member?'

'I'm going to need your help dealing with Richard,' I said, and explained.

Landis listened closely as I spoke, looking like an alert and unusually intelligent greyhound. 'Well, that would explain the mystery, wouldn't it?' he said once I'd finished. He gave a single decisive nod. 'Agreed.'

'The problem is going to be Nimbus. I'm not sure he'll be keen on following my lead.'

'So you want a sheep to jump the fence first, eh?' Landis grinned. 'Not to worry. May be something of a delay, though. However, one slight potential problem does swim to mind. You aren't a little concerned that this isolation ward might end up turning everyone in the shadow realm into a fine red mist, ourselves included?'

'A little,' I admitted. 'But if I'm right, Richard's going to be there too. He'd never do anything like that if he thought there was the slightest risk to himself. And he's a very good diviner. So I'm going to take his word for it, so to speak.'

'Ah, the optimism of youth,' Landis said. 'Clearly you

haven't spent long enough in politics. Well, well, I suppose I'll look into it. Oh, Verus? One other thing?'

'What is it?'

'I understand that Variam is likely to be on the opposing force,' Landis said. 'I'd very much like to do something about it, but I'm afraid I'm going to be rather tied up with command responsibilities. I would take it as a personal favour if you and Miss Vesta could do what you can to get him out of there alive.'

'We were going to do that anyway.'

'Excellent!' Landis clapped me on the shoulder. 'Nose to the grindstone, eh?'

Luna reappeared five minutes later, leading Sonder behind her. I'd withdrawn to the entrance of the Cathedral and met him in the corridor. 'Alex, I'm a bit busy,' Sonder said. He was wearing combat armour similar to Luna's; like her, he didn't look comfortable. 'I need to—'

'This won't take long,' I interrupted. 'That anti-jinn weapon that Richard stole? I need to know its mechanics.'

Sonder hesitated.

'No, I'm not officially cleared for the information; yes, Talisid knows; yes, the Council will clear me if you ask, but only after a lot of time that no one wants to spare.'

Sonder sighed. 'Fine. Off the record?'

I nodded.

'It's a low-level sub-sentient imbued item that uses mind magic,' Sonder said. 'You know how jinn possessions work, how the human acts like a focusing lens for the jinn? Well, the item's designed to attack the lens, sort of like a much more finely targeted mind blast. Ideally it'd destroy the lens and the feedback would break the possession bond completely.'

'And banish the jinn,' I said. 'Would it work on Anne?'

'More powerful jinn have stronger bonds. It'd work on a shaitan. *Maybe* an ifrit. But a marid?' He shook his head. 'I don't think there's any way.'

'So against a marid, what would it do?'

'Well, it'd still destroy the active component of the bond,' Sonder said. 'Force the jinn to rebuild it before it could use its wish magic again. And it'd cause neural shock. Disorientate the host, maybe knock them out.'

'And because it's a new weapon, she might not have a counter,' I said. 'I can see why the Council wants it back. Any drawbacks?'

'The active spell needs a very particular power source. It can't work off a wielder's magical energy the way a focus item can. So it has to rely on its own fuel source, and that's quite limited.'

'Wait, it's an imbued item with a finite energy source?' I said. 'That doesn't make sense. Unless it's powered by captured souls or something.'

Sonder hesitated.

I stared at him. '*Seriously?*'

'They were only able to fuel it with the essence from very specific magical creatures.'

'Jesus,' I said. 'Which creatures? No, on second thought, don't tell me, I don't want to know. At least tell me they aren't planning to mass-produce these things.'

'Well, not now that the prototype's been stolen,' Sonder said. 'Anyway, the point is it's only going to have a few shots.'

I struggled to think of what to say. 'I think we're done,' I said at last.

'Okay,' Sonder said. 'I suppose I'll see you at zero hour.'

Sonder disappeared back down the corridor. 'So,' Luna said. She'd been unobtrusively listening in. 'It won't work on Anne, but it might work on Vari?'

'It's not like they've field-tested it on an actual ifrit,' I said. 'But yeah. If those Council researchers did their job and didn't just sacrifice a bunch of magical creatures for nothing, it's a way to get a jinn out of Vari without killing him.'

'Which just leaves getting it off Richard,' Luna said. 'What do you think? Pick his pocket?'

'Probably not the best idea.'

'Yeah, I didn't think so either. I guess we could wait for the Council to kill him first.'

'This thing with Vari has brought out your ruthless side, hasn't it?' I checked my watch. 'Two hours. I need to find Nimbus, then we're getting out of here.'

My talk with Nimbus was a lot less friendly than my one with Landis. Nimbus stood at a distance, arms folded and his body turned away as I made my pitch. Several other Keepers hovered nearby, watching me with expressions that made it clear I was in enemy territory. Nimbus heard me out but wouldn't make any promises. Instead he kept probing for information. I couldn't answer his questions without giving away more than I could afford, and that just made Nimbus even more suspicious. In the end, he told me that he'd keep his comm open and would listen to what I had to say. I wasn't happy but it was all I was going to get.

I was on my way out when I heard someone shouting my name. 'Verus! Mage Verus!'

I turned, and Luna did too. Jogging across the floor towards us was Ji-yeong.

Ji-yeong came to a stop in front of us. She looked quite different from the stressed and battle-scarred young woman I'd met yesterday – her hair was styled, she was wearing make-up, and she was wearing a new set of clothes with no claw marks or bloodstains. 'Finally,' she said. Despite the run, she wasn't out of breath. 'They wouldn't tell me where you were.'

'What are you doing here?' I asked.

'Getting questioned by your Council police,' Ji-yeong said. 'You're going back, right? To our shadow realm?'

'Alex?' Luna said questioningly.

'Oh, right, you haven't met,' I said. 'Luna, this is Ji-yeong. Ji-yeong, this is Mage Vesta, my former apprentice.'

Ji-yeong gave Luna a very brief nod, then turned back to me. 'So are you?'

'Yes.'

'I want to come with you.'

'Why?'

'Because your Council's been trying to wring me out like a wet mop,' Ji-yeong said, and pointed off to the side. 'They've been asking the same questions all day! And once they were done, they made me write the answers down on paper three times! And *then* they were saying something about verification tests! The only way I got out was by telling them I had to go to the bathroom. They're probably still waiting outside the door.'

'Weren't you one of the ones who kidnapped Anne four years ago?' Luna said.

'No, that was Sam and Darren. I just helped recapture her afterwards.'

Luna did not look friendly. 'And then you tried to stab Alex.'

'I stab lots of people,' Ji-yeong said with a shrug, and looked at me. 'Well?'

When I'd left Ji-yeong last night, I hadn't expected ever to see her again. Apparently between then and now, something had happened to make her change her mind, and I didn't think it was the Council asking her a lot of annoying questions. I remembered her last words: '*I don't understand you.*'

I met Ji-yeong's eyes. 'You follow orders, and you don't make trouble,' I said. 'Understand?'

Ji-yeong nodded.

'All right,' I said. 'Let's go.'

Ji-yeong fell in behind us as we started walking. I saw Luna make a small hand movement and I opened up a mental link. *Go ahead.*

Why are we bringing this girl along when she sounds like she'd be happier fighting for the other team?

Because she knows the shadow realm and she's motivated, I said. *Besides, we aren't exactly drowning in help. Aside from her, our entire rescue team consists of you plus me.*

She was working for Sagash until yesterday.

She's a life mage. If you get cut open in that shadow realm, you'll be glad to have her around.

Assuming she's not the one who did the cutting. Luna sounded resigned. *I hope you know what you're doing.*

We walked through the tunnels of the War Rooms, heading for the exit. Somewhere behind us, a couple of agitated-looking Keeper admins arrived in the Cathedral to question the people there about whether they'd seen a Korean Dark mage who hadn't filled out her paperwork.

I sent Ji-yeong to Sainsbury's with a shopping list while Luna and I gated to the Hollow. It was six o'clock and the sun was dipping low in the sky.

Back in my cottage, I geared up. I changed into a new set of clothes, then put on my armour. Once upon a time it had felt too heavy; these days, its weight was comforting. It's saved my life so many times. I hoped it'd get me through this last battle as well.

Next came the dreamstone and the copper headband. I felt them react to the armour, and I had to work to reassure them. It felt like handling a pack of wary animals: *don't worry, they're friendly, everything's going to be fine.* Once the imbued items had been soothed, I distributed my tools, lockpicks and gate stones between my pockets, along with my new bullet ward. Next I turned to my weapons.

Usually for serious battles my weapon of choice is my MP-7. It's served me well over the years, and I'd considered bringing it out tonight, but in the end I'd decided against it. The most common enemies I'd be facing would be Anne's jann and Sagash's shadows, and neither were good targets for bullets. I could bring it along it as a backup, but wearing it on a sling while using the *sovnya* two-handed would be awkward – it would bump against me as I ran and get in my way as I swung the polearm. Small things, but those small things add up. When you're gearing up for combat, you have to do a calculation on every piece of equipment, setting off the utility it brings against the risk that the extra weight will slow you down just enough to get you killed.

So instead of the MP-7, I strapped on my webbing belt and buckled my handgun into its holster. The old-model 1911 had a lot less firepower than the personal defence weapon, but it was easier to carry. More importantly, against the kinds of enemies I'd be running into, the extra power of the MP-7 wouldn't do much good. Battle mages specifically optimise their shields against bullets – to get a shot through their defences, you generally have to catch them by surprise or get very close. A bigger gun doesn't help you do either. Next, I slipped my knife into its sheath on the other side. Gunmen often underestimate knives, and mages almost always do.

In the past, I'd tended to rely on one-shots for situations like this, using them to cover my weaknesses. Unfortunately, the Council's sentence had cut me off from my usual sources of supply, and by now my stocks had run out. I still had my stun focus and the mind shield I'd used against Levistus, but I wouldn't have a supply of forcewalls and condensers. So for consumable items, I'd had to turn to other sources. I took out a small backpack and opened it to look through the contents, then once I was satisfied that the explosives inside hadn't been messed with, I closed it and slung it over one shoulder.

And finally I turned to the *sovnya*. I'd owned the polearm for only four days, not long enough to get a good feel for its personality, but I was already wary of it. The imbued item had a very clear purpose – to kill magical creatures – and its bloodlust was a constant pressure, like a weight leaning against my mind. I also knew from past experience that it really didn't care about collateral damage. When I ran into Variam and Anne, the *sovnya* would try to kill them with just as much enthusiasm as it had those jann. I would have to fight to keep it under control.

I sighed. As an apprentice, I'd dreamed of power. I'd imagined that it would set me free, open up a world of endless possibilities. But now that I had it, it turned out that real power wasn't something that you could just take and forget about. Real power mostly came from relationships, often with people and entities that you didn't particularly like, and to keep it you had to spend so long developing and maintaining those relationships that you didn't have time to do much else.

There was nothing more to be done. I grasped the *sovnya*, glanced around and walked out.

Karyos and Luna were waiting. Luna had one of my short-swords fastened to her belt, as well as the old duelling wand Arachne had made for her; her hair was tied back and she looked focused and set. Karyos was standing with her hands clasped in front of her, barefoot in the grass, her simple dress a sharp contrast against Luna's battle armour. She wasn't coming with us, and I hadn't asked. This wasn't her fight.

I leant the *sovnya* against a tree before walking up to them. 'We ready?' I asked Luna.

'Yup,' Luna said. 'Also, we've got another tagalong.'

A black nose appeared from behind Luna's legs, followed by a vulpine head. Hermes walked out, sat in the open and looked at me.

'You want to come?' I said in surprise.

Hermes blinked.

Well, come to think of it, Sagash's shadow realm had been his home. 'I guess that makes four,' I said. 'You guys head to the exit. I'll catch up.'

Luna nodded and headed for the gating point, Hermes trotting at her heels. I waited for her to get out of earshot, then turned to Karyos. 'Thank you for your hospitality. I know we took the Hollow by right of conquest, but it's your home.'

'No thanks are necessary,' Karyos said. 'You have done much for me.'

'I've spoken to Luna,' I said. 'If I don't come back, she's going to be your link to the outside world. I've left her most of my contacts. If there's anything you need, she should be able to help, even if it's just knowing where to go.'

'I understand.'

I gave the hamadryad a smile. 'Goodbye, Karyos. I'm sorry we didn't have longer. I didn't have as much time with you as I had with Arachne, but I would have liked to.'

'May I ask a favour?'

'Of course.'

'If you can . . . please bring Anne back,' Karyos said. 'I grew to know her over the long months in my cocoon. We never spoke, but I felt her touch, the weave of her magic. This current form . . . in a sense, she gave birth to me. I do not want the only words I ever have with her to be those we shared when she attacked us.'

'That's what I want as well.'

'Thank you.' Karyos bowed. 'Until we speak again.'

I took a last look at the beauty of the Hollow, then walked away.

7

The Arcana Emporium was quiet. Within the shop, the only noise was the tap of Luna's shoes on the floor. The shelves and tables didn't leave enough space to get up any kind of speed, but there was a little corridor in front of the counter where you could walk in a straight line for about twelve feet before having to turn around. I watched Luna pace to the far shelves, then back, then to the shelves again. Every ten minutes or so she'd realise what she was doing and you could see her consciously stop and lean against the counter, holding herself still. Within sixty seconds, she'd be pacing again.

Ji-yeong was in the far corner, in a chair which Luna had tucked in between the display cabinets at the front window and the side tables against the wall. A Sainsbury's bag with some food was under her chair. I doubted we'd need it, but you never know.

Outside, the city was abuzz with the coming evening. Scattered water droplets hung on the shop window: showers had come and gone, but now the weather was dry again and the streets were filling with the fall of night. The hum of voices and traffic filtered in through the walls, and soon distant music would begin to play as the clubs opened. The sounds of a Friday evening in Camden, familiar as a pair of old shoes.

I checked the time. 7.10. Fifty minutes to zero hour.

My communicator chimed. Luna stopped and both she

and Ji-yeong turned to look as I lifted the focus. 'Receiving,' I said.

'Verus?' Talisid sounded harassed. 'I've double-checked. The ward team confirm that the gate and isolation wards on Sagash's shadow realm have been bypassed.'

'Right now? You're sure?'

'Yes, I'm sure. It would help if you could tell me why you consider this so important.'

'I'm afraid I can't.'

'Wonderful. I assume you've checked in with Drakh?'

'Text only,' I said. I absolutely did not want a real-time conversation with Richard right now. Diviners can learn far too much that way. 'His team will be entering at twenty-hundred, point C.'

'Good. Now I have fifteen other things I need to be doing. Please don't give me any more.' Talisid broke the connection.

'What was that about?' Luna asked.

I returned the focus to my pocket. 'Original plan was for the Council ward experts to bypass the wards on Sagash's shadow realm at the last possible moment before zero hour. I convinced Talisid to do it an hour in advance. He wasn't very happy about it.'

'Mm,' Luna said. She seemed distracted and I wasn't sure she'd heard. She stared off into space, then went back to pacing. I checked the time again. 7.13.

Minutes ticked by. From a street or two over came the muffled sounds of cheering, swelling to a roar and then dying away. Luna's footsteps echoed in the quiet shop. It was taking her five and a half steps to cross the floor each time. One, two, three, four, five, half-step and turn. One, two, three, four, five, half-step and turn.

'Ugh.' Luna shook her head and put both hands flat on the counter. 'This is driving me crazy. It's like before a big duelling match, you know? Except then, if I lost, I'd just go back and train harder and do better next time. It wasn't the end of the world.'

'I know,' I said. 'The waiting for these kinds of things is hard. Funny thing is, what I was thinking of just then wasn't the combat ops I went on as a Keeper. It was exams at school.'

'You used to get that tense about exams?'

'You didn't?'

'I mean, they're just exams. It's not like they really *matter*.'

'Well, not compared to the kind of stuff we have to deal with these days,' I said. 'But when you're a kid, you don't have much variety of experience. If exams are the biggest test you're facing, that's what you worry about.'

'Come on. You must have had stuff you cared about more than that.'

'Well, sure,' I said. 'But that was the only thing I could do that adults seemed to care about. Pretty much the one single thing that my mother and father and teachers could all agree on was that I was supposed to do well at school.' I shrugged. 'Didn't really have any friends, so I didn't have much else to do.'

'Don't take this the wrong way,' Luna said, 'but that sounds really sad.'

'Sounds normal to me,' Ji-yeong said.

'You too?' Luna said.

'Well, not the having no friends part,' Ji-yeong said. 'But when you're in school, you don't get much time to see friends anyway.'

'You can see them after school.'

'That's when you sleep.'

'You've got time to do more than work and sleep.'

'Well, classes and study are about sixteen hours,' Ji-yeong said. 'Once you add on meals and travel, that doesn't leave much.'

Luna stared at her. '*Sixteen hours?*'

'I couldn't believe it when I saw what your schedules are like over here,' Ji-yeong said. 'English children are really spoilt.'

'I'm half-English,' Luna said. 'My father's Italian.'

'Close enough.'

'No, it isn't.' Luna paused. 'What time is it?'

'7.19,' I told her.

'Oh, come on!'

All the time that Luna had been pacing, I'd been checking the futures. At exactly 8.00, the invasion would start. And it would succeed, at least to begin with. Both Council forces would deploy into the shadow realm without triggering the wards. I couldn't see what Richard's group would do, but as far as I *could* see, everything was unfolding according to plan.

Once everyone was inside the shadow realm, the futures blurred into a mess of uncertainty and branching possibilities. The invasion would set off alarms, and we could expect Anne's forces to counterattack. But the whole point of invading like this at so many points was to overwhelm the defences with more threats than Anne could possibly handle. The Council would take losses, but with their numbers and with Richard's forces on their side, they should be able to crush her in a matter of hours.

And at that point, they'd be in position to turn on Richard's forces and crush them as well.

'That sword looks kind of familiar,' Ji-yeong told Luna.

'It's Alex's,' Luna said. She still sounded distracted.

'Did he tell you where he got it?'

'Okay,' I interrupted. 'I think it's time.'

Ji-yeong and Luna looked at me as I took out my communicator and activated it. 'Landis,' a voice said after a moment.

'It's Verus,' I said. 'Go.'

'Understood.' Landis broke the connection.

'What was that about?' Luna asked.

I stood up, stretching slightly. 'We're going.'

Luna looked puzzled. 'Going, as in . . . ?'

'The invasion.'

Luna checked her phone. 'It's still—'

'Change of plans.'

Both Luna and Ji-yeong looked confused now. 'What's going on?' Luna asked.

'Okay,' I said. The futures were starting to shift, and I kept an eye on them as I talked. 'Richard needs the Council to take out Anne. But once Anne's been neutralised, his forces are going to be stuck in a warded shadow realm with a Council army. The Council is going to kill him at the first available opportunity. I know that, and if I can figure that out, so can Richard. Right?'

'Okay,' Luna said.

'So imagine you're Richard,' I said. 'You know the Council's going to turn on you. The obvious way to deal with that is to backstab them first. Except the Council knows you know, so they're *also* going to backstab you first. And the Council have a bigger army. If it comes down to Richard's cabal versus the Council strike force in that shadow realm, Richard's going to lose. So what do you do?' I paused for a second, then went on. 'You stop them from having the bigger army. The key is the isolation ward. Once that's triggered, the Council won't be able to bring in any more reinforcements. Their numbers won't matter.'

'But if he triggers the isolation ward once you're all there, that'll just make it worse for him,' Luna said. 'He won't be able to get away.'

'Which is why he isn't going to wait that long. Richard's going to sabotage the plan right at the beginning and trigger the isolation ward while the Council's still moving that into the shadow realm. Let in a fraction, cut off the rest.'

'Why a fraction?' Luna asked.

'Balancing act,' I said. 'He can't beat Anne on his own. He's planning to let in just enough Council mages to distract Anne's forces and weaken them enough for him to finish them off, but not so many that they can beat him. It's dangerous, but he's been willing to take those chances before. And it's exactly the kind of thing the Council wouldn't see coming, because they'd never do anything so high risk.'

'And you figured all this out by divining it?' Ji-yeong asked.

'Well, not exactly,' I said. 'My divination is telling me that the Council's plan is going to work fine.'

'What?'

'The Council has diviners too. They'll have told the Council the same thing.'

'Then . . .'

'Richard can project false futures. Make diviners see what he wants them to see. He's fooled me with it before.'

'So you can tell this one's a fake?' Luna asked.

'Nope,' I said.

The two of them stared at me.

'Future looks one hundred per cent real,' I said. 'But Richard's a master. If he was creating a false vision, that's what I'd expect to see.'

'So . . . you're guessing?'

'Pretty much,' I said. 'If I'm wrong, I just screwed everything up in a really major way and the Council are going to be very, very pissed off.' I shrugged. 'Let's hope I'm not. Now stay quiet, I need to path-walk.'

Luna and Ji-yeong exchanged glances.

The shop was quiet, the streets outside busy with the bustle of a normal Camden evening. But elsewhere, I'd just kicked over an anthill. Landis was starting the gate spells that would send his team through into the shadow realm, and he'd have notified Nimbus to do the same. Nimbus would rage and order him to stop, and when Landis didn't, Nimbus would call the Council and demand an explanation. And the Council would respond by calling . . .

My communicator pinged. Talisid. I picked up the focus, activated it and spoke into it, my voice clipped. 'Richard's betraying you. He's going to let you start to gate your forces into the shadow realm, then trigger the isolation ward and cut you off. You have to go right now.'

'Verus, what do you think—?'

'No time. You have a few minutes. Don't waste them.'

I broke the connection. There was silence for a few

seconds, then the communicator pinged again. I didn't answer.

Now it was a race. My actions had thrown the futures into chaos, and it wouldn't take Richard long to realise something was wrong. Meanwhile, the Council would be arguing. Could they act faster than Richard?

Normally the answer would be no. But Richard had his own army to deploy, and he needed to maintain the *optasia*. And crucially, he was doing it alone. Richard's cabal was powerful, but the biggest weakness of Dark mages is their lack of trust: if he didn't watch his back then someone like Vihaela would put a knife in it. I was hoping that right now, he had too much to deal with.

The communicator pinged, then pinged twice more. I selected the person I needed to talk to and answered. 'Verus.'

An aggravated voice spoke through the focus. 'Verus, this is—'

'Director Nimbus,' I interrupted. 'Yes, I know what I'm doing; yes, there is a good reason, and the reason is the one you just heard from Talisid. Richard is going to trigger the isolation ward and cut your force into bits. You have to launch the invasion right now.'

'You don't have—'

'I do know that.'

'The Council—'

'The Council diviners are being fooled.'

'You—'

'My authority doesn't matter. I'm the one who knows what's going to happen.'

'*Stop interrupting me!*'

'Nimbus, I know you don't like me,' I said. 'But you

are about to make the most important decision of your career, and depending on which path you choose, you will go down in history in one of two ways. Down one path, you'll be remembered as the visionary commander who sniffed out a trap and defeated Drakh when other Keepers couldn't. Down the other, you'll be remembered as a failure who hesitated at the crucial moment. Pick one.'

'I need confirmation!'

'Landis is opening his gate in three and a half minutes,' I said. 'Then you're going to have to make your decision whether you've got confirmation or not.' I hung up.

Luna and Ji-yeong were still watching, looking slightly nervous. 'Um,' Luna said. 'Can we talk now?'

'Not quite.' I opened the door by the counter and went through into the back room.

Luna had kept some aspects of the Arcana Emporium the same – the back room on the ground floor had an enclave from the rest of the shop's wards in order to allow for direct gate transit. I reached out through the dreamstone and the fateweaver, combining their powers. The dreamstone allowed me to step from here into Elsewhere; the fateweaver allowed me to exploit flaws in the castle's defences. The Light mages working right now were creating large-scale breaches in the shadow realm's wards to hold their gates open for an extended period. By slipping through chinks in the armour and causing the defences to weaken at opportune times, I could create a much smaller breach with a fraction of the effort.

At the same time, I was watching the futures. My divination was still telling me that the invasion was set to start at eight sharp, and with a thrill of satisfaction I knew I'd guessed right. Richard was hiding the truth from us, and he hadn't figured out that we were onto him. Yet.

As I watched, the future seemed to quiver. I'd never seen anything like it before, and it was a strange sensation, as though reality was shaking loose. It made me dizzy to watch, and I had to look around to reassure myself that yes, I was still in the back room.

'Alex?' Luna asked.

'I'm fine,' I said absently. I was still forming the gate. I'd grown better with the dreamstone, and I'd discovered that with a little extra work I could compress the Elsewhere journey down to effectively nothing, placing the gate from here to Elsewhere and the gate from Elsewhere to the shadow realm right next to one another. After all these years, I could finally gate the way elemental mages could.

And then, just as I watched, the futures shattered, a screen breaking and crumbling to reveal new futures, *real* futures, that were a flurry of activity. I felt my spirits lift. I spend so much time looking into the future that having it taken away feels like fumbling around in the dark. Now the lights were on.

'Okay,' I said. 'Gate into the shadow realm is in ninety seconds. Once we get through, things are going to get messy. Ji-yeong, we're coming out in the same spot we left from. You know the area?'

'I know it,' Ji-yeong said. Hermes had appeared at Luna's feet and was watching us, bright-eyed.

'We're going to need a way to get out of sight and escape pursuit quickly. You know a route that'll do that?'

Ji-yeong hesitated. 'I don't know if—'

Hermes yipped.

We all looked down at him. Hermes looked up at me and blinked.

'Okay,' I said. 'Fox has the point.'

My communicator pinged, then pinged again. I didn't answer. Everything had been set in motion and the only question was which dominos would fall first.

And then the air shimmered and a portal opened in mid-air. It was messier than the neat ovals created by gate magic, but through it I could see the yellow stones of the castle and feel the warm sea breeze. The sky above was the dusky purple of twilight.

I jumped through. Hermes followed at my heels and Luna and Ji-yeong came through a second later.

We were in a small courtyard at the base of a tower. Archways and a set of stairs led off in several directions. The four of us looked around, holding our breath. Nothing moved. After the background hum of Camden, the castle was eerily silent.

Behind us, the portal hung in the air. 'Do they know we're here?' I asked Ji-yeong.

'Yes,' Ji-yeong said. She looked tense. 'The alarm's going.'

'What alarm?' Luna asked.

'*All of them.* We can't stay.'

'Just a second,' I said. The futures were shifting.

'Master Verus,' Ji-yeong said, and the urgency in her voice made me turn. 'We need to go. *Now.*'

I hesitated. I wanted to see the isolation ward trigger . . . but then I saw Ji-yeong's expression, and I let the portal back to my shop fade into thin air. 'Hermes,' I called.

A red and white head poked out from the top of the stairs, gave us an impatient glance and vanished again.

I took a grip on the *sovnya*, and together we jogged up the steps.

In the distance, the silence was broken by a wail, rising and falling like a siren. 'What's *that*?' Luna asked.

'Major breach alarm,' Ji-yeong said. 'I don't—'

'Brace!' I snapped.

The world around us *shifted*. There was no other way to describe it. It was like watching a video feed where the resolution changes, or having your ears pop and suddenly being able to hear. I stumbled, catching myself just in time, while Luna went sprawling. It was all over in an instant and I stood up, looking around. Everything seemed normal again, the moment of wrongness already gone.

'That was the isolation ward?' I asked Ji-yeong.

'How should I know?' Ji-yeong said. She was looking around nervously. 'Even Sagash wasn't crazy enough to fire that thing just to see what it looked like.'

'Well, looks like you guessed right,' Luna said, pulling herself to her feet. 'How many do you think made it in?'

'Don't know,' I said, pointing up at the sky. 'But I think I can guess where they are.'

The walls around us limited our view, but between two towers was a gap through which we could see a narrow window of sky. Across it, lit in the fading sunset, a cloud of black dots was drifting. They were very small, almost invisible at this distance. If you didn't look too closely, it could have been a flock of birds.

'Uh,' Luna said. 'Are those . . . ?'

'Shadow constructs,' I said. Anne hadn't wasted any time bringing the things under her control.

'They'll be coming this way too,' Ji-yeong said. 'Now will you listen to me and *run*?'

We ran.

Through the castle, across walkways and around buildings. Hermes dashed ahead faster than any of us, a red flash in the gloom. Above us, the sky was fading from purple to grey. Towers loomed up all around, shadowed and threatening, dark windows hiding what might be within.

Elsewhere in the castle, fighting had broken out. A distant boom echoed from the east, followed by more. Lights flickered, faint and reflected, and I could feel the signature of battle magic. I couldn't tell who was winning, and I didn't stop to find out. The Council army could afford to fight Anne's forces in open battle; we couldn't.

Hermes began to lead us downwards, flights of stairs pointing down toward ground level. As he did, the futures lit up. *Incoming*, I sent to Luna and Ji-yeong.

The shadows in the archway ahead moved. Black figures appeared out of the darkness, spreading out to block the courtyard. Five, ten, a dozen.

I felt the *sovnya* stir. Luna and Ji-yeong slowed and stopped. *Alex?* Luna asked telepathically. *Call it.*

'They're here to slow us down,' I said quietly. I walked between Luna and Ji-yeong to face the creatures. The jann stayed where they were, blocking the way forward. 'We're going through.'

I strode forward. The jann spread out, faces blank and expressionless, welcoming me in.

The *sovnya*'s bloodlust ignited, and I let it fill me.

The world around seemed to fade. Walls, floors, stone – all were shadows. Dead things, useless things. Only the living mattered. The three humans blazed with life, white blooms against the darkness. The things in front, though . . . they glowed an angry red, twisted, *wrong*. Tendrils of corruption seemed to spread from them, warping the space around. As I cut through the first, the tendrils that made up its essence flared, wisping away. Behind it was another, and another. It was methodical work, satisfying, like clearing weeds out of a garden. As each one faded, its tendrils faded too, the world seeming to sigh in relief as the taint was burned away.

The last of the things died. But the castle was infested; there were more, far more. I let my senses spread outwards, searching. Another presence, not as harshly wrong as the others, but still tainted, an aberration. I moved toward it but it slipped away. It was small, agile. Familiar, somehow—

Hermes.

Realisation flashed through me and all of a sudden I came awake. *No!* I struggled, fought the *sovnya*'s influence. It was like swimming in heavy clothing, trying to reach the surface. The *sovnya* resisted. *Tainted. Kill.* I forced it away, clawed upwards, broke clear—

Sight and sound rushed back. I was standing on the other side of an archway. Black bodies lay all around, red light glowing from gaping rents. The ones farther back were already starting to dissolve, vapour drifting upwards.

Luna and Ji-yeong were back in the archway, staring at me. Both had their swords out, the blades a matched pair. '*Alex*,' Luna said urgently. 'Can you hear me?'

'Yeah,' I said. The *sovnya*'s influence was receding, but I could still sense it, waiting and hungry. From the position of the bodies, I must have kept advancing after the last one had fallen. I knew where I'd been going, too. Dimly I could still sense Hermes, a red glow in the darkness, changed by magic, unnatural—

No. I forced the thought away. This was *my* mind, and *my* body. The *sovnya* withdrew . . . for now.

Hermes had led us to a small enclosed courtyard. Sheets of metal leant against the walls and some unidentifiable machine stood rusting in the centre. The high walls blocked any view of the sky, but I could still hear the distant sounds of battle. Hermes was waiting at the far side, next to a doorway that opened into darkness.

I walked closer; Hermes trotted aside, eyeing the *sovnya*. The doorway led into empty space. A vertical shaft dropped away into blackness, cables hanging in the shadows.

Ji-yeong walked up next to me. 'Lift shaft?' I asked.

'Yeah,' she said with a curious look. 'Down to the old levels.' She glanced at Hermes. 'I thought Sagash sealed these off?'

Hermes looked back at her blandly.

'Does it work?' I asked.

Ji-yeong stepped forward to study the controls set into the wall. 'As long as Anne hasn't broken anything . . .'

'It's too quiet,' Luna said.

'I know what you mean,' I said. I looked ahead into the short-term futures. 'Ji-yeong? We need that lift.'

In answer, Ji-yeong shoved one of the levers. There was a screech of rust and a clanking sound, and within the shaft, I saw the cables start to shake and move.

'How long?' Luna asked.

'Until that lift reaches the top, two minutes,' I said. 'Bad news is someone else is going to be here first.'

Luna and Ji-yeong moved instantly towards cover.

Hermes disappeared with a flick of his tail. 'Who?' Luna asked.

'It's Sam, isn't it?' Ji-yeong asked.

'Sam, or Aether, since you said that's his mage name now,' I said. I looked at Luna. 'Lightning mage. He'll be coming from above, shooting on sight. Stay out of view.'

'So she got him too,' Ji-yeong said with a twist of her mouth.

'You knew him,' I said. 'Any advice?'

'He hates fighting up close,' Ji-yeong said. 'You get in range, he'll lightning jump away. You can't catch him, but you can hold him off.'

'Board the lift as soon as it arrives,' I said. 'Ten seconds.'

Silence fell. Ji-yeong and Luna were sheltering behind the buttresses that jutted from the wall. I stayed in the shadows of one of the doorways. Night had fallen and the courtyard was cloaked in shadow.

How many times had I waited like this? Keyed-up and still, seconds dragging by. Then the shift in futures, the scrape of a footstep, the lunge, futures splintering into the chaos of combat.

It was very close now. Was that a sound up above? Sam must have flown in silently, alighted on the rooftop. He should be coming into view of the courtyard right about—

I snapped my eyes shut as the courtyard went white. The flash was bright enough for me to see it through my eyelids, and a numbing jolt went through me as the courtyard rang to a deafening crash of thunder. Air rushed past, blasting my hair, then everything was still.

I opened my eyes. From a dozen places in the courtyard, faint trails of smoke were rising. The blast had been concentrated near the lift shaft. The mechanism was still moving, though I couldn't hear anything except for a faint whine. The air stank of ozone.

Nothing moved. Luna and Ji-yeong had been smart enough to stay hidden. There would be no way for Sam to know how many people were waiting in the shadows, and that would make him cautious. Mages from the air sub-family don't like to drop down into close quarters. His first instinct would be to wait, to keep his distance—

Sam dropped down into the courtyard.

Surprise skittered along the edge of my thoughts, but I was already moving, closing on Sam in a silent rush. Sam spun, electricity crackling around his hands, and I narrowed my focus to the next couple of seconds. The first lightning bolt went wide; the second would have hit but I pushed with the fateweaver and felt hot air wash over my head. Before he could strike again, I was on him. I could see his shield, hardened air crackling with static, but air shields are more flexible than strong; an enchanted weapon like the *sovnya* would cut through like paper. I started my swing and took in the futures in a wide-angle glance, a single glimpse with a hundred variations of the next half-second, searching for one in which the polearm cut through cleanly so that I could use the fateweaver to—

There wasn't one.

The *sovnya* hit the side of Sam's shield and bounced off, the shock vibrating down my arms. The impact made Sam stumble, but he recovered almost instantly and looked at me with flat, shadowed eyes from less than five feet away.

Sam fired a lightning bolt into my chest.

8

The Alex from ten years ago would have died in that courtyard. The lightning would have burned straight through his body, killing him instantly. The Alex from five years ago would have survived the first blast, but the shock would have left him stunned. The follow-up attack would have killed him a few seconds later.

But I was very different from my younger self. I had my imbued armour, and the fateweaver's magic. More than that, I had its mindset. The fateweaver had been designed to command a battlefield, and the battlefield was where it was most at home.

In the split-second before Sam fired, I took in hundreds of possible futures. Nearly all of them saw me die in the next ten seconds. The first blast wouldn't kill, but it would daze me enough that Sam could easily finish me off. In a few futures I was able to hurl myself out of the worst of the blast, but I'd still be caught by the edge of it. There were no futures in which I dodged: I was too close and the fateweaver couldn't nudge Sam's aim far enough off course.

But there *was* one future in which I broke away.

The lightning burst out from Sam's hands, blindingly bright, and I pushed with the fateweaver, straining for the future I needed. The lightning forked as the fate-weaver guided it, finding pathways in the air. Some of the charge went around me; more crackled through my armour. But there was too much power in the bolt to guide it all away, and instead of trying, I took the hit on my lower body, letting the electricity go through my legs and into the ground.

Every muscle in my legs and feet spasmed, and I kicked off from the courtyard like a gymnast. I did a full mid-air somersault, hit the ground, rolled and came up as another blast of lightning lashed the stone.

Sam was more than twenty feet away. It was hard to make out his features in the darkness but he looked surprised. When you hit someone with lightning, you don't expect them to jump like a kangaroo. He recovered immediately, but the second's pause had been enough and I was on my feet and dodging out of sight behind the courtyard machinery.

'Alex!' Luna shouted.

No! I snapped at her through the dreamstone. *Break left!*

Luna had stepped out to attack, her whip coming out in a swing, but as she heard my warning she dived sideways. Lightning crashed through the space where she'd just been.

He's too strong, I sent telepathically. *Ji-yeong, you too.*

Ji-yeong had been circling around for a flank; now she halted. *So what, then?* she asked.

All three of us were briefly out of Sam's line of sight, the tangle of machinery at the centre of the courtyard blocking his vision. *Ji-yeong, stand there*, I said, sending the image of the spot I meant. *Luna, behind the buttress. When he comes over, hit him from all sides.*

Telepathy is much faster than speech: we'd had the whole conversation in two seconds. Now that we weren't poking our heads out, the futures forked. In some of them, Sam blasted the courtyard blind; in others, he advanced or jumped over.

I reached out for the strands of the future I needed and tapped an iron wheel in front of me with the butt of the *sovnya*. A faint *clang* echoed around the courtyard.

Lightning magic surged and Sam came soaring over the machinery in a thirty-foot leap. I was already moving and his strike split the paving stones behind me. Sam landed with a thud, tracking me as he prepared to fire again.

Luna and Ji-yeong came out at the same instant, the three of us forming a triangle with Sam at the centre. Luna's whip snapped out and silver-grey mist lashed into Sam's body. At the same time, Ji-yeong and I charged him from both sides.

Sam was midway through his next attack when he realised what was about to happen. If he blasted either of us, the other would get him in the back. As my *sovnya* began its thrust, Sam's body went white, becoming blinding energy that flashed upwards in a lightning bolt.

Ji-yeong and I skidded to a stop, our blades halting inches from each other. Behind, I sensed the movement of the lift change, and I pointed towards it. *Get in.*

Ji-yeong obeyed instantly, breaking into a run. *What about you?* Luna asked.

I'll follow.

You can't—

We all go down at once, he'll just cut the cables and watch us fall.

Luna hesitated.

I softened my thoughts slightly. *I'll follow, I promise. Go!*

Luna ran after Ji-yeong. The old lift had reached courtyard level, and Ji-yeong was waiting impatiently by the door, a lever in her hand. As soon as Luna ducked through, Ji-yeong pulled the lever and darted after her. The lift descended with a shudder, Luna and Ji-yeong disappearing from sight.

I was alone in the courtyard. There was no sign of Sam. His lightning jump would have carried him out of range but he'd have had time to get back down to the edge of the rooftops. He would be up there now, looking to re-engage.

Parts of the courtyard had overhangs, blocking any direct view of the sky above. I drew back against the wall and called out softly, using the fateweaver and the echoes to twist the sound of my voice. 'You're fast, Sam. Or I guess I should be calling you Aether now.'

Silence.

I moved right, hugging the wall, careful not to let my footsteps ring out. 'I remember that lightning trick from the last time we fought,' I called up. 'You remember? When you and Darren brought Anne here. You were working for Crystal then.'

The walls and shadows were silent. My ears were still ringing, but I could dimly make out the clanking of the lift. If Sam had been focused on the fight, he might not have noticed that it had shifted from going up to going down.

I kept talking, using the fateweaver to throw my voice. The narrow courtyard cast echoes, and it wasn't hard to bounce the sound off a first-floor window, making it seem as if I was hiding in its shadows. 'Crystal's dead, by the way. Anne killed her. And from what I've heard, so's Darren. You're the only one left. But you're *not* really left, are you? Because you're not Sam, or Aether, or any of the other names you used. You're something else, wearing his body. Is the real Sam still in there somewhere? Can you hear what's going on, or is it—?'

The courtyard went white. Lightning split the sky, striking into the window opposite. Stone chips went flying, bouncing and skittering around the courtyard.

'Okay,' I said once the echoes of the thunderclap had died away. 'Touchy subject.'

My feet and legs were still numb. They were moving, but not quite as fast as they should; maybe a ten or twenty per cent drop in agility. 'So, jinn,' I said. 'Ifrit, general, whatever you call yourself. Are you sure you should be trying this hard to kill me? Because I think Anne would much rather take me alive.'

Silence. I'd expected the jinn to have dropped back down by now. I couldn't get a handle on its reactions well enough to predict them. I widened my view of the futures and a variety of different attacks played out before me. The patterns were confusing, different from fighting a human.

'Maybe she was in too much of a hurry?' I called. 'I'd think twice, in any case. She's going to be very upset if you . . .'

I trailed off. One future was eclipsing the others.

The smell of ozone in the courtyard grew stronger. Light flickered and I turned to look. A mote of electricity sparked from a piece of scrap metal in the corner, first once, then again and again. More sparks flickered from the sheet metal piled against the walls, from the iron wheels behind, from the levers by the lift, from every part of the machinery at the centre. Everything metal was sparking.

The sparks grew brighter, crackling. The stink of ozone grew stronger. Electricity flashed, joining an iron bar to a sheet of metal, a piece of scrap to a railing, a wheel to a lever. A distant hum began to rise, faint at first, then growing louder and louder.

From the opposite side of the courtyard, the lift machinery clanked to a halt.

I took one look at the futures ahead, then lunged for the lift shaft.

Electricity exploded outward. It was as if my movement had triggered something, and a hundred tiny bolts of lightning flashed out, connecting every piece of metal in the courtyard with each other, the walls, the floor. I wove a path through them and realised in less than a second that it wouldn't work, there were too many. The lightning was trying to path through me into the ground.

So I jumped. Air magic surged from my headband and sent me flying in a low arc.

Lightning flashed all around me in a lethal spiderweb. I couldn't dodge any more but the fateweaver worked its magic, bending away the electricity, finding a safe path through the maze of death. Seconds seemed to stretch out as I soared through the air, strobing energy all around, every hair standing on end, half-blinded eyes seeing the black square of the lift shaft draw closer, closer—

I went flying through the doorway, slammed into the opposite wall, and fell. The roar and flash of lightning cut off and I was falling through darkness. The *sovnya* scraped the wall, sending me spinning; cables burnt the back of my hand.

I channelled through the headband, air magic wrapping around me. My spin slowed and stopped, my speed dropping until I was sliding downwards at a comfortable ten feet per second. The darkness felt warm, comforting. Light glimmered below and I saw the roof of the lift rise up out of the gloom to meet me.

My feet hit metal with a clang and I rolled forward, coming out of the shaft to drop onto bare rock. I spun instantly, the *sovnya* coming up. The lift was seven feet tall, the gap from the top of the lift to the edge of the ceiling three feet more. I held the *sovnya* back, ready to strike.

Seconds ticked by. My eyes were glued to that three-foot gap. If Sam followed me down, he would drop onto the roof of that lift. For an instant he'd be off guard, and I'd have the chance to cut through his shield and into his legs. I'd have to kill or cripple him with the first strike.

Silence. I held absolutely still. The lift shaft was silent as the grave. I looked through the futures and couldn't find any in which Sam came down the shaft in the next few seconds. I searched further ahead. One minute. Five minutes. Ten.

Nothing.

He wasn't coming.

'Alex?' a voice said from behind.

I exhaled and turned, letting the tension seep out of my muscles. Luna and Ji-yeong were standing just behind me, weapons ready. 'We're clear,' I said.

We'd come down into a natural cavern beneath the

castle bedrock, pitch-black but for Luna's and Ji-yeong's lights. Huge rusting iron pipes loomed up out of the darkness, silent and ominous, running away to the north and south-west.

Ji-yeong relaxed, lowering her short-sword to sheathe it at her waist. Magelights danced around her, four tiny spheres weaving over her shoulders and at her sides, coloured a bright vibrant green. 'I didn't think he'd be that strong.'

'It's not really him,' I said.

Ji-yeong nodded. 'That's it, isn't it? I've always been a match for Sam. But it isn't Sam any more.' She grimaced. 'Everyone's stronger than me now.'

'You get used to it,' Luna said dryly.

'You know where these caverns go?' I asked Ji-yeong.

'This must be the old water main,' Ji-yeong said. 'It'll run to the north caves. The western route should lead to the keep.'

'North it is.'

We started walking. The caverns were ancient, smooth uneven rock that rose and fell under our feet. Luna and Ji-yeong stumbled occasionally, but Ji-yeong's magelights flew low over the stone, illuminating the drops and holes. Hermes appeared briefly, painted green in the glow, then disappeared off ahead. 'I gave you bad advice,' Ji-yeong admitted.

'Wasn't just you,' I said. 'I underestimated him as well.' I'd made the mistake of treating Sam as though he were human, and I'd nearly died for it. The feeling was starting to return to my legs, and with it was coming burning pain.

'It wasn't just the power,' Ji-yeong said. 'His style . . .'

'Jinn don't feel fear or pain the way we do,' I said. 'They don't care about their host getting hurt.' A normal lightning mage would have flinched when he'd seen my *sovnya* swinging towards him, tried to defend or dodge. Sam had just taken the hit and blasted me. 'Even when he jumped away, it wasn't because he was afraid. It was because he knew he was going to get his body destroyed if he didn't.'

We walked for a little while longer while the burning in my legs grew worse. When it became hard to concentrate, I finally let myself stop. 'I think that's far enough. Ji-yeong, can you take a look at my injuries, please?'

Luna stood watch while I lowered myself down to lean against the rock wall. I had to hold back a sigh of relief as I took the weight off my feet. Ji-yeong knelt next to me, green light hovering at her hands as she placed a hand flat against my chest. 'Electrical burns through both legs, especially the right thigh. Looks painful.'

'Anything serious?'

Ji-yeong shook her head. 'No, you were lucky. Internal organs were out of the path of the current. It'll regenerate with . . .' She tailed off, eyes widening. 'What the *hell*?'

'Oh, right,' I said. 'It was like that when I got here.'

Ji-yeong stared at my right arm. 'What *is* it?'

'A symbiotic imbued item. Don't worry about it.'

'That can't be a graft. Is that . . . transmuted flesh?'

'I said, don't worry about it.'

'If something had eaten my arm and was starting on my shoulder, *I'd* worry about it.' Ji-yeong put up her free hand. 'Fine. I won't ask.'

'Thank you,' I said. I could see that Luna was listening

very closely. 'I'm going to path-walk. Stay quiet for a few minutes.'

Ji-yeong was as good as her word, and as her magic got to work the pain from my legs faded. I took advantage of the rest to see what was happening elsewhere in the castle.

Landis's force from the Order of the Shield seemed to be doing reasonably well. They were still skirmishing, but the heavy fighting looked to be over and the futures where I reached out to their minds with the fateweaver were reassuringly free of panic. Whatever was going on, they seemed to have it under control.

Nimbus's force was another story. All the futures in which I tried to open up a link rapidly broke down into chaos, and in a tiny but significant fraction the links cut off in pain and darkness, suggesting that the additional distraction of my presence had been enough to cause someone's death. They were still in combat, possibly one that was not going well.

Richard's group was an enigma. The only two mages from his group that I knew well enough to forge a link with were Richard and Vihaela, and there was no way in hell I was entering into telepathic contact with either. I couldn't even say for sure whether they were in the castle, but all my instincts said yes.

I drew back to the present. Ji-yeong was finishing up, green light glowing softly around her hands, staring into my legs as if she could see through the skin. 'Done?' I asked.

Ji-yeong nodded and I got up. Weakness swept through me and I had to pull myself upright with my right arm, but the pain was gone, and as I tested my legs, they felt far better. 'Much better,' I said. 'Thank you.'

'You'll need to eat in the next couple of hours,' Ji-yeong warned. 'Oh, and I wouldn't go fighting any more jinn until you've had a night's sleep.'

'Well, I've got some good news as far as that goes,' I said. 'Looks like Anne's throwing everything she's got against the Council main force. We should be free to move for the next half-hour.'

'So now that Richard's done his completely predictable betrayal,' Luna said, 'what do we do?'

'We join up with Landis.'

The three of us started walking again. Ji-yeong's light illuminated the curved, shadowed walls of the cave, bright enough to drown out the glow of Luna's torch. Hermes stayed ahead, appearing now and again in a flicker of movement before vanishing.

'So . . .' Luna said. 'Not to ask a stupid question, but whose side are we on?'

'We aren't completely on anyone's side,' I said, 'because no one's completely on *our* side. You and I are here because of Anne and Vari. And Ji-yeong's here because . . . Why *are* you here?'

'I left all my make-up back in my room in the keep.'

Luna and I looked at her.

'You know how hard it is to find decent lip stain outside of Korea?' Ji-yeong asked. 'The stuff you guys have is terrible.'

I kept looking at her.

Ji-yeong sighed. 'Fine. I don't like losing, all right? This castle was my home and I'm not running away without a fight.'

I nodded. I was pretty sure that was true as far as it went, although I knew there was more she wasn't saying. 'Anyway, for now, we can mostly trust the Council. Landis's group, at least. As long as we've got the threat of Anne hanging over us, we're on the same team. Richard is probably more hostile right now than he's ever been. In the past, he needed me because of Anne. He doesn't any more. If he can kill us, he will.'

'And Anne?' Luna asked.

'There's probably enough left of her that she'll want to talk to us at least a little bit before enslaving us.'

'You're a real ray of sunshine lately, you know that?'

We kept going. At regular intervals, I checked on the futures in which I tried to contact Nimbus's force. The combat kept going for another fifteen minutes, then died away.

At last the tunnel began to widen into a cavern. The air began to stir with a breeze, carrying the salt tang of the sea. Hermes came into view in Ji-yeong's light, sitting with his tail curled around his legs. He looked to our right at the wall, where a small doorway led into a spiral staircase. We entered and started climbing. Up, up, up, step after step.

At last I stopped, feeling Ji-yeong and Luna come to a halt behind me. 'Hey there,' I called up softly.

My voice echoed around the spiral staircase. No answer.

'Friendlies coming up,' I called.

A voice called back down from up above. 'No friendlies down there, mate.'

'Mage Verus with my team,' I called. 'Confirm with Landis. He knows we're coming.'

A moment's pause. 'Stay there.'

We waited for a minute before the voice called again. 'All right, come on.'

Three Council soldiers were waiting at the top of the stairs, dressed in body armour and carrying rifles. One of them nodded at me. 'This way, sir.' He led us through a narrow tunnel. Light and the murmur of voices began to grow ahead of us, and as we came around a corner and out into the open, we walked out into bright light and noise.

The room was a huge stone structure built for some forgotten purpose, and had been turned into a combination mess hall and barracks in which dozens of Council soldiers were bustling about, laying out bedrolls and readying gear. Electric lights made the stone walls look almost friendly. A portable kitchen had been set up in the centre and men were lining up with bowls; I could hear sizzling and smelt frying sausages. In the corner was what looked like a small field hospital, marked out with white banners holding red crosses.

'What are they doing?' Ji-yeong sounded slightly insulted. 'Camping?'

The man leading us acted as if he hadn't heard. 'Captain's this way, sir.'

We walked through the men. I recognised a few and nodded. Many looked cheerful, and I heard the odd laugh. The hospital didn't seem very crowded – it had four camp-beds, one of which was empty. Whatever the battle had been like, they'd obviously come through in good spirits.

Landis came ducking out of a doorway ahead. 'Ah, Verus!' he called cheerfully. 'You and Mage Vesta made it in one piece, delighted to see it.' He shook my hand

and gave Luna a nod. 'Oh, and Lady Ji-yeong, excellent! My men and I are very grateful for your briefing. Extremely clear and helpful. If you need anything, just ask.'

'Uh.' Ji-yeong looked taken aback. 'Thank you.'

'I should be the one thanking you, dear girl. Well then!' Landis clapped his hands. 'Time for some tea.'

'Seriously?' Luna asked.

'Absolutely! Right this way.' Landis wove through us and headed for the portable kitchen. 'I don't know about you, but between the battle and all the jawing, I'm quite parched.'

'Um,' Ji-yeong said, hurrying to keep up with Landis's long strides. 'Mage Landis? I don't mean any disrespect—'

'Of course! But a more profound form of disrespect is an unwillingness to come forward, wouldn't you say?'

'—but isn't this dangerous? If there's an attack . . .'

'Four cups, please,' Landis said to the man behind the stove, who nodded and turned to some sort of chrome and brass contraption that looked very similar to one I'd once seen in Landis's house in Edinburgh. Landis turned back to Ji-yeong. 'My dear girl, when it comes to military life, there are three things you're always short of. Good intelligence, a hot meal and enough sleep. Whenever you have the chance to give your men the last two, you should take it.'

Ji-yeong looked around.

'No, he's not crazy,' I told her. 'If he's let his men set up camp like this, it means we're not due any attacks.' I glanced at Landis. 'At least not for a while?'

'Not for a few hours, I'd expect. Thank you, Jamie.'

Landis accepted a steaming mug from the man behind the stove and blew on it before addressing us. 'Sugar's on the table there; do help yourselves. Even milk, God forbid. Well, as I was saying, we managed to bring the entire force through before the isolation ward activated and the gate collapsed. Our arrival triggered the alarms and their rapid-response force arrived in six minutes. By then we'd set up fire zones around the windmill, and the jinn and shadows were taken care of easily enough. The second wave was a little more troublesome, a mage by the name of Sagash. Acquaintance of yours, I believe?'

I sighed. 'I'd been afraid of that.'

'It did get rather sticky for a few minutes,' Landis agreed. 'A few bumps and bruises, but no fatalities, I'm happy to say.'

'You fought off Sagash without anyone getting killed?'

'We did have something of an advantage of numbers.' Landis blew on his mug and took a gulp. 'Tried to catch him, but he's a slippery bugger. We've got pickets if he tries for an encore, but I rather suspect he'll give us more respect next time.'

'If Anne's got Sagash, does that mean she knows everything about the castle defences?' Luna asked.

'Safe bet,' I said. 'Landis? What about the other force?'

'Ah, yes,' Landis said. 'As they say, there is balance in all things. Director Nimbus, unfortunately, saw fit to delay his deployment while he attempted to verify your analysis. When he did send his force, it was a little late. The gate closed partway through.'

I swore. 'How many—?'

'Once through,' Landis continued, 'he took the remaining part of his force and attempted to follow the original attack plan. Unfortunately, this did rather attract attention and Miss Walker deployed the bulk of her forces against him. The fighting didn't fully stop until ten minutes ago and I'm afraid it was rather bloody.'

'How bad is it?'

'Between dead, wounded, and those left behind, I'd estimate Nimbus's force is down to around forty per cent strength. In light of this new development, the assault has been put on hold for the time being.'

'On that subject,' I said, 'aren't you supposed to be attacking?'

'Absolutely!' Landis said, waving his mug around. 'According to the assault plan, established by no less an august presence than our very own Senior Council, all of us are driving on the keep at this very moment. Of course, that plan may not align perfectly with the current state of affairs as it might appear to us from our limited perspective here on the ground, but I have every confidence that the after-action reports will draw a veil over any such irregularities.'

Luna, Ji-yeong and I looked around. A collection of soldiers and Keepers from the Order of the Shield were listening in on the conversation with mugs of tea steaming in their hands. None of them looked as though they were about to go assaulting any keeps.

'Well then!' Landis said. 'I really must go check on the pickets. Do have some of the sausages. Jamie is quite excellent at turning any rations you give him into a thoroughly pleasant meal. After all, what's the point of extradimensional storage if you don't get a good dinner out of it, eh?' He clapped me on the shoulder and paused. 'Oh, and Verus, I'd recommend giving Nimbus a little time to cool off. He isn't in the best of moods right now and I rather suspect any conversation would turn out badly. Toodle-oo.' Landis strode off. Two Keepers peeled off to follow him.

'I'm going to talk to Tobias,' Luna said. She walked over to the remaining Keepers.

Ji-yeong was staring after Landis. '*That's* your captain?'

A nearby soldier laughed. 'Stick around,' I said. 'You'll see why they follow him.'

'If you say so.'

'He was the one who took on Sagash, miss,' the soldier told Ji-yeong.

Ji-yeong looked startled. '*He* fought *Sagash*?'

'Landis is one of the best battle mages I've ever seen,' I told her. 'And a good commander. Look around.' I nodded at the soldiers and mages talking and laughing among themselves. 'They just went through an attack, and they're telling jokes.'

'At least he's confident . . .'

I sighed, my brief good humour fading. I took my mug of tea. *He wasn't*, I sent to Ji-yeong through the dreamstone.

Ji-yeong gave me a surprised look.

Today was just the warm-up, I told her silently. *A day from now, a good number of the people in this room are going to be dead. Get some sleep. Tomorrow will be bloody.* I walked away without waiting for an answer.

9

Outside was dark and still. A blurry moon shone down through the haze, the castle battlements looming up all around. From up ahead I could hear the slow *creak . . . creak . . . creak* of the windmill.

I walked around the castle walls, my feet soft on the grass. The windmill was a hulking shadow in the gloom, its sails turning slowly in the sea breeze. Far below, the sea crashed against the rocks.

There was a man leaning against the windmill, invisible in the darkness. 'Ozols, isn't it?' I said.

'Ah, Verus, yes?' Ozols sounded pleased. 'Yes, yes.'

'Brought you some tea,' I said, walking up and handing him the mug. 'All quiet?'

'Yes, yes,' Ozols said in his thick accent. 'Those demons, they watch. No move.'

'Jinn, not demons,' I said with a yawn. 'But close enough. I'll be in the windmill.'

'Inside is warmer,' Ozols said with a chuckle. 'I call if they attack, yes?'

'Thanks, Ozols.'

'Is no problem. Thank you for tea!'

I walked past Ozols into the windmill. The inside was pitch-black, lit only by stray moonbeams. I climbed the stairs until I came to an open room on the upper level. Windows opened up on all four walls, giving views onto the castle and out to sea.

I sat down against the wall with a sigh. The after-effects of Ji-yeong's healing were setting in and my limbs felt heavy and tired. My stomach was also telling me in no uncertain terms that I was hungry, and I knew the sensible thing would be to go back to Landis's camp and get a hot meal and a nap on one of those camp-beds.

I rummaged in my bag for a protein bar instead. My stomach growled in protest.

I stared up at the sky as I chewed. From my angle, I couldn't make out the moon, though its beams cast the opposite wall in blue-white light. A few stars were visible through the haze. The first time I'd come to this castle, Anne and I had spent the night in this windmill. She'd been afraid and vulnerable, but she hadn't given up, staying awake and on the run for days. Only when I'd found her had she allowed herself to finally fall asleep. It had been right in this room, and I'd been against the wall . . . here?

No, it had been the other side. I got up, ignoring the angry complaints from my legs and back, and dropped down against the opposite wall. I shuffled over a little bit until, as far as I remembered, I was in the exact same spot. Once I did, I closed my eyes.

That was it. I'd been against this wall, just here, and Anne had been on my right. I'd had my arm around her, and that was how she'd fallen asleep, her head on my shoulder. I remembered how she'd looked, white skin pale in the moonlight, strands of black hair falling across her cheek down to my coat, the slow rise and fall of her chest. Had that been when I'd started to fall in love with her? Memories . . . waking in Arachne's lair as Anne healed me, lying side by side with her on the grass of the heath, training together in Wales . . .

It had been here that I'd first met Anne's shadow, too. Maybe that was where things had started to go wrong.

Anne's shadow had been a danger for a long time. Not the kind that creeps up on you, but the kind that sits and waits and is just a tiny bit bigger every time you look. The more I'd learned, the more worried I'd become. I'd tried talking to her; I'd tried getting help; I'd even travelled into Elsewhere to face it. In the end, none of it had really made a difference. Arachne had told me in her letter not to blame myself, that Anne's doom would have fallen with or without me. But I still felt as though it was my fault.

Maybe that was why I was here.

I kept my eyes closed. As long as I didn't move, I could pretend that Anne was next to me, just for a little while.

I felt the change in the futures before I heard the footsteps. They climbed the stairs. I didn't open my eyes.

Luna appeared in the doorway. 'Hey.'

I held up a hand.

Luna put a plate down next to me, the plastic clacking against the stone. 'I brought you something.'

I could smell the sausages from the kitchen. My stomach growled again. 'Thanks.'

Luna sat back against the wall, and I sensed the silver mist of her curse spreading out. Luna keeps it under tight control when people are close, relaxes it once they're at a safe distance. She does it automatically these days. 'Landis is quizzing Ji-yeong about the castle.'

I nodded.

'Still think we can trust her?'

'Sagash taught Ji-yeong one way to live,' I said. My

stomach wanted me to eat, but I didn't reach for the plate. 'Now she's realising that there are others. As to which one she'll pick . . . I think she's still figuring that out herself.'

'Are you okay?'

'Tomorrow's going to be ugly,' I said. 'The Council's going to launch an all-out attack. They'll probably spend all night arguing about it, but in the end it's not going to make a difference, because it's the only choice they've got. Landis knows it, I could see it in his eyes. A lot of people are going to end up dead.'

'Okay,' Luna said, and paused. 'That wasn't really what I was asking.'

'I know, I know. You just want to know about Vari.'

'No!'

I looked up in surprise. Luna was frowning at me. 'Alex, give me some credit, okay? Yes, I'm here because of Vari. But I know you'll do everything you can for him. Right now, I'm more worried about you.'

'You don't need to worry about me.'

'You think I haven't noticed?' Luna asked. 'Those conversations with Karyos? The way you've been giving me access to all those bank accounts, "just in case"? You aren't planning on coming back from this shadow realm. And you act different as well. You don't tell jokes or make fun of me or even smile. You're just . . . distant and focused.'

'I've got a lot to be focused on.'

'That doesn't mean you're supposed to act like a machine.'

'What do you want from me, Luna?' I snapped. I had too many things to worry about, and I didn't need this now. 'You just said that I'm going to do all I can for Vari. Well, you're right, I am, and it's going to be *really frigging hard*, because I've been counting up the numbers and I don't like the answers I'm getting. If I'm right, then saving him means solving a problem I don't know how to solve, on top of saving Anne, which means solving at least two *more* problems I don't know how to solve, and that might not be even *possible* to solve, but I *have* to solve them, because if I don't, there's nobody else. So excuse me if being friendly and approachable isn't high on my priority list!'

Luna was silent and I looked away, already regretting my words. I knew I shouldn't have lost my temper, but I was strained to breaking point.

'You remember when we went into that bubble realm in the British Museum?' Luna asked. 'When we were going after the fateweaver the first time?'

'Yeah.'

'We ran into Cinder and Deleo,' Luna said. 'They were caught in a trap and couldn't get out. I thought we should just leave them. You didn't. After they were gone, I asked you why you did it. You remember what you told me?'

'If you can't get another ally, next best thing is to give your enemy another enemy.'

Luna nodded. 'But when I kept asking, you gave me another answer. You remember?'

'Honestly, no.'

'You said there was another reason.' Luna was looking at me steadily. 'You said whenever you kill someone, it gets a little bit easier to do it the next time. You said if you're making the decision to do that, when you're doing it deliberately, to be really sure you know what you're doing. Because you're going to have to live with it for ever.'

I hesitated. Had I told her that?

I couldn't remember.

That bothered me.

'It's been a month since you took the fateweaver,' Luna said. She hadn't taken her eyes off me, and in the moonlight, I could make out her steady gaze. 'How many people have you killed since then?'

I didn't answer.

'Alex?'

I spoke quietly. 'I've lost count.'

The answer hung in the silence for a long moment before Luna started speaking again. 'Back when I first met you, I wanted to be a badass. You know: tough and strong and good at fighting. Like you. Even when I started to get into your world and met Dark mages and Light mages who could throw me around like I was nothing, it didn't put me off. It just pushed me to get better. It was why I got into duelling. I wanted to go up against mages and beat them. Even when I got hurt, it didn't put me off, I'd just drive myself harder. I think . . . I think in some weird way, I felt like I was fighting my curse. If I could get strong enough, go far enough, then I could beat it. So I kept training and pushing myself.

'Then there was what happened with White Rose. You remember that battle at the end, where Vari and I were with the Keeper strike team? I saw men killed right in front of me. And afterwards, watching them carry away the bodies . . . it made me realise something. The normals and the adepts killed in that battle, they trained too.

They wanted to be tough too. And in the end it got them . . . nothing. They died for nothing.

'I tried to forget about it, but for a long time after that, every time we heard about someone getting killed, I'd remember those bodies and I'd think: hey, that was someone who trained and practised and wanted to get stronger, just like me. And the more I thought about it, the more I realised . . . if you keep on fighting, if you keep trying to prove how tough you are, then that's the *only* way things can end, isn't it? And when you die, it's not going to be some heroic last stand. It'll be some pointless fight in a back alley, or a battle where neither side even knows what it's for. Most fights aren't about good and evil. I mean, even this one, right now. We're here because of Anne, but Anne would never have ended up like this if Richard and the Council hadn't been using her as a playing piece in their stupid chess game.

'So when I was picking my mage name, I decided I didn't want something that sounded cool and dangerous. I would have, once. Now, though . . . I've looked down that road, and I've seen where it ends. So I picked Vesta. The goddess of hearth and home and family. Maybe I'll get to have those things someday, maybe I won't. But even if I don't, it's worth a try.

'So the way you're acting now . . . it feels really wrong. Because you were the one who turned me *away* from all that. You taught me to look ahead, think about the future. But now it doesn't feel like you *care* about the future. When you told me to take that lift, and I hesitated . . . it was because I was wondering if you were going to follow us down.'

'I was always going to follow you down.'

Luna waited. I hadn't answered her question and we both knew it.

'But . . . there's probably going to be a time very soon when I won't.'

Silence fell. A sea breeze blew through the open windows. From far below, I could hear the rush of the waves against the rocks.

'I'm sorry,' I said. 'I haven't been setting you a very good example lately, have I?'

'I don't need an example. I'm not an apprentice any more. I'm *worried* about you, Alex, don't you understand that?'

'I do,' I said with a sigh. 'And you're right. It's just . . .' I trailed off, trying to figure out how to say it. It was an effort to find the words; this was a place in my mind I'd been shying away from. 'After I got away from Richard, I made a promise to myself that I wouldn't be like him. I knew I wasn't a good person, I was never going to be the hero. But I could be different from him. Running a shop . . . it's good, for that. No one expects much from a shopkeeper. You buy and sell, maybe give a little advice now and then. It's safe. But it can be lonely. So I started making friends. Arachne. Anne, Vari. You. And I came to realise over the years how much I cared about you all. I wouldn't give you up, and I'd fight if I had to.' I paused. 'Those were the two things that mattered to me. Not being like Richard, cold and manipulative and evil. And protecting and being loyal to all of you. It was why I wouldn't join with any of the factions. Didn't want to compromise. So I stayed apart.'

'Until?' Luna asked quietly.

'Until what happened with Anne,' I said. It was hard

to say all this, but I had to. I'd been keeping it bottled up too long. 'Two pillars. Not being Richard, and my friends. I'd been walking a tightrope between them. Figured I could keep my balance. Hadn't thought of what I'd do when the rope ran out. Anne being lost broke . . . everything. Couldn't leave her or she'd die. Vari, too: he was never going to walk away. But couldn't stop her, either. Not as the person I was.' I paused. 'Two pillars. Myself, all of you. Had to let one fall.'

'And you chose the first,' Luna said. 'You stopped trying to be different from Richard.'

'Funny thing?' I said. 'How easy it was. Just had to stop holding back.' I turned to look at Luna. 'You know all the times the Council screwed us over, or some Dark mage tried to kill us? Remember how after the dust settled we'd get together and talk? And you'd be furious, wanting to hit back, and I'd tell you to calm down and think?'

Luna nodded.

'You ever wonder why I didn't get angry?'

'A few times.'

'I did get angry,' I said. 'When Caldera acted like it was my fault for fighting back when she tried to arrest me. When Undaaris sold us out. When Levistus told me how he'd destroy us. When Bahamus voted for my sentencing. When Alma tried to remove me from the Council. When Talisid double-crossed me. When Onyx hurt me just because he could. When Vihaela boasted about torturing children. When those Council mages tortured Anne. Over and over. Every one of those things, they'd spark a tiny little white-hot drop of fury. But I couldn't let it loose, because they had the power and I didn't. So I'd force that little drop down below the surface, and it would stay there, burning away. And year after year, those drops kept building up.' I took a deep breath and let it out. 'So when I finally stopped holding back . . . let's just say that fire had a *lot* of fuel.'

'I did wonder,' Luna said. 'You were *too* calm about some of those things. But you don't act angry now.'

'Yeah, well, it turns out that when you store up that much anger for that long, then let it burn its way out, it's not good for you,' I said. 'It's hard for me to feel much of anything now. Too much pain, too much death. And I'm responsible for a lot of it.'

'Then shouldn't you be dealing with that?'

'I can't afford the distraction.'

'You're not cold enough to keep this up,' Luna said. 'Not long term.'

'Luna,' I said, trying to make my voice gentle, 'there isn't going to be a long term.'

Luna stiffened. 'You—'

I spoke over her. 'The fateweaver's spreading. Eventually it'll reach my heart. And once that happens, my emotional health isn't going to matter very much.'

'You could stop using it.'

'It's the only chance I've got of winning.'

'But—'

'The dragon told me this would happen,' I said. 'I've had time to accept it. And honestly, at this point, it might be for the best.'

Luna stared at me. Futures shifted; a hundred possible Lunas argued, protested, pleaded, shouted. One future eclipsed the others. Luna rose to her feet and left.

I listened to her footsteps descending the stairs, then rested my head back against the wall with a sigh. I hadn't wanted to open up that far, but Luna and I had been through too much for me to brush her off. She deserved the truth.

I still didn't feel happy about it.

With an effort, I put it out of my mind. The food Luna had brought me was nearly cold, and I ate without tasting, searching the futures as I did. Once I was done, I leant back and closed my eyes, willing myself to sleep. There was someone I needed to talk to, and tonight might be my last chance. As the world faded away, my last thought was to hope Luna would be feeling better by tomorrow.

The sky in Elsewhere was overcast. Brooding clouds stretched to the horizon, dark and ominous. Only a weak half-light made it through to the abandoned city below.

The conversation with Luna was still replaying itself in my head, calling up feelings as it did: tension, pain, worry, guilt. I forced the feelings away, centring myself. Breathe in, breathe out. The past was done; what mattered was the present. Once I was calm again, I set off, walking along a raised path above street level.

The sky stayed dark, the clouds thickening. I already knew from path-walking that Anne was asleep, though I hadn't been able to find out much else – divination isn't much use for looking into Elsewhere: it's too fluid. Trying to track her down like this was dangerous, but I had to try.

Trees rose up in front of me as I drew closer to the border. Beyond was Anne's kingdom . . . or world . . . or prison. I came to a stop at the edge of a plaza. Thirty feet ahead, the stones of the plaza broke up into clumps of grass that turned into a meadow that turned into a forest. Black storm-clouds roiled the sky.

I sent out a call. There was no sound, but my skills in Elsewhere were far advanced beyond what they'd once been, and I knew that Anne had heard me. I stood and waited.

Nothing. No shift.

She wasn't coming.

I walked forward into Anne's Elsewhere.

Instantly, the world changed. I could feel a presence in the air, charged and alive. The wind whipped up around me, hissing through the trees and rising to a roar. I'd crossed into something's territory, and it had noticed me.

I changed direction, moving next to one of the trees. It was a huge oak, hundreds of years old, great branches rising up into the sky. I leant against it and let the essence of the tree flow into me, feeling the earth, the water, the leaves. Anne's Elsewhere is its own world, sculpted over many years. It's not my world, but I loved Anne, and this place was made in her image. I knew it because I knew her.

The colour of the tree's bark spread to cover my body, its leaves hiding my hair. My feet ran down into the earth. I took my essence, the core of myself, and muted it, smoothing it out below the surface of the forest around me.

The storm hit seconds later. A roaring gale lashed the trees, rain hissing through the leaves. Through the canopy above, I had a vague image of a monstrous shape, legs like mountains, its head hidden in the clouds. I felt its attention turn towards me, massive and terrible. It brushed across the forest like fingers sweeping a carpet, huge yet strangely delicate. With a crash, a branch broke above my head, smashed down into the earth nearby, the sound almost drowned by the scream of the wind . . .

The presence passed over without finding me. It groped away to the north, fading, and was gone.

I stayed quite still for maybe a minute, neither moving nor breathing. The rain above died away to a drizzle and stopped, and the wind fell off until it was only a breeze.

I pulled my consciousness together again and stepped away from the tree. The broken branch was lying nearby, jagged and wet from the rain. I put my hand on the tree trunk in silent thanks and set off through the forest. Far away to the north, the storm raged.

I slipped through the trees quickly and quietly. When the wall of black glass loomed up in front of me, I jumped it in a single bound. I came down in an open courtyard, the only feature the black tower rising up ahead.

The sounds of the storm felt muted here. The wind blew less strongly and the hostile presence was weaker. I could still sense it, but there was something between, a kind of shield. The thing could still find me, but it would take time.

I crossed the courtyard and entered the tower, absent-mindedly creating a doorway that closed behind me. The inside was made of the same reflective black glass, soft lights glowing at intervals from the walls. I climbed a spiral staircase and opened a door.

The room within was the one that I'd come to think of as Dark Anne's drawing room. A long dining table of dark wood occupied the centre, with a sofa off to one side. The room was barer than I remembered: the chairs by the sofa were gone, as were most of the ones at the table. The sofa was green, as were the glass bowls on the table, contrasting sharply with the black walls and ceiling. Open arch windows at the far end looked out onto a spectacular view.

Dark Anne was leaning on the table with her head propped up in one hand. Her dress was the vivid red one that she'd worn to our first meeting, but it was rumpled, as though she'd been sleeping in it. With her free hand, she was playing with a long knife. Her eyes flicked up as I walked in.

'You could at least answer when I call,' I said.

Anne flipped the knife into the air, catching it by the blade.

I crossed the room and walked past her. There was one other chair, placed opposite from Anne, but I didn't sit down. Anne's eyes tracked me as I moved.

The view from the windows was just as amazing as I remembered, the forest beyond the walls stretching away into a fantastic landscape of tower-sized trees, mirrored lakes and distant mountains . . . but there was a difference. The first time that I'd been here, most of the world had been bathed in sunlight, while the tower and the walls around it had received only the murky light of an overcast day. Now the contrast was the other way round. The tower was still overcast, but the world outside was covered in black storm-clouds. Lightning flickered around the mountains, and the towering trees swayed in what had to be gale-force winds.

Dark Anne's prison hadn't changed. Everywhere else had.

'I've got to say,' I said, 'I don't really like what you've done with the place.'

She shot me a look.

'Your jinn tried to catch me on the way in,' I said conversationally. 'You know, when you only see them in the outside world, it's easy to forget how powerful they are. Having to act through a possessed human really limits them. Here, though . . . they're like a sea monster in the ocean.'

No answer. I turned, leaning my elbows on the window-sill. Dark Anne was spinning the knife between her fingers, watching me out of the corner of her eye. 'Just as well, I suppose,' I said. 'It's so powerful it's hard for it to find me. Like a giant hunting a mouse.'

Dark Anne finally spoke. 'Are you going to talk all day?'

'You're trapped here, aren't you?'

'Right, because I've got nothing better to do than come running when you call. Get over yourself.'

I shrugged. 'You're not a prisoner?' I pointed out through the window. 'Then step past those walls and back again.'

Dark Anne scowled.

'I can even tell you when it happened,' I said. 'It was last night. You were thinking about paying your family a visit, weren't you? I mean, you've dealt with everyone else. So after you took down Sagash, you figured it was time to go settle some old scores. Only the jinn didn't want that, did it? It was happy to feed you all the power you needed as long as you were using it to fight Sagash. But once it had his shadow realm, well, it wasn't going to put all that at risk just because you had a grudge against your two pain-in-the-arse cousins. Of course, you weren't going to take no for an answer, so you forced the issue. After all, you've done that lots of times, and the jinn's always backed down, right? Except that was when you discovered that all the times it did that, it wasn't because it was weaker. It was because it was biding its time. And now that it's stronger than you, it doesn't need you any more. Which is why you're slumped over your dinner table, feeling sorry for yourself.'

'Oh, screw you!' Anne snapped. 'Like you've done anything to help!'

'I haven't helped?' I said, and suddenly my voice was harsh. 'How about all the times I told you this was going to happen using these *exact fucking words*? I told you the jinn wasn't your friend, I told you it was stronger than you, I told you only a complete *moron* would let a marid into her head and expect to be the one running the show. And you just rolled your eyes and sniggered. Well, you going to laugh at me now? How about it, Anne? Still think it's funny?'

Anne glowered at me but didn't speak. 'Four weeks,' I said. '*Four weeks!* That's how long it took you to end up here. You know what's really ironic? When I first met you, you were a prisoner in this tower. You finally get your freedom, and it takes you less than *one month* to end up stuck right back inside the same prison you were trying to get away from!'

'I've noticed, okay?' Anne snapped. 'Is that all you came for? To say "I told you so"?'

'The only reason? No. But now I'm here I'm going to do it, because I am *really pissed off*. I expect this shit from the Council. They don't trust me and they don't know whose side I'm on. But you knew damn well I was giving you that warning because I loved you. I'm one of the foremost experts in the British Isles when it comes to possession and imbued items, I know a fair amount about jinn, and I can see the future. I am one of the best people in the *entire country* to give advice on *not* getting possessed. And your response was to do literally *the exact opposite of what I told you*!'

Anne stared at me, then suddenly broke into a grin. 'Aww, you still love me? That's cute.'

I threw up my hands. 'Damn it!'

'All right, all right, cool it.' Anne leant back in her chair, but her back was straighter and she seemed more alive all of a sudden. 'Fine, I might have made a few mistakes. No need to make a big deal over it.'

I drew in a breath to explode, then stopped myself. I was fairly sure she was just baiting me at this point.

'So,' Anne said. 'You going to help?'

'I've wanted that jinn out of your head from the beginning. Why the hell *else* do you think I'm here?'

'Works for me.' Anne jumped to her feet. 'Let's do it.'

'Do what?'

Anne nodded towards the window.

'Wait,' I said. 'Your plan is . . . what? Fight it?'

'Yep.'

I stared. 'Are you serious?'

'Uh, yeah?'

'Anne, you just went up against this thing last night,' I said. 'It kicked your arse. And if I had to bet, it probably wasn't even trying.'

Dark Anne scowled. Something I'd learned about Anne's shadow – she *really* hated looking weak. 'It caught me by surprise, okay? I figure we can manage with the two of us. Are we doing this or what?'

I looked at Anne for a second. Then I pulled out the

spare chair, sat down and covered my face with both hands. 'Oh my God, you're an idiot.'

'Hey,' Dark Anne said. 'I gave that thing a hell of a fight. Yeah, it pushed me back here, but it didn't have an easy time of it.'

I took a deep breath, took my hands away. 'Anne. The reason it had trouble pushing you back is because it had to work really, really hard to do it without killing you.'

'No, it didn't.'

'You saw that thing.' I pointed towards the north wall. 'You seriously think you are going to beat *that* in a contest of strength?'

'*She* did it.' Dark Anne never uses her other half's name. 'And I'm stronger than she is.'

'Okay, number one,' I said. 'She fought back *instantly*. Possessing entities gain power the more you rely on them, and she didn't. As soon as I woke her up, she went for the jinn all-out, with everything she had. No compromise, no hesitation. You've been letting the jinn act through you for weeks. You lost your chance a long time ago.' Anne started to speak and I held up two fingers. 'Number two. One of the last pieces of advice that Arachne gave me was that if I went into your Elsewhere and tried that same trick again, it wouldn't work. The jinn will swat me like a mosquito.'

Dark Anne put her hands on her hips. 'You got a better plan?'

'As a matter of fact, yes.'

'What is it?'

I just looked at her.

'I'm not hearing anything.'

'I've told you enough times.'

'Told . . . ?' Anne trailed off and her face darkened. 'Oh no.'

'You knew this was coming.'

'No.'

'There is exactly one way you're going to have a chance against that jinn,' I said. 'And that's to stop flying with one wing.'

'No.'

'Even your other half wouldn't be able to do it on her own any more.'

Dark Anne's face was set. 'No.'

'Come on, Anne!' I rose to my feet, started pacing. 'What's your endgame here? Even if we could get rid of the jinn with just the two of us – which we can't – you seriously think you and your other self can keep on living with some supercharged magical version of multiple personality disorder?'

'Worked so far.'

'No,' I said. 'It hasn't. The whole damn reason the jinn could possess you in the first place was by wedging itself into the crack between the two of you. You were going to fall apart anyway, Dr Shirland was pretty clear about that. The jinn just sped things up.'

'So you want me to do what, kiss and make up? Screw that.'

'Listen—'

'No, you listen.' Dark Anne pointed across the table at me. 'That bitch kept me locked up for years. Shut away from light and feeling and . . . everything! She got everything! The only reason you're even here is because of her. You don't care about *me*.'

'Anne—'

'Screw you. I'm not giving her anything.'

'You can't manage on your own! Neither of you can! She can't handle violence or confrontation and deals with problems by pretending they don't exist. And you're a violent criminal with the impulse control of a rabid wombat.'

'Yeah, well, I'd rather be me than her.'

'You're going to end up dead, enslaved, or worse.'

Dark Anne shrugged.

I threw up my hands. 'What does it take to get through to you?'

'You think you're so clever, you figure out some way to fix things,' Dark Anne said. 'Something that doesn't involve her.'

'There isn't one!'

'Well, then I guess you're out of luck.'

I stared at her. 'You really are this short-sighted, aren't you? If you were on a plane that needed two people to fly it, you'd let it crash rather than work together.'

'Sounds good to me.'

Frustration boiled up inside me. How could *anyone* be so *stupid* as to . . . ?

. . . except I already knew the answer, didn't I? I'd said it myself. Because she was violent and short-sighted with no impulse control. Trying to reason with Dark Anne was like arguing with a hungry tiger. There was a damn good reason the other Anne had kept her locked up.

I wasn't going to solve this by talking.

Light Anne had to be in this tower. If I could find her . . .

'You try and break her out,' Dark Anne said, 'and I'll fight you with everything I've got.'

That's the trouble with being close to someone. They can read you too. 'It's the only way you're getting out of this.'

'Bullshit.' Dark Anne's face was set. 'You just want your girlfriend back.'

We stared at each other across the table. I knew she wasn't bluffing. I'm far more skilled than Anne in Elsewhere, but this was *her* Elsewhere and she was on home ground. If it came to a fight then I might be able to get past her, force my way down to the basement, where Light Anne was trapped . . .

. . . but there was no way I could do it without drawing the attention of the jinn. It'd come down on us both like a hurricane.

'Fine,' I said, and straightened. 'You win. You get to stay here, just the way you are. Enjoy it.'

Dark Anne shrugged.

'You remember the first time we met?' I said. 'You told me that if there was one thing the two of you agreed on, it was that you weren't going to be a slave again. You told me you wanted to be the one in charge, the one who made the decisions. You told me you wanted to be queen.' I gestured to the room around us. 'How's that working out for you?'

Anne said nothing, and I turned and left. I could feel the jinn's presence, drawing closer. It wouldn't take it much longer to find me.

I opened a door in one of the black-glass walls and stepped out of Anne's Elsewhere, back into my own dreams.

10

I woke up next morning in a good mood. The morning sun lit the castle and glittered off the sea, the air smelt fresh and clean, and the waves made a soothing sound on the rocks below. Everything seemed bright and clear.

I really shouldn't have been so happy. Anne was possessed, Variam was a prisoner, the marid was planning an apocalypse and I had maybe a day to live. But I was in a good mood all the same, and it was because of the conversations I'd had last night. I'd been carrying around an enormous amount of pent-up stress, and it had been a relief to let it out. Even getting to tell Anne that she was an idiot had made me feel better. In a weird way, it had been the most honest conversation we'd ever had.

Nothing had really changed, and all the horrible things due to happen today were still going to happen. But there's really only so long you can keep on feeling miserable about stuff. Eventually you just have to accept that this is the new normal and that's how things are. And I'd already decided I wasn't going to waste my last day moping.

I got up, stretched, worked the kinks out of my muscles while enjoying the view from the window, then went downstairs to wash my hands and face in the pond. There was a new sentry outside the windmill; I chatted with him, asked if the night had been quiet (it had), then once I'd freshened up I headed for the barracks.

The barracks was busy with morning bustle. I got a few hellos as I waited in line for breakfast. Once I had a moment, I reached out through the dreamstone. *November?*

November's reply came instantly. *Oh, Mr Verus. I'm glad to hear from you, I was becoming a little worried.*

November's physical shell was back in our world, in a south London flat, but I could talk to him as easily as if he were right next to me. Dreamstones are handy like that. *So what's been happening with the Council?*

A constant stream of rather frantic communications, November said. *With the tail-end of Nimbus's force not making it into the shadow realm and the reserves being cut off, the Council were somewhat concerned. They demanded reports, but since the mages they were demanding them from were under attack at the time, they had some trouble getting an accurate picture. Still, things apparently quieted down after the first hour, and since then they've been in more or less constant contact with Landis and Nimbus and their seconds for, well, the entire night as far as I can tell. I've never seen the Keeper net so active.*

I'd got close enough to the front of the line to see that the cook – it was Jamie again – had done a fry-up. The soldier ahead of me scooped bacon, fried tomatoes and mushrooms onto his plate. The smell reminded me that I was very hungry. *Active with what?*

The Council's first priority has been trying to re-establish a gate link, November said. *However, the teams working overnight have confirmed that the isolation ward has, as expected, caused a divergence of various universal constants within the shadow realm.*

Mm-hm. Wait a sec, I'm getting breakfast.

I loaded up my plate. My stomach growled at the smell and I headed towards the folding tables set up in the middle of the room. *You were saying?*

This divergence is cause for some concern.

Right. I sat down and ate a forkful of eggs and bacon. It tasted amazing. *Didn't you say that messing with these universal constants could cause us all to explode or something?*

Oh no, nothing like that.

I poured myself some orange juice from a jug on the table. Landis clearly believed in treating his men well. *Well, that's good.*

It would just cause your bodies to stop functioning.

I paused with the glass halfway to my lips. *What?*

Well, the biggest area of concern was the dielectric constant. It governs the vacuum-electric permittivity of free space, which is fundamental to biochemistry.

November? Layman's terms please.

Ah . . . November said. *Changing this constant to any significant degree would cause virtually all biological processes within the shadow realm to stop working.*

Which would kill everyone.

Yes.

I see. I took a sip of orange juice. *Given that I'm still talking to you, can we safely assume that this hasn't happened?*

Well, so far.

So far?

The Council teams within the shadow realm have been conducting experiments, and apparently the results have differed in such a way as to lead them to believe that the shadow realm's physical constants are continuing to diverge from baseline at an accelerating rate.

Wonderful, I said. *Any good news?*

Well, so far the most pronounced changes appear to have been to the speed of light and to the gravitational constant, which should have relatively little effect at human scale, November said. *And divinations suggest that the shadow realm is unlikely to become entirely uninhabitable in the near future.*

I really don't like how many qualifiers you put on that last sentence. Okay, so this makes the Council's attempts to establish a gate a bit more urgent. How well are they doing?

Not very, November said. *Standard gate spells were rather designed under the assumption that the universal constants of physics would remain, well, constant. They're attempting to compensate but even after that they'll still have to defeat the regular gate wards. From what I'm overhearing, I'm afraid they don't sound very confident.*

So no reinforcements and no exit strategy, I said. *Just as well my expectations weren't high. Anything else I ought to know?*

I understand that the Council have authorised a battle plan, which they've passed to Director Nimbus. I imagine you'll hear about it quite soon.

I'll be in touch.

I broke the connection to see Luna weaving through the crowd. She looked as though she'd been up for a while, and walking alongside her was a Keeper called Tobias. 'Alex,' Luna called.

I gave her a wave. 'Had some breakfast?' I asked once I'd swallowed.

'Verus,' Tobias said agreeably as he ambled up. He was a tall, strongly built Keeper from the Order of the Shield with dark hair that he for some reason hid behind a large Stetson hat. I'd never got an explanation for the hat. 'Briefing in twenty minutes in the ready room.'

'I'll be there.'

Tobias headed off on some other errand. 'So?' Luna said. 'Learn anything last night?'

'Yes, and also this morning.' I finished my orange juice, grabbed the last three hash browns and rose. 'Let's take a walk.'

Once we were outside and away from eavesdroppers, I filled Luna in on my conversations with November and Anne. 'Well, crap,' Luna said once I was done.

'Sums it up.'

'I guess now we know why no one uses isolation wards.' Luna walked for a few seconds more before shaking her head. We were out in the morning sunlight, making a circuit on the grass around the millpond, the sails of the windmill creaking overhead. 'Well, I suppose if there's nothing we can do about it, there's no point worrying. Do your Elsewhere gates work?'

'They're blocked too,' I said. 'Might be able to find a way around it with enough time, but that's not something we have a lot of. Which brings us to Anne.'

Luna nodded. 'So is it still the same plan?'

'Which plan?'

'You stun Anne with that anti-jinn weapon, open up a gate and drag her into Elsewhere, get Anne's two sides to team up and banish the jinn, then you get out of Elsewhere and back to our world.' Luna looked at me expectantly. 'Right?'

'You're . . . skipping over a lot of problems.'

'But that's your plan, right?'

'Okay,' I said. 'Problem one: that anti-jinn weapon is currently in Richard's pocket. Problem two: the wards on this shadow realm are stopping me opening a gate to Elsewhere. Problem three: Anne's two sides hate each other and refuse to work together, and problem four, I've no idea how banishing a jinn actually works.'

'But that's still your plan,' Luna said. 'Right?'

I sighed. 'Yes.'

Luna shrugged. 'Four problems doesn't sound so bad.'

'Problem five,' I said. 'Klara warned me a while ago that using the fateweaver would accelerate its spread. I think using it in Elsewhere does the same, but much faster. When I destroyed Rachel in Elsewhere, the fateweaver jumped from my elbow to my shoulder. I think it's okay as long as I just dip in and out, but an extended battle against something like the jinn . . . I've got the feeling this is something I'm only going to be able to do once.'

'Oh,' Luna said. She glanced around; apart from a couple of sentries, we were alone out on the grassy space. 'This was why you didn't want to talk about this in front of the Council.'

'Yeah,' I said. Of course, even if I could banish the jinn, there was the issue of Anne's split personality. But I'd been thinking back to my conversations with Dr Shirland, and it had given me some ideas.

'What about Vari?' Luna asked.

That problem, on the other hand, I had no answer for at all. Entering Elsewhere was the only card in my hand that I thought gave me any chance at all of banishing a jinn. If I could only do it once, then when I came to Vari I was going to do . . . what? Get him and Anne in the same place and drag them through together? Threaten Anne into ordering the jinn out of him? Knock him out and hand him over to the Council and hope their mages could un-possess him?

All of those plans sounded terrible.

'I don't know,' I admitted at last. We finished a circuit of the millpond and started round again.

'Look, we need that anti-jinn weapon off Richard anyway, right?' Luna said. 'So we mug him first, deal with Vari second, and go after Anne last of all. Use that weapon to get rid of Vari's jinn, and save your Elsewhere trick for Anne.'

'Okay,' I said. 'What you just described is something most mages wouldn't be able to pull off in ten years. You're suggesting we do it in a day.'

'Well, a day's what we've got.'

'And there's no guarantee this weapon is going to break Vari's possession.'

'Do you have any better ideas?'

'. . . No.'

'So that's it then, isn't it?' Luna said with a shrug. 'If this is the only way it can work, then this is the way it'll have to work.'

I sighed. 'You really have turned into a chance mage.'

A group of soldiers emerged from the castle, carrying crates. A mage was leading them, and to my surprise I recognised her. Her name was Lumen, a Keeper auxiliary seconded to the Order of the Star. Why was she here?

'What are they doing?' Luna asked.

'No idea,' I said with a frown. Lumen pointed the men towards the windmill, and they crossed the grass to disappear inside. I couldn't see what was inside those crates, but from the way the men were walking it looked heavy. As we watched, more soldiers appeared from the castle, also weighed down with cargo.

The twenty minutes Tobias had given us were up. We headed for the ready room.

Landis's ready room was packed with people. It looked as though every Keeper of the Order of the Shield who'd made it into the shadow realm was standing in a cluster on our side of the room; they were talking and drinking from mugs, looking relaxed. A few nodded to us as we entered. The air smelt of coffee.

Landis and Nimbus were leaning over a projection table, deep in conversation. Two other mages were standing nearby, Sonder and Rain. As I watched, Lumen came through the door after us and walked over to join Sonder. Last was Talisid, or an image of him. The Council mage was a translucent projection of light, hovering in one corner.

I left Luna and walked over to Talisid. 'Hey,' I told him.

'Verus.' Talisid's voice echoed from the focus on the ground.

I couldn't resist. I leant forward and swiped my hand through him.

Talisid's image fuzzed and re-formed. 'Yes, Verus, very amusing,' Talisid said. 'Was there something you needed?'

From behind, I could sense Luna stifling a laugh. 'So you didn't make it into the shadow realm,' I said. 'Let me guess, you were at the end of the line?'

'I was in the rearguard, yes.'

'That's what you get for leading from the back.'

'I'm glad you find this entertaining.'

Being locked out of the shadow realm meant that Talisid – and by extension the Council – would have limited influence on today's battle. On the one hand, that made it less likely that Alma would betray me at a critical moment. On the other hand, it also meant that Nimbus had near-total authority.

I looked across the room at Nimbus. The Director of Operations of the Order of the Star was making forceful hand gestures as he spoke to Landis, who was standing with his arms folded. Nimbus and I had rarely crossed paths, but from the little I knew of him he seemed ambitious, inflexible and proud. The few times I'd watched him in action, I hadn't been impressed. That might have come across in our conversation last night. On the other hand, the information I'd given Nimbus *had* been accurate. Maybe that might have raised his opinion of me?

As if sensing my thoughts, Nimbus glanced up and saw me. His eyes narrowed.

I sighed inwardly. As if I didn't have enough problems.

'Right, then!' Landis called, clapping his hands. 'Friends, mages, Keepers, lend me your ears.' I was fairly sure Landis hadn't slept, but he looked as energetic as ever. 'Director Nimbus will now grace us with his plans for our day's entertainment.'

The murmurs of conversation died away. All eyes turned to Nimbus.

Nimbus frowned, clearly not appreciating the levity. 'The Council has spent the night gathering information and exploring options,' he announced. 'We now, for the first time, have a clear understanding of our enemy's intentions. As a result, it has finally been possible to devise an effective counter-strategy.'

I glanced sideways to see that Luna had moved next to me. I reached out to her through the dreamstone.

Nimbus gestured and the projection table lit up with a three-dimensional image of the castle, sculpted in pale yellow light, a perfect scale model reaching to Nimbus's waist. If the Council ever runs short on money, they could make a fortune selling their projection tech to Games Workshop.

'Our forces currently control the western, north-western and south-eastern sections of the castle,' Nimbus said. Sections of the castle lit up in blue as he spoke. 'Drakh's forces are confined to the north-east, while the jinn have been driven back to the central keep and to the north.'

Driven back? Luna asked.

They withdrew, I said. *But 'driven back' is how he's reporting it to the Council.*

'Through analysis of the data collected during the battle last night, and through divinations performed by the Council, we have been able to decipher the enemy's plans,' Nimbus said. 'The marid intends to perform a large-scale ritual which will bring the shadow realm as a whole closer to the dimension from which jinn are summoned. Our attack has forced the marid to accelerate these plans, and it set them in motion last night.'

Nimbus gestured towards the image of the castle. When nothing happened, he frowned at Sonder.

Sonder started. 'Sorry.' Four small white diamonds appeared within the corners of the keep, glittering against the dark building.

'Mage Sonder,' Nimbus said.

'Yes,' Sonder said. 'Right.' He stepped forward,

fumbling a little. 'So, as you remember from the briefing, the wards over the shadow realm are all anchored at the— in the keep. This includes both the realm-wide gate wards that prevent external access, and the smaller but more powerful wards over the keep itself that protect it from intra-realm gating or scrying, as well as from physical and magical attack. The ritual uses that existing ward structure for leverage, allowing An— the marid to affect the shadow realm as a whole.'

'Which means,' Nimbus said, 'that the ward system is the key. Bring it down, and at one stroke we both stop the marid's plan and open up access to and from the shadow realm.'

Nimbus paused for effect. The Keepers from the Order of the Shield looked back at him.

'Director,' Tobias said with a nod. 'We were given to understand that the reason we couldn't gate out of here was due to the isolation ward.'

'It's both,' Sonder said. 'The teams at the War Rooms say they can open up a gate through the isolation ward, or through the gate wards. It's having to break through both at once that's too much for them.'

There were a couple of whispers from the crowd, but no further comments. They didn't look enthusiastic. *What are they upset about?* Luna asked.

They're wondering if he's about to order them to do a frontal assault on that keep.

When no one spoke, Nimbus cleared his throat. 'There is an additional problem.' He pointed to the north-east corner of the castle, marked by a splotch of red. 'Scouting reports indicate that Drakh's forces have fortified themselves within this area. Our divinations indicate that he does not intend to launch an attack in the short to medium term, but as long as he holds this territory, he represents a threat we cannot ignore. Though his force is inferior to ours, should we attack the keep, we would be vulnerable to him attacking our flank or rear.'

'While this absolutely is a problem to address,' Landis said, 'I think everyone is exceedingly interested in learning what our plan is for dealing with that keep.'

'I was coming to that,' Nimbus said. 'In the absence of external fire support, we will be deploying an accumulator.'

That got people's attention. 'We brought one of those?' a Keeper asked.

'I had Compass pack one,' Landis said cheerfully.

Nimbus shot Landis a look. 'The Council has emphasised that this does not represent a change in established doctrine. However, given the circumstances . . .'

What's an accumulator? Luna asked.

Magical siege weapon, I said. *It's like a giant battery that can draw in ambient magical energy. The range is enormous – miles. Then once you're ready, you get a mage to channel that energy in a directed attack. I'm not surprised Landis had to smuggle one in, the Council hates them.*

Why?

They're banned under international treaties. Also, they're not actually very useful because of the warmup time.

'What about the warmup time?' a Keeper asked.

'Well, we've taken measurements,' Sonder said, 'and actually, it turns out that conditions here are ideal for an accumulator. Between the isolation ward, the jinn ritual and the confined nature of the shadow realm, the ambient magical index is gigantic.'

'So how long are we talking?'

'Ah, based on our projections, to achieve minimum power level to break the keep's wards . . . twelve minutes.'

The Keeper frowned but didn't speak.

Is that slow? Luna asked.

No, it's actually really fast for an accumulator, I said. *The problem is that the charge-up process is* really *obvious. Once that thing starts building up power, literally every mage in this shadow realm is going to know where it is and what it's doing. And twelve minutes is more than enough time for Anne's jinn to fly or gate over there and destroy everyone and everything in the area in about eight different ways. This is why no one uses accumulators. They're useless in a police action because they're overkill, and they're useless in a military action because in the time it takes to charge up your shot the people you're aiming at can either attack you first or just gate somewhere else.*

Landis seemed to think it was worth bringing one.

Yeah, trust him to find the one time a giant explosive siege weapon would actually be useful.

'Seventeen to eighteen minutes if we're being safe,' Sonder was saying.

'That enough to blow up the keep?' Tobias asked.

'Not the *whole* keep,' Sonder said. 'But we don't need to. Those four points on the projection are the anchor points for the ritual. Destroying any one of them will cause the entire effect to collapse, which will cause a chain reaction that will destroy the wards on the shadow realm as a whole.'

'Excellent!' Landis said. 'Now I think we should address the marid in the room, as it were. What are we going to do when our mutual acquaintance notices what we're doing and takes exception?'

'This brings us to our plan of attack,' Nimbus said. 'Both Drakh's forces and the jinn have the potential to threaten the accumulator as soon as it begins to gather a measurable level of power. It is therefore necessary to engage both enemy forces before the accumulator can be activated.' He gestured and a blue arrow appeared in the castle's north-east. 'Captain Rain?'

Rain stepped forward. Tall and dark-skinned, he had a calm, measured way of speaking. He'd been my and Caldera's boss back when I'd been working in the Keepers. 'Our force will be acting as a sieging unit in this operation.' He gestured and the blue arrow moved towards the red blotch of Richard's forces, then moved to encircle it. 'We'll establish a perimeter around Drakh's forces and set up wards and an interdiction field. No one gets in, no one gets out.' He glanced around at the Keepers and at me. 'I know several of you have recent combat experience against Drakh's cabal. Once we're done here, I'd appreciate anything you can tell me.'

'Sieging the keep itself, however, is not an option,' Nimbus said. 'The perimeter is too large and its wards would defeat any kind of interdiction field. This is where you men come in. Captain Landis, you will take your force and attack the building upon the stack off the island's northern face.'

The castle was built upon a tall rocky island, with cliffs dropping into the sea. To the island's north was a stack – a pillar of rock – separated from the castle by a stone bridge. Upon the stack was a huge forbidding-looking structure made up out of the same yellowish stone as the rest of the castle. Ji-yeong had called it the tombs.

'According to our intelligence, the building upon that stack contains the spawning infrastructure for the shadow constructs that we've been fighting since we got here,' Nimbus said. 'Destroying their regeneration source will eliminate the shadows and thus remove half of the marid's army.' Nimbus looked around. 'It is an attack the marid cannot afford to ignore, and it will respond accordingly.'

'Respond as in, in person?' a Keeper asked.

'No, that shouldn't be possible,' Sonder said. He pointed, and a small glowing white symbol appeared at the centre of the keep in between the four diamonds. 'She— I mean, the marid was able to attack us last night because the ritual hadn't been started. Now that it's been set in motion, it needs constant supervision.'

'As such, we expect the marid to deploy its jinn against the attack to the north,' Nimbus said. 'Divinations have confirmed that we can expect our attack to be answered by ifrit-possessed mages as well as jann.' He looked at Landis. 'Your task will be to press the attack sufficiently to draw in the ifrit, and either destroy them or keep them engaged so that they cannot redeploy. Once this has been accomplished, you will send the signal to the accumulator team. The code word is "trident".' Blue arrows stabbed against the red on the northern island. Nimbus pointed at the map and a thin beam of light extended from one of the castle towers. It pierced through the keep and touched the nearest of the four diamonds, and with a flash the whole corner of the keep disappeared. Nimbus stepped back. 'Any questions?'

'So who has the honour of using the focus?' Landis asked.

Nimbus nodded to one side. 'Mage Lumen will use

the accumulator's reserves to launch a directed-energy attack.'

Directed-energy attack? Luna asked.

Lumen's a light mage, I said. She was a small woman with neat brown hair in a pageboy cut, and didn't look especially happy to be here. *She'll launch an attack spell and the accumulator will supercharge it. Basically it'll be a giant laser cannon. Hang on a sec.* I held up a hand. 'Director Nimbus?'

Nimbus looked at me, thin-lipped. 'Yes, Verus?'

Several other Keepers stopped talking and turned to watch. 'What happens when the accumulator gets attacked?' I asked.

'The purpose of the diversionary attack on the northern island is to ensure that the marid has no available forces to spare.'

'And what if it does?'

'An attack on the accumulator is not a concern,' Nimbus said stiffly.

The Keepers watching Nimbus didn't look away. Their expressions clearly indicated that they were waiting for a better answer.

Nimbus gave an irritated sigh. 'Sonder?'

'We're using an experimental apparatus to transfer the energy flow from the accumulator through a specially modified gateway,' Sonder said. 'I'll be monitoring the situation at the accumulator through a video link. As soon as it looks as though the accumulator's under threat, I'll give Lumen the signal to fire. So anyone watching will sense the energy build-up in the accumulator, but they won't know where the attack's going to come from until it's too late. We won't activate the focus until it's time to fire, and the video link will be non-magical, so there'll be nothing visible on magesight to warn them.'

'Understood?' Nimbus said, paused for only a second, then nodded. 'Good. Auxiliaries Sonder and Lumen and Captain Rain will remain here to answer any further questions. Captain Landis, I need to discuss assignments of your men.'

11

The briefing broke up. Nimbus disappeared off with Landis, while most of the Keepers had gathered around Sonder. Tobias had walked over to Talisid's projection and was questioning him about timings.

Could you follow all that? Luna asked.

It's simple enough, I said. *Scorpion tactics. Pincers hold; tail strikes.* I reached forward and closed my thumb and forefinger in the air. *Rain's force pins down Richard.* I did the same with my other hand. *Landis's force pins down Anne.* I arced a finger over the top. *Accumulator fires.*

Oh. Why didn't they just explain it like that?

I noticed that Rain wasn't occupied and walked over. 'Captain Rain.'

Rain had been frowning down at a tablet; now he glanced at me. 'Verus,' he said in his deep voice. 'Been a while.'

'Glad you're not under orders to arrest me any more,' I said. I'd always rather liked Rain. 'How's it look?'

Rain hesitated and I saw futures flicker as he decided how honest to be. 'Not great,' he admitted.

The tablet held a list of names, with separate columns for killed and wounded. 'How many did you lose last night?'

'Counting all serious casualties . . . a hundred and three.'

'Jesus.'

'We were supposed to be bringing over five hundred, with as many more in reserve.' Rain didn't let anything show on his face, but his voice was grim. 'Right now, we've got maybe two hundred and forty effectives. We're missing half our main force and all of our reserves and we've barely scratched them.'

So they'd been able to bring about three hundred and fifty into the shadow realm last night. And they'd lost almost a third of them already. 'How were you hurt so badly?' I asked. 'Anne?'

Rain gave a nod. 'She'd hit from the flanks, then fade away as soon as we brought mages to bear. Used those jann and shadows as distractions. She couldn't stop our main force but she damn near bled us dry before Nimbus gave the order to fall back.'

I glanced towards the door where Nimbus had left. 'Surprised he was so confident.'

Rain hesitated again, and through the futures I could see him caught between worry and discretion. He shook his head as he made his decision. 'He's not,' Rain said, lowering his voice. 'He spent half the night arguing with the Council. Wanted to hold position until they could bring in reinforcements. He's only doing this attack under direct orders.' Rain's eyes flicked in the direction of Talisid's projection, still talking with Tobias. 'Your friend there's watching to make sure Nimbus does as he's told.'

'Well,' I said. 'That's . . . not good.'

'No shit,' Rain said. 'Listen, Verus, I know this woman's your girlfriend, but . . . we're going to need you for this one.' His dark eyes bored into mine. 'You with us?'

I was silent for a moment. 'It's not my girlfriend making the decisions any more,' I said at last. Anne would never have fought as Rain described; Dark Anne would have gone in swinging, and Light Anne wouldn't have attacked at all. 'I'll do all I can.'

Rain gave me a nod and went back to his tablet.

It was strange, but Council politics felt simpler these days. It was as though I'd only started to really understand the Council after I'd been kicked off it. Maybe you can't see an organisation clearly until you've looked at it from both inside and out.

Luna had joined the Keepers around Sonder. I moved over to listen in. '. . . would have taken part in the ritual,' Sonder was saying. 'Each of them would have invested one of the focus crystals to reinforce the overall structure. They were doing that through the early hours of the morning.'

'Suppose that's why they've been leaving us alone,' one Keeper said.

'Can we bring down the ritual by killing the ifrit?' another asked.

Sonder shook his head. 'All you'd do is kill the host.'

'Sonder?' Luna asked. 'You said you'd been researching these ifrit generals? What did you learn?'

'Not very much,' Sonder said, scratching his head. 'Just a lot of battle reports, and those don't go into detail. We do have their names though – it was only the marids that were unnamed, not the ifrit. They translate from Old Arabic as Lightning-amid-the-Storm, the Sun That Brings Death, the Eternal Sand or the Endless Sands – I'm not sure which translation is right – and the Water of Life.'

'Sound lovely,' a Keeper said.

'How powerful are they?' Luna asked.

'We're not sure,' Sonder said. 'But Lightning-amid-the-Storm was supposed to be the weakest, and the Sun That Brings Death the strongest.'

'Lightning-amidst-the-Storm is the one possessing Aether, I think,' I said. 'Sagash's old apprentice.'

'Is that anti-jinn weapon going to work on them?' Luna asked.

'It'll certainly weaken them—'

'I mean is it going to banish them?' Luna interrupted.

Sonder hesitated. 'That's . . . unclear.'

'Really not what you want to hear going into battle, Sonder,' a Keeper commented.

'Well, I'm sorry, but it's true. It's not as though we had the chance to test it.'

'Bit of a moot point, isn't it?' another Keeper said. 'Since the bloody thing got stolen.'

Lumen was standing on her own. Like Sonder, she wore Keeper battle armour; like Sonder, she looked uncomfortable in it. I walked over. 'Lumen.'

Lumen looked at me in surprise. 'Oh, Verus. Last time was . . . Syria, wasn't it?'

'Nimbus is counting on you pretty heavily for this,' I said.

Lumen grimaced. 'I wish he wasn't.'

'I'm guessing this wasn't the original plan?'

Lumen shook her head. 'They were supposed to set up a forward siege base with special equipment. They had a team of specialist mages, heavily protected.' She sighed. 'Unfortunately, they were *so* heavily protected that they were put in the rearguard. So they never made it in.'

'And you're the substitute,' I said. 'Can it work?'

'I mean, it *can.*' Lumen raised a hand and a pinpoint of light glowed at her finger. 'All you need for something like this is control. I don't have the strength for proper battle magic, but the accumulator handles all the buffering.'

'So your spark of light turns into a giant laser beam,' I said, looking at the glow. 'Will it be enough?'

'Oh, power's not the problem. Give it enough time and it'll take out the wards and the whole corner of the keep with it. It's the warmup time I'm worried about.'

'Where are you going to fire from?'

'Nimbus said we shouldn't decide on that until we were ready,' Lumen said, 'and for once I agree with him. Sonder and I will be moving around until we're ready to take the shot. No, what I'm worried about is what happens when they home in on the accumulator. There's supposed to be no way to trace the signal to us, and we'll be running dark so we won't ping on magesight. But I still don't like it.' She glanced over towards Tobias. 'Excuse me.'

The meeting was breaking up. I found Luna and we left the ready room. 'Anything else?' I asked her.

'Sonder says Anne's ritual is going to take about twenty-eight hours from start,' Luna said. 'So about 6 a.m. tomorrow. But the veil will start thinning before that – she'll be able to summon jinn more easily starting from about eight this evening and it'll get worse through the night.' Luna looked at me. 'Oh, and something else. Sonder thinks that the wards on the keep are stabilising the isolation ward. They're stopping everything in the shadow realm from going completely crazy.'

'So if we blow it up . . .'

'Yeah,' Luna said. 'They'd better be right that taking those wards down will let us gate out, because it sounds like we won't have much time.'

Ji-yeong walked up. She looked fresh and well-rested, and had somehow found the time in the middle of an invasion to redo her make-up. 'Hey, guys,' she said. 'What did I miss?'

Luna and I filled her in on the Council's plan.

Ji-yeong considered. 'Will it work?'

I had to think about it. 'It's not the worst plan I've ever heard,' I admitted. 'I don't think much of Nimbus as a commander, but . . . once the accumulator is active then neither Anne nor Richard will have much time to react, and if they're pinned down fighting then they might not be able to redeploy fast enough. And they're right that the marid needs to defend those tombs. Those shadows are half its army, and if we occupy the place we can shut them down easily enough.' I looked at Ji-yeong. 'Right?'

Ji-yeong nodded. 'But?' Luna asked.

'But there isn't a backup plan if things go wrong,' I said. 'And in operations like this, something *always* goes wrong. If I were running this, I'd set some forces aside as a mobile reserve.'

'Would they listen to you if you told them that?'

'No.'

'So what are we doing?' Ji-yeong asked.

'Okay,' I said. 'There are three Council forces. We can go with one of the three, or we can strike off on our own. Attacking on our own is obviously stupid, and I don't like going with Rain's force to siege Richard either.'

'He's the one with that anti-jinn weapon,' Luna said.

'Yeah, but they're not trying to take it; they're just bottling him up. We go with them, best case, we sit around while the battle's decided elsewhere.' I looked between Luna and Ji-yeong. 'That just leaves Landis's force and the accumulator team. The accumulator can win the battle if it goes off, but again, if we go with them, we'll just be sitting around.'

'So you're going with Landis,' Luna said.

'It's dangerous, but it gives us the best chance to make a difference. And if the tombs are under threat, there's a good chance Anne's going to send everything she's got to reinforce. That means Variam.' I looked at Luna. 'Maybe that good luck of yours can do something.'

'I've played worse odds,' Luna said with a nod.

I looked at Ji-yeong.

'I'll stick with you,' she told me.

I nodded. 'Zero hour is 10 a.m.'

It was a few minutes past nine. A group of men stood on the grass near the windmill, chatting and smoking. A sea breeze was blowing in from the cliffs, sending ripples across the millpond and making the sails of the windmill creak as they swung.

I'd spotted Landis and Nimbus standing on the other side of the windmill. They were talking – maybe arguing. I couldn't get close enough to eavesdrop, but their body language was tense. For once Landis wasn't smiling: his eyes were boring into the other mage.

Nimbus gave a final order with a chopping motion of his hand, and left. Landis stared after him for a moment, then turned and began walking slowly towards the men on the grass.

I intercepted him under the sails of the windmill. 'What's wrong?' I asked.

'Director Nimbus has issued the personnel assignments for the attack,' Landis said. His voice was quiet and he was looking past me at the men out in the open. 'He's reassigned men to the accumulator team.'

I followed Landis's eyes. There were a little over twenty men on the grass, some sitting, some standing. They'd checked their gear and weapons and looked ready to go. 'That's the security contingent?'

'That,' Landis said, 'is the force that will be guarding the accumulator while it charges.'

I frowned. 'No mages?'

'No,' Landis said, his voice clipped. 'I need to brief them. If you'll excuse me.' He brushed past.

I watched him go, still frowning. That wasn't very many men for such an important job. I recognised several of the men and many were veterans, but even so . . .

Actually, I recognised a *lot* of the men. Sergeant Little, who I'd met in that bubble realm in Syria. Nowy and Peterson and Lisowski from my old team that I'd led in the early months of the war. Two others that I recognised. In fact, I recognised the whole group. I'd seen them recently. Desert sands . . . where had it been?

Hyperborea. It was the same team that had been sent with Avenor and Saffron into Hyperborea. Saffron had ordered them to arrest me, and they'd refused to fire.

I remembered what Sonder had said at the briefing. They were setting up a focus that would transport energy from the accumulator through a gateway. While the enemies homed in on the accumulator, Sonder and Lumen would be watching through a video link from far away.

I stood dead still for five seconds, then whirled and headed after Nimbus.

I slammed the door to the ready room open with a crash.

Nimbus started. He was alone in the room but for Sonder and Lumen, and looked like he'd been giving orders. 'Verus? What do you think you're—?'

I slammed the door behind me and stalked towards Nimbus. His eyes went wide and he took a step back, magic coming up around his hands. 'You're leaving *twenty-three* men to guard the windmill?' I asked.

'Your point?' Nimbus snapped.

'I ran into one of those ifrit hosts last night,' I said tightly. 'I had Luna and Ji-yeong with me. Three experienced combat mages, and all of us together could barely scrape a draw. And according to Sonder, that one was the runt of the litter. Twenty-three Council security is not even *close* to enough to hold the windmill against something like that.'

Nimbus raised his eyebrows at me. 'You're accompanying Captain Landis, I understand? Then the solution seems simple. Make sure the marid has no spare forces to send.'

'Don't give me that crap! If that accumulator fires, the marid loses, and if I can figure that out, it can too. It'll make damn sure it gets someone here, even if it has to lose half its ifrit in the process. Why would it care? All it'll be losing is host bodies. It can just get more.'

Nimbus turned. 'Mage Sonder, Mage Verus appears upset. I suggest you escort him from the premises.'

Sonder hesitated.

'You aren't expecting to hold the windmill or the accumulator,' I told Nimbus flatly. 'That's why you're setting up the video link. Those men are a screen. The idea is that by dying, they'll buy enough time and give enough warning that when those jinn smash down the door to the windmill, Lumen can fire her shot.' I looked at Sonder and Lumen. 'Tell me I'm wrong.'

Neither Sonder nor Lumen met my eyes.

'Verus, I really don't have time for this,' Nimbus said. Unlike the others, he wasn't looking away; he looked irritated. 'Given your recent activities, you clearly have no compunction about sacrificing men.'

'If all you want is a sacrificial force, you don't need to assign men at all. You could use traps, or automated defences—'

'Which would not slow an attacker for long enough,' Nimbus interrupted. 'Human defenders raise the possibility that any of them could be a mage. This requires the jinn to neutralise each in turn before moving forward.'

'Then,' I said quietly, 'maybe you could explain why *every single one* of those "human defenders" is from the same squad that disobeyed orders to arrest me last week in Hyperborea.'

Sonder and Lumen both looked at Nimbus. Apparently this was news to them as well.

'Sacrificing troops is standard Council doctrine,' I said. 'But this? This is over the line even for you.'

'Why?' Nimbus sounded impatient. 'Council security are used as a screening force. You know that; they know that. They know the risks when they take the money.'

'And you've told them that, have you?'

'If the accumulator fires, the marid loses,' Nimbus said. 'Your words, not mine. The chance of winning this war is well worth twenty-three casualties.'

'Then if it's that important, fortify this place properly. Mages, more men—'

'Who would then be at risk,' Nimbus said. 'Ideally Captain Landis will be able to pin down all of the ifrit with his own attack, but the marid will do all it can to redeploy them here, and yes, it is possible that it will succeed, in which case a significant number of those defending the accumulator will die. With that in mind, any forces stationed here must be considered expendable.'

'And those twenty-three are the most expendable?'

'Mages are a limited resource,' Nimbus said. 'Normals are not. Particularly unreliable ones.'

'You don't need—'

'I'm sorry, Verus,' Nimbus interrupted. 'Were you reassigned to the Keepers when I didn't notice? Were you promoted from journeyman to lieutenant to captain, and then to director? Did you spend twenty years working for the Light Council until you were recognised and promoted for your efforts?'

I looked at Nimbus through narrowed eyes.

'No,' Nimbus said with a curl of his lip. 'You never rose beyond journeyman Keeper, and that only because a Dark mage was able to force you in through a loophole. And now you think that because your friends on the Council have managed to cover up your crimes, you can waltz back in. Well, Verus, you have no friends here. You're a jumped-up Dark mage who reached your position through nepotism and corruption. Nothing more.'

'Talisid gave you orders to listen to me,' I said. But it was a weak reply and I knew it.

'Which I have done,' Nimbus said pleasantly. 'If you

have objections to how your advice has been received, you are of course free to tell Talisid your reservations.'

I was silent.

'I'm glad we understand each other.' Nimbus began to walk past me, then paused. 'Oh, and Verus? This is the second time in two days you've spoken to me with this level of disrespect.' His voice hardened. 'I am Director of Operations of the Order of the Star and if you do it a third time I will have you thrown into a cell. Do I make myself clear?' Without waiting for an answer, he strode out.

Lumen and Sonder hesitated, looking at me, but the futures in which they spoke flickered and died. They followed Nimbus out and I was left alone.

Fifteen minutes to go.

The barracks had been abandoned, the contents packed away into spatial storage. Landis was delivering a last briefing to his assault force, gathered on the grass before the windmill. Luna and Ji-yeong were there, but I was keeping my distance.

The accumulator had been set up in the windmill, along with a big flat-screen monitor providing a video link to Sonder and Lumen. Deployed around the windmill were the men being left to guard it. Light machine gun emplacements had been set up on the towers overlooking the area, and on top of the windmill itself. I could see their barrels pointing up to the clouded sky. They'd do nothing to stop an ifrit.

I hadn't even tried talking to Talisid. I knew what he'd say: Nimbus was in command, casualties an inevitable part of the operation, very regrettable, et cetera.

And if I kept pushing, he'd raise an eyebrow and make some comment along the lines of how my hands weren't exactly clean either.

I looked out over the sea. Much as I hated to admit it, Talisid and Nimbus had a point. I'd killed more than twenty-three people over the past month. A lot more.

Was I just being a hypocrite here? I didn't like Nimbus – he was arrogant and cold. But if I picked any random mage from the British Isles, admitted everything I'd done over the past month, then asked them to compare that to what Nimbus was doing now . . . they'd judge me as worse.

It's a disturbing feeling, realising something like that. As far as most people were concerned, I was one of the bad guys, and I wasn't sure they were wrong. The part that really bothered me was that, when I looked back on the decisions that had brought me here, all of them had made sense at the time. There hadn't been a moment where I'd had a clear choice between good and evil. I'd just had to choose between bad options, over and over again, and things had kept getting worse.

Was there a point at which it had all gone wrong? There had been the point at which Anne picked up the ring, and I'd kept it secret. Then after she'd been possessed, when I'd tried to cover up what she'd done in San Vittore. The attack on Arachne's lair. The choice I'd been given in Richard's shadow realm. Facing Abithriax in the bubble realm . . .

Maybe that had been it. That, at least, had been a clear choice. I'd sought out Abithriax, challenged him for the fateweaver and killed him.

But if I hadn't, Anne and Variam would be dead . . .

I shook my head. No easy choices, no easy answers. And now I was keeping company with generals and politicians, the sort of people who make these kinds of choices every day. Pick option one, these people die. Pick option two, it's some other people instead. Pick option three, and both groups live, but the problem isn't solved and will come back at some unspecified time in the future, at which point it'll probably be worse. Make your choice, and don't take too long, because tomorrow you'll have to do it all over again.

Maybe this was how you turned into someone like Levistus. Having to fight for your own position while also having to decide between life and death for the people below you every single day. Over time you'd get numb to it, and eventually you'd stop feeling anything at all. Was I becoming like that?

I didn't know, and that frightened me.

Five minutes to go. I walked over to Landis.

Landis was going over the attack plan one final time. 'Remember, the bulk of the enemy forces are going to be shadows.' He was all business now. 'Cut through them quickly and don't slow down, because they won't stop coming and we need to push as far as possible in the first three minutes. The primary threat will be the two ifrit.' He glanced over at me. 'Still two?'

I nodded.

'Rearguard, remember, your duties are screening *only*. If enemy reinforcements push across the bridge towards you, pull back immediately. We are anticipating a full-strength push from the keep and I do not want you to get in their way! Rejoin the main force if possible, and if worse comes to worst get out of the line of advance and sit tight. They won't want to slow down for stragglers.' Landis looked around. 'Everyone understand?'

There were nods.

Landis looked to his left. 'Compass?'

Compass stepped up, a small pixie-like blonde woman with a spring to her step. One of the few women in the Order of the Shield, she was a space mage and Landis's gate specialist. 'All right, boys, it'll be two gates!' she shouted. 'Three minutes!'

There was no more chatter. All around, soldiers were doing final checks on their weapons, mages testing their shields. Luna walked quickly over. 'The ifrit mages in the tombs,' she said quietly. 'It's Caldera and Barrayar, right?'

'Yes.'

'They were the first ones Anne took,' Luna said. 'So they're probably possessed by two of the generals, right?'

'Yes.'

'But you haven't seen Variam in any of the futures.'

'No.'

'It's supposed to take a while for her to summon up one of those jinn,' Luna said. Her eyes weighed me up. 'And she must have spent most of last night on that ritual. So . . . maybe she hasn't had time to possess Vari?'

I didn't answer.

'What do you think the chances are?'

'About zero.'

Luna sighed. 'I figured.'

'Two minutes!' Compass called. I felt the signature of space magic as she started her spell.

Ji-yeong walked over to us. She had her shield on her left arm, and was adjusting her sword in its scabbard.

The Council communicator focus in my ear pinged. 'Nimbus to command group,' Nimbus's voice said. 'All teams report in.'

'Alpha team ready,' Rain said in his deep voice.

'Beta team ready,' Landis said briskly.

'. . . Gamma team, ready,' Sonder said.

'Gamma team, status,' Nimbus said.

Lumen spoke over the focus. 'Accumulator is primed. We can activate remotely at any time.'

'Confirm charging time estimates.'

'Minimum charging time to break the keep's wards and threaten the focus crystal is twelve minutes,' Sonder said. He sounded nervous. Sonder's not a battle mage, and this was probably the first time he'd been involved in something on this scale. 'To guarantee complete destruction of that entire section, we'll need to charge for seventeen and a half minutes before firing.'

'Understood,' Nimbus said calmly. 'Captain Rain, Captain Landis, you are required to keep your targets engaged for seventeen and a half minutes. Confirm.'

'Received and understood,' Rain said.

'Received and understood,' Landis said. Whatever he was feeling, he didn't let any of it show in his voice.

'Begin final countdown,' Nimbus ordered.

'One minute!' Compass shouted.

'I don't like this,' Luna said quietly to herself.

'Ji-yeong, stay close to me and Landis,' I said. 'If we get tied down with the ifrit, we'll need you to deactivate the shadows' spawning mechanism. I'll cover you while you do.'

Ji-yeong nodded.

'Thirty seconds!' Compass shouted.

'Confirm ready to attack,' Nimbus said.

'Ready,' Landis said curtly.

'Ready,' said Rain.

'You are cleared to attack,' Nimbus said. 'I repeat, you are cleared to attack.'

'GO!' Landis shouted, his voice booming out over the crowd.

On either side of Compass, just above the grass, a gate shimmered and formed. The first Council forces went through at a run.

12

Luna, Ji-yeong and I jumped through.

We came down on a stone bridge over the sea. Behind was the castle with its looming walls and towers; ahead were the tombs, a single curving building with arrow-slit windows mounted on a rocky pillar rising out of the water.

There was no time to look around. Keepers and soldiers were moving through the gates in a steady stream, crossing the bridge at a jog. I caught a glimpse through the crowd of black shadows guarding the entrance to the tombs: gunfire stammered, there was a flash of magic and the next I saw the shadows were gone.

I stepped to one side, motioning Luna and Ji-yeong next to me. The Council forces kept streaming past for a few seconds more, then the flow stopped. Compass was the last one through, letting the gates close behind her.

Gunfire echoed from within the tombs, and I could sense battle magic: fire, lightning, ice. Over the tactical channel, I could hear combat chatter: progress reports, terse directions. Landis's men were fanning out, destroying any shadows they found. A soldier called out an alert for jann; a second later there was a flash of magic and the order to move up.

Tobias was directing a group of soldiers and mages at the entrance to the tombs. '. . . hold here,' he was saying. He glanced at us as we walked past, then turned back.

'Remember, look out for humans. If they're serious, that's . . .'

I glanced back up at the looming castle. No sign of movement. 'Come on,' Ji-yeong said. She was staring at the tombs, keyed-up and eager.

'Patience,' I said. 'You'll get your chance to fight.'

The inside of the tombs was gloomy and cold. I led Luna and Ji-yeong up the stairs. No shadows or jann were left. We passed one soldier with a bloody arm, leaning against the wall while a medic bandaged the wound, but it looked as if there hadn't been much resistance. That wouldn't change until—

'Mage contact!' a soldier called over the comm. 'Mage contact in the central chamber. Force magic attacks, one man down.'

'Hold position,' Landis replied instantly. 'Second and third squads, converge on the central chamber.'

'Go,' I said.

We ran up the stairs, our footsteps echoing on the stone. Inside my head, I was counting off minutes. As soon as Anne – the marid – realised what we were doing, it'd send reinforcements. We had to do as much damage as possible before then.

And then we came out, and there was no more time for thinking about anything except the battle in front of us.

The main chamber of the tombs was a wide, flattened oval, coloured in browns and greys. Magelights glowed from holders spaced around the room. The walls were lined with sarcophagi, each set back into the stone, with walkways joining them in giant rings. There were rows and rows of sarcophagi, each stacked on top of another and set a little back, running all the way up to the ceiling. Hundreds and hundreds. I knew from Ji-yeong that each was the birthplace of a shadow.

Fully half of the sarcophagi were respawning their inhabitants. Inky darkness would gather around the stone, then slowly coalesce, taking the shape of a smoky humanoid with white eyes and wings. The process was slow, but there were a lot of sarcophagi, and a steady stream of shadows were forming, coming awake and flapping clumsily down from their balconies to fight.

Fight, and be destroyed. Landis's men were spread throughout the first third of the room and they were destroying the shadows one after another with bullets and spells and charged blades. The stammer of gunfire and the flash of spells filled the room. Most of the shadows died before even reaching the floor.

But the real threat wasn't the shadows. Halfway across the room were two figures, one bulky, one slim, engaging Landis's mages with earth and force magic. Caldera and Barrayar.

I took it all in at a glance and broke into a run. The room was chaos, screams and shouts and flashes, fifty men and a hundred shadows all fighting at once. Somehow, though, it all made sense. Through the fate-weaver I could sense the lines of the battle, the inflection points. The shadows weren't important – Caldera and Barrayar were the obstacles. A shadow got in my way and I cut through it without slowing down. I could feel the *sovnya* pulling me towards Caldera and Barrayar. It didn't want constructs; it wanted the jinn.

Caldera was fighting two mages at once: an ice mage called Hoarfrost, and an air mage I didn't know. She was outnumbered, but shadows kept flapping down to distract the mages, splitting their attacks. A Council soldier lay crumpled against the wall.

Hoarfrost threw a volley of ice spikes. They shattered against Caldera's skin: she threw out a hand towards the air mage and some spell knocked him backwards, then I was charging Caldera and she spun to face me.

Caldera's eyes met mine for a second. I expected recognition, anger, but she might have been looking at a piece of furniture. She started some sort of ranged spell, realised at the last second that I was too close and swung a punch.

My armour wouldn't do a thing against a blow like that. I turned my attack into a diving roll; Caldera's punch passed over my head as I came up behind her. The *sovnya* slashed out, and Caldera batted it away with a *clang*.

She's faster. I jumped out of range of Caldera's counter. A shadow tried to grab me from behind; I skewered it and circled left to come at Caldera again. Caldera turned to face me – and Ji-yeong stabbed her in the back.

Caldera staggered. Ji-yeong had been shadowing me and had darted in as soon as Caldera had been distracted. Caldera started to turn, and Ji-yeong drove her short-sword into Caldera's side, under her ribs.

Caldera barely seemed to notice. She finished her turn, wrenching the sword out of Ji-yeong's hands, and drove a punch straight at Ji-yeong's head.

And that would have been a dead Ji-yeong, if she'd been a normal human. But the Korean girl had the enhanced speed and strength of her life magic, and enough combat experience to not freeze up. She jumped away, Caldera's blow just barely missing her, and Caldera started to turn back towards me.

I brought the *sovnya* around in a full-strength swing that cut Caldera nearly in half.

Caldera staggered again, losing her breath in an *uff*. The *sovnya* sang in triumph. The blade had cut upwards through her body, under her arm, and now red light ignited around it, burning away flesh and blood and—

—sand?

Caldera straightened. The *sovnya* was burning her up from the inside, but now that I looked, I could see that sand was flowing in to heal her wound. Grains blackened and charred under the *sovnya*'s flame, but they kept coming, sealing up what should have been a fatal strike. Caldera twisted around to stare at me. We were less than five feet away, linked by the shaft of the polearm.

Uh-oh.

Caldera punched, her right arm extending past human reach.

I shoved against the *sovnya*, using it as leverage to drop down. Pain flared in my fingers as the blow went overhead, then I yanked out the polearm and rolled out of range.

Caldera aimed her palm at me and a cone of sand and grit blasted out.

There was no room to dodge. I spun and hunched over as the blast struck with a howl, drowning out everything around me. Particles of sand slashed at my back, trying to tear through my armour, rip the clothes from my skin and the skin from my bones. Tiny streaks of fire cut across patches of exposed skin. I couldn't see or hear; all I could do was trust my armour—

My armour held. All of a sudden, the blasting sand was gone and light and sound came rushing back.

I sprang away. Hoarfrost was hitting Caldera with ice

blasts, one after another, and Caldera was forced to turn from me to shield her face with one bulky arm. I could see a burnt patch across her torso, but she was moving as though she wasn't even injured.

How the hell do you fight someone who can turn into sand?

When you can't solve one problem, work on another. I turned towards Barrayar.

Barrayar had been nearer to the entrance, and Landis's mages had focused on him. A perimeter was holding back the shadows, shooting down any that came near, while four or five mages were hammering Barrayar from all sides. Barrayar's business suit was slashed and tattered, and his shield was barely holding under the attacks. But at the same time, I was sensing the battle on another level, attacks curving through space and time to the point at which they'd intersect. I knew it would take only a few seconds more.

A blast of fire from Landis knocked Barrayar off his feet. As Barrayar rose, a death mage stepped in behind him and rammed a blade of crackling black energy through Barrayar's shield and body and out the other side. It was a fatal strike.

'Back!' I shouted at the death mage. He glanced at me in confusion.

Barrayar reached across under his arm, touched the death mage's stomach and fired a narrow lance of force right through him.

The man's eyes went wide in pain and he staggered back, collapsing. The blade through Barrayar's chest fizzled and disappeared. Barrayar straightened up; blue light glowed around his wound and when it was gone the skin beneath his ripped clothes was unbroken and whole.

'Oh, come on!' Ji-yeong said in frustration. She'd stepped in next to me. 'They can *both* do that?'

'Different mechanism,' I said absently. 'Water magic.' My thoughts were whirling. This must be why Anne had chosen these two for her defence team: the ones that were hardest to kill, slowest to get past. A shadow dropped down towards Ji-yeong and I cut it in two; she jumped aside as the flaming halves fell where she'd been standing. I could sense the lines of fate that marked Barrayar's future. It wasn't quite the same as my divination, though the divination helped. It was an awareness of the battle, a sense of its flow. I tried to use the fateweaver, guide the futures into the right channels—

The futures wavered and broke. Too many people, too many conflicting decisions. The Keepers were keeping Barrayar and Caldera busy, but they weren't killing them. We needed to break them before reinforcements arrived.

I opened my senses, looking for some weakness. My divination couldn't see far enough – too chaotic. But I could sense the lines of fate where Barrayar's future ended. I couldn't guide them in, not myself, but . . .

I reached out through the dreamstone. *Landis, Luna. I think I can see how to kill Barrayar. I'll need your help.*

Well, he certainly doesn't seem inclined to do it himself. Despite being engaged with Barrayar, Landis sounded detached and calm. *What did you have in mind?*

Luna, channel your curse into him, I ordered. *Landis, cover.*

Landis didn't argue. He gave quick commands over his focus and the mages shifted formation. Luna had worked her way around the right side, near the wall; now she stepped up and levelled her whip, a line of silvery mist springing out from her to Barrayar.

Barrayar turned to focus on Luna, his hand coming up. Luna flinched but stood her ground. Beams of force flashed out, powerful enough to punch right through Luna's armour and her body as well, but Tobias had moved next to her, his water shield expanding to cover them both. Blue light flared and the force attacks glanced away.

Luna kept her whip aimed at Barrayar, a steady stream of mist pouring into him. Shouts and gunfire echoed from all around, and from behind I could hear the *boom* of other mages fighting Caldera, but I couldn't spare any attention. All of my focus was on that future I'd sensed through the fateweaver, drawing steadily closer. *Landis, when I give the word, hit him with an incinerate spell*, I said. *Full power.*

That type of spell—

—is bad against shields, I know. Trust me.

The silver mist around Barrayar was a bright glow, beautiful and deadly. Barrayar's eyes were locked on Luna and he was still launching a steady stream of attacks but Tobias was blocking every one, glancing between Luna and Barrayar as he and Luna backed slowly away. Luna kept her wand aimed at Barrayar, her face set. Barrayar was advancing, shrugging off attacks from Landis and two other mages. It wouldn't be long before he had them pinned against the wall.

I felt the futures shift. Luna's curse had reached critical mass and it was looking for a way to discharge. Possibilities flickered: the ceiling collapsing, shadows mistaking Barrayar for a target, attacks aimed at Caldera striking him instead, ricocheting bullets . . .

Now, I told Landis, and pushed with the fateweaver. One future out of the dozens grew stronger. Luna's curse latched onto it and the other futures winked out.

Landis struck. The world seemed to darken for a second before a roaring blast of flame exploded all around Barrayar, and just as it did, the mist of Luna's curse flared and Barrayar's shield collapsed. It was so fast that I didn't see why. One second Barrayar was striding forward, aiming another force lance; the next his shield was gone and the air around him was incandescent fire.

Barrayar never had a chance to scream. His body flared, clothes and skin and flesh igniting in a single flame. A wave of heat washed over me, carrying the scent of ash and burnt flesh.

It was over in an instant. The charred remains of Barrayar finished the step he'd been taking and collapsed into a pile of scorched carbon. Only a few half-melted bones were left. For a moment, I saw *something* at the edge of my vision, a black winged shadow expanding outwards, then it was gone and somehow the atmosphere in the tombs felt less oppressive, the daylight from the windows a little brighter.

'Regenerate that,' I said to Barrayar's remains. Then I turned to Caldera.

Caldera was looking at the charred bones. As every other Keeper in the room turned towards her, she sank into the flagstones beneath her, disappearing from view.

'Stone glide,' Landis said curtly over the comm. 'We have an earth ifrit loose. All units report if you see it.'

I swore. Master earth mages can merge with earth and stone, passing through it like water and making them virtually impossible to catch or stop. Caldera had never been able to do it before, but apparently that was yet another ability the ifrit had given her. 'Ji-yeong,' I said, and pointed across at the other side of the room. There was a raised platform level with the second ring of sarcophagi, and mounted on it was what looked like a control interface. 'Shut it down.'

Ji-yeong took off at a sprint, dodging around those shadows in her way. Landis issued orders: long-range fire lanced out from the Keepers, striking down the shadows on the stairs and far platform.

And as it did, I felt what I'd been waiting for and dreading. A flicker of space magic directly above.

'Enemy gate!' Compass called out over the comm. 'You have enemies gating in directly above the tombs.'

Back! I sent to Ji-yeong. Ji-yeong had made it halfway up the stairs and was only seconds away from the platform. She slowed, hesitating.

Black light flashed. With a rumble, stone blocks fell from the ceiling, smashing down around the spot Ji-yeong had been aiming for. A column of sunlight came down through the hole in the roof, flickering for a second as it was blocked by a body.

Sagash glided down to land on the far platform.

It had been a long time since I'd seen the Dark master mage, and he hadn't got any better looking. Yellowed skin was stretched tight over tendons and bones, and the lips were pulled back from his mouth to show his teeth in a fixed, unchanging grin. Pinpoints of yellow light glowed from his eyes as he stared down at Ji-yeong.

Ji-yeong took a step back, staring up at her ex-master with wide eyes. 'Um,' she began.

Sagash raised a hand.

Black death flashed out, and Landis's magic darted to meet it. Orange-red fire met Sagash's deathbolt and the two spells annihilated each other in a flash and a clap of thunder. Ji-yeong went tumbling down the steps and scrambled away out of range.

'Ah, Sagash!' Landis called out cheerfully. He'd marched forward and was standing at the front of the Keepers in the middle of the room. 'Where were we?'

Sagash turned to fix Landis with an unblinking stare. A few shadows flapped in, but as Sagash gazed down they swerved away, pulling back to the sarcophagi. Around us, the gunfire died as the Council soldiers dropped back into a guard position, watching the shadows warily.

I spoke quietly into the comm focus. 'Verus to command group. Reinforcements have arrived. Recommend you initiate immediately.'

Rain's deep voice sounded in my ear. 'Rain to command group. Perimeter established, Drakh's forces contained. Ready to initiate.'

A pause, then Nimbus's voice came in. 'Verus. Please have Captain Landis confirm.'

'Landis is occupied facing Sagash,' I said through clenched teeth. It took serious effort not to add 'you idiot' to the end of that sentence.

Another pause. 'Captain Landis. Please confirm.'

On the platform behind Sagash, sand and stone rose up from the platform, re-forming into the shape of Caldera. She folded her arms and stared at the mages beneath her.

What are they waiting for? I looked ahead—

Orange-red light bloomed from above and Variam came floating down. There was no obvious magic supporting him; I could sense some spell, but it wasn't the fiery wings he'd used before. He just drifted, gliding sideways to touch down on one of the upper balconies above Sagash and to the right.

'Captain Landis,' Nimbus said into my ear, infuriatingly calm. 'Please confirm.'

Landis cocked his head and spoke a single word. 'Trident.'

'Confirmed,' Nimbus said. 'Lumen and Sonder. Begin.'

'Understood,' Sonder said over the circuit, his voice strained. 'Accumulator is active.'

Variam gazed down onto the room below. It had been three days since I'd seen him, and to a casual glance he looked much the same: his work clothes and black turban were clean and neat, and he didn't look hurt. He didn't radiate the same aura of menace that Caldera and Sagash did. Yet somehow, looking at the three mages facing us, it was him my eyes were drawn to.

I felt my heart sink. *Oh no.* It was what I'd been afraid of, right from when I noticed that Anne had taken five mages instead of four.

Variam's voice rang out from the balcony. 'You trespass.' Standing still, the creature could have passed for Variam; speaking, the illusion was broken. The voice was measured, dispassionate . . . wrong.

Okay, four generals, Luna said over our mental link. *First three are in Aether, Barrayar and Caldera, right?*

Sagash is the fourth, I told her.

So Vari's got a weaker ifrit? Luna asked hopefully.

It's not an ifrit.

'Master Jinn,' Landis said courteously. 'Delighted to make your acquaintance. I do hate to burst in unannounced, but I'm afraid that on behalf of the Light Council, I must inform you that we rather take some objection to your sultan's plans.'

'Yes,' Variam said.

Landis, I said urgently through the dreamstone. *Stall.*

'I don't suppose you'd be interested in discussing the matter?' Landis asked.

'This realm approaches eternity.' There was a weird dissonance to Variam's voice, like an echo at the edge of hearing. 'In contemplation you may understand.'

Landis paused. 'Well, that's certainly . . . interesting.'

'What are we waiting for?' someone muttered from behind me.

I spoke through the communication focus, my voice low and urgent. 'Verus to beta team. The creature possessing Keeper Talwar is a marid jinn that used to be bound in an item called the monkey's paw. Do *not* engage.' Beside me, I heard Luna draw in her breath.

'Excuse me a moment,' Landis said to Variam, then spoke quietly into his communicator. 'Verus. Analysis.'

'Caldera and Sagash will attack first chance they get,' I told him. 'The marid won't attack until you reach the platform.'

'Understood. All units, hold fire.'

Alex? Luna asked. *Tell me you've got a plan.*

It's been two minutes, I said. *Accumulator will be ready in ten to fifteen more.*

I don't mean the accumulator!

I'm working on it.

Screw it. Luna stepped up next to me and called out across the room. 'Vari!'

Variam turned his head slightly to look at her. From across the room, I searched his eyes, hoping for some spark of recognition, of humanity . . .

'You're not a marid,' Luna called out. 'You're not a jinn, or the monkey's paw. You're Variam Singh, and I want to talk to you! Not the thing inside you!'

The marid looked back at Luna through Variam's eyes.

'*Talk* to me!' Luna shouted. 'Don't just stand there!'

The marid's voice was as calm as before. 'The storm does not pierce the earth.'

'You can't do this!' Luna shouted. 'Variam isn't some set of clothes for you to wear! He's a person, and he matters to me!'

The marid seemed to focus on Luna. 'Thought and feeling bend to law.' The echo in Variam's voice was stronger, as though other voices were trying to speak at the same time. 'Your words are those of many, but they are in vain. Desire is what calls me from slumber, yet desire is not my banishment; the spark kindles the blaze but cannot bring its end. Only law is eternal.'

Somewhere away to the west, I felt something on my magesight. A sense of power, still weak, but growing. The accumulator was charging, and my eyes flicked between Sagash and Caldera and Variam. How long before they noticed?

'What law?' Luna said. 'Martin signed a contract with you. Vari didn't!'

The chamber was silent but for Luna and Variam; all around, Landis's soldiers had their guns trained on the shadows or on the mages ahead of us. Landis stood at the front, his head slightly tilted so that he could listen to Luna without taking his eyes off Variam and Sagash. For now, everyone was obeying Landis's order to hold off, but you could feel the tension in the air. It would only take one man to pull a trigger.

'My allegiance was ancient when the creator of your mantle was young.' Variam's voice was calm, implacable. 'The spark does not move the stone.'

Luna's fingers clenched white on her wand. 'Okay, fine,' she said, and her jaw set. 'Then maybe you'll listen to this.'

My precognition warned me just in time, and my hand shot out to grab Luna's wrist as she started to raise her wand. *Don't.*

Luna's eyes snapped. *Get out of my way!*

It won't work, I said silently. I could feel Luna's curse sinking into my arm; with an effort of will I forced myself to keep hold. *Luna, your curse can do a lot of things, but it can't do this. Please.*

I could see the anger in Luna's eyes, feel it through the mental link, fury and frustration, wanting to lash out. With a jerk, Luna pulled out of my grip, then she stared down at the silver mist swirling around my arm. Slowly she began to draw it back in, soaking into her own aura. It wasn't as fast as usual.

'I must admit, I'm a little curious as to what you mean by allegiance,' Landis said. 'Perhaps you could explain . . . ?'

Variam opened his mouth, then paused. He turned his head.

Adrenalin spiked through me. *Get ready*, I told Landis.

Variam stared west a second longer, then turned to look at Sagash and Caldera. They didn't speak, but I could feel something passing between them.

'All units, prepare to engage,' Landis said quietly. 'Do not allow those jinn to leave this room.'

Variam looked up towards the hole in the roof and crouched.

Landis spoke into the silence. 'Fire.'

Everything happened at once.

Variam jumped, and as he did bolts of fire and ice slammed into him. His shield flared, absorbing the attack, but he was sent flying into the wall behind. The roar of automatic weapons filled the room, shadows twisting and falling. Sagash disappeared in a bloom of multicoloured light and Caldera was knocked back a step as a dozen bullets hit her.

The light faded to reveal Sagash standing, unharmed. He raised both hands, sparks flashing as bullets sank into his shield, and I felt magic gathering, dark and terrible. A point of darkness appeared above his head; it grew quickly, spinning as it did, becoming a ball of black fire.

I felt what was coming, images and movement, a hundred things at once. 'Hoarfrost, right!' I shouted over the noise. 'Travis, down! Sanders, get—!' Even as I spoke, I knew it wasn't enough. Too many people; too many conflicting directions. I caught Ji-yeong's arm and yanked her aside just as the black sun above Sagash flared, bright enough to cause pain.

Beams of black light flashed out, spearing through the crowd. I saw one barely miss Hoarfrost, his eyes going wide as it cut through his shield and went over his left shoulder; Travis ducked as another went over his head. Others weren't so lucky. Sanders screamed as a beam burned through him, his shoulder and chest flaring into ash.

The black sun twisted and the beams scythed across the room; I ducked and more screams sounded behind me. Over the comm I heard Landis snapping out orders; spells sprang out to touch the black sun and it guttered, its beams going out.

Behind Sagash something appeared in my magesight,

a lattice of power, some kind of magic I'd never seen before. It formed a column linking the platform to the hole in the roof. Variam jumped up through it, lifted on fiery wings.

Hydroblast spells flashed out, aimed by Tobias. They struck Variam with perfect accuracy . . . and winked out as they hit the column. They weren't deflected, as by a shield: they just vanished. Variam disappeared through the hole in the roof.

Shit! I knew where he was going. *Luna, Ji-yeong, I'm going after Vari. Stay alive.* I crouched, calling upon my headband, and leapt.

Air magic wrapped around me, carrying me upwards. I had a brief panorama of the battle below, soldiers fighting shadows and spells flying back and forth and Landis engaged with Sagash in a deadly long-range duel, orange-red fire meeting black death. Caldera saw me and flung out another stream of flaying sand, but the range was too long and I was already bending the futures; the sandblast flashed past below. I alighted on the window ledge, the sun dazzlingly bright after the gloom of the tombs.

As my vision cleared, I saw a small dark figure, soaring on wings of flame. He was heading for the castle walls, angling west towards the windmill.

I tightened my grip on the *sovnya* and leapt into the sky.

13

Air rushed around me as I soared. I'd never pushed the headband to see just how far and fast it could go, and now I gave myself over to it. I felt the item come alive, exulting in the open sky.

The bridge was far, far below, Landis's rearguard black specks against the stone. 'Verus to command group,' I called as I flew. 'A marid jinn has broken away and is inbound towards the accumulator.'

'Did you say a *marid*?' Sonder asked.

'Gamma team,' Nimbus said. 'Status on the accumulator.'

'Sixty per cent,' Lumen said, her voice tense. 'We need at least five minutes.'

'Acknowledged,' Nimbus said calmly. 'Beta team, engage the marid and slow its advance.'

Now that I was out of the tombs, I could feel the accumulator clearly, a glow of power behind the castle's western corner. Up ahead, I saw Variam dip out of sight beyond the walls.

The castle's north wall was coming up to meet me. I was reaching the top of my arc, and my eyes were telling me I was going to slam into the ramparts and fall. Despite myself, I glanced down: the castle's walls fell away sheer and vertical, down and down to the rocks and crashing surf far below. My stomach lurched and I pulled my eyes up towards the crenellated wall, closer, closer—

My feet sailed in between two of the merlons and I touched down on the rampart, turning the landing into a run. I searched for Variam and found him, below me and to the left. He was soaring westward on fiery wings, jumping from walltop to walltop.

He wasn't moving as fast as me, but he was fast. He'd reach the windmill in much less than five minutes. And once he got there, he was going to level that place and everyone around it.

The *sovnya* tugged, pulling in Variam's direction. I shut it out; instead, as I ran along the rampart, I searched through the futures, calculating angles. *There.* I leapt, then leapt again, off the wall towards Variam.

Variam was flying towards a towertop that would give him a view over the western castle. I soared high, my arc carrying me over his. As I flew, I unclipped a grenade from my belt, pulled the pin, waited two and a half seconds, then threw it downwards just as I passed over Variam's head.

The grenade went off in Variam's face with a flat *boompf*. His shield absorbed the impact, but while Variam might be immune to shrapnel, he wasn't immune to Newton's laws of motion. The blast slowed his momentum, and all of a sudden the arc that would have carried him onto the towertop was falling short. Variam slammed into the wall and fell out of sight.

I alighted and jumped again. 'Verus to gamma team,' I said. 'Stalled the marid for thirty seconds.'

A pause, then Sonder replied. 'Can you do that a few more times?'

'No,' I said shortly. 'Verus to accumulator team, friendlies coming in, repeat friendlies coming in, hold fire, hold fire.'

I came flying over the western walls and down towards the windmill. I saw the muzzles of light machine guns turning towards me; they tracked me all the way in but Little's team were veterans and no one pulled a trigger. I landed on the grass by the millpond and turned and ran for the windmill. Men stationed by the building stood aside as I threw open the door.

This close, the accumulator's power was like a furnace, filling the windmill with leaking energy. The focus looked like a thick white cylinder with a rounded top, connected by some arcane mechanism to a polished blue disc that I knew was the gate linkage. On the right side, Sergeant Little was speaking into his comm, his voice low and tense. The far wall held a big flat-screen monitor, and on it I could see Sonder and Lumen against a background of ramparts and sky. Below the monitor, a camera was pointed at me.

I strode into the room. Just being around the accumulator felt tense, like being in a room with a ticking bomb. 'How long?' I asked.

'Four to nine minutes,' Lumen said through the video link, her voice strained. She was holding a focus the size and shape of a spearhead that I knew would channel the blast; a silvery wire led away from it out of view. 'What's going on with the marid?'

'Still coming. Two minutes out.'

Across the room, Little looked up and shook his head. 'No reinforcements,' he told me. 'Orders are to hold with what we have.'

I hesitated, futures and battle plans unfolding. Little and me and twenty-two more, with rifles, three light machine guns and a handful of grenades. Against a marid . . .

We couldn't win. Not even close.

I turned to the video screen. 'Sonder. I need you here.'

Sonder's eyes widened. 'What?'

'We don't have enough to stop this thing,' I said. Mentally I was tracking how long we had until the marid landed. One minute, forty seconds. 'Your magic could do it.'

'I can't—'

'A stasis spell.' I spoke quickly. 'It's the only thing that's got a chance of working.'

'It won't—'

'It'll land, I'll make sure of it. Hurry.'

Sonder hesitated, the futures shifting. One second, two seconds, then his expression firmed. 'No.'

'Sonder!'

'Our orders are to stay.'

'We can't hold against a marid on our own! If we try, everyone here is going to die!'

'Then go,' Sonder said.

I stared at Sonder, then towards Lumen. Lumen didn't meet my eyes.

'I'm not going out on a limb for you this time,' Sonder said. He hesitated for an instant. 'I'm sorry.' He reached out towards the camera and my feed cut off.

I stared through the video link. All I could see was a black screen. 'Sonder!' I shouted.

There was no sound but for the whine of the wind.

Slowly I turned away. Sergeant Little was watching me, his face blank.

I couldn't beat a marid. Not with the *sovnya*, not with the fateweaver. But Sonder had said it – I could go. Little's men were under orders to hold this place. I wasn't.

I hesitated, remembering the men outside. They were

Council security, most of them veterans of the war, and I'd led many of them, learned their names. They had a dangerous job, with the usual profile for those in dangerous jobs: poor, low status and male. About two-thirds were lower-class British, the rest immigrants, most from Eastern Europe. If this were a Hollywood movie, they were the kinds of characters who'd be played by extras. No one would care if they died in a movie, and few would care if they died here.

I remembered what Nimbus had said when I'd confronted him. Security men were expendable; mages weren't.

Thirty seconds.

'Sir?' Little said.

Little's men weren't going to make a difference to the battle. Cold calculation told me to abandon them.

Expendable . . .

'Screw it,' I said out loud. 'Little, pull your men back.'

Little paused. 'Orders—'

'I am giving you new orders,' I said harshly. 'On my authority, get your men out of range of the accumulator and hold fire until further notice. Clear?'

'. . . Clear, sir.'

I turned and walked out.

I strode out of the windmill, the *sovnya* in one hand, its blade low above the grass. The sun was directly overhead, dazzling and bright.

I came to a stop in front of the pond, then took a deep breath. 'Marid!' I shouted at the top of my voice. The echoes bounced off the castle walls, travelled on the wind. 'Face me!'

The wind died away. The sails of the windmill above me slowed, the creaking coming at longer and longer intervals until it stopped. There was a hush.

Variam dropped out of the sky on wings of fire. He landed on the other side of the millpond with a *thud* before straightening to look at me.

I heard Nowy speak quietly over the tactical circuit. 'I have a shot.'

'Do not engage,' Little said instantly. 'Nowy, you pull the trigger on that LMG and I'll stuff your dick down the barrel!'

Variam studied me dispassionately from across the water. Even if I hadn't seen what he could do, I would have known it wasn't him: his movements were wrong, too slow and too measured, as though he were used to brushing aside anything in his path. Flame flickered around his hands and feet, then died. 'You challenge your doom,' he said in that weird, too-old voice. He nodded towards the windmill behind me. 'Stand aside.'

'I will not.' I levelled the *sovnya* at Variam; it quivered in my hand, eager to strike at the creature inside him. 'For nearly ten years, you stayed with me. You slept under my roof, within the monkey's paw, waking only to take your victims. I was your host, and you were my guest. You said as much when I spoke to you in the Hollow. Well, I am *still* your host, and under the laws of hospitality, you may not raise your hand against me!'

Variam paused.

I knew that I was gambling with my life. If the marid chose to attack, it could obliterate me. But I'd noticed back in the tombs that the marid from the monkey's paw seemed different from the other jinn. The ifrit and the jann had acted like extensions of the sultan's will, usually attacking us on sight. But Variam had spoken, drawing a line in the sand and waiting for us to step over it. The sultan cared only for war and death, but the marid inside Variam was a creature of law. That was how it had taken its victims back in my shop. It had offered them a contract, then extracted its price.

If I was right, I had a chance. If I was wrong, I was dead.

But the marid didn't strike. It looked at me through Vari's eyes, dark and unreadable. 'The emperor commands. Stand aside.'

'No,' I said. I could feel the magic radiating from the accumulator behind me. It wasn't fully charged: if Lumen fired now, everything we'd done would be wasted. 'You want to destroy it, you'll have to go through me.'

The marid stared at me. The futures shifted, slow and sluggish, and I felt a chill. The marid was making up its mind. 'Intractable,' it said. 'You force a contradiction.'

I heard Nimbus through the focus in my ear, demanding an update. Sonder and Lumen said something that I didn't hear. All my attention was on the marid.

Futures shifted, branching. I saw Variam's eyes shift up to the windmill. He might try to strike past me, blow up the accumulator that way . . . I shifted position slightly, blocking a direct attack, and one of the futures faded out. The marid's eyes shifted back.

Everything was silent. I held my breath, feeling the coin spin.

'The contradiction is resolved,' Variam said. He turned; fire ignited around him and he leapt up into the air, soaring away over the walls and out of sight.

I stared after him, checking and rechecking just to make sure he wouldn't turn around. Nothing.

Variam was gone.

A wave of exhaustion rolled over me and I sagged, my knees going weak. There's a special kind of fear you only get when your life is in someone else's hands. All of a sudden, my limbs felt like lead.

Nimbus was still yammering on over the command channel, demanding updates. 'Oh, shut up,' I told him wearily. 'The marid's gone.'

'Gone where?' Nimbus asked. 'Accumulator team—'

'Verus!' I heard Nowy call down from the walls. 'You okay?'

I gave Nowy a half-wave, then walked slowly back to the windmill and pushed open the door.

The inside of the room was empty; Little had obeyed my orders and got everyone out of range, himself included. The monitor was once again displaying Sonder and Lumen on their towertop. Apparently they'd turned the camera back on once they didn't have to worry about looking me in the face.

'Alex?' Sonder asked hesitantly.

'It's gone,' I said. 'No thanks to you.' It was an effort to speak. I'd gone from fighting my way through the tombs to the chase over the castle walls to facing Variam, and right now I was running on empty.

'Verus,' Lumen said urgently. 'Is the windmill clear?'

The accumulator was humming with power, filling me with tension. 'Windmill is clear,' I said. 'Fire your damn weapon so we can get out of here.'

'Sonder, charge,' Lumen said.

'One hundred and fifteen,' Sonder said, checking

something off-screen. His movements were jerky and quick.

'How long to full?'

'Three minutes, twenty seconds. Come on, Lumen, just fire.'

Lumen paused an instant, then nodded. 'All right.' She turned away from the camera, lifting the focus.

A soft voice spoke from out of view. 'I think not.'

Sonder and Lumen whirled.

Green light flickered. Sonder and Lumen froze in place, every muscle locked and still. Footsteps sounded, and a figure walked out in front of the camera.

It was Anne, but it wasn't. The first time I'd met Dark Anne, I'd felt as though I was meeting another person who just happened to be sharing Anne's body and voice. This was the same, but worse. She had Anne's long dark hair and slender grace; she wore the black skater dress that Arachne had given her at our last meeting together, and her bare arms and way of moving and the soft green light glowing around her hands were all those of the woman I loved. But then she glanced towards the camera, and it felt like a knife through the heart. The creature looking out from behind those reddish-brown eyes wasn't her. I'd known that Anne had to be fully possessed, I'd had a long time to prepare for it, but I hadn't been ready for how badly it would hurt. Actually *seeing* it was like being stabbed and then having the blade twist in the wound.

'You,' the marid told me. 'I should have known.' It turned towards Sonder and reached out, pale fingers resting delicately against his armour. Sonder was trembling, eyes wide with panic, struggling to move against the paralysis spell. 'Worth keeping?' the marid mused.

I tried to think of what to do. All I could think of was that last-resort idea I'd had about Arachne's dress, but I was on the other side of a camera and—

The marid killed Sonder then killed Lumen. Their bodies dropped, dead before they hit the ground.

I stood frozen, trying to process what I'd seen. It had been so fast that it was over before I'd realised what was happening. There had been a flash of green light, something flickering into Anne from the bodies, and that was it.

'No,' the marid decided, and turned back to me. 'I dislike being distracted from my work. Abandoning the nexus in this manner will delay the alignment. More importantly, I have been forced to perform with my own hands that which should properly have been attended to by my servants. This irritates me.'

I stared at the marid, then down at Sonder's body.

'I know who you are and what you desire,' the marid told me. 'Should you wish to save this human, seek me at the heart. Until you do, we will not meet again. Now.' It reached down, picking up the focus from Lumen's lifeless hand before studying it. 'Human weapons have changed, but are apparently no less inferior. Ah, I see. This is linked to the device behind you. You intended to draw my retaliation towards your location, rather than here.' The marid looked towards me. 'I presume this is primed to project energy. I wonder what would happen if I aimed it back at that device itself?'

I looked down at the focus in Anne's hand and saw Lumen's magic still radiating from it, ready to be unleashed. My eyes went wide.

The marid pointed the focus at the portal.

I turned and ran.

I burst out of the windmill, sprinting with everything I had. I could see the futures converging ahead of me, narrowing in on a single event with a terrible finality. Three seconds. Two seconds. No time to get clear.

I dived for the millpond.

A beam of incandescent light flashed past, streaming away over the cliffs towards the horizon. I could sense the magic within it, the most powerful attack I'd ever seen, pure light and radiance. I'd already turned my face away to avoid being blinded, but I felt the heat burn the back of my arms and head.

But terrible as that beam was, it lasted only an instant. It hadn't been targeted at me but at the accumulator, and as the accumulator was destroyed, all the energy it had gathered in the past fifteen minutes was released at once.

The windmill exploded behind me.

I dived into the pond, cold water engulfing my body. An instant later, I felt the water shudder as the shockwave hit. Through my divination I caught a confused glimpse of the windmill expanding outwards, the explosion rising up through its stories to burst upwards past the castle walls. A mushroom cloud of dust and white fire rose into the sky.

I floundered underwater, my clothes and armour making my movements heavy and slow. I heard muffled thuds as debris hit the grass, then missiles were raining into the pond. I twisted clumsily; a chunk of grey-yellow brick the size of a beachball crashed through the water's surface and sank past my head. Then the sunlight was blotted out as something far bigger came flipping down and hit the pond with a *boom*, leaving me in shadow.

The thunder of falling debris stopped, and all I could hear was the rush of water. My lungs were burning; I hadn't had the chance to take a breath, and I pushed off the bottom of the pond, swimming heavily upwards. My fingers scraped something and I broke the surface only to bang my head painfully against a wooden strut and go under again. Only after two more tries was I able to get my mouth above water and gasp in air.

The object lying flat on the surface of the pond was one of the windmill's sails. The wooden struts made it hard to get my head up but there were a few inches of air and I got a grip on the struts and tilted my face so that I could keep pulling in breaths. Once I'd recovered, I kicked towards the edge of the pond, pulling myself hand over hand until I came out from under the sail and could see.

The windmill was gone. Only its foundations were left, and even they were hollowed out into a wide melted crater. Grass had been burned black all the way to the edge of the millpond. The castle wall had withstood the blast, but you could see damage all along its length where pieces of the windmill had been driven into the stone. Rubble and charred timbers were scattered everywhere, and a dozen small fires were burning.

I hauled myself from the water, clambering out onto the far side, where there was still some flattened grass. The shaft of the *sovnya* was sticking out from the shallows where the explosion had driven it into the mud; I pulled it loose and tossed it to the ground. Water ran from my hair and clothes as I crawled on hands and knees until I could twist around into a sitting position. All of my body ached.

I realised there was a voice shouting into my ear. Nimbus was speaking through the comm. '—gamma team, report! Mage Sonder, Mage Lumen, report! Accumulator team, what was that blast? Verus! I want to know what's going on out there! Are you receiving me! Report immediately! This is a direct—'

I pulled the focus out of my ear and shut it off. The shouting fell silent, replaced with the soft hiss and pop of fires, and the whine of the wind. I stared at the smoking crater while in my mind's eye I saw Anne killing Sonder, over and over again.

Sonder was dead, Lumen was dead, and the accumulator was destroyed. The Council's attack had failed utterly.

Water dripped from my hair and ran down my face. I sat by the pond, cold and alone.

14

Time passed.

Men filtered through the smoke, guns sweeping left and right. One saw me and called; after a minute, Little walked up. 'Mage Verus?'

I nodded.

'You all right, sir?'

'I'm not hurt,' I said. It was an effort to talk.

'I'm pulling the squad together,' Little said. 'No one's dead, but we've got some injuries and Lisowski was thrown from the wall. We're going to need medevac.'

I nodded again.

Little paused. He looked as though he wanted to say more, but then the moment passed and he signalled to the men beside him, then turned and left.

I sat alone for a while.

Something nudged my left hand and I looked down to see a vulpine head and amber eyes. Hermes poked his nose into my hand, then looked up at me.

'Hey, you,' I said tiredly. 'You're good at getting out of trouble, aren't you?'

Hermes blinked, then curled up next to me and settled down. His fur was a solitary patch of warmth against the cold.

The wind blew, chilling my wet clothes. The image of Sonder's death played over and over in my mind; again and again I saw that deadly green flicker, watched him slump lifeless to the stone.

Sonder and I had been friends once. I'd met him the same year I'd met Anne, and for a few months Sonder and Luna and Anne and Vari and I had formed a little group of five, meeting in my flat in the Camden evenings to laugh and talk and play board games. My friendship with Sonder hadn't lasted, but it had never quite been forgotten, a lingering memory of happier times.

And now he was dead, and the fact that he was dead at Anne's hands made it so much worse. For the first time since we'd entered the shadow realm, I felt helpless. What was I supposed to do?

It was maybe forty-five minutes after the explosion when Luna came picking her way through the wreckage. 'Jesus,' she said, looking around at the devastation. 'I thought they were exaggerating.'

I pulled my eyes up to look at Luna. She looked like she'd been through a lot, but she didn't seem hurt. 'What happened at the tombs?'

'We won, I suppose,' Luna said. 'Though it doesn't feel like it.'

'Losses?'

'I didn't stick around for the count,' Luna said with a grimace. 'Makes me feel like a bit of a coward. But seeing it was bad enough. At least ten or fifteen of those men we went in with are dead. Because of Sagash, mostly. That black sun was horrifying. I think it would have been even worse except Landis and Tobias managed to push him back just long enough for Ji-yeong to sabotage those controls. The moment she did, Caldera and Sagash stopped attacking, just like that.

Caldera opened up a hole in the wall and they did a disappearing act.'

I nodded.

Luna hesitated. 'Is it true about Sonder?'

I nodded again.

Luna looked shocked. 'I got told over the comm, but . . . Anne would do something like *that*?'

'It's not Anne any more,' I said tiredly.

'He probably thought he was picking the safest place,' Luna said. She looked sad. 'Only group that wasn't supposed to be in combat. Poor Sonder. He always did try to stay away from fights.'

We sat in silence for a little while.

'So Vari's got the monkey's paw,' Luna said.

I nodded.

'That was what you meant last night, wasn't it? I was wondering why you weren't pushing more to get that weapon off Richard.'

Nod.

'Damn it,' Luna said. She paused, then shrugged. 'Well, we'll just have to figure something out.'

Luna kept trying to talk but I didn't have much to say and eventually she got up and left. I knew I should do the same, but I couldn't muster the energy.

I was still sitting by the pond when Landis came striding over. 'Ah, Verus, there you are,' he said. He gave Hermes an inquisitive look. 'Is that a blink fox? Fascinating.'

Hermes tilted up his muzzle and blinked.

Landis squatted down next to us and offered his hand for Hermes to sniff. 'Losses from the tombs are nineteen dead, including two Keepers,' he told me, his voice brisk and business-like. 'Fourteen more seriously wounded, some of whom will almost certainly die in the next twelve hours if we can't get them back to the healers at the War Rooms. Chop-chop, Verus, no time to sit about.'

'We just put everything we had into that attack, and we're right back where we started,' I told Landis. There was an edge in my voice. 'What do you want to do, find another accumulator and do it all over again?'

Landis held up one finger and recited:

'If you can make one heap of all your winnings,
And risk it all on one turn of pitch-and-toss,
And lose, and start again at your beginnings,
And never breathe a word about your loss.'

'I'm not really in the mood,' I told him.

'I understand the men stationed here took casualties,' Landis said. 'You took command of them, I believe. So what are you doing sitting out here?'

I looked at Landis resentfully.

Landis met my gaze with clear, calm eyes. 'Footsoldiers are allowed to complain and feel sorry for themselves. Commanders are not.'

'I'm not in command.'

'You entered this shadow realm in order to save Anne and Variam, and to prevent Drakh and the marid from carrying out their plans. Is that correct?'

'Yes.'

'Has that changed?'

'No . . .'

Landis nodded, then touched my clothes with one finger. Fire magic pulsed; the water soaking my clothes and hair evaporated into warm vapour. In an instant, I was completely dry.

Landis straightened. 'Then get to work.'

I looked up at Landis, then down at Hermes. The fox gazed up at me and blinked.

'All right,' I said. I pulled myself to my feet.

Landis and I started back towards the castle. Hermes shook himself and trotted after us.

'Right, Rain,' Landis said. 'Let's hear it.'

We were back in Landis's ready room, looking over the projection table. The focus had been zoomed in to show the north-east of the castle, a closely packed area of tall buildings overlooking small courtyards. It looked tighter and more confined than the areas we'd fought in before. The north and east sides of the projection showed the castle's edge; to the south and west was an irregular arc of blue marking the positions of Rain's men.

'Drakh's forces have gone to ground here,' Rain said, his voice slightly tinny through the speaker. His figure was a small holographic projection floating next to the castle; unlike Landis and me, he was on site. 'Scouting reports put his numbers between a hundred and thirty and a hundred and fifty.'

'Composition?'

'Some mages, but the majority seem to be adepts.'

'All the rest will be adepts,' I said. 'Don't expect any normals.'

'Current status?' Landis asked.

'They didn't contest the perimeter or the interdiction field, but they've pushed back hard the couple of times we tried to probe,' Rain said. 'We haven't forced it since

Nimbus's orders were to keep them pinned. And speaking of, where the hell *is* Nimbus? I've been trying to contact him and all I get is orders to hold.'

'We've heard no more than you,' Landis said. 'Can you hold?'

'Against the adepts, sure,' Rain said. 'The problem's Vihaela.' He made a gesture and half a dozen target marks appeared on the map, spread out over his forces. 'She's been sniping at us ever since we moved in and she's deadly. We've lost one Keeper and sixteen security just to her. All dead, no wounded. She pops up somewhere we're not expecting, kills one before we even know she's there, kills another as the rest scatter, then vanishes.' Rain's projection turned its head towards Landis. 'She's picking us apart and it's wearing down morale. No one wants to stick their heads out. And when they ask me what the plan is, all I can do is tell them to sit tight.'

'We'll have to—' Landis paused and put a hand to his ear, then looked at Rain. 'It's Nimbus.'

'About bloody time.'

Landis strode out of the room and began speaking quietly into the focus. 'How's Vihaela moving around without your mages spotting her?' I asked.

'Wish I knew,' Rain said. 'Between our Keepers, we've got mindsight, lifesight, deathsight, detection for air and cold and heat and at least three things more, and Vihaela's not showing on any of them. She's flitting from one side of the perimeter to the other without anyone noticing. We could use your help.'

'You'll have it, but I'm not sure it'll do much. Drakh's got a way to block my divination too.'

Rain swore. 'What's keeping Nimbus? We're sitting ducks out here!'

I started to answer, then paused and turned. Through the door I could see Landis standing stiff and still. He said something into the comm, his manner curt: whatever Nimbus said back, he clearly didn't like it.

'Verus?' Rain asked.

'One sec,' I said, frowning. Landis and Nimbus were speaking through a private channel, but they weren't too far away . . .

'What the hell?' I muttered. *That doesn't make sense.*

'What's going on?' Rain asked.

'He's about to tell us,' I said absently. I looked ahead, sorting through the futures in which we contacted Talisid.

Landis broke the connection with a sharp movement and strode back through the door. 'Director Nimbus has issued new orders,' he told us. His expression was flat, giving nothing away. 'Rain's force is to pull back.'

'For what, an attack on the keep?' Rain asked.

'To Nimbus's command post.'

'I don't get it,' Rain said.

'We're not attacking,' Landis said, his voice clipped. 'Nimbus's orders are to establish a defensive position and wait until the Council can break through the wards on the shadow realm and reinforce us.'

'What?'

'That'll take days,' I said. I was still busy with the futures, pushing our conversation aside with the fate-weaver to explore possibilities. 'If we're lucky.'

'This is ridiculous,' Rain said. 'Landis, I don't want to launch an attack either, but . . . this is just stick your head in the sand and hope.'

'I agree,' Landis said curtly. 'Unfortunately, Nimbus holds command. I'm going to have to go over his head.'

'Won't help,' I said. 'Council are divided.'

'Talisid?' Rain asked.

'Nimbus has told Talisid that a ground attack is hopeless,' I said. 'Talisid isn't willing to overrule him without something more to go on.'

'Dammit!' Rain said.

I made my decision. It was surprisingly easy. 'Rain, keep your troops where they are,' I told him. 'Landis and I will come over to see the lay of the land.'

'And Nimbus's orders?'

'I'll deal with it.'

Rain's projection looked dubious, but he nodded. 'All right. I'll meet you at point K.'

Rain's image winked out and I turned to Landis. 'Could you gate us please?'

Landis was watching me closely. 'What are you planning, Verus?'

'I think I can see a way to make this work,' I said. 'But . . . I'm going to need you to trust me.'

Landis's eyes rested on me, considering.

We came through the gate to arrive in a small room inside a castle building behind Rain's lines. Rain was waiting with another Keeper called Ilmarin. 'All right, Verus,' he told me. 'Where to?'

'Easternmost point of your lines,' I told him. 'That big flat rooftop.'

Rain led us out on a snaking route through narrow passages and halls. 'Vihaela's been using some sort of custom spell,' he told us as we walked. 'Launches a small conductive bolt wrapped in a shell designed to pierce shields. When it hits, it discharges a death pulse that stops the heart. Very low signature, very hard to detect. We're trying to close off her firing angles, but . . .'

We were passing the men (and occasional women) of the sieging force, deployed in small groups behind walls and improvised barricades. They were huddled behind their cover, hiding or waiting or just sitting slumped. Few met our eyes. The difference compared to Landis's force was like night and day, and it worried me. Battles are usually won or lost by morale; a combat force will break and run long before they run out of men. These soldiers had taken heavy losses last night, they'd had bad news all day, and right now they were being forced to sit and hold a position under sniper fire. I wasn't sure how close they were to falling apart, but it didn't look good.

We came out onto the rooftop, squarish in shape with a waist-high parapet. A couple of soldiers gave us brief nods but stayed down on the staircase, out of sight. 'Keep your eyes open,' Ilmarin warned. He was a long-faced air mage, one of the few Keepers from the Order of the Star who didn't seem to have a problem with me. He seemed to be acting as Rain's second. 'We're about due for Vihaela to take another shot.'

Rain looked around the bare rooftop. There was no cover, not unless you went right up to the parapet and ducked down. 'Sure you want to stay here?'

I nodded.

Landis glanced towards the complex of buildings to the north. 'So this is where our old friend Drakh has chosen to make his stand, hmm?'

The three of us left Ilmarin at the stairs and walked out to get a better view. To the north we could see where Richard's force was gathered, a close-packed sprawl of one- and two-storey buildings laid out across the castle's north-eastern corner. Dozens of windows looked down over small courtyards, mostly hidden from our view.

'Yes . . . just a second.' Rain put a hand to his ear, then looked at me. 'Nimbus wants to know if we've started to withdraw.'

'Tell him we're staying,' I said.

Rain and Landis looked at me.

'I'll handle Nimbus,' I said.

Rain raised his eyebrows but spoke quietly into the focus. Landis was studying the buildings to the north. 'Does look like a challenge, doesn't it?' he said conversationally. 'You think you can assault the place, Rain?'

Rain cut the connection and looked up. 'On paper, we're stronger. In practice . . . ?'

'I might be able to do something about that,' I said.

'All right, Verus,' Rain said. 'You've dragged us up here; let's hear it.'

The futures that I could see looked brooding and still. But with Richard somewhere in those buildings, I didn't trust my divination for something like this. Instead I reached out with the fateweaver. I knew what I was looking for, and began to shape the direction in which the futures would go, sketching out the rough lines of what I needed.

'I'm sure the Council's told you about the item I have,' I said, lifting my right hand for a second before letting it drop. 'So far I've been using it for personal combat, but that wasn't what fateweavers were made for. They were tools for commanding armies. During the attack on the tombs, I got a sense for how that would work.'

'Were you using it?' Landis asked.

'I tried, but every time I'd try something on a large scale it'd fizzle out. I'd try to bring about a favourable outcome, but every single person on our side was trying to do the same thing on a smaller scale in different ways and they'd pull the futures in a dozen different directions. It was only later that I realised what the problem was. In the Dark Wars, fateweavers were carried by generals.' I looked between Rain and Landis. 'To make this work, I need tactical command. The Keepers and soldiers in the attack have to be following my direct orders.'

Rain snorted.

'It's not a joke,' I said.

'Verus, there's no way in hell Nimbus is giving you command,' Rain said. 'Hate to break it to you.'

'It's not Nimbus's support I need,' I said. 'He might be director, but it's the two of you that the Order of the Star and the Order of the Shield really trust. Being assigned command doesn't matter a damn if the troops won't listen. But the Keepers *do* listen to both of *you*.'

Rain and Landis looked at one another.

'I think I can win this battle,' I said. 'With much fewer losses than we'd take otherwise. But I'll need you two to vouch for me.'

'Even if we take your word for it,' Landis said, 'might I raise the inconvenient point that we have been specifically ordered *not* to attack, and that we are, furthermore, disobeying our orders right at this moment by continuing to stand here?'

I nodded. 'On that subject, I think we can expect Nimbus any minute now.'

Rain and Landis didn't say anything more, and neither did I. We stood and waited on the rooftop. The midday sun shone down, heat radiating from the stone.

We heard Nimbus coming before we saw him. Raised voices sounded from below roof level, drawing closer. *There.* I pushed with the fateweaver, aiming for a point five or ten minutes away.

Nimbus came striding up the stairs, looking pissed off. Two Keepers were trailing him, Slate and Avenor; I knew both, and neither liked me. 'Rain,' Nimbus demanded as he walked towards us. 'What are your men still doing here?'

Rain glanced at Landis.

'I'm afraid a withdrawal isn't viable,' I told Nimbus.

'I wasn't talking to you,' Nimbus snapped. He came to a stop ten feet away, with Slate and Avenor standing a step back. Rain, Landis and I stood facing him, the six of us forming two sides on the sunlight roof. Back at the stairs, a few other men hovered nervously.

'We've got some concerns,' Rain said.

'I don't care if you have concerns! You've been doing nothing but bending my ear about the attacks you've been taking. Well, now you've got orders to pull back. I'd have thought you'd be grateful.'

'And then what?' Rain asked.

'That isn't your concern! I am in command of this task force and I am giving you a direct order. Withdraw your men *now*!'

Behind Nimbus, I saw Slate shift. He and Avenor didn't show anything on their faces, but I could tell they were uneasy.

'Your command authority over this task force is delegated to you from the Council,' I said. 'You were granted that authority on the understanding that you'd use it to complete the mission's objectives.'

'A withdrawal is the best way to achieve them.'

'How?' Rain asked bluntly.

Nimbus looked as if he wanted to explode, but controlled himself with a visible effort. 'With the loss of the accumulator, we no longer have a means to destroy the wards on the keep,' he said, his voice tight. 'Withdrawing will allow us to set up a strong defensive perimeter where we can wait for the Council teams to overcome the wards on this shadow realm. Once they do, we can bring in reinforcements as well as specialised siege equipment and end this battle without further casualties.'

'The last I heard from the Council ward teams, they had no estimate for how long it would take them to break in,' I said. 'It could be hours, days or weeks. You're gambling on something completely out of our control.'

'I did not ask for your opinion, Verus!'

'Second,' I said, ignoring him, 'anything that gives *us* time also gives *them* time. Drakh is going to be fortifying his position and laying contingency plans. He's seen us attack once; next time he'll be better prepared. And the situation with the marid is even worse. We killed Barrayar, but we didn't kill the ifrit inside him. All the marid needs is another host body, and it can summon it straight back. Or summon something worse. The marid is an escalating threat. Pulling back and leaving it alone is the worst way to fight it.'

Nimbus looked at me in fury.

'Director, I'm afraid I do rather share Mage Verus's concerns,' Landis said politely. 'In addition, I feel we should bear in mind that the men comprising this portion of the task force are somewhat dispirited. They suffered heavy losses last night and they've heard what happened at the windmill. Add on the losses they've taken over the last few hours, and it's starting to look rather like an unbroken string of defeats. If we order them to retreat, I'm quite certain they'll do it, but I rather suspect that once they're inside that defensive perimeter, they won't be willing to leave.'

'They'll obey the orders they're given,' Nimbus said, his voice hard. 'As will you.'

Silence fell. Neither Rain nor Landis moved, and the six of us stared at each other across the rooftop. The only sound was the whine of the wind.

'Director, we were told that the marid represented a threat to the whole country,' Rain said quietly. 'If we're not stopping it, what the hell are we doing here?'

Nimbus looked about to snap, then drew in a breath and seemed to calm himself. 'All right,' he said. He glanced around: no one else was in earshot. 'You want to know the real problem? We've been in this shadow realm less than a day and we've got six dead Keepers and four dead mage auxiliaries. *Ten mages.* If the wounded don't make it, it'll be fifteen. We started this war with less than a hundred Keepers in the Order of the Star and a third of that in the Order of the Shield, and we've been bleeding numbers ever since. We just lost over ten per cent of our remaining combat-effective Keepers in *one day*. You want to lose even more? The Keepers are the backbone of the Council. The reason anyone does what the Senior Council tells them is because we're out there making them. We go away –' Nimbus snapped his fingers. '– and that's it. Won't matter who's won.'

'If the marid is able to carry out its plans and begin mass-producing jinn-possessed mages,' Landis said, 'then it will matter *very much* who won. How exactly are you expecting us to maintain the Council's authority when there are twenty or thirty Calderas and Barrayars running around?'

'Then we call in help,' Nimbus said. 'Or step up security recruitment. It doesn't matter. There's a line for acceptable losses and we're over it.'

The futures looked peaceful – too peaceful. It couldn't be much longer now. 'Council orders were to stop the marid,' Rain said. 'At any cost.'

'Oh, come on,' Nimbus said impatiently. 'You know what the Council means when it says something like that. If we win this battle but lose most of our Keepers, you think they're going to care when you point to that order? Maybe they won't put us on trial, but it won't matter. It'll be round our necks for ever.'

'This is bigger than you or me,' Rain said.

'You going to tell yourself that when they pension you off?'

Rain looked at Nimbus in disgust.

'Look, Rain, it doesn't matter what you think,' Nimbus said. 'The Keepers here aren't expendable. End of story.'

'You don't understand the Council as well as you think, Nimbus,' I said. 'In the long run, everyone's expendable.'

'Maybe *you* are,' Nimbus said, his voice hard. 'The rest of us? Not so much.'

I could feel the futures through the fateweaver, strands of fate drifting around us. I felt them brush over the men on the rooftop, considering. Slate and Avenor were ignored after only a touch. Rain was measured, then discarded. It was between me, Landis and Nimbus.

'We have the opportunity to finish Drakh's forces and end this war,' I said.

'It doesn't matter what you think,' Nimbus said.

Me, Landis, Nimbus. Landis, Nimbus, me. I pushed with the fateweaver, feeling the strands of fate shift under the pressure. It was harder without my divination, but combat is a chaotic thing. There are always little things, gusts of wind, shifts of position, tiny events that can nudge someone to choose one target over another.

'Enough of this,' Nimbus said. 'Withdraw those men.'

Landis and Rain looked back at him.

Me, Landis, Nimbus. Nimbus, me, Landis. Landis and Nimbus. Nimbus and Landis. Nimbus. Only Nimbus.

The moment of stillness before the shot.

'I will not ask again,' Nimbus said, biting off his words. 'I am issuing a direct order and you *will* obey or—'

The projectile came darting in too fast to see. Nimbus's shield flared in my magesight, triggered by the incoming spell; the projectile pierced it in a green-black flash. Nimbus jerked and fell.

Shouts rang out across the rooftop. Shields flew up; Slate threw a deathbolt in the direction of the attack; Ilmarin came running across the roof. 'Incoming!' I shouted.

Another shard of green-black death came flashing in.

Landis's magic met it at the edge of the rooftop and exploded it into light and heat, then he, Rain, Slate and Avenor all struck back. The corner of the building from which the attack had come disintegrated under a barrage of fire.

Ilmarin grabbed Nimbus's body, and he and Avenor dragged him back towards the stairs. Landis and Rain covered them, backing away with their shields glowing red and blue. I ran after.

Avenor and Ilmarin didn't set Nimbus down until they were back at ground level, the buildings around us blocking our view. 'He's not breathing,' Ilmarin said.

'He's not going to,' Slate said, his face twisted in anger. 'He was dead before he hit the roof. Fucking Vihaela.'

We stood around the body. After the brief flurry of combat, everything was quiet. Soldiers were peering out at us from where they'd been stationed, their eyes going down to rest on Nimbus. The former Director of Operations of the Order of the Shield was lying on his back, eyes open in a last expression of surprise.

'Well,' I said, and turned to Landis. 'I suppose that puts you in command.'

Landis looked at me. I returned his gaze, my face showing nothing.

'Captain?' Ilmarin asked.

'. . . Yes,' Landis said. The futures flickered for just a moment, then he turned away, business-like once more. 'Ilmarin, please take Nimbus's body to whatever you're using as a morgue. Have your healer take a look, though if Slate says he's dead, I'm sure he's dead. Rain, assemble your Keepers at your forward command post with as many of your squad leaders as you can afford to pull off the line. Order the rest of the men to stand down. Briefing is in ten minutes.'

The people around Landis looked around, then began to disperse. I joined them. I felt Landis's eyes on my back as I walked away.

15

The room Landis had chosen for his briefing was crowded. There was no projection table this time. Keepers, other mages and sergeants stood waiting for Landis to begin.

'All right, boys and girls,' Landis said without preamble. He was standing on a box so everyone could see him. 'We don't have much time, so I'll make this quick. We are going to destroy Drakh's force and remove his ability to project power within this shadow realm. Elements of the Order of the Star will hold the western perimeter while all remaining forces will push up from the south in standard sweep formation. We keep going until everyone in Drakh's force is dead or captive, or until we run out of castle, whichever comes first. Now, I'm sure you have questions, but Councillor Verus has something to tell you.' Landis stepped down.

I stepped up onto the box. The men looked up at me with expressions ranging from neutral to unfriendly. The bulk of these mages were Keepers, and up until three days ago, their job had included hunting me. I didn't have many friends here.

'Before you go into this battle, I'm going to tell you what you're fighting for,' I said, trying to copy Landis's confidence. 'We entered this shadow realm under a truce with Drakh. As you know, he betrayed us immediately. Now, the Council's assumed that this was just Drakh doing what he always does and trying to weaken the

Council to give him an advantage in the war. And that's true, he was. But there's another reason.

'About a week ago, Drakh's forces attacked the Southampton facility and stole the Council's prototype anti-jinn weapon. Then two days ago, when Drakh met the Council for negotiations in Concordia, he told them that the marid's ritual worked by granting the marid's host, the mage Anne Walker, the power to more effectively summon greater jinn. We now know that that was a lie. The ritual affects the shadow realm, not the host.

'So why did Drakh lie? Because he wanted to draw attention towards Anne – towards a *person* and away from the *place*. His goal was never to stop the ritual. He wanted to let it complete, then take control of the marid himself. The Council's divinations confirmed that we could expect swarms of greater jinn coming out of this shadow realm. They didn't say who'd be controlling them. We've been assuming that it would be the marid. Drakh intends that it'll be him.'

'Now that isolation ward's been triggered, this shadow realm's a ticking time bomb,' Rain said. 'How's he planning to use it as a base?'

'He's not,' I said. 'Not any more. That part of his plan has failed. But the fact that he's still here means that he still believes he can turn this into a win. Drakh's got the item that the marid was bound into, Suleiman's Ring. With that and the weapon, he probably thinks he can bring the marid back under his control. It'll mean starting from scratch with a new host, but Drakh's patient. If he gets out of here with that jinn, then sooner or later, in a few months or a few years, this whole thing is going to start all over again. The Council is not willing to let that happen. Neither am I.'

I held up my right hand, the too-pale fingers gleaming in the light. 'This is a fateweaver,' I said. 'Those of you hunting me this past month will have been briefed on what it does. They were intended as tools for commanding armies. That's what I'm going to use it for today.'

People looked around. 'Commanding?' someone said. 'Hey, you're not . . .'

Landis spoke loudly from my side. 'Councillor Verus will have tactical command for this operation.'

A storm of protests and complaints broke out. 'Are you frigging—'

'—a Dark mage—'

'—killed Levistus—'

'—not going to—'

'—crazy—'

'ENOUGH!' Landis roared at the top of his voice.

Silence fell. 'I have spoken to Verus!' Landis said, his voice ringing out. 'I believe that he is the best choice to carry out this mission with the minimum amount of lives lost. This decision is final!'

A few people looked towards Rain.

'I agree with Captain Landis,' Rain said loudly. 'We both vouch for Verus on this matter. You have a problem with it, take it up with us after the briefing.'

No one spoke, but their eyes turned back to me. They looked even less friendly than before.

'The fateweaver gives me the ability to alter the flow of battle,' I said. 'I will direct you through comms and through a telepathic focus called a dreamstone. Sometimes I will give you orders to move, or attack, or pull back in a way that makes no obvious sense. When that happens, I need you to trust that I know what I'm doing, and obey immediately.'

'Why should we trust you?' a Keeper asked.

It was the big question. 'Most of you have been fighting against Drakh for less than fifteen months,' I said. 'He's been my enemy for over fifteen *years*. I have far more reason to hate him than any of you will ever have. On top of that, I struck a bargain with Councillor Alma before coming here. My half of the deal was to make sure Drakh ended up dead. I intend to keep it.'

'From where?' another Keeper asked derisively. 'Back at the command post?'

I smiled without humour. 'No, Keeper . . . Travis, was it? I'm going to be at the front. Try to keep up, because I'm not planning to hang around.'

Silence fell once more. I looked around to see if there'd be any more challenges. No one spoke and after a few seconds I hopped down off the box.

Behind me, Landis stepped up and started ordering squad deployments. Other mages crowded around him and Rain. I imagined that most were there to complain about me.

Luna and Ji-yeong appeared out of the crowd. 'That was pretty good,' Luna said. 'Where do you want us when the fighting starts?'

'Watch my back,' I said.

'Against Richard's lot, or ours?'

'Ours. Let's get to the lines.'

The three of us stood waiting, our backs against a wall. The sun shone down from right overhead, casting small shadows beneath our feet. Luna was glancing around and spinning her wand between her fingers. Ji-yeong leant against the wall with her arms folded. I had my eyes closed, the *sovnya* in one hand.

'Eastern perimeter is ready,' Rain said over the comm. 'Interdiction field holding.'

'Understood,' Landis said. 'Last southern elements are moving up now.'

The building we were up against was blocking our view to Richard's position, but it didn't matter. Between my divination, the fateweaver and the dreamstone, I was only a moment's thought away from knowing the position and status of every man and woman in the attack force. We had nearly four hundred in total, but I'd chosen to deploy less than a hundred and fifty for the initial attack, with the rest tasked to the reserves or the perimeter. A smaller group was easier to control, and I'd worked with Landis to make sure we had the right men for the job.

'Verus,' Landis said. 'How effectively can Drakh block your divination?'

'Very effectively, but he can't be everywhere. He'll focus on where he can do the most damage, probably using Vihaela. If we don't give him space to weave those false visions, he'll only have time to do it once or twice.'

'Understood. All units, two-minute warning.'

There was a subtle distance in Landis's manner that hadn't been there before. A message and a warning: *I know what you did, and I don't like it.* I was just glad he wasn't taking it further.

'Verus to all units,' I said over the comm. 'Once again: the first line of defence is mines, the second is poison.

Once that's been cleared, wait for orders before advancing further. Confirm.'

A chorus of confirmations came back. A few of the Keepers still sounded suspicious, but as far as I could tell, they'd do as they were told.

I'm leading a Council army into battle. Who'd have thought.

'Once more into the breach,' Luna said under her breath.

I studied the futures. It was time. 'All units, advance towards the first line,' I said quietly and calmly. 'Go, go, go.'

The futures and the minds around me shifted and moved, beginning to roll forward.

Richard's first line of defence was antipersonnel mines: claymores and improvised explosives with hidden triggers. I'd already mapped them out, and now sappers moved forward, Council security men with explosives experience. Each sapper had three riflemen and a battle mage to cover him.

Gunfire sounded over the rooftops. Richard had positioned scouts and snipers to shoot at anyone trying to defuse the mines. The futures began to scatter into the chaos of combat, and I shifted my focus to the fateweaver, letting myself sense the flow of the battle and its direction. There was resistance to our west, and I narrowed my focus to find out why. 'Verus to Travis, your target has been reinforced,' I said. 'Expect heavy fire. Verus to Avenor, there's a battle mage waiting to ambush you. Chimaera, advance to support Avenor.'

More gunfire stuttered. There was the flash of battle magic, followed by a *boom* as one of the mines went off.

The Council forces suffered their first death. One man from Slate's group was advancing to support his sapper when his presence suddenly faded. A lucky shot, maybe, or a mine I'd missed. The battle moved on.

Avenor and Chimaera's groups reached their target, enveloping the enemy mage and adepts. Landis's group were clearing the south-east corner. The centre groups had opened up a hole in the enemy lines; I reached out through the dreamstone, urging them forward.

Battle magic flashed, again and again. There was a distant scream.

'Target down!'

'Tobias, first line is clear, advancing.'

I turned and began walking towards the sounds of battle. Luna and Ji-yeong followed. Another explosion echoed from up ahead, followed quickly by two more. More gunfire.

'Move in!' Avenor's voice was hard. 'Move in!'

I spoke over the comm. 'Central teams, move to the second line and hold. Air mages, sweep those buildings of poison gas. Ilmarin, sweep from the east, Lizbeth, from the west.'

We passed what had been the first defence line. The entrance to the doorway was blackened; I could smell gun smoke and the chemical scent of plastic explosives. The dead body of an adept lay within, a weapon still clutched in his hands.

I felt air magic up ahead, sweeping through the next line of buildings, purifying the air within. The gas being flushed out was colourless and odourless: if we'd advanced into it, dozens would have died. But I could feel through the fateweaver that our advance was stalling, and I paused to find out why. We were clearing out the gas, but more was being laid. Where was it coming from . . . ?

There. 'Wait here,' I told Luna and Ji-yeong, then ran forward. 'Verus to Ilmarin, move west,' I called into my focus. 'Skip the next building, sweep the centre.'

'Acknowledged.'

I came around the corner upon one of the attack teams. A big Keeper called Trask – Slate's friend – with his four men. They whirled to face me, ready to fire, then held off as they recognised me. I ran past them, out across an open space, then sprang from a low wall onto a pillar up onto a roof. I heard a shout but didn't stop; the *sovnya* clanged on stone then I was running across the rooftop, crossing the width of the building in seconds before dropping onto its far side.

I came down behind two of Richard's adepts. They whirled, eyes going wide; one was holding a handgun and the other some sort of focus weapon, but they'd been facing the building, watching the doorway, and they were a second too slow. The first died before he could raise his gun; the second scrambled back, whipped out a knife, realised too late that a knife was no match for a polearm. He opened his mouth to shout and the *sovnya* drove through his ribs. He coughed, choking on blood.

I wrenched the *sovnya* out of the dying adept and moved to press my back against the wall. I could hear shouts and gunfire all around; my dash had taken me behind Richard's lines and I knew most of the voices I could hear were enemies, but they hadn't yet realised I was here. I could sense air magic to the east, sweeping through the buildings as Ilmarin transformed the poison gas into breathable atmosphere. Running footsteps sounded from within, and I reached down and unclipped the flap on my holster.

A man burst out of the doorway, running past me. He was dressed in dull green and wore a long-beaked mask with goggles; canisters were mounted on his back. I could sense magic around him, toxic and deadly, and as he saw the adepts' bodies, he twisted, one hand coming up.

I had my 1911 aimed and ready. I shot the mage twice, centre mass, then as he staggered I put a third bullet through his head. He went down and didn't get up.

There was something wrong with the shape of the futures. I'd taken my attention off the larger battle, and now I scanned hurriedly, trying to catch up. Something was off— *There.* I spoke urgently into my comm. 'South-east teams, get to cover, there's—'

The sky lit up in a green-black flash. Through the dreamstone, I felt a cluster of minds wink out.

'South-east teams, report!' Rain called.

'Avenor's down!' It was a new voice, sounding frightened. 'It's—' I felt another pulse of magic and the voice cut off.

'It's Vihaela,' I said into the comm.

'South-east teams, get eyes,' Landis said.

'I see her!' Chimaera called. 'She's running north!'

'Do not pursue,' Landis ordered. 'All teams, continue your advance.'

Ilmarin came running out of the same doorway the poison mage had used. He skidded to a stop as he saw me, then did a double-take at the bodies at my feet. Two soldiers came out behind him.

'Air clear?' I asked.

Ilmarin pulled his eyes away from the bodies. '. . . Nearly.'

'Finish your sweep, then bring up the men,' I told

him. Ilmarin nodded and disappeared back into the building.

The shouts and gunfire were receding, leaving an eerie silence. I looked ahead, searching the futures in which I ran north. I hadn't yet been able to see through to Richard's inner defences. For a moment everything looked clear . . . no, that made no sense. I widened my search, checking the futures in which I cut east and west. This was a false future, I was sure of it. I just needed to find a gap.

Something flickered to the west. Richard's *optasia* was good, very good, but he was having to cover a wide area in a short time. As I focused on that tangle of futures they blurred, becoming a placid screen, but I caught a glimpse of myself falling, a hand cut from my body—

—and gone. But I'd seen enough.

'Eyes on Vihaela,' Chimaera said urgently. 'We can catch her.'

'Do not pursue!' I ordered. 'There are monofilaments ahead. She's luring you into a trap!'

I felt the futures ripple and our advance slowed. Mage-spun monofilaments are nothing like the kind that get sold for fishing line. They're razor-sharp and so thin as to be almost invisible, and they can cut through flesh as though it were butter.

'Change formation,' Landis ordered. 'Mages to the front. As soon as the gas is cleared, steady advance. Focus your magesight and look for faint signatures of metal or matter magic. Destroy the filaments on sight.'

I moved up, staying behind cover. One of Rain's teams appeared behind me and I signalled them forward. Our forces were advancing on both sides, and I could sense flickers of magic as mages cut and burned away the filaments blocking their path.

More gunfire sounded from the front lines, along with the flash and roar of battle magic. Richard's forces were still trying to withdraw, but they were running out of castle and their movements were starting to look jerky, reacting to our attacks instead of following a plan of their own. Richard's adepts were used to Council forces that advanced slowly and cautiously, pausing at setbacks. This kind of aggression was new to them.

Darkness bloomed to the north-west, an inky cloud that sucked in light. 'Shroud spells!' a mage called. 'Can't see anything!'

'It's Tenebrous,' I said over the channel. 'Don't advance into it: you'll take too much fire. Wrap around his eastern flank instead. West perimeter, advance and cut in from the north. Tenebrous is only covering their south-east corner. We'll trap him in a pocket.'

The battle raged just out of my line of sight. Men and women fought and died from bullets or fireblasts or stabbing blades. Someone was wounded and screaming, the sound almost lost in the gunfire.

I could sense something through the fateweaver, a key point in the flow of battle. A room in one of the buildings up ahead . . . orders, decisions. It was close. I could reach it in less than a minute, kill the people inside . . .

. . . no, I'd made that mistake once already. I was a commander now, not an assassin. 'Verus to Landis,' I said. I sent him a mental image of the building through the dreamstone, focusing on the room at one corner. 'Suspected enemy command post.'

'Thunder, Aegis,' Landis ordered immediately. 'Artillery strike. I'll paint the target.'

'Roger that,' a new voice said. 'Moving up.'

The fighting had stalled in the south-west; Tenebrous's shroud was still holding the Council forces back. Our reserves were moving in from the west to cut in behind him.

'Aegis in position,' a voice said. I could feel spells building.

'Fire,' Landis ordered.

Battle magic flared, force and lightning. The ground trembled beneath my feet and I heard the rumble of falling masonry, then the air flashed white as lightning struck out of a clear sky, not once but again and again. Thunder crashed, hideously loud.

The echoes died away. I watched the battle. At first there was no change, then I started to sense a shift, movements becoming undirected. 'Verus to all units,' I said. 'Envelop the shroud.'

Through the fateweaver I sensed mages and soldiers moving in behind Tenebrous's position. I could see the exact moment at which the adepts there realised they were being trapped. A ripple of panic swept through their forces, and their resistance weakened. The shroud contracted.

'Advance on the shroud,' Rain ordered. 'Tenebrous is the priority target.'

I was already looking elsewhere, searching for Vihaela. This was when she'd strike. I couldn't sense her in the futures, but through the fateweaver I could feel where our forces were vulnerable. Not to the east . . . the centre . . .

There! No time to talk. Through the dreamstone, I sent information flashing into Landis's mind.

The green-black of Vihaela's death magic flashed in the centre of our lines in an area we'd thought clear. Landis's magic mirrored it, fire leaping out to intercept. There was a *crack*; shouts echoed and two soldiers fell, but none were killed.

'Eyes on!' a Keeper shouted. 'She's running!'

'Pursue but do not engage,' Landis ordered.

There was battle magic and gunfire everywhere. Information poured in, more than I could process. Tenebrous's pocket crumbling as Rain directed his men; Ilmarin and Landis leading attacks from the south; reinforcements from the west pressing in. All across the lines, Richard's adepts were wavering and falling back.

To my west, the shroud vanished, its magic fading. 'Tenebrous is gone!' Rain said. 'Wounded and fled.'

'Lost Vihaela!' someone shouted. 'Trying to— Wait—'

There was a scream, abruptly silenced. 'Move in on Vihaela,' Landis said, his voice hard. 'Do not let her out of sight.'

That last death had given me Vihaela's position. I broke into a run.

I reached Vihaela less than a minute later. She was in an L-shaped courtyard, backed up against a building that looked like a mausoleum; six-foot tombs in the courtyard provided cover. Landis's men were on the south side and up on the building to the west, firing down. Vihaela was fighting with a small group of adepts supporting her.

A fireball from the south flew towards Vihaela's position; she blew it up in mid-air, then blocked a hydroblast from the west. An adept popped up to throw some kind of glowing red bead and a Council marksman shot him. Vihaela sent a black line scything across the courtyard and the marksman's head came off his body in a spout of blood; the remaining Council soldiers hit the deck and the mages ducked out of sight.

All of a sudden everything was quiet. Smoke and the scent of blood hung in the air. I'd reached the corner on the short side of the L; if I took another step, I'd be in plain view. The mages and soldiers ahead of me stayed down, catching their breath.

I heard footsteps behind me and glanced back to see Landis. He was advancing towards me, more men at his back. 'Vihaela!' I shouted around the corner.

'Hi, Verus,' Vihaela called back. 'Come to join the party?'

A low voice spoke into my ear. 'This is Ilmarin. We're on the east roof.'

'Hold,' Landis said quietly as he walked up next to me. 'Wait for my signal.'

'Vihaela, listen closely,' I shouted. 'I'd love to see you dead, but right now, Drakh's a priority and you're not. Surrender and I'll guarantee your life. Refuse and we do this the painful way.'

'I think I like the sound of the painful way,' Vihaela called back.

'This isn't your fight,' I shouted. 'You're going to die for Drakh?'

'I'm not dying for anyone,' Vihaela called. She didn't sound afraid; I actually had the feeling she was smiling. 'None of you are good enough to take me. But you're welcome to try.'

I felt Vihaela start to channel a spell. 'Kill her,' I told Landis and his men.

Landis strode past me into the open.

The courtyard lit up, red-green-black. Spells stabbed from the rooftops, flashed across the open space. The stones of the castle splintered and burned. I caught a glimpse of the security men, ducked down with their heads low. The sound was a steady roar, mixed with the *crack* of discharging energy.

The adepts died in seconds. Vihaela didn't. She was duelling Landis and the mages behind him and the ones on the rooftops all at once, using the blocky tombs to mask line of sight, popping in and out of vision and firing deathbolts as she did. She was so fast and deadly that even splitting her attention as she was, the mages she targeted were forced back. There were six mages on her, but she was moving so that no more than two ever had line of sight at once. And there was something more, something fuzzy about her signature on magesight. I snatched a glance around the corner, catching a blurred glimpse of her form—

A mist cloak. It had been a long time, but I recognised it instantly. That was how she'd been able to strike unseen.

Fire exploded off Vihaela's shield; a counterattack nearly killed the mage to Landis's left and Landis had to step in to block as Vihaela disappeared again. The fight was so fast I could barely follow it. Landis was throwing fireballs and pinpoint bursts of heat, the other mages were using water blasts and blades of force and air. Death was raining on the tombs, but Vihaela was slipping through, everything just barely glancing away. Both sides were going all out.

A bolt from Vihaela carved away the corner of the wall I was hiding behind; I felt the tingle as death magic missed me by a foot. A column of bricks fell with a groan towards Landis's men. Two jumped back; Landis ran forward, a few stray bricks vaporising against his shield.

The fire on Vihaela slackened for a moment and she took the opening, sprinting away.

I saw the futures in a flash. Vihaela was trying to get back into the mausoleum. If she could make it inside with the mist cloak, we'd never catch her. Landis's view of her was blocked for two more seconds. The only one who could reach her was Ilmarin, on the east roof. But if he did he'd be exposed.

I hesitated for half a second, then sent an impulse through the dreamstone.

Ilmarin reacted instantly, springing up out of cover and throwing out a wall of hardened air. Vihaela hit it, bouncing off, but as she did she twisted like a snake and green-black death flickered from her hand. Ilmarin jerked and fell.

The impact and the attack had put Vihaela off-balance. For just a second, Landis on the ground and Tobias on the roof had a clear shot.

I threw all my energy into the fateweaver, forcing one future through.

Water and fire slammed into Vihaela's shield and the angles lined up in just such a way for the attacks to bring the maximum energy to bear. Tobias's spell glanced off. Landis's struck the same spot a tenth of a second later, and the weakened section of shield collapsed. Fire speared through shield and flesh, and Vihaela fell.

'Target down!' Tobias called.

'Ilmarin's down!' I called at the same time. 'Get someone to that roof!'

'All units, overwatch,' Landis ordered. 'Hold position.'

All of a sudden everything was quiet. After the shouts and the crash of spells, the courtyard was eerily silent. Landis strode forward, his shield flaring bright, and crouched down next to Vihaela. There was a pause.

'Cease fire,' Landis ordered. 'Move up.'

I was already advancing, scrambling over the rubble and walking across the courtyard, craning my neck to look upwards. There was a soldier up on the east rooftop where Ilmarin had fallen, but as I looked into the futures I saw what he was going to say. I felt something wither inside me; pain stabbed from my arm.

Vihaela was lying where she had fallen, eyes closed but teeth bared as if she'd struggled to the last. Most of her torso was charred, and the stench of burnt flesh was in the air. I forced myself to look into the futures where I pulled open the body.

'Focused beam through the upper abdominal cavity,' Landis told me. 'Superheats the bodily fluids and organs and sends a shockwave up into the brain. A quick death. Better than she'd have given us.' He looked down at Vihaela a moment longer, then turned away.

I could feel a stiffness in my upper chest, and without looking knew that the fateweaver had spread. I'd been using it heavily, and the fighting wasn't over yet.

Up on the rooftop, the soldier finished checking Ilmarin's body and began to report in. I turned away.

16

By the time I reached the front lines, the battle was all but over. Richard's remaining forces had been driven back to a long, low structure up against the northern wall that might once have been a set of kitchens. Rain and Landis's forces were surrounding it to the east, south and south-west; to the north was the castle wall and the sea. There was nowhere left to run. The fighting had fallen silent as both sides hunkered down and checked their weapons, ready for the final push.

Landis and I walked up to Rain, who was talking to Slate and Trask. We were barely a hundred feet from Richard's position. 'Numbers?' Landis asked Rain.

'Slate counts eighty-five hostiles remaining,' Rain said, nodding to the death mage.

'Might be eighty-three by now,' Slate said. He ignored me, talking directly to Landis. 'They got a lot of wounded.'

'Verus?' Landis asked.

I studied the futures, looking for any sign of Richard's tampering. Nothing jumped out at me. 'They haven't got many mages left,' I said. 'But they're dug in for a fight and those buildings have basements.' I glanced at Landis. 'Best way to attack something like that?'

'A dug-in force with no hope of escape?' Landis said. 'I'm afraid if they really are that determined to fight to the death, then our best option is to simply level the place.'

Landis was talking about an artillery bombardment. I'd seen it a few times during the war. Any defenders at the windows would be killed or driven back, then water and earth and force mages would demolish the building, bringing it down on the heads of everyone inside. It was a last-resort option used when the Council didn't consider anyone or anything in the area worth retrieving.

Rain and Landis were looking at me. If I gave the order, this would end the battle. We'd take very few casualties, possibly none at all. As for Richard's force, virtually all of them would die. They and everything they carried would either be crushed under tons of falling rubble, or entombed in the basements until their air ran out. The few remaining mages might escape, but the adepts wouldn't.

I spoke over my shoulder to the mages behind me. 'Compass.'

'What's up, chief?'

'White flag please.'

A tiny portal appeared at Compass's hand; she reached into it and pulled out a piece of folded cloth. Space mages can create a pocket dimension that works as personal storage; some use it to pile up all kinds of junk, but Compass seemed to pack with an eye to the battlefield. I opened up the flag and began tying it to the *sovnya*, just below the blade.

'Do bear in mind that the men and women in that building have just taken rather heavy losses,' Landis said. 'They may not be in the most reasonable frame of mind.'

I shook out the flag, checking that the ties would hold. 'Get your men in position,' I told Rain and Landis.

'If one or two take shots at me, ignore it. If they all do, launch the bombardment.'

'Understood.'

A good couple of dozen mages and soldiers stood watching, waiting to see what I'd do. I took a breath, then walked up to the corner and stuck the *sovnya* out in plain view.

Silence. The white flag stirred in the breeze. I'd expected a shout or a bullet, but there was nothing. I waited thirty seconds; then, when there was still no reaction, I walked around the corner.

The building where Richard's adepts had gathered for their final stand was two stories high, with the north wall of the castle overshadowing it from behind. Square windows lined the ground floor, dark and threatening. My eyes spotted shapes at a couple of those windows; my divination told me of a dozen more. I shouldered the *sovnya*, letting the white flag hang down over my head, and marched forward.

My footsteps echoed from the buildings as I advanced. All my instincts were telling me to run: there were a lot of weapons being readied at those windows, and I was the only target. I knew that the buildings behind me and to my left and right were filled with soldiers and mages, all poised to attack, but it would only take one adept with an itchy trigger finger to set everything off. He'd die moments later, but that wouldn't be much consolation to me.

I came to a stop in the middle of the courtyard. I could feel hundreds of eyes on me from all around. I planted the butt of the *sovnya* on the stone and took a deep breath. 'I am Mage Verus of the Junior Council, commander of the Light task force,' I shouted. 'Who speaks for you?'

Silence. The futures swung crazily. The fateweaver would be little use here: too many independent decisions. I waited, holding still.

Then the futures settled. Up ahead, there was the rattle of bolts being drawn, then a door opened in the kitchen wall and Richard Drakh stepped out into the sun.

Richard didn't look like someone who'd lost. His clothes were neat and he carried no weapons or armour . . . at least none visible to normal eyes. My magesight told a different story. His clothes were a suit of reactive armour similar to mine, though less bulky and maybe a little weaker, and half a dozen kinds of magic radiated from the matte-black pouches hanging from his belt. But it was his manner that was most out of place. He walked towards me as though taking an afternoon stroll.

Richard came to a stop fifteen feet away. 'Alex,' he said with a nod.

'Richard,' I said flatly. There were spells twined around him. Space magic, force magic, some universal effect I couldn't identify. None were standard protections.

'Commander of the Light task force, is it? You've done well for yourself.'

Richard was just barely out of range for a lunge. The *sovnya* tugged, sensing the thing inside him. It wanted to kill him. So did I. 'Like master, like apprentice, I suppose,' I told him. 'Are you willing to surrender?'

'Should I be?'

I knew that every marksman and mage on the buildings behind me had their sights trained on Richard. Richard Drakh had been at the top of the Council's most-wanted list for years, and the Keeper or soldier who killed him could name their own reward. If Alma and Druss were here right now, they'd give the order to fire, and to hell with the flag of truce. They wanted Richard dead more than anyone.

But Richard had to know that too. There was no fear in his brown eyes as he looked calmly towards me, and that scared me. All of a sudden, none of the men backing me up seemed to matter. It was just the two of us, like it had always been, and like always, I knew deep down in my bones that I was outmatched.

'Over fifty per cent of your adepts are dead or wounded,' I told Richard loudly. I kept my voice hard, not showing any fear. 'Vihaela has been killed, and the rest of the mages of your cabal have fallen or fled. You are surrounded by a superior force that outmatches you in every way.' I looked past Richard to where the people behind him were listening. 'You gathered these adepts to your banner claiming that you were creating a mutual defence association. You promised them power and independence. What you've led them to is death. If you want to prove you really do have their best interests at heart, this is your last chance. Order them to lay down their weapons.'

'I'm afraid that what you want will take more than speeches and threats,' Richard said. 'We all know how the Council treats its prisoners.'

Richard was too calm. What was he planning? 'I can't promise amnesty,' I said. 'But I can promise your forces that if they surrender, they'll leave this shadow realm alive. If they don't, they'll be killed to a man.'

'And you want to spare them?' Richard said with a faint smile. 'Be honest, Alex. That isn't why you're standing there right now. You aren't here to save my adepts, and you're not here to protect those Council soldiers either.'

I could feel eyes on me from all around. I kept my face expressionless. 'Choose, Richard,' I said. 'Life, or death.'

Richard nodded, then pulled back the flap on one of his pouches.

I tensed, ready to strike. But instead of attacking, Richard reached slowly into the pouch and pulled out a pair of items, his movements steady and unthreatening. He held them out in one hand. 'I believe,' he said, 'that what you truly want is this.'

In the palm of Richard's hand were two items: an ancient, ornate ring, and a lattice of gold and silvery metal, curved so as to fit around the fingers like a knuckle-duster. It was the first time I'd laid eyes on either, but I knew what they were. The Council's weapon, and Suleiman's Ring.

'Hear me!' Richard shouted suddenly. His voice rolled around the courtyard, strong and commanding. 'The Council care nothing for your lives! They are here to kill me, but more than that, they are here to seize the marid and return it to their control! And these items are the means by which they plan to do it. Bear witness, and know that I shall return!'

The echoes of Richard's voice died away. Richard looked me in the eye; his mouth quirked and he spoke again, this time so quietly that I could barely hear. 'And you, Alex, are here only for your lover. For her, you would sacrifice every other living being in this shadow realm. How long will they follow you once they learn that?'

I stood quite still, muscles tensed. The *sovnya* sang to

me, pure in its urge to kill. I could reach him with a step and a lunge.

But in the second it would take me to cross that distance, Richard would have time to activate those spells. I wasn't afraid for myself, but my plans for saving Anne hinged around that ring and that weapon. If either were destroyed . . .

Slowly, Richard bent down and laid the ring and the gold lattice upon the stone. Then he straightened up again. He watched me as if waiting for something.

'Step away,' I told Richard.

Richard took two steps back.

The futures were steady, calm. My divination was telling me that Richard would let me pick up those items. I didn't trust it. When he made his move, I'd have only my reflexes.

I walked forward.

Richard stood still, watching. The world seemed to hold its breath.

I was within range for a strike. The *sovnya* trembled, pulling at me. With an effort of will, I silenced it. Holding the polearm in my left hand, I crouched, reaching down with my right. I didn't take my eyes off Richard.

Richard looked down at me, waiting.

My hand touched the ring.

The spells around Richard activated. Space magic twisted and he vanished in a *bang* of imploding air.

Startled shouts and cries echoed around the courtyard. Two shots rang out; a bullet whined past my ear. 'HOLD!' I roared at the top of my voice, then spoke into the communicator. 'Landis! Compass!'

'Teleport effect!' Compass called over the comm. 'He managed to bypass the interdiction field. We don't know how!'

I was standing alone in front of Richard's army. A mutter of voices sounded from ahead, angry faces appearing at the windows, the noise swelling.

The futures were only seconds away from violence. If the shooting started again, it wouldn't stop. 'Drakh has left you!' I shouted at the adepts. 'So let's try this again! I offer terms of surrender. Who speaks for you?'

Silence. I held my breath. If they chose to fight now . . .

'I do,' a voice called from the door Richard had used.

A figure walked out. It was a young man, no older than twenty-five, with a thin beard. He wore patched-together armour and carried no weapons; his hair was dishevelled and blood was on his forehead. He walked forward, eyes boring into mine.

I took one look into the futures and saw what was going to happen. I slipped Richard's items into my pocket and grasped the *sovnya* two-handed.

The adept stopped in front of me. He had a look I'd seen before, the blank expression of one who'd watched everything they believed in fall apart. 'Who's in command of your forces?' I asked.

The adept didn't take his eyes off me. 'Drakh.'

'Who's your second in command?'

'He was at the front headquarters. You hit him with lightning.'

'Third in command?'

'She was at headquarters too.' The adept's eyes stared into mine. 'Trying to get the wounded away.'

Dammit. 'Fourth?'

The adept's lips curled in a snarl. 'That would be *me*!' At the last word, glowing daggers appeared in the adept's hands and he lunged.

I was already twisting aside, bringing around the *sovnya*. The blade gashed his arm as his rush carried him past. He spun to attack again, and I skewered him through the chest.

The adept jerked. He tried to move forward, but the six-foot polearm held us apart; the blade had gone through his ribcage. I gave the *sovnya* a twist and yanked it out; the adept stumbled, went down to one knee, then slowly collapsed.

All of a sudden, my fear was gone, replaced by rage. I wasn't afraid that the adepts would fire. I was sick of everything, sick of killing people and sick of this stupid pointless war, and I turned back to the kitchens and shouted at the top of my voice. 'I DO NOT HAVE TIME FOR THIS SHIT!' I kept yelling, all of my anger and frustration boiling over. 'Every one of the Council soldiers behind me would like nothing more than to just pull the trigger on you all and go home! I come out under a flag of truce to talk and you do *this*?' I pointed the *sovnya* down at the adept's body; the white flag flapped, stained with his blood. 'You are not heroes! You were not brought out here to fight for freedom, or justice! You were brought here as cannon fodder for a war you don't understand! If you die here, you will not be remembered as martyrs for a noble cause! You'll be remembered as a bunch of *idiots* too stupid to figure out that they'd already lost!'

The courtyard was tense, silent. I glared from window to window, daring anyone to challenge me. 'What do you want?' a small voice called.

'I want you to surrender!' I called back. 'Those still able to walk will come out one at a time, lay their weapons down at my feet, and go past to the men waiting behind. We'll fetch the wounded later. Co-operate, and you will not be harmed! But if you choose to fight, then the mages behind me will tear that building down right on top of you and I swear to God that once they start they will not stop until every last man, woman and child among you is dead!'

There was dead silence.

A figure appeared at the door. It was an adept, a big, burly guy holding an assault rifle. He walked forward, stopped in front of me, looked into my eyes. Then he laid the rifle down on the stones with a clatter. I turned my head to watch as he walked past the way I'd come.

A second adept appeared, then a third. Through the futures, I could see that they would keep coming. The last faint possibilities of violence flickered, then died away.

I stood there in the courtyard, the *sovnya* planted in front of me, watching the adepts pass one by one, the pile of weapons at my feet growing steadily larger. The white flag, spattered with red, hung from the *sovnya*'s blade. Behind me, I could hear Landis and Rain giving orders to organise the prisoners. Only once the adepts at the very end of the line had left the building, limping and staggering, did I give orders for the soldiers to move in.

Luna found me half an hour later.

I was sitting on the roof of the mausoleum, my legs hanging off the edge, looking down into the courtyard below. At the far end, two Council auxiliaries and a mage were talking. Ilmarin's body had been retrieved from the east roof, but the rest of the corpses, including Vihaela's, were still there.

Luna walked across the roof and sat down next to me with a sigh. 'I wondered where you'd gone.'

'You get through okay?'

'Barely saw any fighting,' Luna said. 'After we got separated, I didn't have a clue what was going on. Then Ji-yeong got roped in as a medic, and I figured I'd be more use watching her back than trying to catch up with you.'

I nodded.

'I got there for the tail-end of your speech,' Luna said. 'Pretty impressive.'

'I suppose.'

'Did Richard really just give you those things?'

I reached into my pocket and took out the ring and the lattice, setting them down on the roof. Luna tilted her head, focusing on them.

'They're the real thing,' I said. I'd already had the chance to study them. The lattice, the Council's weapon, had been the easier of the two; all I'd needed to figure out was the command word. The ring was another story. Heavy and ancient, made from solid gold, it wasn't something I knew how to use. But it had bound the marid once, and it might be able to do so again.

'Then why did he . . . ?' Luna asked.

'Hand them over?' I said. 'I don't know.'

'Landis and Rain are planning the assault on the keep,' Luna said. 'They want to know if that weapon's going to work.'

'Oh, it'll work,' I said. 'Channel a thread of magic and

say the command word, and it'll project its effect over a narrow cone to a thirty-foot range. But as to whether it'll stop an ifrit . . . well, it's not like we've got one to test it.'

Ji-yeong appeared in the courtyard below. She exchanged some words with the disposal team, then began picking her way over towards the mausoleum.

'The security guys are talking like you practically won the battle on your own,' Luna said. 'I wasn't expecting you to be celebrating, but I didn't think you'd be . . .'

'Doesn't feel like much of a win.'

From fifty feet below, Ji-yeong glanced up at the two of us, then walked across towards where Vihaela had fallen. 'I mean, we did just beat Richard's entire force,' Luna said. 'Yes, people died, but it sounds as though if you hadn't been there we would have lost a lot more. Even Keepers that I thought hated you were admitting it. I know you had to kill that adept, but I'm really glad you convinced the rest to surrender.'

In the courtyard below, Ji-yeong reached Vihaela's body and stopped. 'It's not about the adept,' I said.

'Then what is it?'

'I killed Ilmarin,' I said. It was hard to say it, but Luna was maybe the only one left in the shadow realm that I could talk to. 'Got him killed, I mean, but it comes to the same thing.'

'Ilmarin's dead?'

I pointed. 'Over there, on that rooftop. Last seconds of the battle with Vihaela. I saw her getting away, and Ilmarin was the only one in position to stop her. I knew if he did, there was maybe a seventy, eighty per cent chance she'd kill him. I ordered him to do it anyway.'

'Why?'

'Because if I hadn't, we'd have lost her,' I said with a sigh. 'She was just too good. If I'd played it safe, Vihaela would have made it into the mausoleum, and once she was out of sight she'd have used her mist cloak and we wouldn't have been able to track her. Probably. But the truth is, that's just a guess. Maybe once she was inside she wouldn't have been able to find a way out, and we'd have been able to trap her. Maybe she'd have decided to do what Richard did and just break off and disappear. I wasn't willing to take the chance and so I rolled the dice and they came up wrong, and Ilmarin's dead.' I looked at Luna. 'Do you think I was right?'

'. . . I don't know.'

We sat in silence for a little while. 'Ilmarin was one of the witnesses from my apprenticeship ceremony,' Luna said eventually.

'He was, wasn't he?' I said. It had been six years ago. 'You know, when I found out about Nimbus's plan this morning, I was furious. I was so outraged that he was going to sacrifice those men to buy time. But I just did pretty much the same thing. I knew what was going to happen when I gave Ilmarin that order, and I still did it. He was one of the only Keepers from the Order of the Star who always treated us decently, and now he's dead because of my decision.'

Below us, Ji-yeong was still looking down at Vihaela's body. 'I'm still thinking about that ceremony,' Luna said. 'You remember who was there?' She began ticking people off on her fingers. 'Talisid swore me in; Anne was my second; Ilmarin was the other witness; Sonder was there too; and we all went to Arachne's afterwards. Now

Sonder's dead, Ilmarin's dead, Arachne's gone, Talisid tried to kill you last week, and Anne . . .' Luna tailed off, a sad look on her face. 'We've lost so much.'

The simple way that she said it hurt. I wished I could tell her that the worst was over.

I looked away from Luna, down at the courtyard. 'You were right,' I said. 'I'm not cold enough to keep doing this.'

Luna reached out, her curse pulling back, and put her hand on my shoulder. She left it there a few seconds before taking it away again, letting her curse flow back out to her fingers. We sat together in silence for another minute or so.

At last, Luna got to her feet. 'I'll tell them you'll be there soon,' she said, then hesitated. 'Alex? About whether you were right . . . I still don't know. But for what it's worth . . . these decisions, about who lives and who dies? I'm glad you're the one making them, and not Nimbus or Talisid. And not me.'

Luna walked away. The disposal team at the far end of the courtyard was bagging up the body of the soldier Vihaela had decapitated. As for Ji-yeong, she hadn't moved.

I picked up the ring and lattice, then pushed off the roof and let myself float down to the courtyard below.

I landed a little way from Ji-yeong. She glanced over, then went back to staring down at Vihaela's body. I walked to her side.

'Did you know her?' I asked when the Korean girl stayed quiet.

Ji-yeong shook her head.

'But?'

'I knew about her,' Ji-yeong said. 'She was a legend. When we'd talk about the most powerful death mages and life mages, we'd argue about numbers two and three, but never about number one.'

'Did you want to be like her?'

Ji-yeong hesitated. 'I don't think so?' she said at last. 'But she was the strongest.'

'True,' I said. 'She might have been the best battle mage I've ever known.' I nodded down at the body. 'You'll end up like that some day.'

Ji-yeong looked up, startled.

'The only way to be as strong as her, and as feared as her, is to walk the same path she did,' I told Ji-yeong. 'That's where it ends. Anything else you need here?'

'. . . No.'

I nodded and turned away. Ji-yeong took a last look down at Vihaela, then as I kept walking she abandoned the body and followed me.

17

After the battle came clean-up. Soldiers cleared away the bodies while medics and members of the healer corps tended to the wounded. Richard's surviving adepts were searched and disarmed, then put under guard.

'That's the plan,' I said. 'Thoughts?'

Landis, Rain and I were back at the projection table with half a dozen of the more senior Keepers. The rest were out supervising the clean-up work and standing guard; a few of Richard's mages were still at large, not to mention the jinn. The projection table was showing a close-up of the keep at the centre of the castle. Four white diamonds within the corners marked the ward anchor points we'd failed to destroy this morning.

'Well, Compass, it's your call,' Landis said. 'How close do you need to be to those wards?'

'Two hundred feet would be nice,' Compass said. 'I can manage three, but the closer the better.'

Rain glanced down at the projection. 'So . . . ?'

'Here,' I said, pointing to an L-shaped building off the keep's south-east corner. 'Two hundred and twenty feet at the closest point. If we can't make it that far, second best building is the one to the south-west.'

'South approach, then,' Landis said.

I nodded. 'Start from the courtyard, sweep north. I don't see much point trying anything fancy. We need to secure the area and that means eliminating everything in our path.'

'What are we looking at?' Rain asked.

'Jann and shaitan,' I said. 'They've got a skirmish line out to here, and once we hit it they'll reinforce fast. Main problem is going to be the three ifrit. Sagash, Caldera and Aether.' I touched my finger to a tall, ornate building to the south of the keep. It was huge, more than half the height of the keep itself, and loomed over the southern section of the castle. 'If I had to guess, they'll occupy the cathedral. It's got an elevated view over the whole southern approach.'

Landis nodded. 'We'll have to take it. Barrayar's ifrit?'

'Hasn't been re-summoned, at least not yet.'

'And the marids?' Rain asked.

It was the big question. 'I don't think they're leaving the keep.'

'Heard that before,' Tobias observed.

'I know,' I said with a nod. 'And I know last time they caught us by surprise when they did. But so far – *so far* – I can't see any futures in which Variam or Anne's marids go outside the keep walls. I think the sultan prefers to use lesser jinn whenever it can. As far as it's concerned, jann, shaitan, even ifrits are all expendable. It loses any, it can just re-summon them. Losing Anne or Variam is another story. I have the feeling it won't deploy them unless it feels under threat.'

'You sure you can get through the local wards?' Rain asked Compass.

'With enough time,' Compass said. 'But it's not going to be fast and I am going to be *really* vulnerable while I'm doing it. You guys better make sure I don't go the same way as Lumen!'

'Yeah, I think we've all learned our lesson from that,'

I said. 'We'll be right next to you. Any of the jinn want to reach you, they'll have to go through us.'

'Which leaves one rather pressing question,' Landis said. 'At the risk of counting our chickens, what exactly will the consequences be should we succeed?'

I looked at Compass.

'Not great,' Compass said. 'When I talked to Sonder this morning, his theory was the isolation effect was trying to pull this shadow realm apart and it was only the wards that were holding it together. I did a few spatial scans over the past hour and I'm pretty sure he was right. As soon as we blow one of those anchor points, the whole ward net collapses, and once that happens we need to evacuate *really* fast because the shadow realm's going to go with it.'

'What about the marid?' Slate said. With Ilmarin's death, he'd taken over as Rain's second. 'We just going to leave it?'

'I'm afraid we don't have much choice, dear boy,' Landis said. 'Once the wards go down, we'll be able to gate again, but the marid will too, at which point it'll have mobility advantage and no ritual to tie it down. There'll really be no practical way to force an engagement.'

'I've got some ideas as far as that goes,' I said. 'I doubt the marid will run from me if I'm alone. But we're getting ahead of ourselves. Any more suggestions for the attack?'

We discussed it for another fifteen minutes, then dispersed to make final preparations. I went looking for Ji-yeong and Luna.

I found them both in the barracks. Ji-yeong had been pressed into service as a medic again – normally a Dark mage wouldn't be trusted with something like that, but either Landis's influence was making the Council forces a bit more easy-going, or they were just desperate enough not to care. I filled them in on the plan. As I expected, Luna quickly homed in on the last part.

'You're going to face Anne and Vari?' Luna said. 'Alone?'

'Should be okay with one or two more.'

'That sounds like a really bad idea,' Ji-yeong said with a frown. 'We saw what those marids can do and you want to duel them?'

'I don't want to duel anyone,' I said. 'But if we send in an overwhelming force then Anne will just gate out. It's like playing poker. If she *knows* she can't beat us, she'll fold. Only way she stays in is if she thinks she can handle whatever we throw at her. Also . . . that marid told me to find it. I think it wants to tell me something.'

'Tell you what?' Luna said. '"You're a human, I hate you, now die"?'

'I'm hoping for a slightly longer conversation.'

'Okay, look,' Ji-yeong said. 'Taking the castle back is one thing. But I think a marid is out of my league.'

'What about Vari?' Luna asked.

'He'll be between us and Anne,' I said. The thought no longer brought fear. I would do what I must. 'We'll handle him first.'

The Council troops formed up. There was little discussion this time. Once everyone had their assignments, they dispersed, checked their weapons and prepared to move.

The fight with Richard's adepts had changed the Council forces. There was a sense of purpose, a confidence, that hadn't been there before. And beyond that was something harder to place, a kind of cohesion; they acted less like a collection of individuals and more like a single entity. Maybe it was the fateweaver; maybe it was the high from the victory; maybe it was as simple as finally having some trust in their leadership. Whatever it was, it was making a difference.

We gated to the castle's south and advanced on the keep. Immediately, we encountered jann. They were scattered and solitary, and they didn't even slow us down, but they'd been put there to raise the alarm, and they did. By the time we made it halfway, Anne's main force was waiting for us.

The jinn numbered in the hundreds, if not thousands. They seemed immune to pain, and fought to the death. But the claws of a jann were no match for the assault rifles of the Council soldiers, which could shoot them down at a hundred feet. Nor were the abilities of a shaitan any match for the magic of a battle mage. The jinn hurled themselves at the Council lines, trying to break through and turn the battle into a mêlée, where their numbers and resilience would give them the advantage. But with the fateweaver and my divination I could see each attack before it was made, and by the time the jinn came charging towards our lines I had soldiers and mages ready for them. Machine guns scythed across lines of jann; battle magic froze and burned them in their tracks. One by one the attacks were shattered, and after each was broken the Council forces would re-form and march forward over the bodies of their enemies.

Only when we reached the cathedral did I see what I'd been waiting for. 'All troops, hold,' I said over the communication link. 'Ifrit mages occupying the cathedral. Stay out of line of sight of the roof and upper windows.'

'Who are we looking at?' Landis asked.

I concentrated. Future versions of myself leapt forward over the rooftops to come soaring down onto the cathedral's roof and through its windows. I studied the variety of attacks that hit them, then returned to the present. 'Aether on the roof, Sagash on the upper level, Caldera on the ground floor.'

Landis and Rain issued orders, reorganising the troops. While they did, I considered the problem. Out of the three ifrit, Aether and Caldera were the most mobile – Aether could fly, Caldera could sink into stone. Sagash was more powerful in direct combat, but he had no easy escapes. Conclusion: kill Sagash first.

With the decision made, a plan fell into place, details springing to mind as though I'd done this a hundred times before. 'All troops, surround the cathedral on its east, west and south faces,' I ordered. 'Soldiers and auxiliaries maintain a perimeter and target enemy jinn. Mages will advance; be ready to shield against lightning and death magic attacks from above. Once you've reached the cathedral, ascend to the upper level and enter on my mark. Do not enter via the ground floor: you'll be at risk from the stone gliding ifrit. Primary target is Sagash. Confirm.'

Terse acknowledgements came in. Through the dreamstone, I felt the troops under my command moving to encircle the cathedral on three sides. The castle was eerily silent. Occasionally the quiet would be broken by a burst of gunfire, signalling that a Council team had run into an uncooperative jann.

The Council forces were nearly in position. I turned

back to Luna and Ji-yeong. They'd stayed with me, acting as point defence so that I could focus on the larger battle. I made a quick beckoning gesture to the two of them, then spoke into the focus. 'Go.'

I strode forward, Luna and Ji-yeong at my back. Up ahead, the shape of the keep loomed over the castle buildings. Lightning flashed, first once then again and again, and the hollow *boom* of battle magic echoed off the walls. We entered a wide courtyard with stairs leading upwards that I remembered from my first visit. There were burn marks on the stone, cartridge casings scattered behind firing positions. A soldier was propped up against a pedestal, his breath coming in short gasps; his ribs had been opened by a jann's claws and an adept with the shoulder patch of the Council healer corps was working on him. Another soldier stepped aside to let us pass.

But most of my attention was on the battle ahead. Aether and Sagash were raining down attacks from above; the shields of the Council mages were holding, but they'd be vulnerable once they tried to ascend. I selected strands of fate, reinforced them, sent images through the dream-stone. Flying mages from the eastern wing took to the sky, engaging Aether from the air. The fire on the advancing mages fell off, and I pushed the eastern and southern forces up while Sagash was busy with the ones to the west.

My magesight picked up mobility spells, force and fire and air. Mages scaled the walls of the cathedral, jumped up to the windows and doors. Sagash countered with that jinn magic I'd seen in the tombs: the black sun. Through my divination I saw which mages were at risk, and sent urgent messages through the dreamstone to duck back. Black beams carved through wood and stone, but no one was killed. Below, Caldera was about to join the battle, and I detached two mages to block her.

More mages were reaching the cathedral, and the battle was intensifying. I sped up, following the route from the south that Sagash and Aether were now too busy to watch.

By the time I reached the cathedral, the battle was raging at full force. The cathedral was a single huge building with elevated entrances to the north and south. I walked up to the southern entrance, Luna and Ji-yeong still following, and stopped just to one side of the double doors. The roar and crack of battle magic echoed from within, and I looked into the futures for a clear view.

The interior of the cathedral was a vast, empty space. The lower floor was broken with a giant rift running through the centre, and the upper floor consisted of a railed walkway with a catwalk spanning the cathedral from north to south. Lines of windows opened out to east and west, and the mages of the attack force had used them to force their way through; broken glass was scattered on the walkway.

Sagash was at the north end, almost hidden behind his shield. Above his head hovered a black sun that drank in light. Beams of death speared from it, cutting through anything in their path, while magic attacks of every kind poured in through the broken windows, ice and fire and force all slamming into Sagash's shield as though drawn by a magnet. The noise was incredible, a continuous thundering roar.

My plan had been to use the distraction of the fighting

to get close to Sagash, then disable him using the Council's weapon. Looking at where the Dark mage had made his stand, I realised it would never work. To reach Sagash I'd have to cross nearly a hundred feet of open catwalk; he'd tear me to pieces before I got half that far.

We'd have to do this the old-fashioned way.

Quickly I issued orders. Caldera was still fighting below and Aether above; I assigned three mages to contain each of them while the rest converged on Sagash. Sagash hammered at the mages at the windows with deathbolts and beams from the black sun, and I let the mages give ground, sending impulses through the dreamstone for them to back into cover when threatened. Only when everyone was in position did I begin.

From my position, it felt like a game of chess. Hoarfrost and Tobias struck at Sagash from the west, then as he turned to answer I had Slate and Trask attack from the east. Slate's death magic disrupted Sagash's shield and as Sagash took a moment to repair it I directed Landis and another Keeper to strike at the black sun. The magical construct dissolved under a counter-spell; Sagash tried to re-form it, and as he did Hoarfrost hit him again.

It was like a pack of wolves bringing down a bear. With the ifrit's power, Sagash was stronger than any of the Keepers, maybe stronger than any three of them put together. But I didn't give him the chance to use it; every time he tried to focus on a single target I'd have a mage hit him from the other side, knocking him off-balance and forcing him to split his attention. From Sagash's position, it probably felt as though he was holding his ground. He reacted to the flow of battle, attacking targets and countering their strikes, fighting with all of his power, each move natural and logical and taking him step by step towards his death.

I felt the exact moment at which Sagash lost. The currents of fate tipped and began to flow, first slowly then faster and faster. To an observer, it wouldn't have looked like anything. A novice chess player doesn't notice when he makes the move that loses him the game. He keeps playing and trading pieces, and only at the end, when it's far too late, does he come to understand that he's lost, not now but many moves ago.

Strikes of fire and ice slammed into Sagash's shield, staggering him. Sagash tried to recover, hurled a counter-attack at Hoarfrost, but a force blast from Aegis hit him in the back, throwing his spell off target. Sagash tried to re-summon the black sun; counter-magic from Landis and Tobias flashed out, disrupting the effect and causing the sun to collapse in on itself. More spells hit Sagash and now the Dark mage wasn't attacking at all; it was all he could do to block the incoming fire. Sagash's shield flickered, struggling to hold under the rain of attacks.

A lightning bolt from Thunder slammed into Sagash. His shield took it, channelling the electricity away down into the catwalk, but a firebolt hit a second later that weakened his defences. An ice strike from Hoarfrost pierced the damaged shield, freezing Sagash's flesh. Sagash tried to recast his shield, but I'd already chosen the future I needed and a spell from Landis exploded around Sagash, the fire magic overloading the shield entirely.

Another lightning bolt hit, and this time there was nothing to stop it. Sagash's body jerked as electricity coursed through it, and a force blade struck him from behind, severing his arm and shoulder, the limb spinning towards the floor far below.

Somehow Sagash got his shield back up. I didn't know how he was able to stand, much less fight. His lips were still pulled back in that unnatural grin, and with his remaining arm he blocked a water blast from Tobias. I could sense death energy flowing through him, the tendons and muscles of his withered body still obeying his iron will. Once again, he tried to re-summon that black sun.

I pulled in the last strands of fate, and made an end of it.

Battle magic came in from all around, every spell timed to strike at the same instant. Ice, air, force, lightning and fire broke Sagash's shield and met at a single point.

There was a thunderous crash and Sagash disappeared in a ball of multicoloured energy. The cathedral trembled; hot air rushed through the open doors with a roar, followed by silence.

I stepped out into the doorway. Where Sagash had stood, the walkway, railings and stone had been eradicated in a twenty-foot radius. The catwalk ended halfway across the room. Beyond, the cathedral's northern walls were melted in a spherical pattern, still glowing with latent heat. If there were any pieces left of Sagash's body, I couldn't see them.

I scanned the futures. Caldera had sunk into the stone, and Aether was falling back towards the keep. The remaining jinn were in retreat. 'All units, enemy forces are withdrawing. Advance on the primary objective and secure it before they have a chance to regroup.'

I started walking around the walkway. Around me, I could sense the Council forces advancing, sweeping north towards the looming shadow of the keep. Behind me, dimly, I was aware of Ji-yeong lingering, one hand on the walkway railing, looking out at the wreckage where her old master had made his stand.

The Council forces kept going. I directed them, ordering them to quickly burn through any pockets of resistance, using the fateweaver to push through favourable outcomes. Inwardly, I was tense; this was where we were most vulnerable. If Anne decided to come out and fight . . .

But she didn't. The jinn continued to fall back in disarray until they reached the keep. They fled inside, disappearing into its shadow.

'This is Sergeant Little,' Little said over the comm. 'Reached the primary objective. Building is secure.'

'Slate, Hoarfrost, reinforce Little's team,' I ordered. 'Hold that building.'

'This is Thunder and Aegis. The lightning ifrit has withdrawn to the keep.'

'Understood, monitor its position but do not approach. This applies to all units. Do not enter weapons range of the keep. Take and reinforce the target building but go no further.'

The sounds of battle were dying away. Every now and again a burst of gunfire would echo through the castle, but each time, the interval between shots would be longer. A lull settled in the battle, both sides catching their breath.

I strode across courtyards and down alleys, heading north. Luna hurried at my back, and Council security advanced with me, covering windows and doorways down the sights of their rifles. Over the walls and roofs ahead I caught glimpses of the keep, a huge, foreboding presence. We'd come far, but as long as Anne held that keep, the castle was still hers.

A soldier opened a door for us to stride through. A corridor and another doorway led us into an L-shaped room with open windows along both sides of the L that looked out onto an open courtyard. At the other side of the courtyard was the huge dark-stone shadow of the keep. More than a dozen people were there already, with more arriving all the time.

'Sir,' Little said with a nod. He was standing next to the door, his weapon pointed at the floor. 'Should we set up on the roof?'

'No,' I said. 'There's a fixed emplacement on that south-east tower. You try to put heavy weapons up there, they'll have a clear field of fire right down onto your heads.'

'Snipe the emplacement?' Hoarfrost said. 'Could take out the tower . . .'

'It's reinforced,' another mage said.

'No, we stick to the plan,' I said. 'Compass?'

Compass was lying flat on the stone, head tilted to one side, sighting up through the window towards the keep. 'Sec,' she called, her voice slightly muffled.

I walked to Compass and knelt by her side, balancing the *sovnya* with its butt against the flagstones. I lowered my head and looked up, following Compass's line of sight.

The corner of the keep was a rounded tower, made of dark grey stone. It looked forbidding even to normal sight. To magesight, it was more so. Protective wards ran through the stone, reinforcing it against both physical and magical attack, and tied into it was a gate ward designed to harden the area within against any kind of spatial disruption. The lines of power flowing through the wards were thick and powerful; if they had flaws, I couldn't see them.

Footsteps sounded behind us. 'Well?' Landis asked.

Compass sighed and scrambled to her feet, brushing dust off her hands and clothes. 'It's going to be tight.'

'Verus?'

'I can feel the anchor point,' I said, standing. 'It's less than thirty feet beyond the wall.' Behind the walls of the keep, halfway to the top within the south-east tower, was a concentration of power where the lines of the wards converged. That was one of the four anchor points that we'd seen on Sonder's map this morning. That anchor point was supporting the wards protecting the castle, the wards stopping us from leaving the shadow realm, the marid's ritual, and, ultimately, the shadow realm itself. Knock it out, and all the dominos would fall.

'Well, Compass, it's all on your shoulders,' Landis said. 'Gate or assault?'

Compass hesitated for a long moment. The futures hovered, then shifted decisively. 'Gate.'

Soldiers took up positions by the windows; others were sent out to make room. Mages gathered: Landis, Rain, Tobias, Slate, Hoarfrost, Aegis. All would be protecting Compass.

'Up a bit,' Compass told Rain. 'Left . . . There.'

A beam of blue light stabbed from Rain's hand at a forty-five-degree angle, disintegrating a neat twelve-inch tunnel through the ceiling. Rain held it a second longer, then cut it off precisely as it went through the wall above. Compass sighted through the hole, and nodded.

'Jinn have been cleared out,' Slate said. 'Think that lightning kid's in the keep, but hard to tell through the wards.'

'Caldera?' Rain asked.

'Can't see her.'

Compass looked tense and focused. 'Don't talk to me once I start.'

'Understood,' I said. 'Package?'

A portal appeared at Compass's feet; she reached in and heaved out a hiking backpack. It was the size of her torso and she struggled to lift it; I grabbed it with my right arm before she could drop it, then hefted it one-handed and walked towards the others. 'Ozols,' I called.

'Yes, yes,' Ozols said cheerfully. He walked forward and took the backpack, shifting under its weight.

'Try not to bloody well kill everyone, all right?' Little told him from a safe distance.

'Is fine! No worry!'

Ozols carried the backpack over to the far wall, set it down with a grunt, and pulled it open. Several mages stepped away. Landis wandered right up and peered over Ozols's shoulder.

'Ji-yeong, you're on point defence,' I told her. 'Cover us and Compass.'

Compass looked at Luna. 'Mage . . . Vesta, right? How long do those blessings last?'

'The more danger you're in, the faster it burns off,' Luna said.

'Then save it for the gate,' Compass told her. 'If I mess

up suppressing the ward, we just have to start over. If I mess up the *gate*, it'll be a lot worse.'

'All right,' I said, looking around. 'Everyone ready?'

No one objected. Even Slate gave a terse nod. The only one who didn't respond was Ozols, still busy with the contents of the backpack.

I drew in a breath, let it out, then spoke over the comm. 'Begin.'

Compass raised a hand towards the keep and began her spell.

Just as locks caused the invention of lockpicks, gate wards caused the invention of spells to pierce gate wards. And just like a lock, any gate ward can be broken with enough time and effort. Right now, Compass was probing the lines of power in that ward system, figuring out how to suppress them for just long enough.

But beating a ward system that's *defended* is a different story. Compass was using as little power as she could, but the more progress she made, the harder it would be to hide what she was doing. If she was discovered – *when* she was discovered – our enemies could try to repair the ward network and fix the hole in their defences faster than she could bore it. Or they could just attack this building and kill her. Given the way this day had been going, I was betting they'd go for the second option.

'No movement,' Slate said, his voice tense.

'Verus will give us warning,' Landis said calmly. 'Keep it quiet, boys.'

Thanks for the vote of confidence. In truth, giving warning was about all I could do. The lines of space magic that Compass was tracing were too complex for me to follow – bypassing gate wards like that is a specialised skill, and I didn't understand it well enough to use the fate-weaver to help.

Minutes ticked by. I felt the lines of magic in Compass's spell shift, then shift again. A soldier coughed, then fell silent. The sun was still high in the sky, and the room was hot. I saw a bead of sweat trickling down Compass's forehead.

There was a shift in the futures. It was small, but I'd been watching for it. 'Movement,' I said.

'When?' Landis asked.

'Wait.' I pushed with the fateweaver. A branch of futures was opening up, danger and violence and death. I tried to suppress it and guide us down a different path.

It didn't work. 'Got incoming,' I said. 'I'll stall them as long as I can.'

The futures branched, possibilities spreading out. I pushed them down the path which seemed the least violent, and pointed towards the west wall. 'Hundred and ten feet that way. They're trying for a closer look.'

'Tobias,' Landis ordered. 'Shroud.'

Tobias stepped forward, pulling something from his pocket. Blue light glowed, illuminating the brim of his hat from below, and I felt a fuzzy hard-to-see shell of magic envelop the building's western end.

Magic flickered from the west. We couldn't see it through the walls, but I knew that someone had just appeared. 'It's her,' Slate said sharply.

'Nice and quiet, boys,' Landis said calmly. 'Let her think there's nothing to see.'

Thirty seconds ticked by. Sixty. The soldiers at the windows scanned the courtyard through their gunsights. I could feel the futures shifting. No one said a word.

The futures tipped. 'She's moving,' I said. I pointed to the courtyard between us and the keep. 'Popping up there.'

'She's going to see it,' Rain said.

'Hoarfrost, Slate,' Landis ordered. 'Don't let her get a clear look.'

Hoarfrost and Slate moved to the windows. 'Ten seconds,' I said.

'On Verus's mark.'

I watched the futures shifting. 'Seven,' I said. 'Six— four. Three. Two. One—'

The stone of the courtyard rippled, and Caldera rose from its surface.

Ice and death struck like vipers. Caldera flinched under the attack and sank back into the stone, but for a moment our eyes met through the window, and I saw her gaze flick from me to Compass.

It was only an instant, then Caldera was gone, leaving nothing but a circle of frost on the flagstones. But it was Caldera, one of the best investigators on the Order of the Star, who'd been passed over for promotion so many times but who'd always refused to quit. Last year, when I'd tried to cover up what Anne had done, she'd been the one to figure it out. So many times, back when we'd worked together, I'd seen her piece things together from just a couple of clues.

The futures shifted decisively, and in the distance, at the edge of my hearing, I heard an echoing whine like a hunting call. 'Incoming!' I snapped.

'Positions,' Landis ordered.

A wind rose in the distance, carrying the sound of movement. Jinn were converging on our position. 'Jinn,'

Thunder called in over the comm. 'North, west and north-east.'

'Contact west,' a soldier called. 'Shit, there's a lot of them!'

'All units, fire at will,' Landis ordered. 'Do not let them reach this building.'

Gunfire opened up. Some of the mages moved to the windows, scanning for targets. A rifle stuttered as Nowy engaged a target; others fired a second later. The smell of gun smoke filled the air.

'Verus,' Landis said.

'Watching,' I said briefly. It was Caldera I was waiting for.

More and more soldiers opened fire. The air was heating up, becoming smoky and acrid. Hoarfrost and Tobias added their magic from the windows, icebolts and hydroblasts. Shouts and warnings sounded over the comm. The chaos was making divination harder, bringing my view of the futures down to seconds at most.

If I were Caldera, this would be when I'd strike. I narrowed my focus, concentrating on the immediate futures around where Compass was standing. I closed my ears to the shouts and gunfire, closed my eyes to the flashing spells and the rush of movement. I focused my senses on the ground beneath my feet and what would be coming up from it. The battle around didn't matter. There was only me, Compass and Caldera.

Nothing.

Nothing . . .

There.

Caldera was underneath, rising fast. I threw my energy into the fateweaver. She was too close to push away – all I could do was affect who she'd home in on. I made a snap decision, pushed the futures down that path, threw warnings into the minds of the mages closest to me and then I was out of time.

Caldera breached the surface like a shark lunging from the ocean. But she came up under my feet, not Compass's, and as I jumped away her clutching hand missed my ankle. The focus was on my left hand; I twisted in mid-air, aiming the gold and silver lattice like a knuckleduster, and triggered it.

Energy surged out, engulfing Caldera as she finished rising from the stone. She staggered; the spell she'd been about to launch at Compass collapsed and Caldera fell to her knees.

'Freeze!' Slate shouted. Ji-yeong halted, her sword raised above Caldera's head. Compass didn't move, all her attention on her spell.

Rain came striding forward. 'Verus. Is she—?'

'Jinn's lost control,' I called over the gunfire. I was watching the futures very closely. 'For now.'

Rain knelt down in front of Caldera and put a hand on her shoulder. 'Caldera,' he said in his deep voice. 'Wake up.'

Caldera raised her head. Her eyes were muddy and confused, but they were human again. '. . . Rain?'

'You've been controlled by an ifrit jinn,' Rain said. A burst of gunfire stammered from the window nearest to him, but he didn't take his eyes off Caldera. 'Hold still.'

'Rain . . .' Caldera said. 'What did I . . . ?'

The futures shifted; looking ahead, I felt a chill. The jinn was rebuilding its connection to Caldera, and it was doing it fast. Very fast. *It's coming back*, I sent through the dreamstone to Rain.

'We're going to get you out of here,' Rain told Caldera.

The building shuddered as a lightning bolt struck the roof. Fear flickered in Caldera's eyes. 'It's coming.'

'Fight it,' Rain said urgently. 'You can do this.'

The futures were coming closer and closer. None of them were good. *Rain*, I sent. *It's not going to work.*

Emotions flashed back through the link at me; anger, frustration. Caldera drew a ragged breath, fixed her gaze on Rain. 'Get away,' she said hoarsely.

Rain didn't take his hand off Caldera. 'Fight it.'

Rain!

'Shut up!' Rain snapped.

Caldera's eyes flicked from Rain to me. Fury flashed, replaced in an instant by that deadly blank stare.

'Caldera, you—' Rain began.

Caldera's fist swung in a short, deadly arc. There was the *crack* of breaking bone and I caught a glimpse of Rain flying through the air, his head twisted at an impossible angle.

Caldera surged to her feet, turning towards Compass, but I was faster. The *sovnya* rammed through Caldera's chest, pinning her in place.

Caldera swayed back but held her ground. The *sovnya* flared, trying to incinerate Caldera from the inside, but as the flesh around the blade blackened it turned to sand. Caldera – the thing inside her – fixed its gaze upon me. It reached forward, took hold of the shaft of the *sovnya* and pulled itself forward, impaling itself to get closer to me.

I pulled my hands back, gripping the *sovnya* by its end. A paralysis spell from Slate slammed into Caldera, along with an ice blast from Hoarfrost. Caldera kept going, pulling herself further along the shaft.

One more pull and she'd be in reach. Caldera was pushing me towards Compass and she was staggeringly strong; it was all I could do to hold her back. Ji-yeong's sword clanged off Caldera's side. 'Landis!' I yelled.

'The focus,' Landis called. Fire was dancing at his hands, but we were too close for him to loose his spell.

My muscles were screaming at me; only the strength of my right arm was letting me hold my ground. The lattice was still on my left hand but both of my hands were locked in a death grip on the *sovnya*'s haft and if I let go Caldera would be free. Caldera pulled herself along the shaft one last time and now I could smell the scent from her body, scorched sand and flesh. Blank, empty eyes stared into mine as she reached for me.

A blue ray flashed across my vision and disintegrated Caldera's head.

Caldera wavered. Her arm was still raised, but her head and neck were gone, a neat spherical pattern carved out of shoulders and collarbone. Staring down into her body, I could see white bone and spine, red blood replaced with flowing sand. The sand pooled, began to pour upwards as if to try to re-form, but the ifrit had expended too much power. The sand darkened, slowed, stopped. Caldera's body fell with a crash, yanking the *sovnya* out of my hand. Something seemed to move at the edge of my vision, a shadow expanding down into the earth, then all was still.

The futures were quiet. I looked towards where the ray had come from.

Rain was lying against the wall, one arm still raised. His finger pointed towards where Caldera had fallen.

Slate hurried to Rain and I turned back to Compass.

Somehow, in all the time that Caldera had attacked, fought and died, Compass hadn't stopped working on her spell. 'Aether falling back to the keep,' Thunder reported over the comm.

'They're running!' a soldier called.

'Vesta,' Compass said tightly. 'Now.'

Luna stepped up, touching Compass's back. The grey mist around her shimmered, turning to gold as she directed the full power of her curse into Compass. The futures seemed to clear, random possibilities flaking away, leaving only one glowing path with slight variations.

I was looking down at what was left of Caldera's body. It was dissolving into sand and for a moment it was as though I saw a patchwork of my memories of her. Our first meeting in the shop. Drinking in the pub, working in the office. Caldera standing between me and a pack of enemies. Caldera facing me on the roof of Canary Wharf, chasing me into traffic, shunning me in the halls. Caldera in the basement of Levistus's mansion, bloodied but coming for me one last time.

A flash of pain went through my mind and I forced the memories away. 'Ozols, set for six seconds,' I said. 'Activate on my mark.'

Ozols nodded and hefted the backpack. 'Twenty seconds,' Compass said, her voice tense. I could feel the gate taking form.

'Aether is next to the node,' I told Landis. 'Need cover.'

'Hoarfrost,' Landis ordered. 'Aegis.'

The mages lined up behind Compass. The futures wavered one last time, then set, and the golden mist around Compass ebbed. Luna stepped quickly away as a portal formed in the air.

The portal was a circle instead of the standard oval, six feet in diameter. It appeared in front of Compass, revealing a room tiled in dark stone. In the centre of the room was a vertical spike of black metal that radiated power.

But it was hard to see the spike through all the jinn. The room was packed with them, and Aether was hovering over their heads. They'd felt the gate coming, and as it opened death and lightning exploded out through the portal.

A triple shield flashed up from Landis, Aegis and Hoarfrost, fire-force-ice, concentric layers stopping the attacks cold. 'Mark!' I told Ozols.

Ozols twisted something inside the backpack.

I grabbed the backpack by one strap, my artificial arm taking the weight, and darted forward. I curved around Compass and the mages, spinning like a hammer thrower, then swung back in and flung the backpack through the gate.

Aether threw up a shield of air. The backpack *thumped* into it, bounced off a jann's head, landed flat on the floor.

Aether looked down at the backpack, then up at me.

Behind me, Compass cut the spell. The portal vanished, and Aether, the jann, the metal spike and the room vanished with it. I looked up through the hole that Compass had been using to sight with.

Back when we'd been laying plans for this assault, I'd looked through the contents of Compass's spatial storage. And just as I'd thought, she packed with an eye to the battlefield. She'd been Landis's gate expert and space mage for some time, and she'd learned to bring the kinds of things he asked for. Which, apparently, mostly consisted of tea, good food and high explosives.

As it turns out, a hiking backpack can fit a lot of high explosives.

There was a massive hollow *whump*, as though someone had dropped a sandbag the size of a building.

Halfway up the tower, a section of the keep bulged and cracked. Dust and smoke burst outward in a cloud, and stones came plummeting out of the sky to slam into the courtyard. With a groaning noise, the upper part of the tower slumped, stones cascading down until the collapse stopped.

But for all the destruction, it was dwarfed by what I could see in my magesight. The node that had acted as the anchor point for the keep's wards was gone. Not damaged, gone. The complex net of wards around the keep was shrinking, collapsing in on itself, the lines of power tearing. It was like watching a massive tower with one of its legs cut away; the remaining nodes held out a few seconds longer, then the second collapsed as well, followed by numbers three and four.

A thunderclap shook the air. Magical energy surged, flashing outward, all the spells unravelling at once. The shields in our room flared, reacting to the discharge. All around us, I felt the ward network dissipate. I could use the dreamstone to enter Elsewhere again, and the Council forces could gate home.

The sultan's ritual had failed. The battle was over.

18

Landis started issuing orders to the troops. I clapped Ozols on the shoulder, then walked over to Rain.

Rain was propped up against the wall, with Slate kneeling next to him. '. . . don't think I'm walking out of here,' Rain was saying.

'We'll handle it,' Slate said, then looked up at me with a frown.

I stopped a few feet away from Rain. 'How the hell are you still alive?'

Rain closed his eyes, resting his head against the stone. 'Transmutation,' he said, his voice raspy. 'Turn the broken bone into liquid, reshape it, turn it back.'

'I didn't even know water mages could do that.'

'There's a reason they don't,' Rain said. 'Have a guess what happens if you get it wrong.'

'Well, glad you didn't.'

There was a moment's pause. Behind me, the first soldiers were moving out.

'I'm sorry—' I began.

'Not now, Verus,' Rain said. He didn't open his eyes. 'Okay?'

Behind me on the floor lay the pile of sand and tattered clothes that had once been Caldera. Slate was staring at me, his eyes cold, and I could sense a barrier between me and the two Keepers. They'd put their grudges aside, but only for the battle. Now it was over.

There was nothing more to be said. I walked back to Luna and Ji-yeong.

Luna was looking tired but satisfied. 'Too bad it wasn't Barrayar in there,' she said. 'Remember how he mined my flat with explosives? Would have been kind of poetic justice.'

'We're at the endgame,' I told them both. 'Any last things you need to do, do them now.' I bent down to pick up the *sovnya* from Caldera's remains and headed for Landis.

Landis was talking with Tobias and Compass. '. . . already deteriorating,' Compass was saying. 'It's only a matter of time before the drift is serious enough to collapse the realm's link to our world.'

'How long?' Landis said.

Compass raised her hands helplessly. 'An hour? A day? Five minutes? There's a reason no one uses isolation wards!'

'Well, it's not five minutes,' I said, walking up. 'But there's too much noise in the futures for me to see any further. Landis?'

'Evacuation's under way,' Landis said.

'Are you taking a shot at Anne?'

'No,' Tobias said.

I nodded. Now that the ritual had failed, an attack on the keep was pointless. The marid would just gate away. 'Guess this is goodbye then.'

'Verus,' Landis said. His expression was serious. 'I know I asked you to rescue Variam, but that was before we discovered his situation. I don't want you and Mage Vesta to throw away your lives.'

'Like I said, we were doing this anyway.' I looked at

Compass. 'If all goes to plan, I'll have a last few evacuees for you. If you could keep the gate open, I'd appreciate it.'

'I'll try my best,' Compass said.

Landis extended a hand. 'It's been an honour, Verus.'

I shook Landis's hand, then shouldered the *sovnya* and walked back to Luna and Ji-yeong. 'Let's go.'

Luna, Ji-yeong and I faced the keep.

We were maybe a hundred paces from the front gate. A flagstone avenue, bordered with lanterns of black iron, ran in a straight line from our feet to the double doors. In the distance I could hear the faint calls of the Council forces as they co-ordinated their evacuation, but nearby there was nothing. The keep loomed above us, cracked and broken but no less threatening. A wind blew over our heads, catching the trails of smoke rising from the south-east tower and carrying them away to the north.

As we stood, a quiver seemed to go through the castle, like a tremor in the world. It wasn't as violent as the shockwaves we'd felt earlier, but there was something disquieting about it.

'Wards are definitely down,' Ji-yeong said. 'But I can't see the jinn.'

'They're hanging back,' I said.

'So,' Luna said. 'Just to review. Once we go into that keep, we're going to be facing two marids and God knows how many lesser jinn. Not only do we have to beat both marids, we have to do it without killing Anne and Vari in the process. Does that sum it up?'

'Don't forget that the shadow realm's going to collapse soon.'

'Right, thanks for reminding me. Next point. Based on what we've been through since coming to this shadow realm, I think it's fair to say that if it comes down to a fight, either of those marids is more than a match for the three of us.'

Ji-yeong raised a hand. 'I'm not fighting a marid.'

'Correction, the two of us,' Luna said. 'So, Alex. I don't want to make it seem like I'm always coming to you for help. You know, I'm an independent mage now, I solve my own problems. But I really, *really* hope you've got a plan. Because I've been trying to think up a way to make this work and I'm drawing a blank.'

'We've got a few cards left to play,' I told her. 'First is the Council's focus. It worked on Caldera. Although that said, doing that burnt up about a quarter of whatever fuel this thing uses, and I think the marids are going to take more than that. Card number two is an idea I've had floating at the back of my mind about Anne's dress. That dress is the last thing Arachne gave her. Arachne foresaw what was going to happen to Anne – well, maybe she foresaw this too. She might have woven in something to help.'

Luna looked sceptical. 'I hope you've got a card number three.'

'Card number three is the big one,' I said. 'I don't think the marid possessing Vari wants us dead. It serves the sultan, yes. But every time we've faced it, it's chosen to interpret the sultan's orders in ways that don't involve killing anyone unless it has to. I had it in the Arcana Emporium for nearly ten years and all it did was make a contract with a new host every twelve months or so. Maybe it might be willing to make a contract now.'

'Well, it's a better idea than fighting it.'

I looked at Ji-yeong. 'How are you doing?'

'I don't think I'm getting my make-up out of my room.'

'Ji-yeong.'

'What?'

'I know you weren't especially close to Sagash or Aether,' I said. 'But you're allowed to be upset.'

Ji-yeong was silent for a second. 'I knew something like this could happen one day,' she said. 'I just didn't think I'd be on the other side.'

Diviner curiosity is a funny thing. Even this close to the end, I couldn't help but wonder what was keeping Ji-yeong at our side. It couldn't be just self-interest or she'd have deserted long ago. Was it really just that she didn't like to lose? Or did she see something in us, a way of living that was new to her?

Our footsteps echoed off the walls around as we approached the keep. I felt another barely perceptible shudder go through the castle. It was hard to be sure, but it felt a tiny bit stronger than the last one.

The double doors of the keep were closed. Luna covered us while Ji-yeong and I pulled them open to reveal a long corridor floored and walled in black stone. It ran straight as an arrow as far as the eye could see, disappearing into darkness. Small ominous-looking slits were spaced along the walls at regular intervals.

'This is a trap,' Luna stated.

'Barbican corridor,' Ji-yeong said. 'Wards are meant to kill intruders. At least when they're working.'

I walked in. Behind me, Ji-yeong cast a light spell and Luna clicked on a torch. The green and white lights cast two shadows from my body, bobbing and wavering as we moved, stretching out into the darkness. Our footsteps continued to echo, three times as loud, the sound bouncing up and down the tight corridor. The air seemed to grow colder the further we went. This was Sagash's lair, the heart of his power. For decades he'd schemed, seeking to become immortal. Now he was dust and ashes, but his presence remained, dark and brooding.

A door appeared out of the darkness. My twin shadows bobbed, drawing together. As they touched each other, I stopped.

Ji-yeong halted just behind my left shoulder, and I could feel her staring at the door. 'He's there,' she said.

'Luck, be with us now,' Luna said quietly.

Ji-yeong took a breath. 'Master Verus?' she said formally. 'These past few days, I've been learning my limits. A marid is outside them.'

'Fair.' I turned to face Ji-yeong. 'It's been a dangerous road, and you've walked it well. Once you get back to London, if you need anything, use that phone I gave you and ask for November. For now, our agreement's at an end. You're free to go.'

Ji-yeong hesitated, then nodded. I looked at Luna. 'Ready?'

Luna bit her lip. 'Let's do it.'

I pushed open the doors.

The space within was wide and square. Lamps along the walls cast a feeble glow, swallowed by black stone. The room looked like a final defensive position to hold any intruders; beyond were corridors to the left and right, and a central staircase at the back.

Variam stood at the centre. His black clothes and turban faded into the shadows, making him look like a disembodied face floating in darkness. Luna and I started forward, me holding the *sovnya*, Luna holding her whip. Ji-yeong hung back. Variam watched us approach, hands clasped behind him.

'Halt,' Variam ordered once we were ten feet in.

Luna and I stopped. 'Marid,' I said.

'Host.'

'I have a matter to discuss with your ruler.'

'Yes.'

I could almost forget that Variam was possessed while looking at him, but as soon as he opened his mouth, the illusion broke. His voice was dissonant, inhuman. 'Will you let me pass?' I asked.

'You are to be admitted,' the marid said. 'Others are forbidden.'

'I'm not here for Anne,' Luna said clearly. 'I'm here for you.'

'You are neither bearer nor host.' Variam's gaze rested on Luna, dark and clear. 'This bearer wishes you no harm, cursed one, but should you force a conflict, all your fortune will not spare your life.'

'We don't want a conflict,' I said. 'But neither do you.'

Variam looked at me without expression.

'You lived under my roof a long time,' I said. 'Ten years next January. If you really wanted humanity destroyed or subjugated, you've had plenty of chances. I don't think you want this war any more than we do. "Only law is eternal" – that was what you told me, wasn't it? I think the only reason you're obeying the sultan's orders is out of a sense of obligation.'

'Allegiance binds as a contract,' Variam replied. 'Desires crumble and fade. Only the eternal remains.'

'Then how about this?' I said. 'I make a contract with you. A new contract, with a clean slate. What you're doing right now, using Variam . . . it's against the principles you've always followed. Back in my shop, you'd take victims, but you'd always give them a choice. Vari didn't get a choice. He was taken against his will.' I looked at Variam. 'So?'

The marid studied me for a moment. 'No.'

My heart sank. That answer had been final and certain. 'Why? Is it because I'm your host? You can't grant wishes to me?'

'No.'

'Then what? Tell me!'

'A contract is of the future,' the marid said in that weird dissonant voice. 'Both promise, and price. But you, Mage Verus, have no future with which to bargain. For you, what is, is what must be.'

I stared at Variam. He didn't move, and as I looked at the futures I saw that there was nothing I could say to change his mind.

I thought about the focus in my hand, the fateweaver in my arm. I didn't know if it could banish the marid, and I didn't think I'd survive another trip into Elsewhere. But I had no other ideas.

Screw it. I took a step forward, my left hand tightening around the lattice. Battle plans and tactics began to flow through my mind. I needed to—

'No!' Luna said.

I stopped. Luna stepped up beside me, and as she did the silver mist of her curse brightened, glowing in my sight. 'He may not have a future,' Luna said, her voice sharp and commanding. 'But I do. You lived in the Arcana Emporium when Alex owned it. Well, now it's passed to me. I'll offer you the same deal. Leave Variam, return to the monkey's paw and the Emporium. You can take your victims, as long as they're willing. One per year, no more. Leave us in peace, keep to those terms, and I'll let you use the shop for as long as it's mine.'

'I am commanded to stand guard,' the marid said.

Luna nodded towards the stairs. 'No one but Alex to be admitted, right? Fine. I won't go up there, and I won't let anyone besides Alex from our group go up there either. You have my word.'

The marid paused. I felt the futures shift, and hope leapt within me. *It's actually thinking about it.*

Luna's curse blazed like the sun, so bright it was hard to look at. 'This violates neither command nor allegiance,' the marid mused. 'There is no contradiction.'

Luna stood very still, her curse flaring around her. I held my breath.

'When the shop passes on, you will find another to fulfil your obligation,' the marid said. It studied Luna with those unblinking dark eyes. 'Fail, and I will take both this bearer, and you.'

Luna hesitated for a long moment. 'Agreed.'

The marid looked at me. 'You relinquish the position of host?'

'I do,' I said.

'Step forward.'

Luna did. The marid let her approach; she stopped within arm's reach.

'The contract is offered,' the marid said. It held out a

hand to Luna; resting on Variam's palm was the blue and white cylinder of the monkey's paw.

Luna shifted her whip from her right hand to her left. She reached out for the monkey's paw and her hand met Variam's, the blue-white cylinder forming a link between them.

The marid spoke one final time through Variam's lips, and this time its voice was deeper, louder. 'Done.'

The word echoed around the chamber, growing louder: *done-done-done-DONE-DONE*. I felt a snap of power, like a thunderclap without sound. Every light in the chamber went dark, then flicked back on again.

The light went out of Variam's eyes. His eyes slid closed and he slumped to the floor.

Luna staggered backwards. The silver mist around her shrank, fading to a sliver. Luna bent forward with her hands on her knees, breathing hard.

'Holy shit,' I said. 'You actually made that work.'

Luna gave a shaky laugh. I wasn't sure she had the breath to talk.

Variam was lying unconscious on the floor and he wasn't getting up, but he didn't seem hurt. The monkey's paw was lying where it had fallen from his grip. Luna bent and picked it up.

As she rose, I glimpsed Luna's face, side-lit by the lights, and caught my breath. There was something in her expression I'd never seen before, something distant that spoke of knowledge and the burden of old choices. For a moment, I felt as though I were seeing Luna as she'd look in ten or twenty years. She didn't look like an apprentice, or a young woman. She looked like a . . .

. . . *Mage.*

I blinked and the moment was gone. Luna stared at the monkey's paw, then shoved it into her pocket and looked down at Variam. 'He's not getting up, is he?'

I turned my head and called back towards the entrance. 'Ji-yeong?'

Ji-yeong stepped out from behind the doors. For a while back there, she'd considered leaving. I'd felt the moment she'd decided to stay. 'Would you mind?' I asked.

'You want me to carry your luggage now?' Ji-yeong said, then rolled her eyes. 'Oh, fine. It won't do my reputation any harm to come out with a marid host over my shoulder.' She walked to Variam.

'Well,' I told Luna. 'Guess this is goodbye.'

Luna looked tired but she stepped up next to me and reached out a hand. The last flickers of silver mist around her turned gold as she touched my forehead, and I felt something warm flow into me. 'Last blessing. Maybe it'll help.'

I nodded, turning to go. Beside us, Ji-yeong hauled Variam up in a fireman's carry.

'Alex,' Luna said.

I paused.

Luna was looking straight at me. 'You said last night that if you didn't come back, it might be for the best. Well, I didn't say this then, but I'm saying it now. If there's any way you can make it back from this – *any* way – you take it. You don't give up; you fight to the end. You understand?'

I nodded.

'Promise me,' Luna said. There was a fierceness in her eyes.

'I promise,' I told her.

Luna said nothing more. I took a last look at Variam, slung unconscious over Ji-yeong's shoulder, then walked away. As I entered the stairwell, I glanced back and saw Luna standing there in her battle armour. She was still watching, and as I looked she raised a hand in salute. Then my movement made the walls of the keep come between us and she was gone.

Memories came back as I climbed the keep's central stairwell. The last time I'd been here, I'd taken a route not so different from this, though back then it had been Sagash I'd come to see. Another of those tremors ran through the keep. Definitely stronger.

I listened in on the Council's tactical circuit; the evacuation was in full swing. I waited to confirm that the gates were still open and that Luna and Variam would be able to make it out, then switched it off. I didn't need the distraction.

From the feel of my shoulder, I could tell that the fateweaver had replaced it fully. Its tendrils must be deep into my chest. Well, it didn't really matter any more. I only needed to last long enough to make it into Elsewhere.

Sagash's personal quarters were connected directly to the stairs, a vault door leading off from the landing. A squad of jinn stood guarding it. Their gazes tracked me as I came up around the stairs.

I planted the *sovnya* at my feet and looked up at them. 'Move or die.'

The jinn stared down with malice in their eyes, but they parted. I climbed the stairs and marched through their ranks. None moved to stop me.

The door was massive, made of solid metal, and ajar. I heaved it open, then stepped through. It swung shut behind me with an echoing *boom*.

The room within was cylindrical, with a high gallery. Waiting for me on the far side was Anne.

19

Sagash's duelling arena had two levels: a raised balcony halfway to the ceiling, and a lower floor with a duelling ring marked on the stone. A set of iron stairs joined the two levels, and a door at the far end led into what had once been Sagash's laboratory.

Anne was on the upper level, bare forearms resting against the balcony rail, the pale skin of her legs and arms standing out against the darkness. This room had been where Anne's other self had been born. Perhaps today it would be where she'd meet her end.

'You summoned me, marid,' I told the sultan. 'I have come.'

The sultan studied me through Anne's eyes. 'I assume this is your work.'

'I'd call it more of a team effort. But I was co-ordinating, if that's what you're asking.'

While I spoke, most of my attention was on path-walking, my thoughts whirling with futures and attack plans. The focus was ready in my left hand. It should be able to stun her . . . if I got close.

I focused on the futures in which I interacted with Arachne's last gift, the black skater dress that Anne was wearing. I didn't know if Arachne had seen all the way ahead to this moment, but if she had, she might have modified the imbued item with a back door, some kind of hidden vulnerability that would let me close the distance. I knew it was a long shot. Dark Anne wasn't stupid – she'd have gone over that dress with a fine-tooth comb – but there was always the chance she might have missed something. I looked into the futures in which I channelled into the dress, evading the flashes of combat to the ones where I tried to activate it . . .

And my heart leapt. *There!* A latent spell, subtle and well-hidden. And one that could be triggered from range.

'You think too highly of yourself, human.' The scornful words of the jinn sounded jarring in Anne's soft voice. 'You believe conquering this hovel of a keep is a deed worthy of pride?'

'Sorry it doesn't meet your expectations,' I said. I narrowed my vision into the futures, carefully keeping any trace of excitement out of my voice. 'But look on the bright side. It's about to be destroyed anyway.'

'A suitable fate for the works of your kind.'

I found the future I was looking for, one where I dodged the jinn's attacks long enough to trigger the spell. I saw it activate, unfolding like a flower. It was powerful but almost impossible to detect, and I looked ahead eagerly to see what it would do. A paralysis effect, or a stun? Or – my hopes leapt – something that would banish the jinn altogether? I might not have to use Elsewhere at all. I could get out of here alive. I focused, my heart pounding. The futures parted and I finally got a clear look. It was a spell of . . .

. . . healing.

Some kind of healing effect designed to repair trauma to the mind and body.

It wasn't going to disable the jinn. In fact, from what I could see, it would actually make Anne slightly stronger.

I wanted to sigh. Well, I shouldn't have been surprised. Nothing else today had been easy, why should I expect this to be?

'And were that not enough,' the sultan continued, 'you have required me to go through this whole demeaning process again. Who knows how long it will take to find a new shadow realm and a new set of suitable hosts?' It frowned at me. 'In a more just age, I would have the time to punish you appropriately.'

There was one good thing about listening to the marid: there was no way I could hear its words and still have the slightest illusion that I was talking to Anne. Looking at her face still made my heart twist, but as long as I concentrated on the futures and on what I was hearing, I could forget that I was facing the woman I loved.

I put the dress out of my mind. 'You *did* say you wanted to talk to me,' I told the marid. 'Did you have anything to say, or shall we just skip to the part where we kill each other?'

'Very well,' the marid said. 'You are to become the new bearer for the entity which in your language you call the Sun That Brings Death.'

I blinked. 'Um, I'm honoured. Mind if I ask what I've done to deserve this?'

'You have done nothing to deserve this,' the jinn stated. 'But this host, for reasons that do not interest me, would prefer that you survive. Your opposition bolsters her resistance, which is an irritation that distracts me from more important matters. As such, I have decided that you shall serve at my side. Punishment for your crimes against my person shall be deferred.'

'Well,' I said. 'I'm not quite sure what to say.'

'I have no interest in anything you might say.'

'Okay, here's the thing,' I said. 'The British Council have really not given me many reasons to like them, and the Dark mages looking to replace them aren't any better. So I came in here figuring that I'd at least try talking things out. But honestly, it's taken less than five minutes of listening to you to make me realise that no matter *how* bad the Light and Dark mages of this country are, they're—'

'Silence,' the marid said.

I sighed. *So much for talking.*

The marid pointed to the walkway in front of where it stood. 'Approach.'

I paused, then shrugged. 'All right.'

I walked around the gallery. Another tremor went through the keep, making the balcony sway under my feet. 'Halt,' the marid said once I was close enough.

I did.

'Remove your clothes.'

'Okay, I know you're possessing the one person who can actually get away with telling me that, but I prefer a little more romance.'

'Do not test my patience.'

I looked back at Anne – the jinn – and laughed.

The marid waited for me to finish, and when it next spoke there was a flat, dangerous tone to its voice. 'Your life hangs by a thread.'

I looked at the marid, my smile fading. 'Oh, I'm not laughing at you. It's just . . . you have any idea how long I spent coming up with plans to get this close? And it turns out, all I needed to do was follow your orders.'

'You expect to use that weapon against me?'

'This?' I said, lifting the *sovnya*. 'No, you'd kill me in a heartbeat. But here's the thing about humans. We don't have the powers you marids do, but working together, we can do some pretty impressive things.'

'None of you can—' the marid began.

I put every last bit of power into the disruption focus on my left hand and fired.

An impenetrable black-green shield flashed up around Anne. But the spell in the Council focus hadn't been designed to attack the subject's body, and as it struck the shield it flowed into it, the black wires of the jinn's magic acting like conduits into Anne's mind. Anne's head jerked back and she fell.

Ever since I'd started walking towards the marid, I'd been using the fateweaver, subtly altering the futures to bring about a natural thinning of reality. Now I threw out my hand and channelled through the dreamstone, forming a gate to Elsewhere. It shimmered into existence, ten times faster than normal.

Anne was already recovering. She was on her hands and knees, and now she looked up, life magic flaring. But I hadn't created the gate vertically; I'd formed it horizontally, at her feet.

Anne dropped through. With three running strides, I leapt after her.

Normally when I step into Elsewhere, it's hardly any different from using a gate to travel to our world. You could almost believe you've stepped into the same place you came from. It's subtle and quiet.

Entering Elsewhere this time was neither of those things.

As soon as Anne dropped through the portal, Elsewhere went mad. The ground and walls shredded away, the fragments warping through an impossible range of colours, violet and cerulean and deepest black. Space shimmered and twisted.

The gate that I could normally hold open for minutes tore itself apart in seconds. Anne was falling away from me and with an effort of will I closed the distance, but there was nothing to land on. All around was a spinning kaleidoscope of colours.

This had to be something to do with Anne. I caught hold of her arm; her eyes were closed but her body was blurred, vibrating, as if pulling in three different directions. I tried to shape the space around us, land us somewhere familiar—

And suddenly my feet were on solid ground. The swirl of colours vanished.

We were back in Anne's Elsewhere. I was crouched on a plaza of smooth obsidian, stretching out around me to the high walls that blocked out all but the upper branches of the forest behind. The tower loomed over us, reaching towards the roiling sky. Storm-clouds thrashed and boiled in the heavens above, but the winds didn't touch the air around me.

Anne was lying at my feet, unconscious. Or at least her body was.

Dark Anne and Light Anne were facing each other on the plaza, shouting at each other, their words blending together so that I couldn't understand what they were saying. Their faces were twisted in fury, perfectly alike; the only way I could tell them apart was that one was wearing black and the other white. When I enter

Elsewhere, I do it as a single entity, body and mind. Apparently with Anne, things were a little more complicated.

Thunder rumbled in the distance. The jinn had been torn away, but it had already recovered and it was coming for us. 'Both of you shut up!' I shouted.

The two Annes turned on me with identical looks of anger.

They're getting worse. I could feel the jinn drawing closer; we didn't have long. 'Settle this later,' I told them. 'Your marid is coming and it's not in a good mood. We are going to bind it and that means you two need to work together.'

'No,' both Annes said in echo.

'I wasn't asking,' I told them. I pulled the ring from my pocket and held it up. 'You do this, or I die and the two of you are enslaved for ever.'

'I can't work with her—'

'This is her fault—'

'I SAID SHUT UP!' I shouted. 'All of this insane crap started because the two of you couldn't deal with each other! Now once that marid is gone you can do whatever the hell you like, but right now you ARE going to work together or I swear to God, before I die, the last thing I do will be to figure out which one of you helped least and put the other one in charge!'

Light Anne and Dark Anne glared but didn't argue. I knelt down next to Anne's body, placed the ring on her stomach and clasped her hands over it. The first faint trails of mist were starting to rise from her skin. 'One on each side,' I ordered, pointing. 'We're only getting one shot at this.'

Surprisingly, both Annes obeyed. Far away I could hear something approaching, the distant crashing sound of falling trees.

Ever since I'd stepped into Elsewhere I'd sensed a change in the *sovnya*. I turned to look.

It felt as though I were seeing the weapon for the first time. On one level it looked as it had in the outside world, a long, slender polearm with a black haft and a curving blade. But overlaid upon that was another form, something larger and brighter and more real, something that towered over me from more than twice my height. It was sculpted of black iron that burned like fire, lined with claw-like barbs hooked to rip and tear. The blade was almost as tall as I was, a monstrous thing of twisted metal, etched with glowing letters in a language that stung my eyes. Where the blade met the haft was an eye, yellow and slitted like a cat's, that blinked and roved. Just to look at the weapon was to feel a hunger, a void that could never be filled.

I pulled my eyes away with a shudder. *I've been wielding THAT?*

The *sovnya* didn't seem to notice my reaction. Its attention was turned away, towards the approaching jinn. And that was how it had always been, hadn't it? All it'd cared about was killing, and all I'd cared about was what it could do.

Maybe what I saw looking at the weapon was how Light mages saw me.

I put it out of my mind. The thunder of the marid was growing louder, and I could see a disturbance in the clouds. 'The marid will come at us with everything it's got,' I told the two Annes. 'It can't back down, not now.'

I pointed to Light Anne. 'You have the strength. You never accepted the marid's contract. That gives you power over it.' I pointed to Dark Anne. 'You have the knowledge. You worked with the marid, used its magic.' I looked from one to the other. 'The two of you together have the power to bind it. But only if you commit absolutely. Falter, waver, and . . .' I turned away from the Annes and took a grip on the *sovnya*. 'Get ready.'

The obsidian beneath my feet was shuddering. The crashing of falling trees was a constant roar, mixing with the thunder of the storm. I could feel the *sovnya* trembling with anticipation. There was a vortex spinning in the clouds, glowing with a sickly yellow light. It drew closer until it was just outside the walls.

A towering figure materialised beneath the vortex.

I kicked off the ground, soaring upwards. I couldn't *see* the jinn, not really – my eyes slid away from it, and at some level I knew it was for my own protection, that seeing it fully and clearly would tear something open inside my mind. All I had was an impression, a looming giant with legs like mountains and arms that blotted out the sky. Its steps shook the earth, and its gaze burned like fire, but as I flew up to meet it there was no fear in me, and the *sovnya* in my hands needed no guidance at all. Bloodlust and exultation filled me as the *sovnya* tore into the marid's enormous form.

And the marid flinched. Unfathomably powerful as it was, it could still be hurt, and it was facing a weapon created to be its living nemesis. A fiery gash opened up on the jinn's body as I came around for another blow.

Far below, at the foot of the tower, I heard Dark Anne's voice, ringing out above the storm. 'By my will and power, our contract is ended! I cast you out from my body and mind, and I bind you to your prison in Suleiman's name!'

The marid aimed some kind of attack at me. I couldn't see it and didn't know what it was, but I knew what I could do and somehow I managed to dodge. Behind me, the top half of the tower disintegrated into dust. I struck the marid once more and felt it recoil from the *sovnya*'s dark flame.

Below me, Dark Anne shouted again. 'Twice I bind you! This is my place of power, and you are not welcome here! Be gone, and be bound to your prison in Suleiman's name!'

I could sense something building below, a wave of power. The marid sensed it too and it turned down and away, reaching for Anne's body where it lay helpless on the ground.

I dived in, bringing around the *sovnya*, but this time the marid was ready. Another attack came swinging at me, ponderous and massive. I tried to get out of the way, but it was like trying to dodge a falling tree and it caught me a glancing blow.

My vision fuzzed out. Thoughts frayed and scattered; the jinn's attack was striking both my body and mind and I could feel a horrible *thinning* sensation, as though I was fraying away thread by thread. I clung desperately to my thoughts, my feelings, everything from my memories of Anne to the fight in the shadow realm; I squeezed the *sovnya* in a death grip. For an endless moment, I teetered between existence and the void.

Gradually, I caught my balance. It was like wavering on the very edge of a cliff and pulling yourself back.

Sight and hearing returned and I realised that both my armour and the *sovnya* were blazing with power; both looked weakened but they'd shared the blow, anchoring me. I looked down.

Below me was the kind of scene that you remember for the rest of your life. The marid was looming over the remains of the walls and tower, a titan of darkness, so vast that it seemed the mountains themselves had risen in anger. It was leaning downwards, its attention fixed, bringing all of its crushing power to bear – but where that power met the earth was a sphere of brilliant white-green light. Anne's body lay unmoving on the ground, but Anne's Elsewhere-self stood in front of it, her hand raised up in a command to halt. And the marid had halted. That globe of light looked like a marble caught beneath a giant's hammer, but it was holding the marid back.

I took it all in in a single glance, then dived towards the marid like a thunderbolt.

The *sovnya* flared with a terrible joy. It tore through the marid like a lance, cutting through the jinn's outer self and into its core.

The marid screamed, a noise beyond imagining. Walls cracked and trees shattered, and it reared back in agony.

Dark Anne's voice rose up one last time, somehow audible over the scream. 'Three times I bind you! By my power, by our power, by the strength of this land and earth and life! Be bound to your prison in Suleiman's name!' She drew a breath and when she spoke again it was with vengeful anger. 'Get out and never come back!'

Power boomed with a clap of thunder. The marid reached down, trying to blot us from existence, but something else reached up to seize it, pulling into a vortex. The marid was drawn down into the ring, shrinking. I heard it scream, an awful sound of rage and hatred, as it was pulled in, smaller and smaller until it was a sphere of impenetrable black.

The sphere imploded and a shockwave burst out. The debris from the battle was flung away and every remaining tree had its leaves stripped from its branches in an echoing *boom*.

And suddenly everything was silent.

I sank from the sky, touching down on the plaza. The obsidian floor had been scoured mirror-smooth. Anne lay where I'd placed her, eyes still closed, hands still folded over her stomach, wisps of light trailing from her skin and dress. But the item in her hands . . . I couldn't see the ring beneath her fingers, but I could feel it. It was the same feeling I'd once sensed from the monkey's paw.

The marid was bound again.

Movement made me look up. Light Anne and Dark Anne were getting to their feet. They'd both been flung away, but they didn't seem hurt and as they recovered they began walking back towards me. But as they drew closer to me, they drew closer to each other, and they shot each other looks and slowed until both came to a stop, the three of us forming a triangle fifteen feet on each side.

'We actually did it,' Dark Anne said. For once she didn't sound flippant or angry.

'It's really over,' Light Anne said.

'No,' I said. I looked between the two Annes. 'There's one last thing.'

Both Annes' faces changed. 'I won't—' one began.

'I can't—' the other said.

I spoke over them both. 'Be quiet.'

They frowned at me.

'You do not get a vote on this,' I said. 'William Shakespeare himself could not find the words to express how tired I am of the both of you. I have journeyed through war and blood and death to reach you here, and after all I have sacrificed I am not going to let you pick yourselves up and do the same stupid shit all over again.'

'We're different people, Alex,' Light Anne said.

'You can't shove us together,' Dark Anne said.

'For any other two people, you'd be right. But you're not two people. You're *one* person, and the only reason you stay apart is because the two of you keep it that way.' I gestured. 'Look around.'

Dark Anne and Light Anne did as I said, frowning. The walls around the tower had been rebuilt, sheer and tall once again. So had the tower itself. Hardly any time had gone by, but it was as though the battle with the jinn had never happened.

'You told me, when we first met,' I said to Dark Anne. 'The very first words out of your mouth. You said those walls were to keep things in. But that was only half true, wasn't it? You fight just as hard to keep her out.'

'Can't we just go home?' Light Anne said.

'In fact, you two are *so* split that when I take you into Elsewhere, you can't even occupy your own body.' I gestured back to where Anne's body lay, its eyes still closed. 'Which is bad for a lot of reasons, but right now, the most relevant one is that it means you can't defend yourself very well.'

'From what?' Dark Anne said sharply.

I met her eyes, then raised one hand.

It was Dr Shirland who'd given me the clue to figure it out. Anne's two halves weren't different people: they were just two parts of her that wanted incompatible things. On its own, that was nothing special. But just at the age where Anne should have been dealing with that, when she should have been coming to understand herself, Sagash had captured her and taken her to his castle, and he'd hurt her badly enough that she couldn't handle the things she'd had to do.

So Anne had turned to Elsewhere, sealing off the parts of herself she couldn't accept. Aggression, self-interest, short-term desire – she'd poured them all into this tower, into her other self. But Elsewhere couldn't actually change her into a different person; the most it could do was keep the two halves of her personality apart. The two Annes weren't meant to be separate – they were drawn together like opposite poles of a magnet, and the only reason they hadn't merged long ago was because they were *both* using Elsewhere to maintain the barrier that held the other at arm's length.

And if that barrier was created in Elsewhere, it could be destroyed in Elsewhere.

Realisation flashed into Dark Anne's eyes. 'Wait—'

The walls and the tower were a part of Anne. It had been easy to spot, once I'd thought to look for it. They existed both outside her, and within the mind of the girl behind me. I focused my will, took a deep breath and prayed with all my heart that this was going to work.

Then I snapped my fingers and wiped the barrier from existence.

Both Annes cried out in shock. The tower and the

walls burst, shattering into a million pieces that flared into nothingness. The two Annes were pulled towards each other, their cries ringing out in stereo, their bodies thinning and fading. As they did, Anne's Elsewhere dissolved around us, and both Anne and I fell into nothingness.

It was only for a moment, then we were standing on stone. We were in the Elsewhere-reflection of Sagash's duelling arena, the walls shadowed and grim, holding the echo of all those that had died there. Anne's body was lying at my feet, still unconscious. Of Anne's light and dark halves, there was no sign.

There was no more time. My armour and Anne's dress had given us some protection, but the wisps of light rising from Anne's skin were dangerously bright and I was starting to get the airy, too-light feeling that I recognised as a warning of approaching death. I shouldered the *sovnya*, lifted Anne, and channelled through the dreamstone, feeling for the thin patch where I'd brought Elsewhere together with the castle. A portal opened and I jumped back into the shadow realm.

20

Sight and sound crashed into me as I came back down in the shadow realm, weight and light and feeling. I was standing in Sagash's duelling ring with Anne in my arms and I looked down at her, my heart in my throat. I didn't know how much damage I'd done to her mind, but her chest rose and fell and that meant she was still alive, at least for now. Luna and the others might already be gone; I had to get Anne out of here before—

A terrible pain stabbed through my chest.

I gasped, falling to one knee. For a moment I thought I'd been shot, and I scanned the room, searching for enemies. Nothing. Then why—

Oh.

Klara's words from a week and a half ago echoed through my head: '*. . . your right lung will be transmuted, followed by your heart. This will cause them both to shut down . . .*'

The pain was like nothing I'd ever felt. No, once before – that time in the deep shadow realm, when something that looked like Anne had stopped my heart. It was like a muscle cramp through my lungs, one that didn't stop but got worse and worse. My vision was greying out with the pain and I was feeling light-headed; I was getting a tiny trickle of air, but it wasn't enough.

I kept trying to breathe but it wasn't working, and deep down, I knew it wasn't going to. Klara had warned me this would happen, warned that if I kept using the fateweaver it'd kill me. I hadn't listened, and now I was paying the price.

I couldn't see any more. I'd dropped Anne and the *sovnya*; dimly I was aware that I was lying on my side. The pain in my chest was burning agony, and I found myself wishing it would be over soon. Diviners get to experience a lot of ways to die and suffocation is one of the bad ones, but at least it's quick. A little more and it would be over.

Over . . .

Faces swam up through my memories. My mother, her eyes dark and intense, fingers gripping my arm as she told me *you come back*. Luna, making me promise to fight to the end.

Something rose up inside me with a snarl. *No.*

I reached inside myself, to the fateweaver. It was killing me, but it was still mine. I found the future I needed and *forced* it through, willing my lungs to expand.

Air flooded into my chest with a gasp. It burned, but it was life, and I pulled it in and out as I forced my own lungs to breathe. My muscles did half the work, the fateweaver the other. Air kept cycling through my body, and as I opened my eyes the ceiling above me swam back into view.

Up. Get up. Painfully I rolled over, getting onto hands and knees. Anne was next to me, lying on her back on the stone.

And next to Anne was Hermes. The blink fox yipped at me.

I'm okay, I told Hermes through the dreamstone. I couldn't manage speaking yet. I controlled my breaths, getting them to a steady rhythm until I had enough oxygen again. It was a bizarre, unpleasant feeling, like giving CPR to your own chest. Pain flared in my body with each breath, but compared with a moment ago, it was nothing.

Hermes yipped again. *I'm coming*, I thought, and reached for the *sovnya*.

Hermes shrank down, his tail curling between his legs.

It's all right, I told him. *I won't let it . . . hurt . . . you . . .*

I trailed off. Hermes wasn't looking at the *sovnya*. He was looking behind me, up towards the door.

'Hello, Alex,' a voice said.

It was a very familiar voice.

Hermes blinked away, air rushing in to fill the space as he vanished. I took a deep, mechanical breath, pulling air into my lungs and pushing it out. Then using the *sovnya*, I hauled myself up.

Richard was standing on the gallery, just inside the door by which I'd entered.

A tremor ran through the shadow realm. I felt the stones shift under my feet; trails of dust came trickling from the ceiling. 'Well,' Richard said. He began walking, circling the gallery. He reached the stairs and descended, shoes ringing on the metal steps. 'It seems I missed quite a show.'

My eyes tracked Richard all the way down.

Richard stepped off the stairs onto my level and I took a step sideways to place myself between him and Anne. 'I see you put my ring to good use,' Richard said with a nod towards Anne.

'I was wondering why you gave it up so easily.'

Richard came to a stop, watching me pleasantly from just outside the duelling ring. He seemed in no hurry.

'Why did you let me have the Council's weapon too?' I asked when Richard didn't speak. 'Just feeling generous?'

'You seemed to need it more than I did,' Richard said with a shrug. 'No need to be greedy.'

'You never did value possessions for their own sake.'

Richard inclined his head. There was a pause.

'Did you plan this from the beginning?' I asked.

'Plan all *this* from the beginning?' Richard said, raising his eyebrows. 'Alex, I'm flattered you believe I possess that level of foresight, but you and Anne between you have managed to create such utter chaos that my long-term plans were wrecked weeks ago. You personally have forced me to abandon my entire course of action and start from scratch no less than twice in the past twenty-four *hours*. I don't know who could have possibly anticipated all of the absurd things you've ended up doing. I certainly didn't.'

Another tremor went through the keep, accompanied by another trickle of dust. The battle with the marid had fried my comm focus and I couldn't sense the Council forces anywhere. Richard and I were alone. 'Glad I'm making a difference.'

'Oh, trust me, no one is going to question *that*. I don't know whether to put it down to desperation or sheer stupidity, but dealing with the two of you has been like trying to steer a wild elephant. When Anne was possessed by the sultan, I really thought things might settle down, but you've been quite determined to take up the slack. Take that assault on my forces. You have no idea how much work it took me to persuade Nimbus that a head-on confrontation between my adepts and his Keepers would be too costly. And then just when I've almost found a way to resolve things neatly, what do you do? You assassinate him and send the Keepers in anyway.' Richard gave an exasperated sigh. 'I suppose I only have myself to blame. I did ask you to protect the girl. I just didn't expect you to take it quite so seriously.'

'And let me guess,' I said. 'This is where you take Anne and that marid and start the whole thing all over again.'

'I'll admit, it's tempting,' Richard said. 'To bring Anne to account for her various betrayals, if nothing else. But no. Anne may be powerful and she may be an ideal jinn host, but if I'd known from the beginning just how much sheer aggravation she would cause, I would have shot her myself. Between her conscious self stubbornly refusing to co-operate, and her shadow self wreaking mayhem, she is the most *irritating* girl I have ever had to deal with. Honestly, I have no idea how you put up with her. I'd have thought you could do better.'

'You hang around with Rachel, Crystal and Vihaela, and you're giving *me* a hard time about my choice in women?'

'Well, there's no accounting for taste,' Richard said. 'In any case, take Anne and be done with her. Quite frankly, I'll be happy if I never see her again.'

I didn't move. I knew Richard hadn't come here just to tell me that.

'The ring, however, is another matter.' Richard held out his hand. 'If you don't mind?'

I looked at him.

'I would really appreciate it if you don't fight me on this one, Alex.'

'Do you have a new host lined up? Or are you going to do it yourself for a change?'

'I'm sure you'll find out sooner or later.'

'No, I don't think I will.'

A shudder went through the keep. I heard a cracking,

groaning sound, and felt the floor tremble as something collapsed far below. 'This strikes me as neither the time nor the place,' Richard said.

'Maybe you should have thought of that before triggering that isolation ward,' I said. 'And actually, I'd say that the middle of yet another one of your giant destructive screw-ups is a *very* appropriate place.'

'For heaven's sake, Alex,' Richard said in exasperation. 'The last time we had one of these conversations, you made it clear that the girl was your sticking point. That you were doing all this for her. Well, you've got her, and you even have enough time to spirit her away somewhere safe before you finally fall over dead. Your objective has been achieved.'

I nodded.

'So can you please explain why you are standing in my way?'

'One question first,' I said. 'Why?'

'Why am I here? Why am I talking to you? Why do I—?'

'Why any of it,' I said. 'What was it for?'

'If you can't figure that out by *now* . . .'

'Oh, I know what your plan was,' I said. 'Control the marid, make an army of jinn mages, take over the country. But what was the point? Even before this war, you were one of the most powerful Dark mages in Britain. You had a mansion filled with servants, apprentices vying to be your successor. Wealth, status, women – anything you could have wanted, you only had to snap your fingers. But somehow none of that was enough.'

'I did have such ambitions in my younger days,' Richard said. 'But the trappings of success grow stale.'

'Then what doesn't? More power?'

'Essentially.'

'When does it stop?' I asked. 'Say you'd succeeded, taken over the country, then what? Would you have built a bigger army, aimed for other countries? All of Europe? The world?'

'The world seems a little ambitious,' Richard said. 'But as long as it works . . .'

'You still haven't given me an answer.'

'Honestly, Alex,' Richard said. 'Look at anyone who rises to the top. The Senior Council, the presidents and prime ministers of the modern age, the kings and warlords of olden times. Why do you think they do it? To change the world? Power doesn't need a purpose: power is its own purpose. It is the only goal that has value in itself, because it is the means by which all other goals are achieved.'

'So you're saying it's never enough. There's always more.'

'Alex, I've tried to be patient with you. I have answered your questions and explained my reasons. However, my patience is not unlimited and I do not intend to stand around debating you until this shadow realm collapses. Give me the ring.'

'No.'

Richard rolled his eyes. 'You're as bad as she is.'

'For someone who spends so much time manipulating people, you have some real blind spots about how they work.'

'Enlighten me, then,' Richard said with a sigh. 'You've gone to all these extraordinary lengths to save the girl lying on the floor behind you. And against all odds, you've done it. You've won! All you have to do is hand over an item – one which was not even yours to begin with, I should add – and that would be the end of it. But instead you've decided to turn around just before the finish line.'

'Well, here's the thing,' I said. 'I don't think that *would* be the end of it. I'm sure if I hand over this ring you'll go on your way quite happily. But sooner or later, in a year or five years or ten years, you'll pop up with a new host and a new army and start all over again. Because just like you said, it's never enough. You'll never be satisfied with what you have, and that means you'll keep coming back again and again until someone stops you.'

'I remember a boy who cared nothing for others. Who was quite happy to let them fight, while he followed his own path.'

'I haven't been that boy for a long time. And the biggest reason for that is you. You're more willing to get your hands dirty than the Light Council, but you know one thing you and the Council have in common? You both like to push the dirty jobs off onto someone else. And a lot of that time, that someone has been me. You see it from on high as a chess game between kings and princes. But when I see it from ground level it's a lot harder to ignore the costs.' I looked Richard in the eyes. 'You have left a trail of death and destruction and misery everywhere you have gone. Some of the people you trampled chose to fight you; some were just unlucky enough to be in your way. But no matter what, every part of the world is a worse place once you've been there. You were willing to start a war that could have brought a new age of darkness, all to get one over on the Council.'

'You were the one who decided freeing that marid was a good idea,' Richard said. 'Though I suppose you did eventually clean up your own mess.'

'But worse than any of that,' I said, 'is that you lead *other* people into evil. You built up that army of adepts with promises and honeyed words, and led them to their deaths while you walked away. You started a war between mages and adepts and a whole lot of regular people, most of whom had probably never even heard of you but who just happened to get caught in the crossfire. And if you want the best example, look at your own apprentices. We were supposed to be your legacy, weren't we? The proof of your greatness. Well, take a look how we turned out. Tobruk, dead. Shireen, dead. Rachel, insane and dead. I'm the only one left, and I'm willing to risk my life to stop you. "By their fruits ye shall know them", isn't it? What does that say about you?' I looked straight at Richard. 'You're worse than a warlord. You're a *bad teacher*.'

Richard's smile slipped. In the seventeen years I'd known him, it was the first time I'd seen him genuinely insulted. 'I gave you everything. I *made* you.'

'Oh, all those things you gave me! You made me a Dark apprentice at seventeen, a criminal at eighteen, a slave at nineteen and a murderer by twenty. Every one of the worst things in my life traces right back to that day you walked up to me on the school playground.'

'You were nothing when I found you!' Richard snapped. 'Everything you learnt, you learnt from me! You think I haven't noticed you copying my tricks?' He took a breath, seemed to calm himself. 'Well. I suppose I shouldn't be surprised. But I did expect some level of gratitude.'

'*Gratitude?*' My voice cracked as I finally lost my temper. 'You self-satisfied arsehole. You have *never* taken responsibility for the shit you've done, not once! Even when your jinn nearly wrecked the whole country you blamed it on me!' I tightened my grip on the *sovnya* to stop my fingers from trembling. 'I am *sick* of you, sick of you coming back over and over again to ruin my life. Now I'll make *you* an offer. You turn around and walk away, and you never go near me or Anne or this ring as long as you live. Because if I ever see you again, it'll be the last time.'

Silence greeted my words. Another shudder went through the keep, and I heard the rumble of falling stone. Richard looked at me without expression. 'You don't want to do this, Alex.'

'I have never wanted to do anything more.'

'Stand against me,' Richard said, 'and after I kill you, I'll kill her.'

'You don't know as much about the future as you think.'

'Look, Alex,' Richard said. 'Let's—' He stopped suddenly as his expression changed.

There. I'd been wondering when Richard would see this coming. No more reason to hold back. I flooded the futures with static.

Instantly my precognition was blanked out. When you can use divination all the time, you grow to rely on it. I barely even think of it as magic any more; it's just another sense, like sight or hearing. Now instead of seeing Richard and the room around me in four-dimensional clarity, all the woulds and coulds and mights, my vision dwindled down to only the present, with everything beyond nothing but a blank void. Hard to believe normal people lived like this all the time.

But it was my choice, and that made a difference. I looked at Richard.

'Very impressive,' Richard said tightly. 'Did you learn that from Helikaon or Alaundo?'

I gave him a cold smile. 'Use your divination and find out.'

There was a new wariness in Richard's eyes. *He's afraid.* For the first time in probably years, Richard couldn't see what was coming. He was still deadly dangerous, but his best defence had been stripped from him. 'Last chance to walk away,' I said.

Richard paused. If I could still see the future, I knew that I'd be seeing the shifting strands of him making a decision. Then his expression became flat and unreadable. 'As you wish.'

Sagash's arena was still. The tremors had fallen silent, and the two of us faced each other across the duelling ring.

'So,' I said. 'What'll—?'

A thread-thin black wire flashed out towards me.

Even without my precognition, I'd seen it coming. I knew Richard, and I knew how he fought – a killing attack as the opening move. I brought up the *sovnya*, channelling through the fateweaver, and the black wire curved in to strike the *sovnya*'s blade, the weapon flashing red as it ate the jinn's magic.

I charged.

Richard struck again but I swerved as I ran; the attack missed and I felt a flash of triumph. He wasn't used to fighting without his divination. Richard started a third attack but I stabbed with the *sovnya* and he had to abort his movement to throw up a black shield.

I pressed in, swinging the *sovnya* in tight, deadly arcs. I had to control my breathing through the fateweaver and maintain the *optasia* at the same time, but with no need to keep up my precognition, I had attention to spare. Richard fell back before my assault, face tight with concentration. The black shield around him flickered, flaring when the *sovnya* cut into it. He tried to strike back with those black wires but they were unwieldy at close range and the fateweaver sent them into the walls and floor.

Another tremor shook the keep, and the floor shifted beneath my feet. Both Richard and I stumbled but Richard recovered first and his hand blurred.

Light exploded at our feet, dazzling me. I felt Richard's jinn magic lash out and I blindly pulled it in to catch it on the *sovnya*'s blade. Without my divination, the fateweaver was cruder, a club instead of a scalpel, but I poured power into it and willed myself to be safe and nothing touched me.

My vision cleared, black-purple spots fading as I heard running feet. I was still dazzled but I could make Richard out at the other end of the room. It had been some sort of one-shot, a flash bomb; he'd managed to draw it without my seeing. Now he stood half-turned away from me, right hand behind him while the left held a tangle of spinning black wires. He was working on a spell.

'An impressive weapon,' Richard said. 'Unfortunately—'

I activated my headband and kicked off the ground, soaring towards Richard with the *sovnya* extended.

Richard's mouth quirked in a smile. He let the spell drop and brought up his other hand to reveal a gun.

Richard shot me twice while I was still in mid-air, then dived aside as I flew past. I crashed into the wall, and before I could recover he'd emptied his gun into me, firing until it *clicked* on an empty magazine and the echoes of the shots faded away.

I straightened and turned to face him.

'A *bullet ward*?' Richard snapped. 'You've been saving that this whole time?'

'What can I say?' I'd been channelling a thread of power into the bullet ward since the fight started, and it had deflected every shot. 'You taught me to be prepared.'

Richard backed away. That black shield was powerful, but from the way he was eyeing the *sovnya* he didn't seem to want to test it against a direct hit. Another tremor ran through the floor; I kept my balance this time and as the spots faded from my vision I lunged.

Richard created an attack behind me, black wires lancing for my head, but I'd seen him use that trick before and I used the fateweaver to make it miss. The *sovnya* cut rents into his shield and he had to scramble back. But he was running out of space now, underneath the gallery with the wall behind him. I deflected another shot with the fateweaver, then brought the *sovnya* around, left hand high and right hand at elbow level so that the blade hissed across at waist height in a sweeping blow, impossible to dodge.

Richard dropped his gun and snatched out something small: with a *shing!* noise it expanded into a thin metal staff six feet long. The *sovnya* hit it with a high-pitched *clang*. The staff should have snapped under the blow but it rang and held.

I reversed and struck again but again Richard parried, sliding away. I followed up, not giving him the chance to open the range. The *sovnya* flickered and slashed, but each time that staff stopped it a foot or two short.

The clash of metal echoed through the room, mixing with the stutter and thud of footwork. My breaths came in and out, harsh and mechanical, as I forced my lungs to expand and contract. Richard fought in silence, but I could see sweat on his forehead and his eyes darted to follow my attacks. Stone dust hung in the air. My left hand was sweaty and my muscles burned, but my right arm was tireless and I put all its power into my blows, forcing Richard to block perfectly or die.

I brought the *sovnya* down in an overhead strike. Richard deflected the blow, taking the instant's breather to try to back away, but I reversed to slash at his ankles, forcing him to jump. He landed with a thump and I was on him again; I wasn't giving him the chance for any more tricks. Richard was too busy parrying my blows to attack with his jinn magic; from time to time he had openings to strike with the staff but he didn't take them, devoting all his attention to defence. I recognised the style he fought with; it wasn't so different from the one I'd learnt in his training hall all those years ago. The *sovnya* did its part, seeming to twist and strike of its own accord. It could sense the thing inside Richard and it wanted to cleave his flesh and bone to reach it.

And Richard was struggling. He was good – maybe as good as me – and he had that jinn, but I had the fateweaver and a better weapon and a stronger right arm. A blow battered through his defences, scoring a gash across his body armour; he blocked the next strike, but the one after that tore open a webbing pouch, scattering its contents on the floor. I could hear his breathing, harsh and ragged – was there fear in those brown eyes? Richard tried to call up some kind of spell, but I was on him instantly and this time he took a cut to his forearm. I was pouring everything I had into the fateweaver, forcing the futures towards ones where my blows landed. It was the most energy I'd ever put into the thing and I knew I couldn't keep this up but I wouldn't have to: Richard was being overwhelmed. He wasn't trying to attack or get away any more, all his attention was on the next parry. Sweat soaked my clothes and my muscles were crying out, but Richard was slowing down too. A little more—

Pain stabbed through my chest. I ignored it, brought the *sovnya* down in a crushing blow that cut Richard's shoulder through his armour. He backed away towards the wall and—

—the pain stabbed again, sharper and stronger. It didn't stop; it pulsed, and kept pulsing in time with the beating of—

—my heart.

No! Panic filled me. *No, no! Not now! Not NOW!* Desperately I tried to keep up the attack, but pain flooded my body; my head swam and I stumbled. Richard was backpedalling, watching me with a calculating gaze. I tried to chase after him, but the cramp grew worse, stronger with each beat. I chased him, but I couldn't catch him and the agony in my chest grew worse and worse until it seized up.

My vision greyed out for a moment, and when it came back I was on one knee. I tried to get back up and couldn't.

It was over.

'Well,' Richard said from a distance. 'You certainly made that as difficult as possible.'

I couldn't answer. My breath was coming in short, quick gasps. I could just barely pull enough air into my lungs, but my heart was fluttering, beating in fits and starts. The only way I could keep it going was by using the fateweaver to push through the futures in which I stayed alive . . . except that using the fateweaver was making it worse.

There was no way out.

'What a pathetic ending,' Richard said. He was still breathing hard and he looked hurt, but he could move and I couldn't. He retracted the staff with a metallic *shikk*, then circled to put me between him and the wall; another tremor shook the keep and he paused until the floor had stopped quaking. 'Killed by your own weapon.'

The *sovnya* quivered in my hand; it wanted so badly to kill Richard, but he was staying out of reach. I stared daggers at him but there was nothing I could do.

'I have to admit,' Richard said, 'after all the trouble you've caused, I'm tempted to make this slow and painful.' He considered a moment, then shook his head. 'No, one should stay practical about these things.' He drew a second gun, a small holdout, and levelled it at me. Somehow it didn't surprise me that he had two. 'Die.'

The gun *cracked* and I sent a thread of magic through the bullet ward. The very weakness of the focus saved me; its energy requirements were so low that I could still power it. The bullets glanced away.

Richard paused, then sent a twisting line of black wires at my head. I changed my focus through the fateweaver, and twitched the *sovnya*. The wires curved in to strike the blade and were absorbed.

'Really, Alex?' Richard said. 'You're going to make me do this?' He drew a knife.

Richard walked forward. My eyes flicked past him, around the room, searching desperately for some advantage, some trick. There was nothing. Scatterings of rubble around the edges, the duelling ring under Richard's feet, Anne lying behind him . . .

Anne. Arachne's dress.

I levelled the *sovnya* at Richard, and as I did I reached out with my magic, channelling a thread of power into the imbued item behind.

The dress responded instantly. Spells activated and began to work, weaving at lightning speed. I could recognise the signature of Arachne's magic, tightly woven and subtle. The spell was enormously powerful, but so well-masked I could hardly sense it.

Richard paused just out of my range. I could barely move; once he got inside the polearm's reach, it would be over. I kept the *sovnya* pointed at him with my left arm, while with my right hand I drew my gun.

Agony flooded my body and my vision went white. Richard could have killed me in that instant but I was still blocking his divination, and as my vision came back I saw that he'd used the time to put his shield back up. Black energy flickered where the gun was pointing, while with his other hand he held the knife point upwards. Its edge gleamed faintly in the light.

I'd slumped the rest of the way to the floor, propped up on my side and one elbow. The *sovnya* trembled as I kept it and the gun levelled. Richard held the shield ready to block any shots, his stance wary.

'You're only making this harder on yourself,' Richard

told me. I saw his eyes flicker and knew he was calculating how to get close enough to cut my throat. Behind him, Arachne's spell was working, repairing the damage to Anne's mind, but it needed time. I saw Richard tense, about to move—

Hermes blinked into existence right in front of me.

Richard paused. Hermes crouched protectively in front of my body and gave a sharp, threatening bark.

Richard gave the fox an exasperated look. 'Oh, come on.'

Richard took a step to the right. Hermes shifted to keep himself between Richard and me. Richard moved back to the left, and again Hermes mirrored him.

'For heaven's sake, Alex,' Richard said. 'First you and your girlfriend, now you want me to kill your pet as well?'

I didn't answer. I was keeping up the *optasia*, forcing my lungs to breathe, training my weapons on Richard, and pushing the fateweaver to keep my heart just barely beating. It was straining me to my limit and I had nothing left to guard against an attack.

But Richard didn't know that. I saw his eyes flick between the *sovnya* and the gun and Hermes; none were a threat on their own but there was no easy way for him to kill me without leaving himself open. Hermes growled, his tail bushed up.

Another quake shook the keep, and Richard staggered. The motion jolted my chest and white spots danced before my eyes. My muscles were trembling and it was all I could do to hold up my weapons.

Behind Richard, Anne stirred.

As the floor steadied, Anne rose. She came to her feet

with a liquid flowing movement, like a shadow on the wall. I saw her gaze lock onto Richard; ahead of her, Richard recovered his balance and prepared to move.

I looked up at Richard and smiled.

Richard stared back at me, then understanding flashed in his eyes and he spun.

Anne was sprinting, low to the ground, long legs carrying her across the duelling ring as they'd done so many times before. Richard's arm came up, the magic of his jinn darkening into a black shield, a killing spell gathering at his palm.

I levelled my gun at Richard's back, the barrel trembling. It was hard to see but I put everything I had into the fateweaver, willing Richard's death, and as I did I dropped the *optasia* and saw every future but one blink out.

The trembling stopped.

I fired.

Richard grunted. His spell discharged, going wide; an instant later Anne slammed into him, hand coming up like a knife. Green light flickered, soft and deadly. Richard crumpled, leaving Anne standing over him, spots of his blood on her skin where they'd been flung by the bullet. She stared down at his body.

For the first and last time, I reached out to Richard with the dreamstone. I searched for his mind and found nothing. Gone.

It was over.

I let out my breath and let myself fall.

I heard a rush of footsteps and saw Anne kneeling over me, hair hanging down towards my face. She glanced up and down my body and worry sprang into her eyes. 'Hold still.'

You sound different, I told her through the dreamstone. I'd stopped breathing, but that didn't seem important any more. My heart beat in fits and starts, on the edge of failing.

'Well, you made sure of *that*, didn't you?' Green light glowed at the edges of my vision and I sensed Anne's magic taking shape. 'I've got a lot to say to you, but it can wait.'

The pain was fading. I didn't know whether it was Anne's doing or not, but it felt wonderful. *If you ever see Arachne again*, I told Anne, *tell her thank you.*

'Tell her yourself. All right, here we go.'

I felt Anne's magic take hold, working on my body. Scrapes and cuts healed, and the beating of my heart steadied, but it didn't grow stronger.

I lay peacefully on the stone, looking up at Anne. After all that had happened, it was nice to just watch her. Red-brown eyes flicked back and forth; a frown creased her forehead; her hair brushed my shoulder and she absently pushed it behind her ear. *Your hair looks nice like that*, I said.

'That should have worked,' Anne muttered. She tried again, her spell weaving through me.

Can't heal this, Anne. Anne's healing works by speeding up the body's natural regeneration, pouring energy into it to let it rebuild itself. But my heart and lungs were being transformed, not damaged. There was nothing to heal.

Stop distracting me, Anne said. Her thoughts were focused, abstracted. She started work on a different type of spell, weaving it through her hand as it rested on my chest.

It's not your fault, I said. I felt warm and at peace.

There was nothing to fight or be anxious about any more. How long since that had been true? I couldn't even remember.

I didn't have the strength to keep using the fateweaver. I let go of the path where I stayed alive, letting the futures open freely.

The futures didn't open. The fateweaver kept working, doing it by itself. *It's not going to make a difference, you know*, I told it. I suppose I shouldn't have been surprised: the fateweaver was alive, just as I was, and it wanted to live too. It didn't understand that it was killing me.

Anne's spell failed again. 'Come on!' she shouted. 'Why won't it work?'

It's okay, I told her. *I knew this was coming.* I raised my artificial arm – the only one I could still lift – and stroked her cheek gently. I couldn't see very well but I could just make out her face. *Glad I got to see you one last time.*

Realisation flashed in Anne's eyes, followed by fear. 'No!' She stared down at me with a look of dawning helplessness. 'You can't do this! Not now!'

I felt a cold nose poke against my left hand, and smiled slightly. Hermes. *I did everything I set out to do*, I told her. *Now I get to die in the arms of the woman I love. Good way to go.*

The fateweaver was still holding me to a single future, but I was close enough now to make out the end. It was like riding a train to the end of the line. Beyond was an empty void, though it was white, not black. Had it always been that way?

'There's got to be something.' I couldn't make out Anne's face any more, but I could hear her talking to herself, her voice quick and frantic. 'Rebuild from another organ, no. Amputate . . . too late. Oxygen . . .'

The shadow realm trembled and I heard the grinding crack of breaking stone, followed by a roar. The floor bucked and shook. *You really should get out of here*, I told Anne and Hermes.

'Be quiet! It's the fateweaver, I can't heal you while it's doing that. Have to make it part of the solution somehow . . .'

You can't save everyone this time. The end of the line was very close. *But it's okay. It doesn't hurt any more. I've been pushing myself so long but it's finally over.*

Anne said something I couldn't hear.

Now I can stop, I told her. I let the connection go.

My heart beat one last time, then ceased. Feeling left my body, starting at the outskirts and drawing in. Sight and sound and touch drifted away, leaving only a white void. It was very peaceful.

Dimly, as if from a great distance, I could make out Anne's voice. '. . . no,' she was saying, and there was something dark and furious in her voice. 'You aren't *allowed* to die. Not until . . .' Then all sound was gone.

The train reached the end of its tracks and plunged into a dazzling white sky.

I felt as though I was racing through the clouds and into infinity. *You know*, I thought as my senses faded, *all in all, that really wasn't so bad.*

And then there was nothing at all.

THE END
of the Alex Verus series

(Yes, this is really the end.)

(There's no need to be like that. You had plenty of warning. Alex went into that knowing what was going to happen, and you should have known too.)

(Really, you can put the book down.)

(You're very persistent.)

(Still here?
I told you, Alex's story is over.
But it's true, there are others.
Very well. Where to begin . . . ?
Three and a half weeks have passed.
In London, the sun rises on a cool October morning.
Somewhere in Camden Town is a street, fenced in by the canal and the train lines. On that street is a shop, with letters above the window that read Arcana Emporium. The door swings open . . .)

Epilogue

The bell above the door goes *ding-ding*.

'I don't sell spellbooks,' I tell the guy at the counter. There are two others in the shop already: a teenage girl in a BTS T-shirt and the guy I'm talking to. The new arrival makes three, which is the busiest it's been all morning. Slow day.

'I mean, it doesn't have to be a book,' the guy tells me. He's got messy hair and looks like a student. 'You could send me something I could read on my phone.'

'So you're asking for an ebook with spells.' The new girl's Ji-yeong. I wasn't expecting her today. She gives me a nod and goes to sit in the Emporium's only chair.

'Yeah. Do you have one?'

'No.'

'But I mean, adepts have to write stuff down,' the guy says. 'I mean, sometimes they try a spell and it works and sometimes they try one and it doesn't, so they'd keep records, right?'

'That's . . . not really how it works.'

'I mean, *I'd* keep records. Like, I do that with my phone. The way I used to do it was that whenever I thought of something important, I'd stop and type it into a notes file. But then after I got my new phone I started doing video logs instead, so, and this was something I was thinking, if you wanted a really good record of your spells, you should video it. Because that way you'd get the movements too. You know, no one ever seems to think of stuff like that. I was thinking about that just yesterday.'

I want to sigh and scrub my hands over my eyes. This never used to happen to Alex. After he said 'no' a couple of times they'd go away. Is it because I'm shorter? Because I'm a girl? Do I just look less intimidating?

'Then you could share it,' the guy is saying. 'I've been thinking that could work really well. Because, you know, that's how it works these days, right? You have to be putting yourself out there. I've been reading that social media guy, you know, the one who shares all the political stuff? Well, he was saying something about that and I saw it and I thought . . .'

Maybe it's how I'm dressed? Arachne did always say people see your clothes before they see the rest of you. Maybe I should wear something scarier-looking. What about that dress she made me for the Tiger's Palace, the 'evil queen from Snow White' one? Though that's a bit much if you're going to be behind a counter all day . . .

'. . . so that'd make sense, right?'

Crap, I wasn't listening. 'So . . . you're talking about some kind of record of the things you say and do to use magic.'

'Yeah, that's right.'

'So something with spells in it that acts like a book.'

The guy looks pleased. 'Right.'

'Right,' I say. 'I don't sell spellbooks.'

It takes way too long to get him out the door. After that, the BTS girl comes up to buy a crystal ball. Once she's gone and I'm alone with Ji-yeong, I sigh, close my eyes, and lean my head against the wall.

'That was a complete waste of time,' Ji-yeong says.

'Thank you, Captain Obvious.'

'Why do you even listen to boys like that?'

'Politeness, I suppose.'

'They don't seem important enough to be polite to,' Ji-yeong says. 'Actually, I don't know why you're running a shop at all.'

I don't feel like answering that. I open my eyes and push off the wall.

'I mean, there are easier ways to earn money.'

I don't feel like answering that either.

'And if you really wanted to keep it open, you could just hire someone.'

'Why are you still in London anyway?' I ask her. You have to push back with Ji-yeong or she'll just keep going until you do. I don't know whether it's a Dark mage thing or whether it's just her, but she seems really forward. 'The first week, you said you were going back to Seoul.'

Ji-yeong looks away.

'Then you showed up again right after.'

'I've been thinking,' Ji-yeong says. She's looking out the window at a woman wheeling a pram down the other side of the street.

'About what?'

'Things,' Ji-yeong said. She turns back to me. 'Do you know if Landis is married?'

I give her a look. 'Seriously?'

The bell goes *ding-ding* again, and three people come in one after the other. The first two are tourists, and they head over to the window displays. The third one's something different.

'Uh . . .' the boy says. He's in his late teens, light brown skin, sweating under a ski jacket. 'Can you help me?'

'Depends on the help,' I tell him. The tourists are looking at the ritual daggers. Ji-yeong takes out her phone and starts reading.

'You were . . .' The boy glances around and lowers his voice. 'You were at that battle, right?'

'Not something I can really talk about.'

'Right, okay, it's just . . . There was a friend of mine, I think he might have been there.'

Oh. I don't ask which side he was on. The Council don't recruit that young. 'He was with the association?'

The boy nods.

'You sure he was one of the ones who went in?'

'I think so.'

'All right.' I take the pad on the counter and write a name and number. 'Call this guy and give him your friend's name. The Council have been trying to put together a record of everyone who was there.'

The boy starts to reach for the pad, then stops. 'He's Council?'

I tear off the square of paper and hold it up. 'It's them or nothing.'

He hesitates, then takes it. I make sure my curse doesn't reach his fingers. He turns away.

'Hey,' I say, and wait for him to look back. I don't really want to say it, but I feel like I should warn him. 'If it's been this long and you still haven't heard from him . . . well, just bear in mind it might not be good news.'

A shadow passes over the boy's face. 'I wish I'd been there.'

'No,' I tell him. 'You don't.'

He leaves, but the memories don't. Black tarpaulin bags, six feet long and lined up on the stone. Fear and gunfire in the castle haze. And the thing I brought home with me, the little white and blue cylinder waiting upstairs . . .

The tourists come up to the counter and I shake it off, pushing away the darkness. I bag up their shopping, hear the bell go *ding-ding*, and watch them walk out of the shop into the morning sun.

Ji-yeong looks up from her phone. 'So is he?'

'Oh, come on! Really?'

She looks at me expectantly.

'How would I even know something like that? I'm not a diviner.'

'You were apprentice to a diviner.'

'What's that got to do with it?'

'Apprentices are mostly like their masters.' Ji-yeong says it like it's something obvious. 'Diviners like knowing things, so you're probably like that too.'

'*You* were apprentice to a paranoid murder-happy death mage with delusions of living for ever.'

'So?'

I sigh and look away. Ji-yeong keeps waiting.

'No,' I tell her. 'He's not.'

Ji-yeong nods.

I'm thinking of what else to say when I notice someone's standing outside the door. She's heavy, a little like Caldera but with less muscle, and her name's Saffron. She's looking at me through the glass.

This day is just getting better and better.

The woman pushes open the door with a *ding-ding*, waits for it to shut behind her, then flips the sign from OPEN to CLOSED. 'Morning, Vesta.'

'Morning,' I tell Saffron. If she's not calling me 'Mage', I'm not calling her 'Keeper'.

Saffron looks down at Ji-yeong. 'How about you give us a few minutes?'

Ji-yeong looks up at her.

The friendliness slides off Saffron's face. 'Something wrong with your ears?'

I look at the two of them – the heavyset Keeper staring down at the Dark apprentice – and all of a sudden I'm annoyed. 'She's staying,' I tell Saffron.

'This is confidential.'

'What, asking me the same questions again?' I walk around the counter and over to Saffron, skirts whisking around my feet. I stop before coming into range of my curse – just – and fold my arms. 'I was polite the first time, I was polite the second time, but now this is getting insulting.'

'It's just routine follow-up,' Saffron says. She's wearing her police poker face, but I've got the feeling she wants to lean away.

'It is *not*,' I tell her. 'I know how short-handed you guys are. Variam was pulled off sick leave to take cases from *your* order. So don't tell me that you coming here three times in three weeks is routine.'

Saffron stares at me for a few seconds. I don't back down, and it's Saffron who turns away. She walks around the shelves and herb rack, then leans on the counter and takes out a stick of gum. 'They've done more auguries.' She unwraps the gum and pushes it into her mouth. 'Came out the same. Drakh is dead. Verus is dead. Anne Walker is alive.'

'Okay?'

'Tracking spells,' Saffron said. She chews on her gum, then pushes it into her cheek. 'No reading on Drakh, no reading on Verus, no reading on Walker.'

'Which is what you expect from someone who can do a life shroud,' I say. 'Look, if you're expecting me to help you find her, forget it. The deal was she got a full pardon.'

'She's not the problem,' Saffron says. 'Drakh is. Yeah, the auguries, but he's blocked divinations before. How do we know he's not doing it again? The Council wants a *body*. Something they can hold up and say: look, he's dead, war's over.'

'Yeah, well, they're going to have to get used to disappointment.'

'You know what happened in that shadow realm?'

'I know two different mages sensed Alex and Richard fighting in the keep right at the end,' I tell her. 'A death mage and a space mage, wasn't it?'

'How'd you hear that?'

I'm getting annoyed again. I don't know whether Saffron does it on purpose or whether Keepers are just like this. 'Oh, I don't know, because I was *there*? Where were *you*, by the way? Don't remember seeing you on the front lines.'

Saffron narrows her eyes a bit. *Guess that one got through.* 'Anyway, where was I?' I say. 'Oh right. Now both of those sightings were right before the last Council mages got out. And according to Compass, by that point the whole place was on the edge of falling apart.'

'Anne Walker made it out.'

'Well, it doesn't sound like anyone else did, does it?'

'That's not proof.'

'Look, I don't know what the Council thinks it's going

to get here,' I tell her. 'But if it's really Drakh you're worried about, then for what it's worth, I'm pretty sure he's dead.'

Saffron stares at me, chewing away at her gum. 'All right,' she says, and pushes herself off the counter. 'We're going to need you to sign a statement.'

'I already signed a bloody statement. I'm not doing another because you can't be bothered to dig the old one out of your filing cabinet.'

I expect Saffron to keep pushing but she doesn't. 'Thanks for your time,' she tells me. She walks down the length of the shop, past me and Ji-yeong.

Ji-yeong and I watch her go.

Saffron puts her hand on the door handle, then suddenly looks back. 'Where's Verus?'

For a moment I feel a weird sensation, like a feather-light brush across my thoughts. But I know that trick and I don't let my concentration slip. I keep my thoughts in the present, taking in the shop around me, the sight of Saffron at the door. I look straight at her and think very clearly. *Try and read my mind again, and we'll see how well* my *magic works on* you.

Saffron flinches and the moment's gone. I give her a smile. 'I'm sorry. Did you say something?'

'No,' Saffron says flatly. She looks from me to Ji-yeong. 'You two watch yourself.' The bell goes *ding-ding* and she's gone.

We watch her walk away up the road. Only when she's out of sight do I sigh and let my shoulders slump.

'She's scared of you,' Ji-yeong says.

'Funny way of showing it.' I look at the sign; it's still on CLOSED and when I think about flipping it to OPEN something in me rebels. 'I think I'm closing up for the day.' Saying it makes me feel a bit guilty, but it *is* my shop.

Ji-yeong nods. 'Thanks,' she says as she gets up.

'For what?'

'I would have had to go if she'd pushed it,' Ji-yeong says with a shrug. 'They don't want me here.'

I'm not sure what to say to that. Ji-yeong opens the door.

'Wait,' I tell her.

Ji-yeong pauses. 'If you're still figuring things out,' I say, 'and you want someone to talk to, you can come to me. Okay?'

Ji-yeong thinks about it for a second, then nods. 'Okay.' The door closes behind her.

I watch her walk away in the opposite direction from Saffron, and shake my head. 'Weird girl,' I say to myself, then turn the lock on the door.

I climb the stairs to the flat. There's a text on my phone from Vari; it must have come in while I was with Saffron. He's been pulled in for a double shift and won't be done until midnight.

I still haven't really talked with Vari since the battle. I mean, not properly. He's not hurt – the marid kept its promise – and the Council doesn't seem to be blaming him for anything. But he hasn't been dealing with it all that well. He tells me he's being given these extra shifts, but I'm starting to get the feeling he's just trying to stay busy so he doesn't have time to think. It's what I used to do.

We haven't talked about the deal I made either.

The monkey's paw is sitting at the back of the drawer.

I could point to it with my eyes closed, and thinking about it brings a complicated mix of feelings, like a knot I can't untie. Was I wrong to say yes? Could I have done anything else? What happens when it goes through with its side of the bargain? Can I really just sit there and watch someone walk away with it?

I shake it off and open my laptop. Half a dozen new emails. Two are from adepts about that network. I thought someone else was supposed to be setting it up but they're acting like they're waiting for me. A report from November, three pages long. Another question for the Emporium account. A message from a guy who claims he used to sell to Alex – he's got some new stock and wants to know if I'm interested. I'll have to check whether he's telling the truth.

The flat feels lonely. I use it, but I don't sleep here. It's not really a home.

There's plenty of work but I don't feel like it. I wish Ji-yeong had hung around. She's strange, but I can talk to her.

I could call Chalice. She sent me a message last week saying we should catch up, but I'm kind of suspicious. Chalice has been getting involved with the Council – it's sounding like she's going to be one of the new aides. Problem is, a couple of things she's said make me think she wants me as *her* aide. Right now, most Light mages have forgotten about me, but if I start showing up at the War Rooms then pretty soon everyone's going to remember that I was Alex's apprentice. And once they remember *that*, it won't take long before they start thinking I'm trying to follow in his footsteps. I saw where that got Alex. No thanks.

Still don't want to sit down at that desk.

I shouldn't be complaining. It was only seven years ago I walked into this shop for the first time. Back then I had no money, a rented flat, and a curse I couldn't control. I didn't know anything about magic and I was about two bad days away from suicide. Now I'm an independent mage with a shop and a home of my own. I've got more than I ever dreamed of.

But none of it's worth anything without people to share it with.

You know what? I open the desk drawer and pull out my box of gate stones. They're labelled with little tags, and I rummage for the one I need. *World's not going to end if I take a half day off.*

I come down in a forest clearing, stepping onto grass. Autumn leaves litter the earth, yellow and brown and gold. It's early afternoon – the time difference from London is a couple of hours – and the sky is a clear bright blue.

I let the gate close and set off; there's no track but I know where to go. I've changed into jeans and walking shoes, and fallen leaves crunch under my soles. I find myself relaxing as I walk. I've always lived in cities, but I like how peaceful the countryside is. When I'm in London, I can always hear traffic and voices, but out here the only sound is the wind. It's nice.

It only takes a few minutes for the house to appear. There's a path running through the trees, flagstones laid out like stepping-stones in a grassy river, and the path runs right by the building. It's a log house with a peaked roof, raised a foot or so off the ground. There are windows on the walls with flowers in window boxes, and a veranda with a couple of chairs. I cross the path and climb the steps. 'Hey, lazy,' I tell the fox lying in front of the door. 'Shouldn't you be out hunting?'

Hermes flicks his tail at the sound of my voice. He's sprawled on his side on the wooden decking, and he lifts one paw and twists his head to look at me upside down.

'You're just stealing from her, aren't you?' I say. 'Anyone home?'

Hermes blinks. I step over him, pulling in my curse to keep it out of his fur, and knock on the door. A voice calls 'Come in!' and I push it open.

The door opens into a combination kitchen/living/dining room. Inside, a young woman is rolling pastry on the table. She's wearing an apron over a T-shirt and jeans, and there's flour on her arms. 'Your fox is getting fat,' I tell her, closing the door behind me.

'He keeps eating my pastries,' Anne says with a smile. 'Want one?'

You'd never think to look at her that a month ago Anne was one of the most feared and wanted mages in the British Isles. All you'd see would be a tall, slender girl with long black hair and red-brown eyes. Beautiful, maybe; scary, no. You can't even sense any magic. I know she uses some kind of life shroud, but I can't see it, though my magesight's awful so that might just be me.

Technically I'm not breaking the law by visiting like this, but it's not something I share around. Yes, officially Anne's been pardoned and taken off the wanted list. But the Council lost a *lot* of people in that war. As long as they have no idea where she is, it's easy for them to let it go, but once that changes . . .

I hop up to sit on the table. 'What's in them?'

'Apricot,' Anne says. She puts aside the rolling pin and starts cutting the dough into strips.

'I liked the apple ones.'

'Come on, give apricot a try.'

'Fine,' I sigh. They'll probably be good; I just prefer things I know. 'Ji-yeong's hanging around the shop again.'

Anne puts the cutter aside and takes two of the dough strips. 'Mm-hm?'

'It doesn't bother you, does it? I mean, she *was* Sagash's apprentice.'

'Well, so was I.' Anne starts plaiting the strips together. She makes it look easy, but the one time I tried I made a horrible mess. 'Though it was a bit more voluntary on her part. But given what I did to her master, I think we can call it even.'

Anne's a very different person these days, and to be honest I'm still figuring out how to treat her. On the one hand, she's easier to get on with. I always *liked* the old Anne, but whenever you talked to her, there was this reserve, this sense she was holding herself back. Nowadays she's a lot more relaxed. And funnier. I can talk to her about things where the conversation would have stalled before.

On the other hand, she's also a lot scarier. Like I said, she doesn't *look* scary, but somehow I'm very sure that if anyone ever really threatens her she'll kill them without a second thought. It's like the safety catches that normal people have just aren't there. I suppose some people would say the same about Alex, but I never felt with Alex that he'd turn that on me. With Anne, I'm not so sure.

'Pass the apricots?' Anne asks.

'Where—? Oh.' There's a small bowl at my end of the table with apricot halves, washed and cored. Anne turns towards me and holds out her hand. I reach out—

It's the way she's standing that does it. All of a sudden, it's a month ago. We're in the shop, shadows stretching across the floor, and Anne's in that exact same pose, except she's wearing a black skater dress and above her palm a mass of black wires is spinning faster and faster. She's staring at me with those dark eyes and—

—the moment's gone. I'm quite still, the bowl of apricots half-extended, looking down at Anne's hand. And suddenly I'm very aware that we're on our own in a cabin in the woods with no one who knows where I am and no one close enough to hear a scream.

'You know I wouldn't,' Anne says quietly. She's looking at me and I know she's read my body language.

I take a breath and hand over the bowl. Our fingers don't quite touch. 'I know,' I tell her. But it's forced, and when Anne turns back to her dough, there's a tension in the air.

Most people think Anne did what she did because she was under that marid's control. I'm one of maybe four people who know better. Oh, the marid had an influence, and it got bigger and bigger until by the final battle it really *was* possessing her. But the people she killed before that? All the marid did was give her a push. And I'm not completely sure she even needed the push.

I know it was only part of her. But that part's still there, and the woman standing next to me folding strings of dough around sliced apricots is still basically the same person who went into Jagadev's fortress and Levistus's mansion and killed every living thing that got in her way.

I shake it off and start complaining to Anne about the shifts Vari's working and how I hardly get to see him any more. Anne listens and makes sympathetic noises and we move on to talk about other things, and the tension fades until I've almost forgotten it happened.

The pastries are lined up on their tray and Anne's about to put it in the oven when I stretch and glance around. 'All right,' I say. 'Where's . . . ?'

'That way,' Anne says, pointing. 'Along the path, then turn off onto the track.'

'Didn't even need to ask,' I say with a grin. I look up; that curved spear of Alex's is mounted above the fireplace. 'Are you still keeping that?'

'You never know.'

I nod and hop off the table. 'Back in a bit.'

'Luna?'

I pause halfway to the door. Looking back, I see that Anne hasn't lifted the tray. She's staring down at the pastries, and this time when she speaks, she doesn't raise her eyes. 'You used to say on your bad days, it felt like you weren't bearing a curse, you *were* a curse. That you made everything worse for everyone you'd ever known, just by being alive.'

I nod.

There's something brittle in Anne's words. 'How did you deal with it?'

It's something I used to think about a lot, and what happened with the monkey's paw has made me dig it up again. It's not easy to say, but I speak honestly and hope it'll help. 'I suppose the biggest thing . . . you have to get used to the idea that you're not a good person. Maybe not an awful one either, but . . . You have to accept that what you've done, what you're going to do, there's a lot of bad in there. You just hope there'll be enough good to balance it out.'

Anne stares down a moment longer, then nods, the movement jerky and sharp. She picks up the tray and walks to the oven, her usual grace returning step by step.

I follow Anne's directions and turn off the path about fifty yards upslope. Trees close in around me. I've only been walking a minute when I see a flash of white through the foliage, and when I pause I hear the scuff and rustle of movement. Old habits take over and I soften my footsteps, creeping closer as stealthily as I can.

The trees open up into a clearing, and I lean out from behind a trunk.

Alex is there, wielding a staff. His shirt is off, back and shoulders pale in the dappled sunlight, and he's moving through some kind of martial arts form, the movements smooth and steady. Leaves crunch beneath his feet, and the staff makes a soft *whoosh* as it sweeps through the air.

'Well, look who's back.' Alex's face is turned away and he doesn't stop his movements, but it sounds like he's smiling. 'Shop too much for you?'

'You have no idea.' There's a fallen tree to one side of the clearing and I walk over to sit down. 'How did you get customers to take no for an answer? Because I swear they don't listen to a word I say.'

'Pretty sure I asked myself that a few times.'

I complain for a while. It's kind of selfish, but after a

day behind the counter it's nice to moan a bit. Alex listens, still working through his staff form.

'. . . and then the other customer turns to me with this expectant look, like it's my job to explain why it happened! It's like he thinks Richard was supposed to follow his plan and the fact that he didn't is my fault!'

'Welcome to being a teacher.' Alex turns towards me; he keeps his eyes up as he brings the staff around in a parry, but I swear he's got an amused look.

'I'm not a teacher!'

'You're the only person they can ask about this stuff.' The parry becomes a strike. 'Works out the same.'

'Oh, glad you're getting a laugh out of it,' I tell him sourly. 'You didn't hear this guy. He was doing a play-by-play of the war like he was a football commentator. Except he got like two-thirds of the things *wrong*, and he expected me to tell him why Richard and Morden did them. I'd say he was my dumbest customer of the week, except yesterday was Monday!'

'See?' Alex draws back into a guard. 'You're a shop proprietor, you're a teacher –' He crouches and sweeps at ankle height. '– and now you're becoming an expert on London magical society.' Back to guard. 'Look at all the things you're learning.'

'If you tell me this is all part of my education, I am going to throw something at you.'

'It's all part of your education.'

I throw a stick. Alex pivots smoothly and it glances off the staff with a *clack*. 'Cheat,' I tell him.

Alex lowers the staff and walks over. As he gets closer, I see his skin is dry. 'Still not sweating?' I ask.

'I should be,' Alex says as he sits. 'Anne says the sweat

glands work, but they're not triggering for some reason. Maybe this body just doesn't produce as much heat.'

Alex looks stranger up close. It's not his shape so much – his body's leaner and harder, and the lack of body hair is kind of odd, but none of that looks super-unnatural. It's the colour that's the problem. Alex's skin looks like white marble, only a little darker than the fateweaver. I used to be fairer than Alex, but now when I sit next to him I look like I've been tanning in a sunbed.

I still don't know exactly what Anne did. Both she and Alex tried to explain it, but Anne was really vague, and Alex wasn't in much of a condition to take notes given that he was, you know, dying at the time. As far as I understand it, Anne couldn't heal Alex because the fateweaver was transforming his heart, and she couldn't reverse the transformation because it was too advanced. So she went the other way. She supercharged it, getting the fateweaver to transmute all of Alex's body until his body and the fateweaver were the same thing.

Alex claims she wouldn't have been able to do it on her own, that the fateweaver pushed it to work because it was the only way for it to stay alive. It's weird to think about. I never realised that Anne could do anything like that, but that's what life magic does, right? Dominion over all living creatures. Though even so, I get the feeling this was right at her limit. Anne's had to put a ton of work into Alex's body to get it this far, and apparently she's still working out the kinks.

'Oh, right, Saffron dropped by,' I say. 'The Council still think you're dead, but they've got her sniffing around anyway. I think they've got their suspicions.'

Alex nods.

'Can you keep blocking their auguries? I know that fate magic's powerful, but . . .'

'I'm not blocking their auguries.'

'Then who is?'

'No one.'

I frown at him. 'Their auguries say you're dead.'

Alex just looks at me.

'Okay,' I tell him. 'I don't get it.'

'How do you think tracking and divination spells find someone?'

'Depends on the type of magic, doesn't it?'

Alex nods, then walks over to where his shirt and top hang from a branch. 'Most tracking spells are living family,' he says, slipping on his shirt. 'Life or death type. They look for your biological signature.'

'And yours would have changed,' I realise. 'So Anne doesn't need to shroud you.' I think for a second. 'That wouldn't fool divination though. Are you using that trick from Helikaon?'

'No, my *optasia* isn't good enough.' Alex finishes doing up his buttons and walks back over. 'But even auguries have to look for something. And for mages, one of the standard things they search for is your magical signature.'

'Okay?'

Alex reaches into his pocket and takes out a small plaque. It's metal mounted on leather, coloured silver and gold. 'Remember this?'

'Your Keeper signet?'

Alex nods. 'They personalise them to your magical signature. Like cutting a key from a blank. Once they've been set, they won't work for anyone else.'

'Okay.'

'Mine doesn't work any more.'

'Really?'

'My magic's changed.' Alex sits back down on the tree trunk. 'For one thing, the fateweaver's integrated with me. It doesn't feel like I'm using it any more; it's just part of who I am. But my divination's changed as well. Weaker. My precognition is fine, but it's harder to path-walk, especially long range. Can't focus on it the way I used to.'

'Does that bother you?' I ask curiously.

'Weirdly, no.' Alex leans back on the tree, resting on his hands. 'It would have once, but I suppose I'm . . . just less interested in the far future? The present seems more important.'

'Huh.'

'So you can see why their auguries aren't showing me up as alive.'

'Yeah,' I say. If Alex has a different body *and* a different magic type, what are they going to search for? But still . . . 'You can't hide in the forest for ever.'

'I know.'

'Are you ever going to come back?'

'I don't think we can.'

'Ever?'

'Never's a long time,' Alex says. 'But the fact is, with Richard and Morden gone, we might be the two most hated mages in the British Isles.'

'Not by everyone,' I say. 'People are still figuring out what to think, but from bits and pieces that I'm hearing, most of the adepts and independents out there aren't blaming you. And the fact that you were the one who finally negotiated that surrender is getting a lot of notice. I think another six months and people are going to be seeing you as a hero.'

'Maybe some of them,' Alex says. 'But think about how many people lost friends or relatives because of what we did. We go back, and even if the Council stick strictly to the terms of that truce – and that's a big if – we'll be getting assassination attempts for the rest of our lives. Any place we go will be a potential war zone; any cause we join will be suspect because we're associated with it.' He shakes his head. 'I can't see any path where it's a *good* idea for us to go back. And even in the ones where it's the least bad option, we'd have to wait years. No, I think we're going to be in exile for a long time.'

I sigh. 'I suppose you're right.'

I wait while Alex gathers up his things and puts on his top. 'There's one other reason,' he says as he picks up his staff.

'What?'

Alex starts walking, keeping to a slow pace, and I fall in beside him. 'Those moves I was working through?' he tells me as we walk. 'It's the staff form of a martial art called *carë*.' He pronounces it *kah-reh*. 'Its last living practitioner died around two thousand years ago. There are no records left of the style.'

I look at Alex with a frown, waiting for him to go on. He doesn't. 'Then how—?'

'I remember it,' Alex says simply.

I stare at him for a second, then I get it.

'The fateweaver,' Alex says with a nod. 'Other things too. I've been having dreams. Battles I was never part of, cities I've never seen. They're patchy, like memories from when you're very young.'

'You're remembering things the fateweaver saw.'

'When I realised that, I started thinking,' Alex says. 'And I kept coming back to that conversation we had. The night in Sagash's shadow realm, before the battle. You remember what you told me, about how I'd changed?'

I nod.

'Well, I kept turning it over,' Alex says. We're coming up to the path; he stops and leans against a tree. 'And the more I thought about it, the more I had to admit that you were right. Now, some of it I could put down to Anne and the Council and losing my hand, but when I thought back, the point at which I really started acting differently was when I took up the fateweaver.' Alex looks at me. 'Imbued items are made for a purpose. My mist cloak was built to hide its wearer. The *sovnya* was made to kill magical creatures. My armour's meant to protect. The fateweaver? It was made as a tool for generals. To win battles.'

'But it was you making those decisions, not the fateweaver.'

'Oh, I made the *decisions*,' Alex says. 'But after you've decided what to do, you still have to figure out how to do it. And if you've got an imbued item that's really good at solving problems one particular way . . . well, don't you think it's a funny coincidence that right after I bond to an imbued item built for war, I start facing and killing my enemies on the battlefield? And less than a month after that, I'm commanding an army?'

I look at him.

Alex shakes his head. 'Don't worry, it's not going to take me over. The fateweaver was made as a tool. It's not bloodthirsty like the *sovnya*. But . . .' He looks past me, into the distance. 'Between the two of us, I think Anne might be the less dangerous one now. If I ended up taking power again, I'd still care about right and wrong, but there'd be nothing to soften the edge any more. Justice without mercy.'

'So what, you're staying away just to be on the safe side?'

Alex grins, and all of a sudden he looks like he did in the old days, back when his biggest worries were me and his shop. 'Probably best not to take the risk.'

We walk out onto the path, and I think about asking Alex the question that I've been wanting to ask, the one that's been hovering at the back of my mind. *Was it worth it?* The people we lost – Sonder, Arachne, Caldera, Ilmarin, all of those soldiers and adepts who fought and died. Did it count for anything?

But I know it's unfair. Every one of us who fought in that war played a part in how things turned out. Alex was at the centre, but he wasn't behind it. And most of the ones who *were* behind it are dead or gone. Maybe we've earned some rest.

Instead, as the house comes into view, I ask the important thing. 'Alex? Are you happy?'

Up ahead, the door opens. Anne steps out and turns to wave.

Alex waves back, and as he does his face softens in a smile. It's not the kind of smile he had when we first met; it's fuller, purer. He looks down at me to answer, but I already know what he's going to say. 'Yes.'

Looking at his face, I'm not worried any more. I'm glad I came today.

The war is over, but our stories are just beginning. The afternoon sun shines down out of a clear sky.

We walk together down the hill, to where Anne and Hermes are waiting.

Author's Note

In 2008, I started work on a novel. It was my tenth; out of the previous nine, seven had been rejected by every publisher that saw them, while the last two had been published but failed to sell. So when I sat down to write the first words of what would eventually become *Fated*, my hopes weren't high. The last thing I was expecting was for it to turn into a series.

But it did, and the first three sold well enough that my publishers were interested in more. I wrote a fourth Alex Verus novel, then a fifth. My contracts were extended, then extended again. Year by year, and step by step, and somewhere along the way, without ever noticing exactly when, I went from being a failed author to a successful one. And now it's almost nine years since *Fated*'s release, and for the first time in my life, I'm going to see a series I started be published all the way to its end.

None of this would have been possible without my readers, so my biggest reason for writing this Author's Note is to say a thank you to everyone who's been buying and reading my books. If not for you, the Alex Verus series would probably never have existed, and without your continued support, it could never have been finished.

Ever since I announced that book twelve would be the last, I've had people asking if I could keep the series going. I've always had to say no, and now that you've read this book, you can hopefully understand why. I've never liked it when a series goes on and on for ever, and I'd much rather leave Alex at the end of *Risen*, in the woods with Anne. There's probably room for more stories in the Alex Verus setting, but Alex's one is over. Besides, after everything that's happened, I think he's earned a happy ending.

Instead, I'd much rather move on to something new! Since mid-2020 I've been putting together ideas for a new urban fantasy series, one with some similarities to the Alex Verus setting but a lot of differences too. If all goes to plan, I'll start writing it this year, and the first book will come out in 2022 or 2023.

But that's all in the future. For now, thank you to all of you who've followed Alex on his journey. I wish you the best of luck with your own.

Benedict Jacka, January 2021

extras

orbitbooks.net

about the author

Benedict Jacka became a writer almost by accident, when at nineteen he sat in his school library and started a story in the back of an exercise book. Since then he has studied philosophy at Cambridge, lived in China and worked as everything from civil servant to bouncer to teacher before returning to London to take up law.

Find out more about Benedict Jacka and other Orbit authors by registering for the free monthly newsletter at orbitbooks.net.

if you enjoyed
RISEN
look out for
INK & SIGIL
by
Kevin Hearne

Al MacBharrais is both blessed and cursed. He is blessed with an extraordinary white moustache, an appreciation for craft cocktails – and a most unique magical talent. He can cast spells with magically enchanted ink and he uses his gifts to protect our world from rogue minions of various pantheons, especially the Fae.

But he is also cursed. Anyone who hears his voice will begin to feel an inexplicable hatred for Al, so he can only communicate through the written word or speech apps. And his apprentices keep dying in peculiar freak accidents. As his personal life crumbles around him, he devotes his life to his work, all the while trying to crack the secret of his curse.

But when his latest apprentice, Gordie, turns up dead in his Glasgow flat, Al discovers evidence that Gordie was living a secret life of crime. Now Al is forced to play detective – while avoiding actual detectives who are wondering why death seems to always follow Al. Investigating his apprentice's death will take him through Scotland's magical underworld, and he'll need the help of a mischievous hobgoblin if he's to survive.

Chapter 1

Scones Should Come with a Warning

Deid apprentices tend to tarnish a man's reputation after a while. I'm beginning to wonder when mine will be beyond repair.

Fergus was crushed by a poorly tossed caber at the Highland Games.

Abigail's parachute didn't open when she went skydiving.

Beatrice was an amateur mycologist and swallowed poison mushrooms.

Ramsey was run over by American tourists driving on the wrong bloody side of the road.

Nigel went to Toronto on holiday and got his skull cracked by a hockey puck.

Alice was stabbed in a spot of bother with some football hooligans.

And now Gordie, who was supposed to be my lucky number seven, choked to death on a scone this morning. It had raisins in it, so that was bloody daft, as raisins are ill-omened abominations and he should have known better. Regardless of their ingredients, one should never eat a scone alone. Poor wee man.

None of their deaths was my fault, and they were completely unrelated to their training in my discipline, so that's in my favor, at least. But still. People are starting to wonder if I'm capable of training a successor.

I'm starting to wonder too. And I'd like to have a successor soon, as I'm past sixty and rather wishing I could spend my time on sunny beaches, or in sunny gardens, or indeed anyplace where I might see the sun more often. Scotland is not known for its sunshine. The Highlands get two hundred sixty days of rain per year. But it's no fun for people in other countries to think of us as perpetually drenched, so I believe the popular imagination has painted us with kilts and bagpipes and unfortunate cuisine.

The muscle-bound constable standing outside Gordie's flat in Maryhill and doing a fair job of blocking the entrance held up a hand as I moved to step around him and reach for the door. He was in no mood to give me a polite redirection. 'The fuck ye daein', bampot? Away an' shite,' he said.

'Ram it up yer farter, Constable. Inspector knows I'm comin', so get out ma way.'

Oh, yes, and colorful language. Scotland's reputation for that is well deserved.

My cane is in fact a weapon that a person of my age is allowed to carry around openly, but I pretended to lean on it as I pulled out my 'official ID' and flashed it at him. It was not a badge or anything truly official but rather a piece of goatskin parchment on which I had written three sigils with carefully prepared inks. Any one of them alone would probably work, but in combination they were practically guaranteed to hack the brain through the ocular nerve and get me my way. Most people are susceptible to manipulation through visual media—ask anyone in advertising. Sigils take advantage of this collective vulnerability far more potently.

The first one, Sigil of Porous Mind, was the most important, as it leached away the target's certainties and priorities and made them open to suggestion. It also made it difficult for the target to remember anything that happened in the next few minutes. The next one, Sigil of Certain Authority, applied to me, granting my personage whatever importance the constable's mind would plausibly accept. The third, Sigil of Quick Compliance, should goad him to agree to almost any reasonable order I gave next and make him feel good about it, giving him a hit of dopamine.

'Let me pass,' I said.

'Right ye are, sir,' he said, and smartly stepped to the side. There was plenty of room for me to enter now without contact and no need to say anything more. But he'd been a tad rude and I believed it deserved a proportional response, so I shouldered past him and muttered, 'I pumpt yer gran.' He flashed a glare at me but said nothing, and then I was in the flat.

The inspector inside did not, in fact, know I was coming. She was middle-aged and looked a bit tired when she swung around at my entrance, but she was a good deal more polite than the constable. She had decided to let her hair go grey instead of dyeing it, and I liked her immediately for the decision.

'Hello. Who are you, then?'

There was a forensics tech of indeterminate gender taking digital pictures and ignoring both of us, an actual camera pressed to their face instead of a phone or a tablet extended toward the victim. I deployed the official ID once more and gestured at the body of poor Gordie, blue in the face and sprawled on his kitchen floor. Years of training, his hopes and mine, all spread out and lifeless. 'Tell me what ye know about the man's death.'

The inspector blinked rapidly as the sigils did their work and then replied, 'Neighbor in the flat downstairs called it in because the victim fell pretty heavily and pounded on the floor—or the neighbor's ceiling—a few times before dying. A choking accident, as far as we can tell, unless the tox screen comes back and tells us there was something wrong with the scone.'

'Of course there was something wrong,' I said, looking at the half-eaten remainder sitting on a small saucer. 'It had raisins in it. Anything else of note?'

She pointed toward the hallway. 'Two bedrooms, but he lived alone. One bedroom is full of fountain pens and inks. Never seen the like. Bit of a nutter.'

'Right. That's why I'm here. I need to send that stuff in for testing n' that.'

The inspector's features clouded with confusion. 'He didnae drink any of it.'

'No, no. This is part of a different investigation. We've been watching him for a while.'

'We? I'm sorry, I didnae catch your name.'

'Aloysius MacBharrais. Ye can call me Al.'

'Thanks. And you're investigating his inks?'

'Aye. Toxic chemicals. Illegal compounds. That sort of rubbish.'

'On ye go, then. I didnae like that room. Felt strange in there.'

That idle comment was a huge warning. Gordie must have had some active and unsecured sigils inside. And all his inks—painstakingly, laboriously crafted with rare ingredients and latent magical power—had to be removed. The last thing the world needed was some constable accidentally doodling his way to a Sigil of Unchained Destruction. I'd secure them and preserve them for later analysis, keeping the successful decoctions and viable ingredients, and destroying the rest.

I turned without another word and went to the hallway. There were three doors, one presumably being the loo. Layout suggested that was the first door on my left, so I went to the second and cautiously cracked it open. It was his bedroom, and there was a desk as well with a small collection of pens, inks, and papers—all for normal correspondence. I snatched a sheet of stationery and selected an Aurora 88 pen from my coat pocket. It was presently filled with a rust-colored ink using cinnabar for the pigment and a varnish infused with ground pearls, fish glue, and the vitreous jelly of owl eyes. I drew a small circle first to direct the effect at myself, then carefully but quickly outlined the shapes of the Sigil of Warded Sight, which looked like a red eye, barred and banded over with simple knotwork. Once completed, the sigil activated and my sight changed to black and white, all color receptors dormant. It was the most basic defense against unsecured sigils: I could not be affected by them until this one wore off—or until I destroyed it myself. It had saved me too many injuries to count.

Putting the pen away and hefting my cane defensively, I kept the sigil in my left hand and crossed the hall to open the door to Gordie's study. A waft of foul, funky air immediately punched me in the nose, and I wondered why the inspector hadn't said anything about it before. It smelled like a sweaty scrotum. Or maybe ten of them.

'Gah,' I said, and coughed a couple of times to clear

my lungs. I heard titters coming from the kitchen and realized the inspector had left out that fact on purpose. No wonder she'd told me to have at it. Her politeness had been a ruse to draw me to an olfactory ambush.

But I'd been wise to guard my vision. Gordie had far more than a few sigils lying around. The room was full of them, warding against this and that. The walls were lined with raw wooden workbenches and chairs, and cubbyholes full of labeled inks and ingredients glinted on the left. The main bench for ink preparation was opposite the door, and it was stained with pigments and oils and binders and held stoppered bottles of yet more inks. There was also a labeled rack of fountain pens and trays of paper and cards for sigils, along with sealing wax, a melting spoon, and a box of matches. Several cards pasted on the wall above the workbench had recognizable sigils on them for selective sight and attention that should make me—or anyone else who entered—completely ignore what was on the right side of the room. That's why the detective inspector had felt so uncomfortable. She felt something was going on in there and most likely saw it, but the sigils wouldn't let her mind process it. My warded sight made the sigils ineffective, so I had no difficulty seeing that there was a hobgoblin grunting and straining to work his way out of a cage placed on top of the workbench. That was a sight I never thought I'd see.

Different from pure goblins and more mischievous than outright malevolent, hobgoblins were extraordinarily difficult to capture as a rule, since they could teleport short distances and were agile creatures as well, with impressive vertical leaps aided by their thick thighs.

This one was trying to reach one of several sigils placed around his cage on little metal stands, like draught-beer lists placed on pub tables. His long, hairy-knuckled fingers waggled as he stretched for the sigil nearest him. If he could reach one of them and tear it up, he might have a way out, since the sigils were more of a prison for him than the actual cage was. He froze when he saw me staring at him, openmouthed.

'Wot?' he said.

I closed the door behind me. 'What are ye *daein'* here?'

'I'm in a cage, in't I? Ye must be the cream of Scottish intelligence. Cannae be anywhere else if I'm no free, ya fuckin' genius. But at least ye can see an' hear me. The bird who was here before couldnae.'

'I mean why does he have ye caged?' The fellow didn't appear to be an unusual hobgoblin worthy of capture or study; he was short and hairy, square-jawed, his face adorned with a fleshy nose and eyebrows like untrimmed hedgerows.

'He's a right evil bastard, that's why. Or was. He's deid, in't he? How'd he die?'

'Raisin scone.'

'So it was suicide, then.'

'Naw, it was an accident.'

'He didn't *accidentally* eat a raisin scone, now, did he? So it was suicide.'

I shrugged, conceding the point. 'Who are you?'

'I'm the happy hob ye're gonnay set free now. Unless ye're like him.'

'I'm no like him. I'm alive, to begin with. Answer ma questions truthfully and no more dodges. Who are ye and why did Gordie imprison ye here?'

'Said he was gonnay sell me. He's a trafficker in Fae folk, so he is. Or was.'

'Nonsense.' I stamped my cane on the floor. 'Tell me the truth!'

The hobgoblin stood as straight as he could in his cage—he was only about two feet tall—and placed his right hand over his heart, deploying the phrase that the Fae always used when they were swearing the truth or asserting reality. 'I tell ye three times, man. He's got a buyer. I'm s'posed tae be delivered tonight. And I'm no the first he's sold. There was a pixie in here a couple of days ago, didnae stay long.' He pointed to a slightly smaller, empty cage sitting next to his.

This information was more of a shock to me than Gordie's death. I'd had apprentices die on me before, but none of them had used their knowledge of sigils to traffic in the Fae. Carrying away the inks and pens of my old apprentices had always been a sad affair, because they'd been pure souls who wanted to do good in the world. This situation suggested that Gordie hadn't been such a soul. Trafficking Fae? I didn't know such traffic existed.

'But . . . we're s'posed tae boot the likes o' ye back to the Fae planes whenever ye show up here.'

'We, did ye say? Oh, so ye are like him. Just with a twee dandy mustache, all waxy and twisted.'

I squinted at him, considering how to respond. Hobgoblins tend not to take well to naked aggression, but they have that pubescent sense of humor young boys have, which I can deploy rapidly when occasion demands. 'It's no twee,' I said. 'It's luxuriant and full-bodied, like yer maw.'

The hobgoblin cackled at that, and I noted that his

teeth were abnormally bright and straight. It wasn't a glamour, because my sight was still warded. He'd had some work done. Since when did hobgoblins pay for cosmetic dental work? And his clothing was notable too. I couldn't identify colors in black-and-white vision, but he wore a paisley waistcoat with a watch chain leading to the pocket, but no shirt underneath it. There was a triskele tattooed on his right shoulder, the sort I've seen associated with Druids. Black jeans and chunky black boots. Maybe he was an unusual hobgoblin after all. His eyes glittered with amusement.

'Come on, then, ol' man. Let us out.'

'I will. But ye still have no told me yer name.'

'For wot? Are ye gonnay send me flowers for the Yule?'

'I need to bind ye to leave this place safely.'

'But then ye can bind me for anythin' else ye want in the future. I'm no letting ye have that power. Ma current situation has made me a wee bit distrustful.'

'Well, I don't want tae set a hobgoblin loose in a room fulla binding inks. Do ye know who's s'posed to be buyin' ye? Or for why?'

The hobgoblin shook his head. 'I don't. But yer lad Gordie had some papers over there he liked to shuffle around an' murmur over. The bird had a look an' said they were nonsense, but maybe they're no to an ol' man. Ye look like ye went tae school back when yer hair wasn't white as lilies.'

I moved to the workbench and scanned the papers I saw there. Gordie had been preparing sigils for later use, but there was no helpful explanation of his business dealings. The hobgoblin might be making this all up, and I hoped he was, because otherwise Gordie had been an evil bastard and I'd been a consummate fool. But the fact was, Gordie had done some impressive sigil work in this room. Work that should have been impossible for him. There were sigils I hadn't taught him yet—like the Sigil of Iron Gall—which meant he'd also crafted inks for which I hadn't taught him the recipes. He'd obviously been keeping some secrets, which didn't bother me, because apprentices are supposed to do that. What bothered me was that someone was teaching him behind my back.

'I think I know who ye are,' the hobgoblin said. 'There's s'posed tae be a Scottish sigil agent with a waxed mustache. Are ye called MacVarnish or sumhin like that?'

'MacBharrais.'

'Ah, that's it. Heard ye were sharp. But if ye had that wanker Gordie tossin' around behind ye, maybe ye're no, eh, pal?'

Maybe not. On a scrap pad where Gordie had scrawled lines in different inks to make sure the flow was good before drawing sigils, he had written: *Renfrew Ferry, 8 pm.*

'Ye said ye were s'posed tae be delivered tonight? Was it at eight?'

I got no response except a grunt and the sound of torn paper. I turned to see a triumphant hobgoblin freeing himself from the cage, one of the sigils that dampened his magic having been destroyed. He couldn't have reached it physically—I saw him fail as I entered—so he must have managed to exert some magical pull on it to bring it to his fingers. That was precisely the sort of thing that should have been impossible with multiple copies of it around him. The only explanation was that their potency must have waned significantly, the magic all leached from the ink, and with Gordie dead and obviously not paying attention, it was little wonder.

Cackling and flashing those white teeth at me, the hobgoblin leapt off the table and made for the door. I was out of position and woefully slow; there was no time to even break the seal on a prepared Sigil of Agile Grace.

'Laters, MacVarnish!' he said, and bolted out the door. A thud and screams followed shortly thereafter, and there was a shouted 'I'm glad yer deid!' before a shocked silence settled in the kitchen. I emerged from the room, far too late, to see the inspector and the tech on the ground, holding their noses. The hobgoblin had leapt up and punched them for the fun of it, and Gordie's body now lay twisted in a much different position, having recently been kicked. I could still see his face, though, a look of frozen surprise that this was his end, that his brown hair was mussed and he had a few days' stubble on his neck and jaw, blue eyes widened in horror that he would be literally be caught dead wearing his Ewok pajamas.

'What in the name of fuck?' the inspector cried. 'What was that just now, a pink leprechaun?' She'd had no difficulty seeing the blighter once he'd exited Gordie's room. I'd not seen the hobgoblin's skin color with my vision limited, so I filed that information away for future reference. Her eyes lit upon me and anger flared in them as she rose from the floor. The constable from outside burst into the room, also holding his nose. I needed them out of there right away, because Gordie's entire flat had to be scoured for clues. The official ID came out before they could lay into me and I gave them what for.

'Clear this flat now! Leave immediately and return tomorrow. That's an order. Go! Work on sumhin else!'

They scarpered off under the sway of the sigils and would probably return sooner rather than later when they remembered someone had punched them and they wanted answers. I needed to get answers of my own before then; Gordie had caught me napping, but I was fully awake now.